Mystical Rome

The War of Infinite Regress

Written By

Jason Andrew

Copyrights and Credits

ISBN: 978-0-9794221-4-0

Cover by Mark Henry

Editor: Jen "Loopy" Smith

Copy Editor: Lisa Andrew, Emilynn Henderson

Acknowledgements

This novel is dedicated to my beautiful wife, Lisa. She is my muse and her inspiriation always illuminates the path towards that brighter future.

We're born in this world to make connections and let ourselves be changed and transformed by others. I want to thank those that helped or inspired me along the way; those special people that believed in me, and helped support me over the years: (listed in chronological order) Jan and Wayne Messer, Doug Houston, Michael Dyer, Chris Beron, Mario Medina, Robert Bennett, Jason Carl, Evonne Traffanstedt, Jen "Loopy" Smith, Ally Foxworthy, Emilynn Henderson, Andrea Barr, Jennifer Childs, and Jeffrey Fowler.

Table of Contents

Chapter One: The Vestal Virgin

A gentle breeze billowed through the seven hills of Rome, providing a welcome relief to the crowd that swelled through the streets below to celebrate the Ides of March. The sweltering heat brought a stench of sweat to Rome that permeated everything. Plebeians, patricians, and slaves alike packed the narrow passages, drunkenly celebrating as though it were a bacchanalia. Their boisterous voices blended together into a soft roar like a swarm of laughing bees.

Claudia closed her eyes and imagined that she stood at the beach, at the edge that divided sand and water. "Rome is the heart of the world." A sharp poke to the back of the head woke her from the daydream; she lounged upon a wooden bench nestled at the edge of the balcony to her private chambers. "Adalia!"

The body-slave clumsily moved her hands, twisting a lock of Claudia's hair and yanking it by the roots. This was her third attempt at braiding Claudia's hair into the traditional sini crenes worn by the honored Vestal Virgins. "Apologies. I hadn't imagined the heart of the world would be so humid," Adalia said. "My blood's too thick for such heat."

Claudia laughed through the ache in her head — a mere affectation rather a demonstration of genuine mirth. She refused to express any pain or discomfort in sight of a slave. Any other slave foolish enough to be so rough with her person would be beaten by the house guards. Adalia was somehow special to Claudia's elder brother, Marcus, and thus she withheld punishment. Why would her brother go to the trouble and expense to send a useless body-slave all the way from Gaul? Had she lost her brother's confidence during the time spent on his tour with the Seventh Legion? "Marcus asked I teach you the politics of Rome to better please him."

"I've tried to listen and learn, domina," the body-slave said.

"If you would learn the ways of the Eternal City, you must understand those are not mere cobblestones below us. Those are the arteries that sustain the Empire. And it is the people — the mob — who sustain it all. What do you see when you gaze upon the glory that is Rome?"

Slowly, Adalia revealed a mastery of the language that surprised Claudia. "I look out onto the streets, and all I see is the mob running wild like vermin, consuming more food and drink than the city can provide."

"I would know the logic that gave birth to your words." Adalia held a number of curious opinions seemingly incompatible with one devoted to serve a great family of Rome. She had been completely uneducated in matters of grace or manners when she first arrived. "Speak freely."

Adalia continued her clumsy attempt to master the sini crenes. It might have been amusing on another day, when Claudia was not expected at temple. "I heard the kitchen slaves talking about the price of grain and how supplies are limited."

This slave ha strange concerns, Claudia thought. "Grain is always in short supply during a festival, is it not?" she asked.

"We do not celebrate in such fashion along the Rhine," Adalia answered sharply. "Our gods have no taste for women who have not experienced the pleasures of the flesh. We prepare for the winter that will always come."

The mere thought of living in such a world revolted Claudia. "The Festival of Antony brings joy to the plebeians and patricians alike. We celebrate a hero of the Eternal City who gave of his life so we might all prosper." She neglected to mention how the Festival of Antony drew a number of respected patricians to the Vestal Virgins for guidance about marriage prospects for their daughters. "Marcus Antony gave his life to save his friend from Brutus and his traitors. He gave his blood to usher an age of peace across the world."

She could almost hear disdain in Adalia's voice. "Save for the Caledonians."

"I have faith my brother and the Seventh Legion will bring Caledonia under the peace of Rome soon enough." Claudia turned aside to glance up at Adalia. "How long has it been since Marcus sent you from Gaul?"

"A month by the Roman calendar, domina."

Adalia barely spoke civilized words when she first arrived at the Domūs de Valeria a mere few weeks ago. She had identified her affiliation with the Valeria by revealing the mark of Marcus Valerius Perseus inked upon her thigh and a sealed message to Claudia in a wax tablet. "What have you come to think of the Eternal City?" Claudia asked.

The body-slave finished the last braid and weaved it into the rest of the pattern. "I had not imagined such a world was possible. The campfire tales did no justice to the reality."

The answer felt too perfect and proper to be earnest. This slave was keeping a secret from her. "You came to our home with my brother's mark upon your thigh. Know that to serve me is to serve him. I have his complete confidence in all matters, and if he has a message for me I would hear it."

"I have no message from your brother, domina."

Claudia half-turned towards Adalia, hoping to read her face. "You bear the mark of my brother. I would know more of why you were sent to me. Attend to my questions, lest I have the house guards whip you until you feel more amenable to my desires, slave."

"I gave a sacred oath my purpose here would not be shared with another soul, lest it be compromised." Adalia shook her head defiantly. "I shall not break my promise to your brother, and if you have me beaten, I will not be able to serve as I agreed. Trust in your brother and his love for you, domina."

"The hour grows late, and I must make haste to perform my anointed duties at the Atrium Vestae." Claudia sighed and then stood from her bench. She spoke again without taking her eyes from the mob. "We shall exchange words again in the future. Dress me."

Claudia kept still as a statue while her body-slave dressed her in the traditional ceremonial garb for a Vestal: a white cotton floor-length stola dress with straps, a green palla draped over her shoulder, and a red infula wrapped around her hair. Adalia remained in her simple cotton tunic and grey cloak as was proper for a servant of a great family of Rome. Afterwards, they ventured down the main staircase into the atrium, where a scant number of servants and guards carried about their day devoted to the business of the villa.

Adalia carried an embroidered leather pack of personal necessities for their stay at the Atrium Vestae. "The size of the Domūs de Valeria is impressive, domina." She glanced aside to soak in the architecture and design of the estate. "There are few buildings of this size where I was born."

"Seven great families founded Rome, each with a villa on the hills," Claudia explained. "Only five remain in private hands. A pity really, but you shall not see such splendor anywhere else in the world."

The great door of the Domūs de Valeria was closed. Claudia found it strange, since tradition demanded that the patricians feed any plebian who called upon their hospitality. The colossal monstrosity had been built during the Time of Kings with hardened wood carved in the likeness of the god Janus, protector of doors, gates, and roadways. Encased with straps of iron, the door was engineered to extend outward into the streets to provide shielding for guards fighting intruders during a siege. No other family, patrician or otherwise, had the right to possess such a door, one that would allow them to secure the hill.

The retainers, loyal freedmen under the nomen of Valerius, had pledged to serve the family with their lives. Claudia turned to the steward of the courtyard. "I have business at the Atrium Vestae. Open the door."

The old guardian of the great door acknowledged her command with a respectful salute and then paused. "Apologies, domina. An order's been issued to keep the great door closed today until Darius arrives."

She opened her mouth to inquire why he imagined the doctore had the right to restrict her movement, but then decided against it, lest she lose dignitas in front of the retainers. "Were you also ordered to keep me waiting without drink or place to rest?"

"No, domina."

The guards scrambled to find Claudia a comfortable chair and a copper pitcher of honeyed wine. It was distasteful to be forceful, as only plebeians raised their voices without just cause.

Claudia graciously accepted the offered chair without comment and slowly sipped the wine. If her father had survived, her life would have been quite different at this moment. The Valeria were one of the original seven families that settled Rome under the leadership of the legendary Remus. She would have held a high place of honor within the family and be carefully considering a number of marriage offers from prominent families.

The mantle of paterfamilias had passed over her brother Marcus to her father's youngest brother, Quintus Valerius Orca. Legally, Claudia no longer required permission from the paterfamilias to leave the domūs. She was a vaunted member of the College of the Vestals, wedded to the city of Rome. She lived at the family home by her choice. Orca didn't seem to care what she did, as long as the treasury deposited her salary into the family accounts.

Darius eventually swept into the courtyard, wearing a grey wool traveling cloak over a plain tunic and a sheathed gladius tucked under his belt. He wore his curly dark hair in a traditional cut, salted with the distinguished streaks of grey associated with Valeria blood. His pale skin and light-colored eyes came from the Gauls, however.

The guards halted their respective duties to acknowledge the presence of their doctore with a hearty salute. He had served the family for three decades, training all of the freedmen to fight and defend the family. Darius knelt before Claudia, a respect he rarely showed the paterfamilias himself. "Domina, would you have me break my sacred oath to your father?"

"You show me too much honor, Uncle." Darius had been gracious in his greeting, so she had no choice but reflect it in her response. He was her uncle by blood, if not legally. "Stand."

The old centurion stood slowly, as though reluctant to leave her feet. "As you wish, domina."

"Am I not your niece in blood and affection?" Claudia asked, gently chiding him. "Why do you insist upon titles in our home?"

"It's true that I'm your father's brother by blood, but I'm also the son of a slave." Darius spoke loud enough that all of the men in the courtyard could hear his words. He rarely did anything without purpose. Why was it necessary to do so within the walls of the Domūs de Valeria? Claudia wondered. "Titus Valerius Perseus gifted me freedom and granted me the Valerius nomen. On the day of his death, I swore the sacred words before bloody Mars that I'd protect you and your brothers against all enemies."

Claudia noted with some satisfaction how the guards now moved quickly and with purpose. Lack of respect from the paterfamilias cascaded down the ranks, which could be dangerous to her future if not corrected. "It is not my intention to prevent you from conducting your duties, uncle. Merely to attend to my own."

"It's my hope you will be gracious enough to allow me to escort you to the Atrium Vestae. The streets of Rome aren't always safe, and during festival it's the mob that rules. We cannot risk losing a treasure of the Valeria and a member of the Vestal College to such rabble. What will the other families think?"

Claudia gestured coyly to her body-slave. "I did not intend to walk alone. That would be improper. Adalia will come with me."

"I haven't vetted this new slave, domina," Darius said, shaking his head. "I've word to Marcus, but his cohort is on extended deployment."

"Herman vetted Adalia when she first arrived," Claudia said. "I trust our overseer to ensure our slaves have proper manners. Marcus sent her to me from Gaul. She knows the secret words that only my brother could possibly know. If he trusts her to protect my needs, then so do I."

"Domina, her blood's not of Gaul. And that's not the blessing that it might first appear."

"Uncle, you have the blood of the Gauls in your veins. Why should I fear the Gauls? Caesar invited their chieftains into the Senate."

"A rage has burned brightly within Gaul, since Caesar dragged Vercingetorix through the streets of Rome during his Triumph." Darius studied Adalia, as though seeking any possible sign of threat. She was a pale, strange-looking woman, taller than most of the men on the hill. Her hair was the color of wet hay. "But, you're not a Gaul, are you? I take from your face that you're of Germani tribes."

Adalia did not shy away from his gaze. She remained confident, almost defiant. "Aye."

Darius turned towards Claudia. "Domina, do you know the tale of Teutobod?" he asked. "He was the king of the Teutons. They were one of the Germani tribes that invaded the Republic not eighty years ago. The Legions beat them back time and again, until they surrendered. Their king offered terms handing over three hundred Teuton women to become slaves, as a promise that this invasion would never happen again. Once the women of the tribe heard tale of this, they pleaded to the Romans to be allowed to serve in the temples, instead of enduring slavery."

"Were they allowed to serve the temples?" Claudia asked.

"They were refused, lest the punishment to their tribe not sting and future sons forget the cost of invading Rome," Darius explained. "The women gathered in secret that night and swore they would not live as slaves. When the Legion came to collect their tribute the next morning, all three hundred women were discovered dead. They had butchered each other rather than submit. Be leery of this one."

If Adalia possessed malice in her heart, her face did not reflect it. She kept her gaze even towards Darius, and it might have been her imagination, but she thought her body-slave revealed the hint of a smile. "Surely, my elder brother would not send someone he did not trust completely to serve me."

"Then may I have the pleasure to escort you through the streets of

Rome, domina?"

Claudia glanced about the courtyard. The guards noted the homage paid by their doctore. Dignitas had been maintained. She rose from the chair and offered her arm. "The honor would be mine, uncle."

The great door of the Domūs de Valeria opened, ceasing traffic from the festival along the Velia. Darius led Claudia through the cobblestone streets down Velian Hill towards the Palatine. They walked along the Summa Sacra Way, marked by the Arch of Titus and the Temple of Venus and Roma.

Plebian vendors hawked wares as they passed, offering a variety of cold meats, flavored rice balls, and shellfish. She wanted to sample the variety, but a patrician rarely ate in public, lest they appear to have plebian tastes. Public festivals and feasts provided a notable exception to this taboo, but her role as a Vestal prevented her from engaging with the people. Instead, Claudia allowed Adalia to sample the cornucopia of offerings, politely refusing to eat anything offered to her, despite her hunger.

The roaring murmur of the crowd echoed off the walls of the houses around them. Darius tried several times to speak, but Claudia placed her hands over her ears to indicate that she couldn't understand him. He leaned close to whisper in her ear. "I can vouch for some of these vendors, domina, if you hunger. Their loyalties are secure."

Claudia shook her head. "And did you vouch for the cooks who served father's last meal?"

Darius flinched as though she'd slapped him. He recovered quickly and glanced about them, suspicious of who might be close enough to hear their conversation. The crowd swarmed about them with great revelry; this was perhaps the safest place to speak. "It's a dangerous time for you to make such suggestions about how your father died, domina."

Claudia scoffed. "Orca seems content to collect my salary, as his intrigues seem to do the family coffers no favors. And my brothers are away from Rome, and thus not a danger to him."

"I received word from Nicomedes this very morning warning of danger."

Her youngest brother, Nicomedes Valerius Corvus, had earned a scholarship to the Soothsayer Academy at an early age. Orca had been satisfied both with the honor given unto the family and the fact that he wouldn't have another patrician mouth to feed. "Why would he not contact me directly?"

"I've ways of receiving messages quietly without notice, domina."

Claudia caught herself unconsciously playing with the silver ring her brother gifted her from the Soothsayer Academy, remembering the promise it held. "What was the nature of this warning?"

"Details were sparse, domina. Only that I should follow you everywhere this day."

"Darius, you know you can't enter the Atrium Vestae during the women's ritual, yes?" Claudia adjusted the red infula wrapped around her hair — the very symbol of her status as a Vestal Virgin. "It would be sacrilege before the gods, and the women would leave without sharing news."

Darius once again pivoted, hand upon the hilt of his gladius, keeping vigil over Claudia, protecting her against anyone in the crowd who might venture too close to them. "The secrets of the seven hills are deep as are the passages under them, if one knows the proper way to access them."

"You know the secret of Ariadne's Maze?" Claudia asked, quite surprised. Only a select few were allowed to memorize the passages under the Atrium Vestae. "How?"

Darius scratched his beard. "This face must seem very old to young eyes, but once I was quite the callow youth and a slave of Venus, risking life and limb for love."

Claudia blinked, wanting to avoid diverting the conversation to old glories, instead redirecting it to new dilemmas. "You must not be caught, Darius. The women of Rome speak truths to me on this day that would otherwise be unthinkable."

He acknowledged her command with a nod and a rueful smile. "What would Volesus Valerius Perseus think of such cynicism, domina?"

"He is five hundred years dead, Darius," Claudia said sharply. "I have little doubt that his concerns are beyond us."

Darius stretched his leg as though testing his old battle wound. "The founder of the Valeria family was deified before the start of the Old Republic. His apotheosis has been certified and blessed by the gods."

Claudia could not help but notice the old scars on her uncle's face, just hidden under his beard. She wondered how this man, almost out of his prime, had suffered for little gain. "Yes, and his honor left us poor. The other major families secured the best land rights and the most slaves. Volesus Valerius Perseus bequeathed only honor to us."

"The Valeria have the highest place of honor," Darius protested. "We're trusted more than any other family in the Republic. We've earned this through blood."

Traffic ahead slowed considerably. There were alleys and secret paths available to them, but such were dangerous during festival, even for Darius. They sent Adalia ahead to discover the cause of the delay.

Claudia leaned close to whisper in her uncle's ear, taking no chance that any could hear her words. "Here is the truth we dare not speak, uncle. We are weak. We are not respected in the Senate. Mighty Caesar does not respect us. And thus, we send our men to war in Gaul to maintain the honor we earned for past glories, with no hope for a future."

"Your father would be ashamed to hear you speak these words, domina."

The thought of her dead father sapped Claudia's kind façade. "My father was poisoned by his younger, weaker brother. Orca then took my mother for his wife. That kept her as materfamilias, but marked my brothers and I as the sole members of a dead branch of the family. Gods know that we only survived thanks to your mercy. If we wish to escape Orca's control and build our own family branch of the Valeria, we must be strong and see the world for what it is, not as we might wish it to be."

"You are in a dark mood this day, Claudia."

Had she gone too far? Claudia wondered. They needed Darius and his loyal guards. Claudia knew sentiment would win this battle better than logic. "I merely trust you enough to see my true face and my dark moods. I trust that you will understand."

Adalia returned, excited with news. "It's a pantomime, domina."

Darius looked ahead at the crowd and grimaced. Actors often staged impromptu performances along the roads to the temples to earn a few denarii from families seeking to gain favor from the gods or the Senate. "We could bypass the mob by walking around the other side of the Palatine, but I couldn't promise that it would be any quicker."

The gods were determined to vex her at every turn this day, Claudia decided. "Perhaps a pantomime would improve my disposition, uncle. And if nothing else, we could learn the mood of the city."

The Flamens were the fraternal order to the Vestals, charged with performing religious rituals, so as to maintain the gods' good will and support for Rome. It was expected they would arrange for entertainment during festivals that encouraged piety and reverence for the Eternal City.

Darius pushed a way through the drunken crowd, worming them closer to the stage, until one of the acolytes noticed her infula. "Divinity walks amongst us. Make a path for the Vestal!"

The Flamens hosting the performance mumbled his apologies to Claudia and ordered his slave take them to a comfortable area just under the stage reserved for patricians and their entourages. Servers brought her wine and water, but she passed them along to Adalia.

An old man clad in a black tunic with a gold belt tapped the stage three times with his staff, catching the attention of the crowd. "The Triumph of Antony."

Claudia found anticipation swelling in her chest despite the delay this performance caused for her plans. She had seen this pantomime dozens of times with her brothers. Marcus adored anything related to his famous namesake, and he strove to emulate his hero in all things. Nicomedes focused his attention upon the Soothsayers and any hint of their true power.

Masked actors portraying the mighty Caesar and loyal Antony strode upon the stage together. They wore thick tragedy masks, symbolizing the divinity of their roles before gods and men.

The three Soothsayers halted their progress. Claudia thought the actors' costuming presented them as scions of Charon the Ferryman. Their hoods obscured their faces, and the flesh that could be seen was painted a ghastly white. Claudia spoke their infamous lines in unison with them. "Beware the Ides of March, Great Caesar."

Caesar stepped forward. His head was adorned with a fresh laurel wreath. "What manner of man or beast is this?"

Antony followed. He carried a bound bundle of wooden rods called a fasces, the very symbol of Roman authority and masculinity. "A soothsayer bids you beware the Ides of March."

Caesar swept his arm over the audience. "Set him before me; let me see his face."

The three Soothsayers stepped forward to center stage. They repeated their warning with one voice. "Beware the Ides of March, Caesar."

Caesar scoffed. "They are but dreamers; let us leave them, Antony. The Senate awaits."

Faux thunder echoed from the amphitheater. The Soothsayers spoke once more. "On this day blood shall be spilt. Yours or theirs." The three knelt before Caesar, presenting him with an amulet that bore a sigil of an eagle. "The choice is yours. Accept our blessing and the Eternal City shall encompass the world."

Caesar turned to Antony and stage-whispered, "Men in general are quick to believe that which they wish to be true. It is better not to upset them and simply pass."

Antony pointed to the amulet that remained upon the stage. "There is power behind their words, Caesar. They have disappeared like shades, but left behind the prize. Take it Caesar. Why tempt the gods?"

* * * *

The Atrium Vestae stood between the Regia and the Palatine Hill, before the circular Temple of Vesta at the eastern edge of the Roman Forum. The walls that surrounded the three-story palace towered over the elegant, elongated atrium and the vast heated bathing pool where the Vestals gave counsel to the women of Rome and bestowed the blessing of Vesta.

Darius escorted Claudia to the steps under the columned porch of the Atrium Vestae. They stood in the shadow of the great marble statue of Numa Pompilius. According to the litany of the Vestals, it was she who founded the cult five hundred years ago. "This is as far as you may proceed, Uncle." Claudia kissed him gently on the cheek and gestured to the crowd consisting of the women of Rome. Maidens, mothers, and crones of every station — plebeians, patricians, and slaves — entered the temple.

Darius nodded ruefully. "Be leery this day, domina. Accept the wisdom of Caesar."

She nodded her silent agreement. "Come along, Adalia."

They entered the temple via a door reserved for the Vestals and immediately arrived in the inner sanctum. Her sister Vestals prepared for the ceremony by gathering candles, warming their voices to sing the hymns, and changing into bleached linen robes and white cotton loincloths.

The inner sanctum bustled with laughter and discreet gossip. This was a moment for sisterhood amongst the Vestals, and a wise person could learn a good deal simply by listening, but Claudia had no time to spare. The heat of the day had caused her to sweat through her stola, and it was considered sacrilegious for a Vestal to enter the ritual without properly sanctifying her body first.

Adalia undressed Claudia in the apodyterium staging area and stored her clothing at Claudia's station. She stepped into the warm water of the tepidarium, where Adalia massaged her with scented oils and gently scraped away the dead skin from her body with a small curved metal tool called a strigil.

The dulcimer chime of the sacred bells rang three times, indicating that the rite would begin soon. Claudia stepped out of the water, allowed Adalia to assist her into her sacred ritual costume and then stepped outside into the fabled protected grove where the great and powerful women of Rome worshiped Vesta.

Her robes swayed behind her until she stopped and knelt before the sacred flame burning at the center of the Atrium Vestae. The dutiful, faithful followers of the goddess were already indulging in the sanctified waters of the bathing pool. They were mostly naked before the goddess offering their worship of the sky above while delighting in the pleasures of the water and fellowship.

This was one of the few places a proper patrician woman could indulge in skyclad sunbathing without bringing scandal to her family. The walls of the sacred grove were high, protected by the legions of Rome, and no proper man of Rome would ever dare challenge the right of the Vestals to administer to their wives, their mothers, and their daughters.

Vesta was the goddess of hearth and home. She ruled over marriages and children. This flame symbolized her favor towards Rome. The Vestals' primary function was to keep the flame burning and bestow the blessing of their patron goddess upon the families of Rome.

Claudia slipped out of her linen robe and let it fall to the ground, where Adalia quietly scooped it into her dutiful arms. Claudia wore only the traditional loincloth and, for adornment, the silver ring that Nicomedes had sent her in secret. It was considered a minor eccentricity for a Vestal to bring jewelry to the sanctified bathing pool, but it was allowed without comment because of Claudia's patrician status. Certainly, she needed it this day more than most.

She stepped into the waters, feeling refreshed almost immediately. Her loincloth billowed under the clear water like a flower unfolding.

The Vestals raised their arms towards the blue sky and Father Jupiter. The women of Rome followed their divine example and began singing the Sacred Hymn of Vesta. The ceremonial blessing of the families of Rome – a long, complicated ritual – involved a good deal of singing, symbolic tending of the sacred flame by both Vestals and selected members of the cult, and lighting scented candles believed to bring the divine spirit home from the blessing.

The Virgo Vestalis Maxima knelt before the entrance of Ariadne's Maze and kissed the earth and dirt, symbolizing her connection to Gaia and the world. This part of the ceremony always worried Claudia, as it recalled the Tragedy of Tarpeia who betrayed her vow of chastity and was buried alive in the maze to appease the gods.

Some Vestals from patrician families were given disposition to leave the cult if their families needed them. Claudia hoped that she would be so blessed. If her brothers succeeded in their machinations, she would need to serve as materfamilias. If she had to live her entire life trapped in service, Claudia had little doubt she would suffer the same fate as Tarpeia.

Once the last hymn had been sung, the Virgo Vestalis Maxima released the congregation of the cult to enjoy the refreshing waters and the joy of sisterhood. Claudia observed that all of the great and minor families were present and mingling at the edges of the bathing pool. The wealthy plebeians swam in the middle huddled like schools of fish, hoping to be invited into one of the more elite conversations.

Slaves brought drinks and platters of fruit. Claudia accepted a plump purple fig, sniffed it, and took a small bite out of it. She waded from one side of the bathing pool to the other, greeting every woman who approached her with kind words and the occasional kiss on the cheek.

A great swarm of sycophants and slaves surrounded Nephele of the Aemilii, clamoring for her favor. She waded through the bath as powerful as an orca, scooping the lesser predators into her tide. Nephele, herself a materfamilias, had birthed a militia of exceedingly wealthy sons and grandsons of Rome.

The Aemilii were thought to be related to the Valeria. Legend spoke of twin brothers who conquered the enemies of Rome under the sigil of Mars. Each brother settled down in time and founded two mighty families. The elder brother earned the agnomen "Aemilius, He That Conquers," because of his ruthless persuasiveness with his language and demeanor in the Senate.

Winning Nephele's favor would be important to her plans, but fighting through the herd of desperate women seeking to marry into the Aemilii would only associate her face with theirs. Instead, Claudia ensured that their gazes met from across the pool, and then she ruefully smiled and nodded, as though offering silent support for the other woman's great ordeal of being wealthy and popular.

"Dia! I am so pleased to see you."

She blinked at the use of her childhood agnomen. Claudia turned her head, trying to locate the source of the voice, until she realized that it came from outside of the bathing pool. The speaker, Livia Drusilla, was the second daughter of Marcus Livius Drusus Claudianus. Her father had considered that man to be his brother-in-spirit gifted from the gods. He had loved Marcus so much that he named two of his children after him as a tribute.

The frail woman wore a long cotton stola that covered her legs and a veil that cast a shadow over her face. Drusilla had been a gentle girl born to a family renowned and celebrated for their beauty. Venus had not blessed Drusilla's features, unlike her elder sister. However, Vulcan had seen fit to bestow shrewd wisdom upon the sickly girl to compensate for cursing her with lameness.

Drusilla had been rejected from the Vestal College due to her deformity, and thus Claudia was quite surprised to see her at the temple. "I am so pleased to see you again. Will you not join us?"

The daughter of Marcus Livius Drusus Claudianus shook her head demurely. "Thank you. I had hoped you would have news of Marcus."

They had played together often as children and took lessons from Sextus Clodius, the renowned Sicilian rhetorician who had once taught oratory to Antony. Drusilla was quite devoted to her elder brother, both then and now. "His legion fights the Caledonians upon the shores of Gaul."

Drusilla smiled brightly at a mere mention of her brother. "I have heard tales that he's grown a beard in the style of the wild men of Albion. And he wears a cape fashioned from the skin of a bear into battle."

Claudia blinked, hoping Marcus hadn't been so foolish as to draw that much attention. "I am certain stories are exaggerated as they reach Rome to increase the joy of the telling."

Drusilla continued her verbal apotheosis of her brother. "Father regaled us this very day with a number of tales of his bravery commanding the Third Cohort of the Seventh Legion."

"I am pleased that your father continues to show an interest in the children of his friend." It was a pity that Orca had forbidden direct communication with the Claudians after father died. They would have been keen allies if they had been able to maintain the friendship. "Surely, you did not venture into the temple merely to share tales of my brother?"

Drusilla blushed, covering part of her face with the veil. She knelt down towards the edge of the bathing pool and lowered her voice to a whisper. "I came to tender an invitation to you and your brother to dine with us when he returns to Rome."

If all went according to plan, Marcus would not return to Rome for two years at the earliest, longer if the Seventh Legion did not secure Gaul from Brutus's followers. Marcus had to serve out his term as Decurion to become eligible to petition the Senate for the right to branch out into a new nomen against Orca's wishes. "It would be unwise to promise that Marcus will arrive in Rome anytime soon, Drusilla. The honor of Rome is at stake, after all."

"My father understands the demands of war and family, and is pleased the sons and daughters of Titus Valerius Perseus honor the old ways." Drusilla kissed Claudia on the forehead. Since her younger sister married into Fabii and her mother died, Drusilla served as the unnamed de facto materfamilias in deed if not name. As a sign of displeasure from the gods her deformity prevented any match to a family worthy of the Claudian name. "The paterfamilias of the Claudians bade me to offer any support that might be required."

Claudia tilted her head. Drusilla had just offered her family's binding support towards her cause. This would risk insulting the volatile Porcii, the conservative Fabii, and perhaps the Aemilii. It would be tantamount to declaring war against Orca. Marriage was the only possible price for such support. She imagined the disappointment on her elder brother's face for such a match, but this possibility could be paramount to their plans for revenge. Claudia returned Drusilla's kiss. "My brothers and I are honored by such devotion, and we will strive to be worthy of it, sister."

Drusilla slowly stood, careful to keep her pride by not stumbling in public. "Until we meet again, Dia."

Claudia waved at her departing childhood friend and turned towards the bathing pool, wondering who had noted the conversation and if any suspicion fell upon them. Drusilla had distracted her to the point that Claudia failed to realize she accidently wandered into the wake of Messalina of the Cornelii. The materfamilias possessed a long neck, giant wild eyes, and dyed hair that recalled an ornery peacock.

Messalina bobbed in the water and waved as though she were trying to achieve flight. "Dearest Claudia, please attend me. Gods know I have need of your insight this day."

"Sweet Messalina, all that I have is yours to command." Claudia suspected she already knew what the materfamilias desired and had hoped to avoid this situation. The Vestals were vaunted by the people of Rome, because they provided wisdom and insight from the gods. Such wisdom was not always well received, and this woman could wreak ruin upon her own intrigues if her advice disappointed. "How may I help you?"

Messalina embraced Claudia as a daughter. "I beg of you… the gods are silent to me. What can I do to appease them, so that I might make a proper match for my girls?"

Claudia had hoped to avoid this very dilemma; it placed her between two horns that were as dangerous as a charging bull. Messalina's husband was the paterfamilias of the Cornelii, branded with the agnomen Salvito due to an unfortunate resemblance to an attractive actor in the forums. Fortune smiled upon Publius Cornelius Scipio Salvito when Caesar recruited him for his campaign against Gnaeus Pompeius Magnus, heeding the superstition that only a Scipio could be victorious in Africa.

Caesar rewarded his friends and forgave his enemies as appropriate for a Consul of Rome. It was rumored the Cornelii had quietly supported the exiled Brutus in Albion with men and gold. Thus, Salvito had the opportunity to experience both faces of Caesar, but this isolated the Cornelii from the rest of Rome.

The major families could very well afford to exclude the Cornelii, but Claudia couldn't afford to make them an enemy. They still had many friends in the Senate and other high offices within Rome. Should Claudia offend Messalina, all of her brother's sacrifices would be for naught. Should she provide incorrect advice, then her reputation would suffer. "You need an augury. There is time this very day."

"Would you?" Messalina embraced her once more and kissed her hands in supplication. "I know that this is not the day for such things."

Claudia summoned Adalia to bring her Vestal robes and started towards the steps out of the bathing pool. "Nonsense. What use is divinity if I cannot help a noble woman of Rome when she needs guidance?"

"Would it be possible to employ the Egyptian method?" Messalina asked. "Nephele speaks highly of it. Her husband has imported a number of slaves that brought their ways to Rome."

Nephele's influence amongst the elder patrons of the Atrium Vestae was such that a whim became fashionable to those seeking her favor. Claudia dressed slowly, considering what words she might use to guide the matron. Wind blew down from the atrium, bringing a slight chill to her flesh, but it made standing near the Sacred Flame more pleasurable.

Messalina joined her at the sacred altar with her body-slaves and three daughters. "This shall not be forgotten, Claudia."

Claudia noted that several patrician women glanced towards them, whispering. Vestals rarely offered private consultation after a public ritual save under grave circumstances. Nephele of the Aemilii seemed particularly intrigued, as though the thought of such an honor going to anyone else was simply unfathomable.

Adalia brought a sleeping hen under her arm and Claudia's ceremonial pugio to the altar. Weapons were forbidden in the Atrium Vestae, but a sanctified divine instrument was an exception to the taboo. The pugio had been another gift from Marcus during his campaign in Gaul. The Vestals kept such instruments under close guard, lest they be used in anger by others who sought to abuse their sacred rights.

Claudia accepted the hen and lifted it high into the air. She whispered a prayer to convince Vesta to anoint the sacrifice with her blessing. Claudia tucked the hen's head under her wing to lull her to sleep and then squeezed her neck until it snapped. Her legs fluttered for a moment and became still.

She carefully placed the dead hen upon the altar. Claudia inserted the pugio into the hen and sliced a gash from breast to stern. She wiped the blood on her sleeves as tradition and the gods demanded, and then plunged her hands into the flesh while it was still warm.

Haruspexy demanded that the organs be examined quickly after death to experience the insight of the gods. Claudia probed the heart, liver, and gizzard, seeking to glean wisdom. "You are seeking to pledge your eldest daughter to a son of the Aemilii."

"Yes. What do the gods say of this?" Messalina asked.

Claudia knew that she had to choose her words very carefully lest she ruin everything. "Vesta is pleased with the concept of such a match. It would strengthen Rome."

"Why am I stymied at every turn?" Messalina blinked and peered over Claudia's shoulder to see what might be learned, as though the very answer to her problem had been literally inscribed on the entrails of this dead hen. "Every advance is rebuffed. We are a proud family of Rome."

"Venus is displeased and stands in your way."

Caesar claimed divinity through lineage to Aeneas and of the blood of the goddess of love. Marriage and love were not always connected, but it was a powerful symbol to fight against. "What can we do, Claudia? I've failed Salvito. Three children and no sons. Aulus grows stronger from each victory in Gaul with your brother."

Claudia understood well the ambition of younger brothers and how said disputes were handled. "It is Juno Regina who will reign over this dispute and settle the matter."

Messalina's eyes widened as large as a seedcake. "What does the queen of the gods wish of us?"

Invoking the epithet Juno Regina was dangerous. The queen of the gods had many faces and aspects that she revealed to mortals. She presided over marriage, children, and the state. Juno Regina was one of the triumvirate patron gods of the Eternal City, and she was quite capricious with her favor, which could possibly hurt Claudia at the end. "She desires a show of public support for Rome, and if she is pleased, she will favor the match."

The best auguries provided actionable advice, left the future open to failure in the hands of the petitioner, and yet imparted hope for victory. Messalina embraced her once again and quickly departed with her entourage of slaves and daughters.

Blood on her hands left Claudia unsanctified, and she could not return to the bathing pool. She caught the eyes of the major families on her and decided she should retire and leave them curious as to what she might have said.

She handed the pugio to Adalia, washed her hands in a nearby brass bowl, and excused herself to the Virgo Vestalis Maxima. She led her body-slave into the inner sanctum and the side corridors where the Vestals kept private rooms; a place where many who did not belong to a patrician family lived and worked.

A pitcher of water and sweet cakes were left outside of her room. Adalia brought the tray inside and proceeded to help Claudia wash and dress. "I believe I am tempted by the cake, Adalia."

Adalia brought a slice of the cake on a small clay plate and poured her some water. Claudia reached out to accept the meal, when she felt a moment of hesitation. Her hand felt numb, as though she had just thrust it into a cauldron of bubbling water.

The ring of Nicomedes vibrated as though it were alive. She knew of the power of the Soothsayers and their apprentices, but to witness it frightened her.

Her younger brother's warning flashed to her memory. "The principle is quite simple, Dia. Like is always attracted to like in the universe. I have attuned this metal to every poison I have studied since attending the academy. Should this ring react, you are in the presence of poison and someone is trying to murder you."

Claudia dropped the cake with horror. The clay plate fell to the floor and shattered. She knocked the drink out of Adalia's hand. "Poison! We must flee before they discover we survived."

Adalia did not deign to ask who "they" might be or why they were in danger. She unsheathed the ceremonial pugio with a practiced ease that surprised Claudia. "Which way?"

Claudia recalled the lessons Darius drilled into their brains as children: always run in an unexpected direction and never let yourself be cornered without options. There were a number of passages that vented into the common areas, but if they were being followed, then they would surely be intercepted before they reached safety. If Darius kept his word, he would be waiting for her below in Ariadne's Maze.

Claudia groped along the wall of the hall outside of her room, until she found the lever that revealed secret stairs twisting downward into the subterranean tunnels, leading to the maze.

She moved slowly, feeling her way along the stone walls and the curved steps. Adalia followed her into the tunnels, glancing back at the light that marked the entrance. "Footsteps!"

Three men, bearing lit torches and clad in grey linen tunics, trampled down the steps and into the maze. Scarves covered their faces, and they were armed with long blades of a nature Claudia had never seen before.

"Run!" Adalia spun the pugio in her hand with the skill of a juggler twirling a pin. She blocked the egress downward, so the assassins would have to run through her to proceed. "I'll hold them here."

She lacked the time or fortitude to argue. Claudia continued forward until the light behind her completely disappeared into the turns of the maze.

Ariadne's Maze had been built to serve as a labyrinth where sacrifices were made as part of reparations to the gods. The name came from the story of Theseus and the Minotaur. Wicked Vestals were cast down here to die, but there were secret ways out if you knew the paths. More than one condemned Vestal with the right connections had escaped the Eternal City via these tunnels.

Claudia was confident she would find her way out once her eyes adjusted to the lack of light. She might not be a soldier, but she was clever, and that made her dangerous.

The assassins were silent as the grave, but the walls magnified any sound a thousand-fold. Lit torches cast light far ahead of her pursuers. They were moving rather quickly, having the advantage of light.

She had no time to ponder what might have happened to poor Adalia. Claudia blindly turned left, trusting her mind and muscle memory, hoping that she would find the route out. She took a circular route with as many limited entry points as possible.

It was difficult to breathe in this section of the maze; the air tasted foul. Her head ached, as it become more and more difficult to focus.

The silver ring vibrated once more. Her would-be assassins somehow managed to dose her with poison or magic. Claudia had neither time to escape nor the ability the defeat her enemies, so she elected to go for a bold tactic. "Darius!"

The assassins quickly closed on her. She squinted at the sudden intrusion of light in the maze, and it dazzled her sense of direction for a few moments.

They spoke a strange musical language, and their words echoed around her, sapping her will. She wanted nothing more than to lie in the earth and sleep forever.

Two globes of flickering light came towards her from different directions. The assassins had managed to flank her position. They slowly edged her out of space and brandished their weapons, ready for the kill.

A familiar voice called out from the darkness: Darius. "Down!"

Torchlight flickered off his gladius as it cleaved into the skull of the assassin closest to striking her. Claudia closed her eyes, but could not escape the cries and moans of dying men soon to visit the afterlife. Her heart raged against her chest, desperate to somehow remain alive.

The clang of metal and screams faded into a terrible silence until Darius spoke. "I think it is best to retreat to more secure ground, domina."

Chapter Two: The Centurion

The Third Cohort of the Seventh Legion ate dried quail, drank bitter wine, and stared out into the Atlantic upon Saxone Shore. The meal provided a rare luxury on the battlefield, but it was well-earned after the day's fighting. Centurion Marcus Valerius Perseus read by the flickering campfire and listened to his men's stories and laughter. Caesar cautioned against the natural inclination of an officer to seek solitude after a skirmish, and Marcus was inclined to listen to the words of a man who had conquered most of the known world.

The soldiers gambled in the dirt, wagering their salaries to feel alive after the battle. The Marian Legionary Reforms strictly prohibited such activities at camp. Marcus disdained the vice personally, but as long as his cohort maintained discipline and followed his orders, he felt content to ignore the infraction. Turning a blind eye was a small price to purchase his men's loyalty and love, and he would need that in abundance in the future.

The optio finished his drink and scooped the dice into his hand with a roar of infectious laugher; Milius had served Marcus well this last year as his second. "Probatus! Attend me, now!"

The cohort's newest recruit pushed through the other soldiers to stand before the optio at full salute. His face appeared more boy than man. "Here, sir."

"I've been quite vexed over a weighty question, probatus." Milius jabbed his finger at the disc of signaculum on the young man's chest, which marked him as a new recruit of the legion. "Exactly how long ago did you replace your boyhood bulla for that disc? Exactly how far from your mother's teat are you?"

Cossus remained at attention. "I am of age, sir."

The fresh recruit was from a rich plebian family named Crassus. Much like Marcus, he sought to earn his name and elevate his family. Milius extended his hand, offering the dice. "Care to throw the bones, probatus? I want some of that viaticum coin your rich father passed on to you to buy fat whores and wine after we kill all of the Caledonians in Britannia."

The probatus took the bait and accepted the dice. He crouched down to the earth and brushed aside loose pebbles and grime. Cossus flashed a smug grin to his comrades and threw the bones.

A collective hush washed over the camp, as the dice settled onto the ground. The entire cohort, save for Milius, groaned with disappointment, hoping Cossus would be the one to shatter the old man's winning streak.

The old soldier repressed any hint of emotion on his face. Marcus knew Milius had fought in two victorious campaigns — one in Hispania and one in Gaul. The optio bore an honored lorica that had clearly seen action over the years; an old soldier was a rarity these days. Killing for the Empire was a young man's game, but what else was left for Milius? *How could farming ever feel right to him?*

Marcus tried not to grin. Milius bilking the new recruits out of their wages was practically an initiation ritual into the Seventh Legion.

Cossus reluctantly plucked a coin pouch from his belt and tossed it over to Milius. "Pluto himself is pissing on my luck all the way from

Tartarus." He turned towards the centurion and blushed. "Apologies, sir."

Milius laughed and slapped the new recruit upon his back. "The centurion won't be offended, probatus. The good centurion doesn't believe in the gods."

"What soldier doesn't believe in the gods, once he has visited the Fields of Mars?" Cossus asked. He paused regretfully, "Apologies, centurion. No disrespect was intended, sir."

Marcus waved away the young legionnaire's concern. "Disrespect was neither intended nor received. Quell your fears, Cossus. I greatly admire the ancient stoics of Athens who followed Zeno of Citium. I believe in a natural universe, with logical laws, that I can observe and understand if I put my mind to it. I place my faith in that which I can touch and taste and fight."

"But what of the foreign gods that protect Britannia?" Cossus asked, echoing the unspoken concerns of the cohort. The other soldiers said nothing, but Marcus knew they observed the conversation closely. "The Caledonians have powerful magics to aid their cause."

The damned reavers pillaged Roman villages from Gaul to Hispania with impunity, and then returned to dark Britannia, where the hostile ports prevented Rome from conquering the insurgents. "Tactics and the weight of history have stymied our campaign, not magic or divine intervention." Marcus lifted the scroll he had been studying for months. "Commentarii de Bello Gallico was written by the imperator himself, after the First Gallic War. The natural lay of that wretched island prevents easy landing of soldiers, without facing a dangerously fortified position."

"And what of the storms, sir?" Two invasion fleets carrying legions had disappeared sailing across the Atlantic. Rumor had it the sea swallowed them whole for daring to invade Britannia. "They say that the gods are pleased another Brutus has come to rule the land Aeneas settled after the fall of Troy."

It was no easy task to order men to their deaths against painted savages who serve a traitor of Rome. Maintaining soldiers' morale was important in this war, which seemed to echo into forever. "The storms are a natural occurrence, according to the very words of our imperator," Marcus stated evenly. "Mighty Caesar himself noted the mercurial weather and the difficulty of locating a safe port for landing a legion without being harried, and that was before the traitor Brutus brought them gold and weapons. Cassius taught the savages how to fight properly."

Milius snorted loudly and toasted the centurion. "The dirt worshipers can have all of the heathen gods at their side, as long as we have Marcus Valerius Perseus leading us."

The cohort cheered, appreciating a chance to lighten the mood. Marcus nodded appreciatively. "We have pushed the Caledonians from Gaul and Hispania, and trapped them in that cursed land. It is only a matter of time before we gather the strength required to end this war."

"Aye, sir."

Marcus waved them off to return to the revelry. "Return to your games, Cossus. Try not to lose your boots."

Milius waited until the cohort was distracted and then brought

Marcus a flash of wine. "I wish you hadn't sent Adalia away to Rome, centurion," said Milius gruffly. "When she was here, you were less grim, and you smiled more."

"It was required to protect my sister."

"You can't trust the Germani." Milius took another swig of the wine. "They can't be turned into Romans by your will and cock alone."

Marcus shrugged. "Not by my will alone certainly."

They laughed in a shared moment of brotherhood forged in steel and blood, until Milius tilted his head upward and pointed to the night sky. "Do you see that?"

Marcus followed the gaze of the optio, noting a shadow moving against the black of night. It landed before the campfire, beating its powerful wings.

"An eagle!" Cossus exclaimed. "They never fly at night."

The regal bird, the very symbol of Rome, turned towards Marcus and screeched. Then the impossible happened…

Marcus had traveled much of the known world, seen many strange people, and spoke their languages. He had heard stories of gods and monsters and heroes, and never before had he believed in unnatural law, until the eagle spoke in his younger brother's unmistakable voice. "Return to Rome, brother. Claudia was assaulted by enemies."

The camp guards drew their weapons and stepped back. Marcus stayed their attack with a single motion of his hand. There could be little doubt now that magic was real, and that the Soothsayers had kept their promise. Nicomedes had mastered their art, and danger stalked his siblings.

He turned to Milius. "Send a rider to Legate Agrippa."

* * * *

Marcus paced the length of the legate's tent, eager to speak with his commanding officer. The words from the eagle, spoken with his brother's tongue, loomed large in his thoughts. Why did Nicomedes not disclose the fate of their sweet sister in the message? And in what world would anyone dare to attack a Vestal Virgin in temple? That would be akin to declaring war against all of Rome.

Agrippa's servant brought into the tent a platter of shellfish, roasted clams, and buttered asparagus, and placed it on a wooden cask of Italian wine. The meal would have served as a feast to the men of his cohort.

"The legate commanded that I serve your needs until he arrives. He is speaking to General Varus about your request presently." She gestured to the food, the wine, and then coyly to the bed. "He bids you to make yourself comfortable in his hospitality. Take that which you need to refresh yourself."

She was a local woman with bright green eyes, kissable lips, and sweet disposition. Were it not for his crushing worry over his sister, Marcus might have indulged himself, if only to avoid insulting the legate. "You are as lovely as a nymph, but my heart and head is elsewhere. You may leave."

His bloody two-year campaign against the Caledonian reavers dulled his memory of real luxury, but standing amongst the rich oriental rugs, silk draperies, and statues of ancient tribal gods brought forth a pang of longing to see Rome and his home once more. The true temptation of the tent lay upon the table, where the legate kept the meticulously drawn battle map of the Seventh Legion. Once the servant left, Marcus half-heartedly ate the meal and quickly seized the rare opportunity to study it.

The legate had marked and notated every battle and movement of the enemy in Greek letters. Marcus studied them at great length, reading them over and over, until he understood the enormity of what lay before him: a secret chronicle of the Second Gallic War, from the flight of Brutus and his treacherous cabal from Italia, the battle for Gaul against the rebel legions, and their eventual defeat at the Rhine River.

Marcus Vipsanius Agrippa served under mighty Caesar years ago, before the attempted assassination, during the campaign against Gnaeus Pompey Magnus. He later studied with Caesar's heir Octavian in blessed Apollonia with the philosophers of Athens. The legate possessed a tactical mind shaped by the greatest natural philosophies of the age. This map was a meditation upon the current dilemma facing the campaign. The Seventh Legion had beaten the Caledonians back to the Atlantic countless times, and yet had never been able to deliver the killing blow.

Announcing his presence by the stomping of his feet, Agrippa ducked under the flap and strode into the tent, confident as though returning home in a triumph. He washed his hands and face in the copper basin and then took to devouring the meal. "Do you know the difference between a map made by a Roman and one made by a Greek?"

Marcus stood at attention and saluted the legate. He opened his mouth to request his leave, but decided to answer the question instead. "I do not, sir."

"A Roman will sketch the geography presented on the map by references to known landmarks, such as a road or a bridge. This is practical, and it meets our needs for governance." Agrippa pointed to the series of roads utilized by the Seventh Legion in Gaul and then traced the outline of the coast of Gaul. "The Greeks care more for accuracy than practicality. They calculate their maps by positioning of the stars. The truth is somewhere between the two perspectives."

"What truth have you discovered, sir?"

"You tell me, Valerius."

Marcus cast his eyes on the map once more, trying to glean the secrets Agrippa had divined and the mystery he was attempting to pierce. Brutus fled to Britannia with a failed general, slaves, exiled soldiers from Gaul and Germani tribes, and foreign mercenaries bought with misbegotten gold from the treasury. Brutus of Troy, son of Aeneas, settled Britannia in antiquity, and the wild tribes of that foreboding land took Marcus Junius Brutus as their leader—a king in deed, if not title and crown. Marcus spat upon the hypocrisy of attempting to kill the imperator to prevent him from taking a crown and then practically claiming another to save his cowardly skin.

Yet the map revealed a number of Caledonian failures in their own pitiful schemes for conquest. The insurgents expected a wellspring of support from the provinces that never appeared. Caesar crushed that possibility once he pushed his reforms through the Senate to include representatives from every tribe under the sway of the Empire. That very act sparked the assassination attempt twenty years ago, and now the provinces had the benefits of Rome and civilization.

The answer seemed obvious when the details were laid before him. "How are they supplying their armies?"

Agrippa poured two chalices of wine and handed one to Marcus. "General Varus believes that is the purpose of their raids along the coast, as has been noted in great and agonizing deal in his most recent report to the Senate. And that surely the campaign is almost over."

"That seems unlikely, sir." It was dangerous to contradict a general you served, but Marcus hoped Agrippa took a more enlightened and reasoned approach to leadership. "The men we killed this very day were as well-supplied and trained as any legion of Rome."

"It is pleasing to know you still hold to logic and reason, centurion. I worried you believed in divine intervention after the recent nonsense." Legate Agrippa shook his head, clearly disappointed. "I should have you scourged for frightening the plebs like that. Morale is dangerously low as it is, and now the men are already whispering that the gods have abandoned us."

Marcus shook his head. "I did not arrange said nonsense, legate. The eagle was just as much of a surprise to my eyes as to your ears."

Agrippa paused a moment, as though reading the lines on Marcus's face. "No matter. It is illegal to speak against a prophecy from the Soothsayers by order of the imperator. And that provides us with an opportunity."

"An opportunity, sir?"

"I could not countermand the general's position or orders, but you have been commanded by the Soothsayers to return to Rome." Agrippa waved towards the bust of mighty Caesar. "The name Marcus Valerius Perseus commands some respect back in Rome, if not rank. The tale of your slaying of the bear grows larger each passing day. I heard tell that you wear it as a cape, and you wear your hair long like a Gaul."

"That would be against regulation, sir," Marcus protested. "And it would be a sin against the gods and nature to mar this face with a beard."

"As long as your priorities are in order, centurion." Agrippa tapped his finger on the map to empathize his point. "Caesar shall ask you to report on this campaign personally, if only to be seen with you. You shall repeat what you have seen here."

Marcus grimaced. "Such would make Varus curse my very name to go against his words."

Agrippa nodded, acknowledging the truth in the statement. "Perhaps, but it would also make you a number of friends who are on the rise. Caesar will believe neither report initially until he begins his own investigation, and then he will remember who it was that brought the truth to him."

"Understand that I have other business in Rome, legate."

The legate's face flushed red with anger. "Understand that to leave for Rome without my permission would be desertion, centurion. You would abandon any hope for your name and forever be an outcast. Follow my command and serve both of our purposes and the needs of Rome."

There seemed to be little choice in the matter. "Aye, sir."

"Order your cohort to break camp at dawn. The Fifth Cohort shall replace your duties until you return." Agrippa handed over a manifest sealed with the sigil of General Varus. "See to it that your optio visits the quaestors for the coin to resupply the Third and the Seventh Legions. Milius knows well how to navigate those choppy waters. It will give you a week to complete your business."

The centurion saluted. "Thank you, sir."

"Thank me by completing this task and aiding me in ending this war."

* * * *

The Third Cohort of the Seventh Legion marched along the Aemilia Way, through the Apennine Mountains and onto the hills and plains of Italia, to the Rubicon River. Whirls of dust and thunderous steps marked their passage, as they strode ever-closer to home. Marcus led the march upon his brown and white checkered mare, ensuring that the soldiers kept to a respectable pace. "How long have you been gone from Rome, Milius?"

The optio rode alongside the centurion. The weight of the old man's age could be heard in the wheeze of his voice. "Seven years or more. I've spent the majority of my five decades on this earth out in the provinces, horribly murdering those who oppose Rome."

"Is it still home?" Marcus asked.

"I have cousins in the Aventine who run the local collegia. Made a good living for themselves over the years." Milius shrugged his shoulders. "If the quaestors provide funds as Varus asks, we could make the denarii go far working through them."

"Would it be legal?"

"Best not to ask too much about the practicalities of the deal." Milius shielded his eyes from the sun and gestured towards the other side of the Rubicon. "There's soldiers camped out along the road. Almost three cohorts worth, I'd guess."

Marcus noted that some of the soldiers were stationed to greet those who would cross the Rubicon and attack them while weak from the crossing. "Strange that the imperator would break tradition and risk the outrage from the Senate."

Milius scoffed. "A Vestal Virgin was attacked in the Atrium Vestae. The real surprise is that legions aren't massing in the Fields of Mars. You might think of her as your sister, but to the mob she is a bride of Rome. She belongs to them as much as you in their eyes."

"Know that should I find out who is responsible, I will personally send them to Pluto absent their head, which will become our standard until I am old as you. But that is a family matter, as it should be." Marcus waved away Milius's argument, as though it possessed an offensive smell. "You suggest this attack was some sort of military assault, when clearly it was some sort of symbolic gesture from an ignorant fanatic. Who else would dare such a thing?"

The Third Cohort of the Seventh Legion began to cross the Rubicon. The horses led the way, but the legionaries marched tirelessly across the river.

"Halt!" The soldiers on the other side raised their arms and closed ranks. "Stand and be recognized."

Milius rode ahead. Marcus followed silently. "By what right under the gods and the imperator do you dare to halt returning heroes?" Milius bellowed.

A fresh-faced soldier wearing clean armor rode to meet them. "I am Optio Junius Flavus Numerius and I have been charged by the Senate to watch this pass for intruders who might seek to take advantage of current events in Rome."

"Do we appear intruders, optio? Perhaps burglars out to steal the food from your pots?"

Junius shook his head. "You look like legionnaires, and none have been scheduled to return this month. We must be careful."

Marcus nodded his approval, and Milius handed over the cohort's sigil of authority granted from Legate Agrippa. Junius read over the scroll. "I cannot authenticate this personally, but I'll send a runner over to the gate for permission."

"Fine, fine. We'll sequester our men over to that hill there and let them rest." Milius nodded towards Marcus. "Our centurion has urgent family business in the city and cannot wait. I'll wait with the men and organize the sequester and resupply."

Junius turned as though to leave, stopped, and replied over his shoulder. "I cannot make exceptions, even for an alleged centurion. He will have to wait for orders."

"You ignorant piss-pot! Do you know who this man is?" The optio's face blushed crimson. "This man killed a bear with his own hands! A hero many times in the campaign against the Caledonians. Why in Tartarus would they let a Flavus protect the gates of Rome? Your family hasn't been in a real fight for four-hundred years — since the Etruscans. I should cut off your tongue and wash my balls with it."

Marcus wearily held up his hand. Milius nodded silently and backed his horse. He took off his helmet so his face could be seen and tossed it to Milius. "Optio Junius Flavus Numerius. I am Centurion Marcus Valerius Perseus. I command the Third Cohort of the Seventh Legion under Legate Agrippa. By order of General Varus, I have brought these men to Rome to resupply the legion. I have been given leave to enter the city personally to speak with my sister Claudia Valeria Terza."

"The Vestal Virgin?" Junius asked skeptically. "The one who was attacked?"

Marcus nodded graciously. It was strange his sister was better known to these soldiers than he, but then again, Milius correctly surmised that this guard was really a patrician's young son pretending to fill service for a later political career. "The very same. She is my sister, and as you might imagine, I would see to her needs and comforts immediately. We are all loyal soldiers of Rome."

"How could you have known? The attack was but a week ago. There would have barely been enough time for word to have reached you."

The centurion rubbed his temple and tried to answer in a calm voice. "I was more than six hundred miles away when an eagle landed at our campsite, bringing the words of an apprentice to a Soothsayer and bidding me to Rome. I do not have time to loiter while you verify orders."

Junius puckered his lip, doling out his words cautiously. "This sounds unbelievable, sir."

Marcus slid off his horse, giving Junius the clear tactical advantage and respect: a wild breach in protocol. Junius glanced aside nervously. "Sir, it is forbidden for soldiers to draw blood on the Rubicon."

The Flavians were one of the major families of Rome, and if the Valeria were to build their own house, they would need the Flavians' allegiance in time. "What you've said is true, Junius. What I have said is also true. I am asking for a personal favor as a member of the Valeria. You may send one of your men to escort me to the Domūs de Valeria if my word is not enough."

"And if I refuse?"

"Then I will pull you off your horse and drag you across the river as Achilles did Hector." Marcus nodded towards the soldiers watching the exchange and continued. "I will not mark your face nor will I gouge out your eyes. I will grab you by the neck and choke you until you slumber with Morpheus."

Junius swallowed. His soldiers listened carefully to the exchange. "Thank you for surrendering to my authority, centurion. If you will leave your weapons with your optio, I shall have my men escort you to your home immediately."

Marcus removed his gladius from his belt and handed it Milius.

The old man shook his head. "I don't like it, sir. What if this maggot betrays you?"

Marcus laughed. "Then you will finally have something with which to wash your balls."

*   *   *   *

Marcus felt strange without his armor or gladius, but it was the snaking paths through the mob that truly set his skin on edge. It had been six years since he left Rome, and the city had changed dramatically, and yet was ever the same.

The guards were cautious, having heard of the centurion who killed a bear with his bare hands. Marcus had to admit the story had done him some justice. Milius made up the story after Marcus accidently stumbled onto a bear cub while taking a crap just before a battle. Each successive telling grew bolder.

Two of the men carried his saddle bags with honor, while the third pushed their way through the crowd. Some of the plebeians looked on curiously. The crowds grew thicker as they ascended up towards the Seven Hills of Rome.

The imperator's Praetorian Guard protected the gate that divided the Appian Way. The soldiers in ornate black armor stopped them. "Halt and identify yourselves."

"I am Marcus Valerius Perseus," he said, waving them to part from his path. "I have come home from the campaign against the Caledonians."

They glanced at each other and whispered. "Your arrival was foretold, but unexpected at this time, centurion. We will escort you to the Domūs de Valeria. Follow us, sir."

Marcus relieved the remainder of his escort. "Tell my optio that I'll need the rest of my bags by the end of the day."

They saluted quietly and quickly disappeared into the crowd. Marcus followed the Praetorian Guard until they reached the Palatine Hill, where pilgrims and plebeians sang dirges praising Claudia. Marcus had never seen the mob stirred.

The great door of Domūs de Valeria was closed, but a small clutch of house guards remained vigilant outside of it. Darius was at the forefront, as though he waited specifically for a special visitor. *Strange*, Marcus thought, *it was almost as though Darius was waiting for him. When did his old mentor turn so frail and old?*

"Darius!"

"Marcus?" The old warrior blinked surprised. "You look at though you could pin down Atlas himself. What are they feeding the legionaries these days?"

"Caledonians and bears."

"It suits you, Marcus."

"What of Claudia? Is she well?"

Darius leaned closely to Marcus and whispered. "She escaped the assassin's blade. It was Adalia who caught the brunt of it."

"Adalia? Did Pluto claim her?" Marcus asked.

"She survived, but only just," Darius revealed. "Nicomedes appeared out of nowhere like a snake and cured the poison inside of her. Said that this was just the beginning."

His old mentor's eyes held fear at the mention of his younger brother's name. Marcus did not have time to broach such a subject. "I would see the both of them."

"Claudia and Adalia have been sequestered in my quarters, where none who do not know the way can reach them. Nicomedes returned to the Soothsayers with the heads of the assassins."

"With the heads?"

"Your brother claims that he has ways of making them speak, even now," Darius explained. "I did not have the courage to ask further questions."

"And Orca and Mother?" Marcus asked.

Darius shook his head. "Orca is on a trip to Egypt to visit your mother. She has been on a pilgrimage to Alexandria the last two years for her health."

"Who is running the house in Orca's place?" Marcus asked.

"Decimus. It is said that this is a test for when Orca retires."

Decimus had been a cruel boy who liked to beat slaves and had made leering glances at Claudia. She joined the Vestal Virgins to protect herself while her brothers were away. "Then let us make haste."

They passed through the great door and skirted around the atrium. Darius led Marcus towards his private cottage behind the main house, where there were two guards stationed at the front door. These freemen, distant cousins, were named by the Valeria and loyal to the concept of the house above all else.

Marcus followed Darius into the cottage, wondering if his mentor would betray him as did his mother. Adalia lay upon the bed covered with a blanket. Her face was a web of bruises and stiches. The odds must have been greatly against her to suffer such a beating, Marcus thought. He knelt down to examine his friend, ignoring the priestess tending to her wounds. "How is she?"

"Her fever has broken as Nicomedes predicted." The priestess replaced the dry poultice covering Adalia's skull, revealing hints of scar tissue and stitches. "She saved my life. Why? I was convinced that she detested me."

Marcus blinked, trying to place where he had heard that voice previously. It had been years since he had last walked the streets of Rome. He tilted his head upwards, towards the priestess. She had the proper appearance of a noble woman of Rome, with a luscious aquiline curve to her nose and delicate cheekbones. A familiar feeling was reflected in her dark eyes. "Dia?"

His sister flashed a smile, greeting him home. "I am pleased that you remember me, brother."

The Valeria were an old Mediterranean family noted for their thick, curly black hair and olive skin. Marcus almost forgot the trouble that had brought him to Rome. Claudia had become a woman during his military service, and while not quite matching the legendary beauty of their mother, she was certainly a fine model of Roman virtue. "The last time these eyes laid upon you, you were but a gangly and awkward girl. Who could have imagined such a world where you are such a lovely woman?"

Claudia embraced her brother warmly. The distance of the years seemed to fade immediately. "You were gone for almost five years. It should not surprise you that I have aged. And look at you. Large and strong. A beard like the men of myth. You look like a wild man. Why, you could wrestle Hercules down to the ground if you set your mind to it. I heard you killed a bear with your own hands."

Marcus laughed. "Stories have been exaggerated, sister. I have been at the front and unable to properly groom myself, and I sent Adalia to you."

"Then, you do not have a pelt for me?" Claudia asked, disappointed.

Marcus laughed. "A promise of the Valeria is always kept. It is with my bags. There was a delay at the gates, because rumor has it that one of the Vestal Virgins was attacked."

The humor died in the room. "It was horrible, Marcus."

"Tell me everything," Marcus demanded.

"Nicomedes warned me that there might be an attempt upon Claudia's life," Darius said, speaking for the first time since they entered his cottage. "I changed the rotation of the house guards. Only those absolutely loyal to our cause were allowed to protect her."

"Why in the name of the gods did you not tell me?" Claudia demanded.

"Nicomedes warned me to tell not a soul," Darius admitted. "He said it would alter the possibilities, and that reactions must be natural for events to occur as required."

Claudia coughed. "Yes, that certainly soothes my soul."

"And what happened?" Marcus asked.

"It was the Festival of Antony, and thus I escorted Claudia to the Atrium Vestae," Darius continued. "I was not permitted within the walls, but I remained at the ready under the temple should there be a problem."

"After the ceremony, they attacked from the shadows," Claudia explained. "They seemed to know everything. They knew where I would walk, the arrangements of my chambers and my habits."

"Clearly, the assassins were well-prepared, and that alone is troubling," Marcus said, nodding towards Claudia. "You survived, Dia, and that is most important."

"It would not be so without Darius and Adalia. She almost exchanged her life for mine. Why would a slave do such a thing?" Claudia asked.

"There was a debt between us, now paid in full. Will she recover?" Marcus asked.

"I admit, I would not have thought so, having witnessed the attack," Darius admitted. He gestured towards Adalia with great concern. "She was stabbed several times with a poisoned blade. I had never seen such a reaction in the body. Nicomedes knew the curse immediately and brewed a poultice that drew the venom from the body."

"Nicomedes did this?" Marcus asked.

"Little brother has grown in power and knowledge," Claudia added. "He was frightening. Wild-eyed and cold as Dis Pater. His skin was sallow, as though he were about to journey with Charon. And he stank as though he had not bathed since he left for the academy."

"If his trick in summoning me here is but an example of his abilities, you speak the truth." Marcus turned to Darius. "Where is he now?"

"Nicomedes said that his presence was required at the academy, and he would return this evening to discuss important matters with the two of you," Darius informed them.

This old soldier had killed many men in his day, and the way he spoke of Marcus' little brother chilled him. "He knew when I would arrive?"

"He said he was carefully monitoring your progress, whatever that means," Claudia admitted.

"Very well, you kept the bodies of the assassins, yes?" Marcus asked. "My eyes might be able to identify them, where yours cannot. I have seen many men killed these last years. It might be the Caledonians sought revenge for their last defeat."

"You can see the bodies, of course, but none of them have heads," Darius explained.

"You did not think to keep them?" Marcus asked.

Darius coughed, as though choking on the words coming to his lips. "Nicomedes collected them. He said that they had one last song to sing before he sent them to Hell."

Claudia placed her hand on her elder brother's shoulder. "As I said, brother, there have been many changes in Nicomedes."

"War changes men. I have no doubt his training under the Soothsayers has done likewise." Marcus turned towards Darius. "My man Milius shall be at the gate by nightfall. Please ensure he is brought to me. I need to discuss possibilities with Claudia."

Darius snapped a salute towards Marcus, nodded a farewell to Claudia, and left his own chambers. "You wounded his feelings, brother," Claudia said.

"I will settle the account before the day is done," Marcus promised. "I have feared for the two of you since I left. Orca is mad to put his son in charge."

Claudia scoffed. "Darius protects us as always, even if Mother does not. And now the both of us are prestigious members of the family."

"You are certain he did not arrange this assassination to be rid of you?" Marcus asked.

Claudia shook her head. "My position fills his coffers. You provided me with my only slave, Adalia. Nicomedes does not draw funds from the family. He is fat and content with his victory, so long as we do not challenge his right to lead the family."

"He must know I am seeking to earn my name, yes?"

"I think as long as we took Darius with us, he would be glad to be rid of us." Claudia shook her head. "We would still be under his thrall, but it would be a start."

"One deed at a time, then. Decimus has not tried anything with you, then?" Marcus asked. "I sent Adalia to shield you from him. Assassins did not enter my mind."

"That bastard has not glanced my way since becoming a Vestal Virgin. I am bride of Rome after all." Claudia smiled sweetly, and it made Marcus quite uncomfortable. Mother had the same smile when she was about to assign an unpleasant chore. "And speaking of brides, I have discovered a suitable match for you. She can drag dreams from the ethereal to reality."

"Who?"

"Livia Drusilla of the Claudians."

Marcus was appalled. "The one with the deformities?"

"Her foot is lame, not deformed. She is a good mother and will make you a proper wife. The Claudians would pay well for the match. Her father, the senator, would actively support the split and anoint you paterfamilias of our new family."

"But what of the children?"

"Is not the Valeria seed strong?" Claudia asked. "And I have faith you shall find other men and women to fill your needs as you have them."

"But what if the children are not beautiful?"

"Then they will have to marry better than you, brother," Claudia snapped. "This is the best match for us financially and politically."

"What of Nicomedes?" Marcus asked, desperate.

"No woman would marry him, Claudia stated. "Not one that serves our purposes. He has no desire of his own, save for knowledge."

Marcus shrugged. "Then he would not mind marrying her. Flesh does not delight him, as you say."

"Livia Drusilla loves only you. She spreads word of every victory and shouts down any negative word. Her father dotes on her and perhaps you by extension. And besides, I have the feeling that

Nicomedes has some sort of arrangement."

"With whom?"

"He keeps his own secrets." Claudia poured him a glass of wine. "Come brother, rest. We will make plans this night when Nicomedes returns."

Marcus shook his head. "I fear I smell as bad as little brother. I have the dust of all of Gaul upon me."

"I shall not argue the point, brother, but first I have watered wine and baked bread. Let us share a meal while you entice me with thrilling stories of heroics and perhaps Adalia will wake."

Chapter Three: The Soothsayer

Nicomedes Valerius Corvus removed the sealed lid of the dusty, Egyptian hieroglyph-marked clay pot and peeked inside with morbid glee. Mutated dermestid beetles skittered over the bloated dead flesh of a severed head, seeking the optimal location from which to consume their meal. The Soothsayer Academy used these insects to remove flesh from skulls and bones required for rituals.

He dug his fingers into the flesh to test the state of rigor mortis, and once satisfied with the progress, he closed the lid. Nicomedes turned his attention towards the rune-etched silver bowl on the workbench. He sprinkled a mixture of purified salt and distilled owl's blood into the water and gazed into it with purpose.

A floating, cascading image of Claudia and Marcus, huddling together over the slave within Darius's abode, floated upon the surface as candle light refracted on the water.

Nicomedes felt an ambivalent mixture of pleasure and pride that both siblings survived. Although he had no taste for the trivialities of life, he needed loyal family members to ensure the household possessed enough wealth to insulate him from the world, so he could complete his studies and eventually leave the Soothsayer Academy.

He splashed the water to sever the connection. Scrying via sympathetic magic rapidly tired him, and it limited his potential subjects. Nicomedes routinely spied upon his siblings and delved into their possible futures to look for threats.

On rare occasions, he tried to scry upon their mother, but each time he was blocked by a roaring reverberation of energy that prevented him from locking onto her. He suspected that she was alive and well. The imperator forbade the practice of magic without sanction from the Soothsayers, but Septima Valerius Orca had mastered the Art on her own. She taught him the elements of magic at her knee as a boy. If she was powerful enough to achieve that and more under their gaze, then surely she was clever enough to prevent others from scrying upon her.

Ten years at the Soothsayer Academy, and still he only understood a fraction of the power and insight available to its students. It would take another decade to master concepts he had only begun to understand. Nicomedes had already advanced to the rank of magister within the academy, which was unheard of at his age. Two hours were sacrificed each day to teach younger students the foundations of magic, and an additional hour was spent to research projects and mundane tasks assigned by the magister palatii counsel. The rest of his time was his to study and sneak peeks at the library.

A small knock caught his attention. Nicomedes turned towards the door. *Who would dare knock on his door?* The small series of chambers that served as his living quarters and laboratory were located at the bottom-most cavern under the academy, almost under the river. The imperator granted the Soothsayers the Island of Tiberina in the middle of the Tiber River, which flowed through Rome. Personal claims to space and privacy were at a premium within the academy. It was said the Soothsayers conducted their business at the Lupercal Cave, but it was at this place that they taught their followers.

The other magisters lived above ground near the gardens, but he preferred the quiet. Nicomedes knew from experience a subject could scream in this place and none would hear it. He once lived in the dormitory as a young student and dreaded the lack of privacy. After progressing to the rank of magister, Nicomedes laid claim to his own space and thereafter did not suffer guests or intruders lightly.

* * * *

The students were naturally terrified of him, and it seemed appropriate. Their fear meant his private time was just that — his own to do with as he willed. If a student dared to knock upon his door, then it must be important. "Enter."

A young boy, whose bright eyes peered through curly reddish hair, opened the door. He was very young, still wearing his bulla, but clad in traditional academy robes. "Magister?"

Nicomedes deigned to glance down at the boy and nodded, acknowledging his presence. The student trembled before him, struggling to keep his knees locked into position. His name was Rubio, so named for his thick and distinctive hair that marked him as one of the Aemilii. They were the wealthiest family in all of Rome if the stories were true, and as a major family they held considerable sway. He tried to contain his anger at the interruption. "Speak."

Rubio swallowed - his face appearing quite weaselly – and then stammered when he finally found the courage to speak. "Magister, I have a message."

Nicomedes motioned for the boy to continue, but caught Rubio glancing about his chambers — his mouth agape at the treasures that it contained. The boy's gaze stopped at the workbench, where Nicomedes had been examining the bloody remains of the assassin who had the misfortune to die from the blades of his brother's secret soldier. He imagined Rubio had only witnessed such instruments in his deepest nightmares.

"Must I pry it from your brainpan?" Nicomedes snapped. He resented the delay in his schedule. "I am well aware my brother has arrived in Rome. Inform the messenger I shall attend them when the time is proper.

Rubio coughed, as though dreading the very words that would soon leave his lips. "This message is not from your family, magister."

Nicomedes snapped his fingers to catch the student's attention, forgetting his hands were still moist from the dead man's blood. Rubio forced himself to look away from the vivisected corpse. "You have witnessed that I have a number of projects that demand my complete attention. Who sent this message?" Nicomedes demanded.

"Spurinna, magister."

Nicomedes blinked at the unexpected news. None of his auguries predicted such an occurrence. Why would one of the legendary Soothsayers — the founders of the academy — send him a message through a student? Was this boy important somehow? Was this a subtle hint that Nicomedes should take special notice of Rubio? During his tenure, Nicomedes had physically seen the Soothsayers less than a dozen times over the years. "By the Iron Throne, boy. Speak!"

Rubio stammered an answer. "Your presence is requested at the Lupercal Cave."

Nicomedes noted the pallor of the boy's face and observed the fluttering of his eyes, and found himself impressed that Rubio was still standing. He never felt more like a teacher. "Why is the Lupercal Cave called the Heart of Rome?"

"The lore masters say Lupercal was where Romulus and Remus were found by the she-wolf that kept them alive. The birth of Rome." Rubio coughed, struggling to avoid fainting. "Some believe it is the source of magic for Rome."

He needed an excuse to bind this boy to his service until he could determine why the Soothsayers placed Rubio in his path. "Excellent. For your bravery, I shall reward you by setting a task for you."

Pride reflected in the student's stature as Rubio straightened his back. The patronage of a magister could very well advance his career at the academy. "Anything, sir."

A small part of his soul still felt exhilaration from casual cruelty. Nicomedes knew in time he would have to evolve past such a weakness of character. "Remain here. Touch nothing save for those pots. I need the contents turned over every hour. Do not harm the dermestid beetles. They are more valuable than you at present."

Rubio nodded. He cautiously maneuvered around the table, careful to avoid looking directly at the corpse, and then snuck a peek under the lid of the closest pot. A severed head's partially consumed grimace grinned up at him. Rubio dropped the lid with a loud thud. He glanced up at Nicomedes and swallowed. "Yes, sir."

* * * *

A warm spring rain pelted the empty streets of Rome, finally breaking the heat. The mood of the mob matched the temperature, and they had taken to the streets, angry that the government of Rome had allowed the travesty of an assault upon the Vestal Virgins. Street vendors deserted the Palatine for fear of yet another riot, while soldiers from the Thirteenth Legion patrolled, intimidating anyone seeking to profit from the turmoil. Fat drops of rain forced the crowds to retreat to venues protected by a roof. Shadows of the ancient buildings grew long and thin as the sun set to a glorious field of red and orange.

Nicomedes pulled his filthy slave's frock tightly around himself to mask his Soothsayer's robes and descended down the winding passage that crossed above the Forum Romanum. He paused for a moment to stop at the edge of the cliff that overlooked the colossal Circus Maximus. While they were but boys, Marcus occasionally broke curfew and brought him here to soak in the roar of the crowd cheering the bloodletting.

He paused at the famous cleft at the base of the Palatine Hill — a crack that divided the entire range — believed to have been caused by mighty Hercules when he struck Cacus with his club. Here the marble steps twisted down into the Lupercal cave, where the she-wolf nursed the brothers Romulus and Remus. This was a place of legends and power. Perhaps if the universe was a just creation, Nicomedes would find his own place here.

The Praetorian Guard guarded the path, but Nicomedes waved them away. He walked under the marble avatar statues of the immortal brothers, admiring the craftsmanship of their design and creation. The greatest warriors and poets each dreamed of leaving their own token here when they passed.

He stopped at the statue of Caesar, noting with trepidation the care and lines in his face. It was whispered that Caesar had been a victim of the Falling Sickness until cured by the Soothsayers. *What power and knowledge they must possess, hidden in this place!*

Nicomedes removed his beggar's clothing and entered the cave, discovering a vast antechamber shaped into a large dome that reverberated like a sounding chamber. An effervescent light shimmered, casting strange shadows over the surface of the curved wall and highlighting letters, runes, hieroglyphics, numbers, scripts, and dozens of other markings burned into the stone. He stepped closer, fascinated, trying to decipher their various meanings.

"Nicomedes Valerius Corvus." It was as though Pluto himself shouted his name from the Iron Throne. The Three spoke as one voice, strong enough to shatter stones and break mountains. "We await your attention."

He turned to discover the Three standing before a vast altar crafted from indigo obsidian, polished to such a fine degree that it reflected their images. They wore identical long, tattered, green robes that once might have been made from fine embroidered cloth, but now even the meanest beggars in Rome would have been shamed to be seen in them.

The Three possessed a strange greyness to their pallor, as though they had succumbed to rigor mortis long ago and only the potency of their magic continued to animate them. Dusty hoods covered the top portion of their faces like veils.

Despite the hoods, each of them could be distinguished from the others. The tall, gaunt figure was Trophonius. He pointed a skeletal finger at Nicomedes, as though to accuse him of some unknown sin. It was rumored this Soothsayer had founded a shrine to fabled Aeneas before the founding of Rome. "You seek advancement in the academy."

Sweat beaded his forehead. A strange twitching clutched at his stomach. Nicomedes forced himself to nod without trembling. He had almost forgotten the sweet release of fear and terror. "It would be an honor if you decided that I was worthy, Soothsayers."

The Three glanced aside towards each other, as though communicating via a secret means, and turned towards Nicomedes once they achieved consensus. Apollonius of Tyana stepped forward. He seemed the most human of the Soothsayers — the most preserved as it were — and yet the most dangerous. "Worth is decided through tests of the soul. Should you fail these tests, your life blood shall fall upon the stone and nourish our magic."

A steep price for failure: surely they already knew the likely results of this encounter and any choice he would make in the near future. Had they already found him unworthy? Such a test would be an easy way to justify sacrificing his blood to their rituals. "Are these tests fair? Is it possible for me to pass them?"

"Life is unfair and occasionally cruel." Their words resonated within the chamber, burrowing into his ears with great force. "Why should our tests be any different?"

Nicomedes steeled himself. He had survived bullying from Decimus and Orca's maladroit attempts to poison him. He had crawled his way through the academy. "I am ready."

The Three nodded in unison, as though they fully expected this outcome. How could Nicomedes refuse? "You observed that which is carved into our walls. Why did we labor to complete this task? What purpose does this work represent?"

Nicomedes felt dizzy. How could he know what all of these words meant? It would take a lifetime to master all of the languages, much less understand every principle or proof presented. How could he calculate all of these equations? Some of them he recognized from his education as a child. The Pythagorean Theorem described how to determine the area of a triangle. Archimedes' Law of the Lever — magnitudes are in equilibrium at distances reciprocally proportional to their weights. What clue did they intend for him to glean from them? What did the strange runes and symbols mean? Surely, the Soothsayers did not expect him to understand everything on the walls. How could he know the complete thoughts and knowledge of the world? How could he know what the Soothsayers considered was important?

Wait! Was the answer really so simple? "These are statements that describe the world in ways that can be measured and quantified," Nicomedes stated. "All language, all mathematics, all logic is merely a tool to describe the world. That is the secret of the Art."

The Three gave no evidence of their judgment of his answer. They merely continued to the second question. "How did we strengthen the Art in this world?"

Nicomedes stepped back from the Three. How could they expect him to know their plans? To know the subtle shifts of the Mastery of the Art? Clearly they expected he could reason the answer. Did it relate to the first test? "You warned Caesar of the attempt on his life. Every child in Rome knows this. Caesar gave you the right to teach the Art to the patricians."

Their disappointment was palpable, but they did not strike him down immediately. "But how did this strengthen the Art in the world?"

The meaning of their question became clear now that he considered the matter properly. "Faith. The body follows the lead of the brain. The endorsement of the imperator increased the acceptance of the Art in the hearts of the mob. He shifted their perceptions of this world, and thus strengthened the energy we draw upon when we change the world."

The Three conferred privately once again. Nicomedes felt his knees buckle, terrified of what was to come. Once satisfied, they asked their final question. "Describe the principle of sacrifice."

Surely this question was not part of this test. He had learned this answer many years ago at the Soothsayer Academy — that dolt Rubio could answer this question. "To master the Art, you have to be willing to sacrifice blood and tears to balance the world."

The Three each spoke in turn, their voices a mere whisper floating above a grave, yet the power of their words nearly flattened him.

"We require proof of your willingness to sacrifice."

"We require blood."

"We require tears."

The slumbering forms of Claudia and Marcus appeared on the altar. The Three raised their hoods and revealed their rotten visages. Their skulls were thinly wrapped in putrid flesh. Their eyes were black sockets. "This was the price for the Art in the wild days. We surrendered our blood, our flesh to save the spark. Will you do the same?"

"You want me to kill my family?" Nicomedes asked, horrified and yet a little curious. "You need their blood?"

The Three stood immobile like statues — studying his every movement and expression. "We are sustained by the Art. This is about your needs."

A curved, jagged knife appeared on the altar. Nicomedes accepted it carefully. "I will give my blood and pay the prices."

"Sacrificing what you do not value is worthless to the universe."

"Claudia wished just a few days ago that Orca was her father because he had possesed the strength to take what he desired."

"Do you know the value of strength?"

Would Orca have cared of the coast if it meant that he would seize such power? Could his father have protected them if he had been less kind? Would Orca even bother to protect his sons? Nicomedes dropped the dagger. "I do not need to sacrifice my family. You learned the Art on your own. I can as well."

The glamours of Marcus and Claudia disappeared from the altar.

The Soothsayers covered their faces once more and spoke with one voice. It was easier to endure their presence when he did not have to look into the black pits that served as their eyes. "As you wish, but you are invited to remain. Spurinna shall give you instructions. Follow them to the letter, and you may yet gain your wish."

The Three turned towards each other and nodded one last time before Apollonius and Trophonius departed further into the cave, leaving only Spurinna. She was once a woman, Nicomedes judged by the curve of her body. This was the first time he had spoken to one of the Soothsayers privately. "Your father sought our wisdom and long ago paid for the right for you to attend the academy. Were you aware of this?"

"No, Soothsayer."

"We considered refusing the contract. The potential reverberations of your actions might place certain futures at risk," Spurinna explained.

"Risk to what?" Nicomedes asked.

"You have a lust for power and blood that will never be satiated." The Soothsayer spoke in a whisper, but never had Nicomedes heard words that brought more terror. "We have listened to the cries of your victims in lands never before seen. Cities crumble beneath your steps. And yet, there may come a time when the Soothsayers are joined by a fourth."

"I become a Soothsayer?"

Spurinna tilted her head, as though to study his response. "Only trends may be seen of the future."

"Then why the test? Why worry me?" Nicomedes asked.

"I answer this only so that you might be prepared for the future. We wished to judge if we should let you live."

Nicomedes glanced back at the symbols of the formulae, promising himself that the next time he was here, he would be able to master them. "And I passed?"

"Since we could not agree upon a course of action, you have been given a reprieve, pending the consequences of this assignment."

"What assignment?" Nicomedes asked. "I am presently consumed by my own designs. There is a threat to Rome."

Spurinna raised a skeletal finger to silence him. "We are aware of the assassination attempt upon the Vestal Virgin, and your brother's desire to earn his name."

"And you wish me to sacrifice my design for yours?" Nicomedes asked.

"On the contrary, there are many, many patterns interconnected through a single thread. The Vestal Virgins. Grain shortages. The campaign against the Caledonians. The threat against the legions. The best tool is one used well and to its purpose."

"Am I a tool then?"

Spurinna nodded. "Yes, for the moment, you are our tool. And that is the best place for you and your family to achieve your heart's desire."

"What am I to do?"

The Soothsayer turned her back towards Nicomedes, as though to examine the altar. "Mighty Caesar is presented with a problem from Egypt. The details are obfuscated, and he requires investigators."

"Something is amiss with the grain shipments?" Nicomedes asked.

Spurinna ignored the question. "You will offer the services of your family with our recommendation."

"Is my ignorance part of your design, Soothsayer?" Nicomedes asked.

Spurinna seemed pleased by this question. "Knowledge of our plans might corrupt our design. You might alter a decision merely for spite, and this is too important."

"Why?"

"You would question me?" the Soothsayer asked.

"I cannot perform without knowledge."

"You do not have the experience to understand."

"You are not the only Soothsayers in the world, yes?" Nicomedes asked.

The Soothsayer bowed, clearly impressed. "There are three other groups that we are aware of, each making subtle changes to the world. A stratagem of infinite regress, where the last to act claims eternity."

"And one of these other factions has attacked?" Nicomedes asked, pressing his advantage.

"We know that events are not what they should be. The world is twisted and bent."

"I do not feel it," Nicomedes protested.

Spurinna turned again to the various sigils and equations on the walls, as though this was some sort of clue she was unable to verbalize. "You are a child of this construct. We were the first who bent it to our whims. Others have responded."

"When you saved Caesar and elevated magic," Nicomedes guessed.

"This world would have passed for something crass and ugly. And now other visions are in play. To act directly would be foolish at this time."

"We will serve as your proxy, then?" Nicomedes asked. "What reward do you promise?"

Spurinna drew back her hood and glared. "Reward? You seek payment after all that you've learned?"

Nicomedes found himself holding up his hands, unconsciously pleading for mercy. "I am the youngest brother. You wish to make my brother your catspaw. Marcus has his own plans. He seeks to make his name with service. He cannot leave the legion, because I tell him that it is in his interests. He has two years left before he leaves House Valeria and claims his own branch house. This is vital to our interests."

Spurinna waved away the concern. "The centurion serves at the pleasure of the imperator, who may reward or discharge anyone he sees fit. You may express to Caesar that it is the desire of the Soothsayers and to the benefit of Rome that a new minor branch arise under the Valeria family. This patronage will continue, should this mission be successful according to our designs."

"There is one additional matter," Nicomedes interjected.

"There are other tools we can use" the Soothsayer warned.

"This matter concerns the both of us," Nicomedes argued. "Claudia is a Vestal Virgin. A bride of Rome is forbidden to leave the Eternal City. We cannot take her on this journey while she is bound by office."

The Soothsayer nodded with approval. "And you desire her as the matriarch for your house? Yes, she is destined to produce an important daughter of Rome, like her mother. This may be told to Caesar."

"Excellent. Then what must be done?"

"We have arranged for an afternoon audience with mighty Caesar, when his new wife will be away. You will inform him of our wishes and offer yourself in submission." Spurinna raised her skeletal hand as though to touch him and paused. "You will wish to bathe and clean yourself so as to be appealing."

Nicomedes sighed. He didn't object to the bartering of his flesh; what else was it good for? The whole ordeal of cleaning his flesh and cutting his hair felt like such a waste. "As you wish."

* * * *

Nicomedes felt eyes upon him as soon as he turned into the narrow alley that led to what the plebeians called in jest "Patrician Row." The Praetorian Guard halted his progress as he reached the private entrance to the imperial bath house on the edge of the forum, just a short walk away from the Senate Curia, which catered exclusively to government officials and other prestigious patrician families seeking to engage in the business of Rome.

"The baths are closed this evening," the tribune of the guard bellowed. "Move along, citizen."

He felt no surprise the guards failed to recognize him as an envoy of the Soothsayers. Nicomedes appeared little better than a beggar, with his unkempt beard and wild hair in knots and tangles. It had been more than a season since he had bothered to allow the academy slaves to properly groom him or since he visited one of the local bath houses.

Nicomedes drew back his hood. Fire flashed in his eyes. "I come bearing word from the Soothsayers. Impede my sacred progress at your peril."

Even that dolt Rubio could perform his simple glamour, but it was enough to demonstrate his intent. The guards stepped back and raised their weapons. Nicomedes smiled wryly and raised his hands to offer submission.

The guards gingerly checked his person, taking away his only weapon — an obsidian, ceremonial dagger used exclusively for the Art. The tribune of the Praetorian Guard slid it under his belt and then saluted. "I shall personally hold your weapon until you return."

"Be careful not to prick your thumb upon the blade," Nicomedes warned. "You would not enjoy the experience, I assure you."

"Part way for the envoy of the Soothsayers!" the tribune barked. The red feathers on his helmet billowed as he turned, showing Nicomedes full honors. "Continue, envoy."

Nicomedes bowed. There was no need to make enemies of potential allies. "Thank you for protecting the imperator. I shall inform him of your dedication to your duty."

He ducked into the private entrance, where the attendants stationed in the Apodyterium fumed at his presence. They swarmed about him — disgusted as though they had been asked to swim in the sewers below Rome. They blocked his ingress into the deeper chambers of bath house. “No! No! We can’t have you muddying our waters with your filth!”

Nicomedes raised a finger to silence them. “I have coin for your quickest and most adroit hands. To appear before the imperator without proper grooming would be a great insult.”

The valet scowled and gestured to two of the attendants and snapped his fingers. He was a tall, elegant man dressed in a perfect red tunic with golden bracers. “Ensure that he is presentable. You will be whipped if this house is dishonored.”

“Yes, Aius.”

Nicomedes tried to imagine a world where all of his concerns were locked into the honor of a bath house, and then decided it was not a matter worth quarrelling over. He followed the attendants into one of the preparation rooms. They were young, handsome Egyptian men who wore loose loincloths. He imagined these two were quite popular with those who had a taste for such flesh. Their bare chests were oiled, and their faces were painted in the manner of their people, with florid markings under their almond eyes.

“How can we please you?” they asked in broken Latin.

“Groom me to your standards.” His position was no better than theirs on a certain level. *Was he not here to be the honey for bitter orders?* “A reward will be given if the imperator is pleased.”

The attendants nodded and began their strange ritual. They washed his hair twice and then cut and sculpted it into the fashionable Roman style. His beard was trimmed, and his skin was oiled and then scraped with a sharp strigil. They took him to a cold bath, where they cleaned his skin with a course sponge and then rubbed scented oil back into his skin.

While they completed their tasks, they whispered to each other in a low Egyptian dialect. He comprehended the flow of their conversation, even if the occasional word felt strange to his ears. Caesar informed the valet only this afternoon that the bath house would be his dominion for the entire evening and dismissed the majority of the staff. The valet worked frantically to send messengers to clients, rescheduling appointments while continually venting his frustrations upon the harried attendants — screaming at them for any error. The extra coin that Nicomedes promised would be the only bright point in their evening.

The imperator invoked this privilege occasionally and Nicomedes approved. If you were worried about assassination attempts, then meeting with your rivals naked, surrounded by your fanatical guards, seemed a wise maneuver. Strange that the valet felt brave enough to express such discontent, but then the lives of the plebeians were strange indeed.

Once the attendants finished, the valet appeared. He snapped his fingers, and the Egyptians meekly exited. Nicomedes noted the slaves secretly pocketed the extra coins he had given them.

The valet led Nicomedes through the Palaestra, where a small number of Caesar's men were exercising and socializing. They progressed through the Tepidarium, where Nicomedes disrobed and the valet rinsed his body with a bucket of warm water. Once the valet was satisfied that Nicomedes had been properly sanctified, he brought him to a sealed metal door, opened it, and stepped aside.

The Caldarium was the heart of the bath house. Its vast tiled pool was located directly over the furnace below. The heated water bubbled and steamed, covering the entire room with a warm, steamy fog. His skin tingled from the pleasurable heat.

At the edge of the pool was mighty Caesar — the imperator of the empire. He was a handsome man in the prime of his life, perhaps appearing no more than fifty. Yet the records of the Soothsayers say that they intervened in his life when mighty Caesar had reached his fifty-fifth year, and that was nearly twenty years ago. He had a strong Roman nose and a pugilistic face that seemed born for command, and yet this was one of the brightest minds in the empire.

Nicomedes knelt before the imperator. "Hail Caesar!"

"Dread news must come from the Luperical Cave for the Soothsayers to send it in such a form to please my eyes." Caesar gestured for Nicomedes to enter the pool. "Speak your name and join me. Let us speak of ill-tidings now, lest the anticipation kill all other thoughts of enjoyment."

"I am Nicomedes Valerius Corvus, great imperator." He allowed his robe to drop onto the tiled floor. If the glances from the Egyptian attendants were any indication, his body was still admired by others. Caesar nodded his approval, and Nicomedes stepped into the pool. "I am here to serve all of your needs."

"Forget not your sandals lest the floor scorch your feet," Caesar warned. "The furnace keeps the hypocaust heating at a temperature that would singe your skin."

"I have no need for sandals, Caesar." Nicomedes continued forward until his feet reached the bottom of the pool. The tiles were indeed quite warm, but he had learned long ago to regulate his body temperatures and control the elements inside of his flesh.

"Quite impressive, Nicomedes." Caesar washed his face in the pool and then leaned back along the side. "I knew your father. Titus Valerius Perseus. A loyal man of Rome."

Nicomedes nodded. "Many are said to have loved him. I do not remember him."

"Love does not always protect one from a blade or poison. I lost my best friend to both."

"Did it not save your life, mighty Caesar?"

Caesar shook his head. "Love cost the life of a friend. I was arrogant and thought if forewarned we would kill the so-called Senate Liberators. I showed mercy once too often, and my friend paid the price. Tell me, Nicomedes, your brother is a centurion in Gaul, yes?"

It felt strange for his name to be on the lips of the most powerful man in Rome. "Yes, imperator."

"Then answer this question: once a legion conquers a people, what do they do first above all other things?" Caesar asked.

"I know not, Caesar."

"First, they build a bath house for their officers to cleanse themselves," Caesar explained. "Then, they immediately begin to construct a road that will lead to Rome. Do you know why? The face we present to the world determines our fate in it. This is the face of Rome. We present the baths to the world as proof of the superiority of

Roman culture. Every man, woman, and child of the Eternal City is cleaner than the richest kings of other lands. Our slaves present better hygiene than the so-called great chiefs of the petty tribes that fall under the Pax Romana. We build a bath house to give them a taste of what we offer and seduce them. And thus, we spread the empire that you are no doubt here to tell me is in danger."

Nicomedes had difficulty imagining Marcus digging a bath house. The thought of it brought a moment of pleasure at his brother's imagined suffering. "I have news and suggestions from the Soothsayers."

"Speak them and share their enlightenment."

Nicomedes did as commanded. He spoke of the grain shipments, the proposed mission to Egypt, and the requirements of his family to stave off disasters. Caesar listened carefully, often asking him to repeat Spurinna's words exactly as she spoke them. "A good deal to consider. What do you recommend?"

"The best tool is one used well and to its purpose."

"Do you think I am a tool?" the imperator asked.

Nicomedes considered his next words carefully. "I think we are all tools for the Soothsayers. And they are careful when sharing their vision of the future. I believe that if we follow this path, we shall all achieve our dreams."

"This will not be an easy task, even for the imperator." Caesar dunked his head into the water and popped back up like a swan shaking his head. "Your brother is a centurion with the Seventh Legion of Rome under command of the Senate. Your sister is a Vestal Virgin

— a bride of Rome. We have yet to ascertain who might have arranged the attempted assassination. Should I make this happen, it will cause turmoil in the Senate, and the major families will be offended if I push this through without the proper bribes."

"Coin well-spent, imperator, to secure all the tomorrows." Nicomedes pondered the dilemma. "My sister may have provided cover for our needs. Livia Drusilla seeks to marry Marcus."

"Marcus Livius Drusus Claudianus is her father, yes?" Caesar immediately grasped the political considerations. "He is powerful in the Senate and could smooth such deeds, if he had the mind to do it and draw attention from my hand. This could have a number of other implications that would be beneficial. Would the senator support our cause? He has cooled to reason of late."

Nicodemus recalled his childhood experiences together with his brother, when they would often foster with the Claudians after the death of their father. "My brother is his name-sake, and Drusilla is neither a woman to be ignored or scorned," Nicomedes replied.

Caesar nodded, pleased with that answer. "Words must first be exchanged with your brother, and then I will consider the path presented to us."

"Thank you, Caesar."

Caesar reached over, grabbed Nicomedes by the wrist, and yanked him close. "I have supped the bitter wine, and now it is time for my reward." The imperator wrapped his arms around him and nuzzled his neck.

Nicomedes felt a twinge of surprise as his body reacted to the kisses along his neck. He had never felt the interest to actively seek out others for their flesh and rarely took delight in his own. Once, he spied upon Marcus taking one of the other boys as a lover, but he was more curious about the biology of the act rather than titillation.

Caesar touched his hair lightly, running it through his fingers. "The Soothsayers keep me healthy and vital with their bitter potions, but it is youth that is the real magic. Never squander what you possess in abundance now." Caesar cupped his chin and licked a bead of sweat that dripped from his cheek. "Taste what is human and forget the Soothsayer's charms."

His hands were strong, feverish with desire. Nicomedes enjoyed the sense of hunger from the urgency of their bodies and the sweet smell of his lover's sweat along his neck. Caesar turned him in the water and started to kiss along his spine, until he reached the fleshy part of his ass. He bit it as though it were an apple.

The pain only seemed to make Nicomedes aware of his body in a way that he had never before experienced. Caesar rubbed his excited member along his body, and Nicomedes tingled with the anticipation of what would soon be.

Nicomedes allowed Caesar to heft him onto the side of the pool, forcing him to lay on the tiles upon his belly, leaving his ass open to the elements. Caesar snatched up a bottle containing sweet oils that made his muscles relax and his skin tingle.

Caesar clutched his hair once more and whispered into his ear. "And now, Little Owl, I will know you."

Time dilated — it shrank and expanded at will. Nicomedes no

longer could tell if minutes or hours had passed. He only knew that finally Caesar had been exhausted and that he was worn out, yet strangely sated. They rested with their backs against the walls of the pool, when the metal door opened with a loud creak. Aius entered with his head low.

Nicomedes wiped a strand of his hair from his face and studied the valet's seething face. Aius grimaced. "Shall I escort your guest out, imperator?"

"Leave him." Caesar waved for the valet to leave. "I shall see no more guests this night. The empire shall have to do without my attentions this evening."

"As you wish, imperator." The valet looked from Caesar to Nicomedes with a calculated glance. Nicomedes tilted his head. How was it that this man could walk into the heated Caldarium without sweating? The Egyptian attendants were quite acclimated to the heat, and yet their bodies glistened with perspiration. He stepped closer towards the pool. "Shall I bring you or your guest refreshments?"

"I am quite sated, Aius," Caesar replied laconically. "I may wash myself and travel home. No need to bother yourself."

Aius crept forward, bowing before the imperator. "It is an honor to serve you."

Nicomedes looked closer. The tunic remained dry without wrinkles. The heat from the steam should have caused some sort of reaction on the man's body. He pulled Caesar from the side of the pool, deeper into the water.

Aius creaked his neck — it bent in a manner impossible for human anatomy. Nicomedes studied the valet until he shattered the glamour hiding its true form, revealing a strange hairless canine creature — with an elongated snout and bent ears — that stood in the form of a man. Its skin was an earthy red, covered with mucus and vile, bulbous, white blisters of pus and venom. The creature that was Aius hissed and then swatted towards them with its terrifying claws.

Nicomedes took a large gulp of the water and then concentrated on the elements within it. He long ago learned to change the composition of the air within his lungs and alter his blood. The water changed and pooled into his cheeks, slightly singing them, leaving a loathsome taste in his mouth.

He stepped forward and spewed forth a stream of steaming vapors that caught the monster unaware. Aius screamed as the liquid bubbled and boiled its face. Nicomedes raised his hands —his fingers in the proper configurations to adjust the energies in the room –commanding the water to boil until the creature exploded into a spray of blood mist and bone.

The Praetorian Guard stormed the room, attracted to the noise. Several of the more fanatical guards immediately leapt into the water, forming a protective shield around the imperator. Caesar waved his hands to order them to stand down. "The beast is dead thanks to Nicomedes."

The guards ushered Caesar and Nicomedes to the other side of the room and brought them robes. "That creature appeared as though it was a monster of legend. What was it?" Caesar asked.

"Such creatures are only whispered about in civilized lands,"

Nicomedes admitted. "I have read of monsters known only as ghouls from the lands of the desert. They are shapeshifters that feed on the bone and blood of the living and righteous."

"From where do such creatures hail?" Caesar asked.

Nicomedes knew the answer to this. "I have only heard of them in the Parthian Empire, near the cities that dwell in the desert.

"The very name vexes me!" Caesar spat. "That damnable prophecy. You know of what I speak, yes?"

Nicomedes knew this prophecy well. It is said to be the reason Brutus finally joined the conspiracy to assassinate Caesar. "Only a Rome united under a king shall defeat the Parthian Empire."

"Return to the Soothsayers. Share what you have learned. Send your brother to me tomorrow for his report. And consider what reward you would ask from your imperator."

"You have given me all that I could want from you, Caesar." Nicomedes glanced aside to the remains of the creature. "Save for perhaps the body for my studies."

Chapter Four: The Body-Slave

A cacophony of familiar voices dragged her from the darkness. She squinted — desperate to keep her eyes closed and return to the pleasant dream of the hunt — but sharp spikes of pain drilled into her temples. Adalia tried to shield her eyes from the light, but her hands felt impossibly distant and numb as though she lost the power to command them. She opened her mouth to speak, but her tongue felt dead. It tasted of bile and blood.

"Will she survive, Nicomedes?" She knew this voice. It was Claudia — strange to hear such concern from her. "She shielded my body with her own. I would not have her pass into the afterlife with such a debt upon my soul."

"I have diluted the majority of the venom in her system." This voice was raw, brimming with bitterness and holding the resigned tone of one forced to suffer his inferiors. "The lacerations from the blades have healed quite nicely, thanks to my administrations and the blood of those she triumphed over. I have never encountered this specific poison and thus cannot accurately predict its lasting effects. I suspect this slave is strong in spirit and would wager she will endure."

"Adalia is no base slave." This voice belonged to Marcus. She tried to move, to signal that she heard him, but her body was somehow numb to her will. "And if the past is an indication of the future, she is in possession of more than enough spirit to overcome this coward's tool."

"If she is not your slave, Marcus, then why does she bear your mark inked on her thigh?" Claudia asked.

"A bargain willingly undertaken, so that she might protect Dia's life with her own to repay me for the life of her brother, Armin," Marcus explained. It pleased her that he spoke of her with respect. A man will honor his word to another equal, where he might ignore a promise to a slave. "Politics unfavorable to Rome would have had their uncle slay Armin to secure power. I sent her to Rome under pretense that she would serve as your body-slave to avoid suspicious from Orca and others."

"A worthy seed planted that has already bore fruit," Darius replied. "Patrician eyes fail to see slaves, save for a piece of furniture in the background to be trod upon when desired."

"I had no idea that you had come to subscribe to such libertarian philosophies, brother." Nicomedes replied sharply. Adalia already detested him beyond measure, yet she owed the magister her life.

She opened her eyes, surprised to discover she lay in a real bed with a simple frame. Few slaves were awarded such an honor. *Where was she?* The walls were thick and well-made, but the low ceiling removed doubt of the possibility that she was at the Atrium Vestae or the Domūs de Valeria. Such fine masonry, decorated with a velvet-sheathed gladius and shield, indicated a certain amount of wealth and security.

The siblings sat around a black table adorned with a copper figurine that bore the sigils of the Valeria household gods. Darius paced along the wall of the cottage with a practiced familiarity. He filled the decanter with more wine and joined them. This must be where he lives, she thought.

"This woman killed four of those assassins before finally succumbing to her wounds. These men were well-trained. I killed three only because I caught them by surprise," Darius admitted. "This woman could be a worthy cohort to our cause, especially as we do not yet know the identity of those who tried to murder Claudia," Darius argued.

She tried to remain still as the dead. If she remained as furniture a bit longer, she might at the least come to properly understand the mood of the Valeria siblings. The notion that empathy might have played a part Marcus' motives for helping her brother had not occurred to her. She had thought it was merely another aspect of Roman politics, but now she could see that they were truly orphans like herself and Armin. If her family depended upon the strength of the Valeria, she had best learn their weaknesses.

"Adalia is quite clever. She divined the grain shortage merely by observation," Claudia admitted.

"Surely any debt that once existed has been repaid in blood. Will she not wish to return home?" Darius asked.

"A return to the Rhine would be dangerous to her and to the interests of Rome." Marcus nodded to Darius, who filled their goblets. "Her brother is believed dead, but any children of hers would be considered of divine blood by the tribe and a direct threat to their uncle's power in time."

"Where is this Armin?" Darius asked.

"Such things are better not spoken aloud," Marcus said, shaking his head. "Our words and deeds can be scried from afar now."

"None save for perhaps the Soothsayers could penetrate the ward I have cast over this place," Nicomedes protested. "You may speak securely here for this night."

"You said yourself there are foreign Soothsayers seeking to supplant your patrons," Claudia countered. She placed a maternal hand on her younger brother's shoulder, attempting to mediate between her siblings. "Considering that Spurinna wishes to engage us as her catspaws, other powerful eyes might be upon us this very moment."

"It matters not for our purpose of the moment," Marcus stated. He glanced aside towards Darius. "Let us simply agree that I have learned how to shelter children from uncles who want to slay them for their inheritance."

"Very well, then let us proceed to the crux of the issue at hand. I must go to Egypt as my patrons have commanded, lest I be forced out of the academy or worse. Will you come with me?" Nicomedes asked.

"Do you truly believe that the imperator will simply go along with what the Soothsayers wish?" Marcus asked incredulously. "I find it difficult to believe that a man of reason would simply kneel because the Soothsayers commanded it."

"I have intimate reason to believe that mighty Caesar shall place his trust in us," Nicomedes answered slyly.

"Intimate reason?" Claudia asked. "Is this the reason that you finally elected to groom yourself?"

Marcus caught the tone in his sister's voice and turned to his younger brother. "Exactly why did you meet in the Senate bath house?"

"One does not crow about such trivialities like a rooster, brother," Nicomedes replied coolly. Adalia noted that he scooted just out of Claudia's reach, avoiding her touch. "You either trust my word in this, or the pain of the last five years has been for nothing."

Marcus gulped a large swallow of wine. "He might possess the political power to push such an action through the Senate, but why would he risk it on an unknown nebulous threat? There is a reason we name him imperator and not king or emperor."

"The threat is real. Lest you forget, I killed one of their beasts and saved the imperator." Nicomedes gestured towards Claudia and then at Adalia across the room. "Our sister felt the enemy's wrath. Does not Valeria blood call to justice and revenge?"

"Do you know what the Soothsayers are asking me to sacrifice for their cause?" Marcus asked. "I've served almost five years in the legion. We march to a single motto. '*The Senate and People of Rome*!' I am about to earn my name within the year. Even if the Senate approves of the assignment, the soldiers will only know I abandoned them. These relationships are important for our future. Severing those ties may cost us dearly, rendering that time worthless."

"Ask that your cohort be brought to Egypt with the rest of us," Claudia suggested. "If it is an official assignment, then the honor is maintained, yes?"

"And leave the rest of the Seventh Legion weak? Where is the honor in that?" Marcus asked.

"Caesar would be forced to resupply the troops with those legions under his command," Darius interrupted. "General Varus is under command of the Senate to quell the Caledonians. The Seventh Legion is loyal to him. If Caesar sent one of his personal legions, such as the Thirteenth Legion, then he would have more control over the situation."

"This may be why he agreed in theory to the proposal," Nicomedes admitted. "However he will not agree in full until he has taken the measure of your report come the morning, Marcus."

"And it would be better to meet Caesar with a clear decision in mind, to better argue for a favorite outcome," Claudia added.

"Even should I agree that this is the wisest course of action, it would require marriage to Drusilla. Would you have our dynasty be founded on cloven hooves?" Marcus protested.

"The full support of the Claudians would gain more than a simple vote for a branch family in the Senate," Darius observed. He looked towards their household god. "It would mean wealth and political power. It would mean more than mere survival. It would mean the strength to reclaim the entire family and finally put our boots to Orca's neck."

"Do not forget that it also means that I might have freedom from the Vestal Virgins," Claudia added. "Forgive my selfishness, but I had to leave our home to avoid marriage to Decimus or worse. The Soothsayers added a final temptation to follow their will…the promise of a child. An important daughter of Rome, yes? The very life I've always wanted. I cannot venture out of Rome without the approval of the Senate for this plan. Must I be stymied in my dreams for your vanity, brother?"

"Fortuna seems content to piss upon me," Marcus grumbled. "Brother has taken the imperator as a lover. Sister shall have a family. And I shall engage my life to the gorgon prepared to feast on what remains of my happiness."

"She is actually quite lovely, even if she is conservative in her dress and manners," Claudia reported. "I suspect that you can inject her with the proper cause to lighten her mood. And surely Valeria blood can conquer Claudian defects."

"If we travel to Egypt and look into this mysterious threat to Rome, of which we have neither clues to investigate nor suspects to question," Marcus observed. He knocked his fist upon the table. "Have you considered, brother, that we might simply be a feint designed to risk our lives to be victims to another cause?"

"The best tool is one used well and to its purpose. Spurinna said that. She stated that the best way for us to achieve our hearts' desires was as their tools," Nicomedes replied. "I am willing to endure such a bargain and risk petty concerns such as death."

"If only we knew the identity of the assassins and who dared to send them," Marcus complained.

"This shall be known in the morning," Nicomedes replied.

"How?"

"The severed heads are being cleansed as we speak," Nicomedes explained.

"And how does that serve our purpose?" Marcus asked.

"The skulls will be delivered here in the morning, and then after you speak to Caesar, they will sing every song they have ever heard," Nicomedes said quietly. "And then if I am merciful, I shall release them from Tartarus."

Claudia sipped her wine. "You have never been a pillar of mercy, brother."

"Consider the matter settled, then!" Marcus conceded. "I shall visit Caesar in the morning as commanded to give my report and attempt to read his mood. The efforts may fail, however, as I had intended to have Adalia present to give witness to the tribal politics."

"What a happy coincidence, brother." Adalia felt icy fingers grip her arm. She coughed horribly. "Your ally has been listening to us planning our next venture for the last few minutes."

She blinked as the light from the hearth pained her eyes. Adalia coughed again and tried to sit higher on the bed to meet the others' gaze. "It is rare to hear such revealing honesty from a Roman. The story was so amazing that I had forgotten the mortal wounds I achieved to hear it."

Her stomach itched, as though insects burrowed into her skin. Adalia felt the presence of her arms, shivering and sore. Nicomedes touched her forehead with the back of his hand. "Her fever burns to kill the remainder of the poison. Should she survive the night, she will live."

Marcus grinned widely and knelt beside her. Adalia disliked being in a position of weakness, and he forced her to remain on upon the bed. "Darius has surrendered his own bed to honor your deed. Do not insult the man. His wrath is a thing to witness."

Darius stood over Marcus, folding his arms across his chest. "I take hospitality quite seriously."

"Chatter can resume later, or her strength will fade before the night is out. She must rest, lest we do Dis Pater's work for him." Nicomedes helped her lift her head just enough to drink water and chew on wet bread. "You may listen, but close your eyes and wait for Morpheus."

She settled into the bed like a bear nesting for the winter. She resisted the temptation of sleep, but her vision fogged into a white haze. The warmth of the blanket lulled her into closing her eyes, listening to the others, no longer marking their meaning, simply taking comfort in the tones.

Adalia felt safe.

*   *   *   *

Her tongue felt like the bottom of her sandals. Adalia opened her eyes and painfully pulled herself up into a sitting position. She stank of sweat and dried blood. Darius had left a large copper bowl and towels for her to wish the grime from her face and body. It was a struggle to stand, but she managed to touch the tiles upon the floor and pull herself into an upright position.

Adalia felt along her leg, exploring where she had been stabbed on the outer thigh, just below the curve of her hips. The moment of the strike flashed in her mind's eye. The blade had cut to the bone. *What terrible magics did Nicomedes perform to allow it to heal in a mere week?* There was a scar, but it was thin and fading. If Nicomedes had this power, then what of the Soothsayers? Was it true they had extended the life of Caesar, reverting him to a youthful appearance even in his eighth decade of life?

The door opened, and Adalia instinctively looked for a knife. It was Darius, carrying a tray with a steaming bowl of honeyed porridge and bread. If he was aroused by her nakedness, the old soldier betrayed no traces of it upon his face. "It would appear that you are in good health this morning, Adalia."

"I hardly believe that I live."

He placed the tray upon the table and gestured to where Claudia left some of her clothing the night before. Adalia noted he had brought her knife and pouch. What would have happened if she had lost either? "Do you feel well enough to travel? Marcus is outside with the cohort, preparing to visit the Senate."

She rinsed out the rag in the bowl and continued to clean herself. The smell of the food brought a rumble to her stomach. "Walking may be a trial for me, but I am willing to make the attempt."

"Marcus has ordered that his mother's lectica shall be used to ferry you to the Senate." Darius suppressed a smile. "Decimus nearly had a stroke, I am told. Few wish to argue with the man who killed a bear with only his hands."

"You do know that Marcus was armed, yes?" Adalia asked. "While he delivered the killing blow, he was hardly the only one there who battled that beast."

"Rome is a place where power is determined by the mythology you create. The imperator of Rome claims divinity by the line of Venus."

Darius turned towards the household idol of the founder of the Valeria. "He builds temple after temple dedicated to the goddess of love to remind the mob of his supposed lineage. It is a dedication to vanity. And yet, it is the symbol of his power. The lie told in a crowded room accepted knowingly as truth."

Adalia tied her hair into a knot and continued to clean herself. "A truth unknown to my tribe, where we once crowed about slaughtering the legion, and then fell to Rome because our greatest enemies were each other."

"You heard our words last night. Marcus is convinced our goals are one and that you can be trusted. What do you say?" Darius asked.

"Marcus is a cunning warrior who knows how to predict allies and enemies alike," Adalia answered. She turned towards the table. "The food is appreciated. I would appreciate it all the more, if I were allowed a few moments to properly digest it."

Darius laughed. "The hour is early yet. Marcus has not yet risen. I suspected that you might require extra time to find your balance."

"The thought is very well-received with gratitude, Darius," Adalia replied. "I intend to repay you in kind and vacate your home as soon as I am able."

Darius scratched his beard. "Once, I lay my head upon any spot of ground that I found and felt confident I would find sleep. Old men require comforts. My back calls out to my bed."

"This night I shall return to Domina Claudia's chambers," Adalia assured him.

"Marcus revealed that you were not his slave," Darius replied.

"The pretense is no longer needed in private.

"A lie must be told often, even in private, if you wish it maintained," she countered.

"You saved the future of my blood. The closest thing I shall ever have to a daughter." Darius gave the legionnaire's salute, only given to a fellow soldier. "Should you require anything, consider myself at your service."

Adalia nodded, understanding the honor the Romans considered bestowed upon her, and watched as Darius left his own cottage and closed the door behind him. Claudia had brought her a simple linen stola and a bright blue palla to wear over it. Adalia had learned the political implications at her side, and none could be more clear. The Valeria siblings intended to present her in public, specifically to the imperator, as a woman of importance, not from patrician blood or foreign nobility.

She forced herself to eat slowly, soaking the bread in the cooled porridge and chewing it carefully to avoid aggravating her damaged throat. Once she had eaten her fill, she washed her hands once more and then opened the door to the cottage.

The Third Cohort of the Seventh Legion bivouacked within the walls of Domūs de Valeria. The entire villa had been disrupted. House guards exchanged drinks and turns with the dice, while the servants scrambled to ensure there was enough food for the guests. "There was a rumor that Dis Pater himself threw you out of Tartarus!" A gruff voice, weighted in years and blood called out to her. "Heard tell that he was afraid you'd steal his crown and his bride."

"Milius, I could leave you lot to fend for yourself in this world," Adalia replied. "Then there'd be real trouble."

She gingerly stepped outside into the atrium, careful with each step, revealing only a slight limp from her injuries. "Look at you! Marcus said you were at death's door." Milius laughed. "I've seen worse color on your face after a night of drinking."

"Nicomedes healed my wounds with his magic." She tried to smile, to reflect the comradery, but the mere thought repulsed her. Any movement brought back the memory of the blade and the pain. "Though I slumbered, I suffered through nightmares of the sort to drive you mad. Survival was certainly in doubt."

"Then let the nightmare fade by the light of day." Milius stomped across the courtyard until he reached the ornately carved wooden lectica painted Valeria yellow. She had difficulty imagining riding in such a thing while men labored to carry her as though she were a goddess. "You shall ride through the streets of Rome as though you were the Queen of Egypt."

"Is it true that she's a considered a Roman now?" Adalia asked.

"Merely because she married Octavius?" Milius scoffed bitterly. "The capacity for Roman deceit extends to the whole of the world. How could it not blind their own hearts? The laws of the empire apply to any conquered land that accepts the rule of the imperator and becomes a Roman providence. You can be a citizen of the empire without being a Roman. The heir of the imperator's marriage to Queen Arsinoë is tolerated because of political necessity, but the patricians will never consider her one of them."

Adalia opened her mouth to comment, but the arrival of Marcus and Darius silenced her thoughts. The entire cohort stood at once, ready at attention, prepared to enact their centurion's will. Milius called out to the soldiers. "Cohort!"

The cohort maneuvered into inspection formation. Milius stepped forward and claimed his feathered helmet, which marked him as the optio for the unit. "Hail, centurion!"

"Hail, optio. Is the cohort ready?" Marcus asked. He asked this every time as a matter of ritual. Adalia had seen it a thousand times. Milius turned towards the men and they stomped their feet in response. "We march to the Senate. I need four men on the lectica. Do not let a single scratch be found on it afterwards, else my own mother shall have my hide. Half the cohort shall be the spear that divides the mob. The other half shall be the rear guard."

"Do you believe there will be an attack?" Darius asked.

"I think the temptation might be there, and I should show strength to Rome," Marcus replied. He nodded towards Adalia, and she imagined that his features softened slightly. "Some may wish to hinder our project if they are astute enough to see why we are bringing her."

"The freemen of Valeria will man this door and see to it that no harm comes to Claudia," Darius promised.

They exchanged a curious handshake, the likes of which were unknown to Adalia's people. Each reached out and grabbed each other by the elbow, drawing their arms together in a line, and pulling each other chest to chest. She once asked Marcus about this custom, and he replied that brothers-in-arms sometimes needed a last but simple farewell if they did not know if they would see each other come the morning.

The great door of Domūs de Valeria opened. Adalia climbed onto the lectica and four legionaries hefted it into the air. She shivered as they passed the two-faced god, Janus. Here he was the god that protected borders, gates, and beginnings. Her people heard tales of a different two-faced god worshiped across the sea by the Caledonians. She ruled over life and death and encouraged her worshippers to pray to her by consuming the flesh of their enemies.

The cohort pushed through the crowd on the Palatine Hill. Marcus walked alongside her, pointing out historical points of interest, which he had not seen for many years. "The Valeria were once first amongst the major families of Rome as can be demonstrated by the proximity of our villa to the Forum. Our purse might be lighter than some, but the weight of our honor is heavy."

Seeing this city through his eyes sparked some understanding for why he fought out in lands not his own. "Claudia said that the mob was the heart of Rome."

Marcus flinched at the very words. "If that is so, then soon you will see her soul." They marched into the Forum from Sacra Way under the colossal Arch of Antony. "This is the path a general takes during a triumph."

The Forum was a vast rectangular plaza surrounded by marble government buildings at the center of the Eternal City. The crowd seemed to float along the surface, bound to some unknown tide, like flowers of shapes and colors she had never seen nor witnessed upon the surface of a pond in spring. There was a harmony to the motions, some strange law of nature she failed to decipher. Adalia noted the Atrium Vestae on the eastern edge, the opposite side of the Forum. Marcus took pride in pointing out each template, every arch, and every monument to his people. "There is the temple of Castor and Pollux. Father thought his sons should take inspiration from them, and so we ventured there often when Nicomedes was but a babe."

She lacked the heart to remind Marcus she had lived in Rome almost half a year and had learned much of the city. It excited him to speak of it, and so she was content. There would be little enough joy in the tasks ahead.

They circumnavigated the fountains in the center of the Forum, passing near the edge of the Capitoline Hill, where the Tullianum stood alone. Adalia needed no introduction to the prison where the Romans kept foreign generals and kings. Her father had been stationed there when she was a girl.

The exterior of the Curia Julia was built with brick-faced concrete and a huge buttress at each angle to mimic fabled Olympus, with giant white marble columns over the veranda. A single flight of steps led to double bronze doors.

Marcus nodded, and his optio blew a whistle. He offered his hand. "From here we must walk."

"Shall I have some of the men follow you?" Milius asked.

Marcus shook his head and pointed to the smaller building to the left, near the money lenders. "You are needed in the Tabilarium. We promised Legate Agrippa we would attend to the will of the quaestor when the opportunity presented itself. And should the imperator wish for my life, he may have it. It is already his."

The bearers gently set the lectica in front of the steps, as though they were handling a precious egg. Two of them stood guard over it, while the remainder followed Milius in strict marching formation.

Marcus drew aside the beaded curtain and extended a hand. Adalia accepted his help and lifted herself onto her feet. The sandals felt strange on her feet, as though one was clearly not made for the other. He gestured towards the flight of marble stairs that led to the Senate. "Shall I carry you up the stairs?"

"Does this drapery confuse you, centurion?" Adalia tilted her head and released his hand. She took the first several steps slowly and then resumed her typical pace. Her body reacted as though it was wounded, but it was a mere echo in her mind. It felt like it should be in pain, and thus every sensation was magnified ten-fold. "Are you coming?"

They ventured past twin-brass doors adorned with images of Venus and her conch shells into the Senate. Adalia blinked at the audaciousness of the austere surroundings, the likes of which the people of her village could not have imagined. Old men draped in gold whispered, trading in secrets. They wore bleached white togas with prominent red stripes to indicate their rank of senator.

The walls were decorated with painted tiles of marble, detailing the victory of Rome against Carthage, complete with the salting of the earth. Adalia noted with pride there were no stories about the people of the Rhine on these walls.

The centerpiece of the room was the Altar of Victory, which bore a statue of solid gold dedicated to the goddess Nike, holding a palm branch and descending to present a laurel wreath. "The imperator built this shrine to honor his son Octavian's victory in the Battle of Actium to claim Egypt against the mad priest Typhus."

The altar was filthy with tiny mounds of dirt, leaves, and sticks covering it. Marcus reached into his satchel and produced a small pouch. He opened it and poured his own small amount of muck onto the altar. "This is from Gaul, for the victories of the Seventh Legion."

The old men nodded their approval, saluted, and continued to mutter their secrets. Adalia waited until they passed the senators and then spoke. "You bring dirt from every land you conquer?"

Marcus nodded. "Nike requires homage."

"I thought that you did not believe in the gods?" Adalia asked.

"I believe in the power of the gods to motivate others," Marcus answered. "I wish to tell my men the truth when they ask if the deed was done."

They continued until they reached a long, winding line of petitioners. The Praetorian Guard halted their progress. Legend said that these men were hardened soldiers recruited from the most bloodthirsty in the legions. The leader of the troop stepped forward. He was tall for a Roman, with thick black hair and piercing eyes. "What business do you have in the Senate, centurion?"

If Marcus feared these men, it did not reflect in his features. "I am Marcus Valerius Perseus. I have been summoned by the imperator to report upon the progress in Gaul against the Caledonians."

"The centurion who choked a bear to death with his own hands?

Well met, friend. I met your brother last evening. I am Tribune Titus Flavius Petrol, Scion of the Thirteenth Legion. You are expected." The guard in black armor gestured for the line to part for them. "You may leave your woman here. She will be offered the best food and drink in all of Rome."

Marcus remained poised — still like a wolf before the chase — refusing the offered path. "This is Adalia of the Rhine. She has vital information for the imperator alone to hear."

The tribunus remained unmoved. "The imperator said you would be alone."

Marcus nodded, understanding the argument. "He was unaware I had arranged for a witness to answer the very question that he summoned me to address. Time is important, and I am following the direction of an apprentice of the Soothsayers, my brother, Nicomedes. You are aware of his friendship with the imperator."

It must have galled him to say that, Adalia thought.

"My father greatly admired you, centurion, as my name attests. This will not stop me from killing the both of you, should this be some sort of mischief in the making." There was a clear struggle of wills, but Adalia remained silent, not understanding the protocol of the situation. The guard turned towards his fellow Praetorian Guard. "Keep three men on them at all times."

The hall of the Senate was a large domed room, containing dazzling Roman architecture. Five elegant rows of cushioned steps followed the curve of the walls – all facing a single raised platform which held a humble chair. The walls were decorated with stylized rosettes in squares with opposed pairs of entwined cornucopias in green and red porphyry against fields of Numidian yellow and Phrygian purple.

Titus marched forward into the Senate and saluted. "Centurion Marcus Valerius Perseus and Adalia of the Rhine!"

The eyes of the crowd fell upon them as senators, lowly slaves, and guards turned towards them. These faceless old men ruled Europa, Adalia thought, and if they had their way, her people would join them.

She noted with some satisfaction that Marcus had spoken the truth about the Senate. Adalia counted almost a dozen Gaul men uncomfortably dressed in the traditional togas of the Senate amongst the natives. If Caesar kept his word to Gaul, then surely he would do the same for the people of the Rhine.

The imperator did not acknowledge their presence by turning to greet them. Instead he deigned to gesture with his hands to indicate that they should proceed to the center of the room into his view. Marcus accepted the command with a curt nod and did as commanded. She followed, curious to see the visage of the infamous Caesar, whose very name was spoken in hushed whispers across Gaul and the Rhine.

Here was no monster with hooves or horns, but an ordinary man who had mastered fear. He had a handsome face, with a prominent, thick Roman nose and a receding hairline, but also the youth and vigor of a man who could still ride to war. How was it possible this man had several years on her grandfather?

Caesar nodded, and Tribune Flavius stepped forward and tapped the butt of his spear three times onto the ground. "Heed the words of our Imperator Gaius Julius Caesar, Father of all Fathers, Consul of Rome."

Marcus knelt as protocol demanded in the presence of the imperator. Adalia did likewise, not wanting to cause insult.

"Friends, we have weighed and measured these issues together well past the morning. My physician insists I must break for a rest and sustenance." Caesar's words were kind and gentle, but there was a force behind them every person in the room understood. He gestured to a gaunt man who wore a simple grey himation. "Shall we reconvene in three hours' time?"

The proposal quietly passed in the Senate. Caesar coughed. "No meal would be complete without a few friends. Vetus, Creticus, Cicero, and Drusus – will you remain behind to share a meal with an old friend?"

Marcus leaned over and whispered, "Caesar commands the four greatest senators in Rome to attend our words. He takes this matter seriously."

"Do you know them?"

The centurion nodded and gestured to handsome man with dark curly hair, a youthful face despite the grey in his hair, and a disdainful smile that somehow felt inviting. "That is Lucius Antony Creticus, the younger brother of Marcus Antony."

Two senators held back from the exodus from the seats, politely allowing others to pass before them, while sharing quiet words. Marcus indicated the thin man with delicate features and piercing almond eyes.

"Marcus Tullius Cicero, the son of Caeser's greatest political enemy, and now his ally and close confidant."

Marcus gestured to Cicero's conversation partner. He had the look of a hard man softened with advanced age and comfort who appeared to have lived many years burning the candle at both ends. He had large shoulders and girth to match with receding grey hair. "Manius Aemilius Vetus. The richest man in all of Rome. Only his appetite exceeds his wealth."

Adalia turned towards the ancient thin senator with white hair, who walked slowly with a limp. The crowd parted to show respect. "And who is that one?"

"That man is my future father, should Nicomedes and Claudia have their way about my marriage to his daughter," Marcus explained. "Senator Marcus Livius Drusus Claudianus is perhaps the most influential senator in all of Rome. He is a noted conservative and will be difficult to sway."

The Senate slowly dispersed and exited until only those Caesar had personally invited, his physician, and the Praetorian Guard lead by Tribune Flavius remained. The guards unrolled a giant parchment the size of a carpet that covered the distance between Caesar and the senators.

Adalia marveled at the size of the map. She could lay herself down upon it end-to-end three times or more in any direction and still not reach the other side of it. The whole of the known world was depicted upon it, and she could tower over the land like a giant or a god. Her Latin literacy was basic at best, which made understanding the map difficult. She mentally traced the path from Britannia across to Europa — from the shores of Gaul, Hispania, and Germania. There were strange lands to the east she had never envisioned. Adalia glanced down at Italia and the coast of Africa, where Egypt and other lands were delineated.

Caesar turned to his physician, never leaving his chair. "Would you place the markers, Musa?"

The Greek slave placed wooden tiles painted in Numidian yellow upon the map. Marcus leaned towards her and whispered, "Those represent the strengths of Rome's legions."

She noted the number of tiles placed near the Rhine. Some of the tiles were dotted with green marks. These same tiles were placed near Egypt. "Those indicate allied forces under Rome's command, such as your tribe."

Then, Musa placed wooden tiles painted in red on the map near Britannia. "And those are the Caledonians."

Black tiles were placed father south in Africa. Adalia tried to imagine what sort of people lived there. Marcus continued to narrate. "And that is the Parthian Empire."

Caesar turned to Marcus. "Centurion, I have given to understand from Legate Agrippa's message that you have updated information for us regarding the campaign."

Marcus responded with a salute and did as commanded. He altered the formation of the legions along the coast of Gaul and Hispania, and then thinned out the legions in Germania. "Legate Agrippa deployed the legions in this manner to combat the Caledonian reavers."

"Am I to understand that Legate Agrippa disagrees with General Varus as to their purpose?" Senator Livus asked, skeptically.

Was this some sort of trap or attempt to discredit Marcus? Adalia wished he had allowed her to bring her blade to the Senate. Marcus shook his head politely. "Senator, I have been ordered to report that which I have witnessed and observed. I would not speak to the minds of either of my superior officers in this matter without permission."

It was Senator Vetus who spoke next. He was quite handsome in his confidence, with a charming smile. "Centurion, what tactical purpose does this new arrangement of our forces serve?"

"Senator, the Caledonians are targeting populated villages, rather than strategic resources," Marcus answered. He pointed to several villages noted on the map. "These are important trade routes, which have the strongest population of imperial citizens who support Rome. We believe they are trying to expand their reach until they can touch the Mediterranean."

Senator Lucius Antony Creticus scoffed. Adalia saw Marcus flinch. This man was the brother of his hero. "What nonsense is this? You should be protecting the operations of the mines in Hispania. Britannia lacks the proper resources to seize a war. If that should fall to them, Brutus could make a serious run against Rome."

"The Caledonians make no maneuver to seize anything other than people and gold," Marcus explained. "They dump weapons and armor into the ocean rather than see it used to a Roman cause. My optio has brought dozens of Caledonian blades to the quaestor for examination."

Cicero stepped forward to examine the map and the troop

markers. He was a petite man with a weaselly, content face. "I am given to understand that Britannia lacks the natural resources to make such weapons. Are you questioning the word of the imperator?"

Marcus turned towards the imperator. "I have studied Commentarii de Bello Gallico." Caesar smiled at this. "The land is rich with tin along the coast. We do not know what it holds in the center, but that is immaterial to our plans."

Caesar stood and all fell silent. "The centurion believes the Caledonians are trading tin for their weapons."

Creticus scoffed. "Who would dare trade with the enemies of Rome?"

Cicero smiled slyly, as though he had been waiting for such a question. "The Parthian Empire is known for the strength of their blades."

"Perhaps it is the Egyptians," Vetus countered. "This would explain the grain shortages, would it not?"

"You would accuse the son of Caesar of treason?" Cicero asked, horrified.

The imperator raised his hand. The others fell silent. "What say you centurion?"

"Rome has an enemy wily enough to conceal its purpose and move slowly like a jackal." Marcus gestured to Adalia. "They have moved to kill our allies and replace them with those who hunger for power. This is Adalia of the Rhine, daughter of Jarl Segimerus, sister of Armin. And she has a story to tell."

Adalia stepped forward. "My uncle Halas argued long for war

against Rome, until the year my father grew ill. His smile turned sweet as the wolf at winter. His words spoke of Rome as our friend, but we knew the truth."

"What manner of illness struck your father, child?" Caesar asked.

"Our healers knew not the cause of the malady," Adalia admitted. Strange that her pride would feel such a sting to confess this in Rome. "His lips and fingernails turned as blue as the robin's egg. He died peacefully in his bed, surrounded by his new wife and dogs."

"And then Halas became the new Jarl of your tribe, yes?" the imperator asked.

"Yes. We feared that he would speak words against Rome and start another war, but his demeanor changed," Adalia explained. "Where he was once boisterous and proud, he became secretive and sly. He had always lusted after power, but now he seemed obsessed with his station. Gold coins and gifts of strange spices and cloth flowed into his hands. We are not a wealthy people, and even the proud can be turned with such luxuries."

"Strange spices? Can you describe them?" Cicero asked.

"It smelled sweeter than flowers in spring and tasted like a child's laughter," Adalia explained. "We did not have a name for it."

"Why does General Varus not report this? What proof do you have that Jarl Halas turns against Rome?" Caesar demanded.

She reached into the pouch hidden under her tunic for the coin that Adalia had ferried all the way from the Rhine. It was gold, impressed with the stamp of an striking figure with a large bulbous hat and long beard. Strange symbols were etched into the sides the likes of which she had never seen before. "I waited until I believed my uncle would be meeting with the elders in the bath house to speak to the representative of the legions. He returned early, and I was forced to hide. Cloaked men with sharp swords and hidden faces met him in the dead of the woods. They spoke in a devilish language and exchanged these coins for the life of myself and my brother."

She held the coin in the palm of her hand and reached out to the senators of Rome. Creticus took it and examined it closely. "If you did not speak the language, then how do you know they agreed to take your life?"

"My father trained me to walk in the woods so that neither man nor beast could detect my presence." Adalia couldn't help but smile at Marcus, proud of achievements that no Roman lady would dare to claim. "I followed these men to my family cottage, where they sought the life of my brother Armin."

"And how did you escape their blades with your lives?" Creticus asked, incredulously.

"We are a strong people, senator. My brother and I fought them well, but they would have murdered the both of us, had not this centurion interrupted the deed." Adalia gestured towards Marcus. "He saved the life of the future Jarl of the Teutonics, and promised in the name of Rome that our lives would be protected as would our people, under the protection of the Eternal City as members of the empire."

"And how did you make this happen, centurion?" Caesar asked.

Marcus coughed. "The Third Cohort of the Seventh Legion had been given approval for a night's leave, and it happened that I and my optio consumed a great deal of the local brew."

Creticus laughed. "You were drunk and tired from whoring. We have all been soldiers, son. I think I trust your words as real from the knowing of it."

"They refused to identify themselves when challenged, and so we engaged and ended them," Marcus answered. "I spoke with Adalia and her brother, and listened to their story. If true, I saw how Rome could benefit from securing their safety."

"I would know of this benefit, centurion," Senator Livus stated. "Pray tell."

"The old jarl made an alliance with Rome, wishing to join us in full as did Gaul. His children were honor-bound to follow their father's wishes," Marcus explained. "I know what it is to be the son of a murdered father."

Silence reigned in the Senate of Rome, as senators glanced aside, each trying to judge the reactions of others. Caesar coughed, catching their attention. "How did you secure their safety then, centurion?"

Marcus continued, slightly more confident, as none challenged his unspoken accusation. "I sent Armin away from the world, to receive a proper education under a different name. Adalia I sent to protect my sister."

"Might I ask where you are having this future jarl educated?" Vetus asked. "I would see to it that the boy learns to love Rome as we do."

"Apologies, senator. I have sworn an oath upon my family and the flame of Rome to never reveal such," Marcus answered solemnly. He raised his arm over his heart and lowered his head. "And in exchange, I have been promised the loyalty of the Germani people to the Eternal City."

"Who are you to make such a promise for Rome?" the imperator demanded.

Marcus knelt before the imperator. "I made this promise on behalf of me and mine, imperator. I accept any responsibility for it."

Caesar waved away any concerns and motioned for Marcus to rise. "You have done well. I did the same once when I was your age. And the children of Segimerus shall be as my own. What of these foreigners that you killed? Do you know anything of them?"

Marcus shook his head. Adalia answered. This was the moment they had planned for. "I saw such men again only once since that night. They came for the life of Claudia of the Valeria, and I along with Darius Valerius Egnatius, slew them."

Cicero seemed to be quite satisfied with that answer. He turned towards the other senators, as though he were about to crow like a rooster. "The mystery thickens. It is a pity that the Soothsayers will not release the Sibylline Scrolls."

Adalia turned towards Marcus confused. "A prophecy?"

Caesar laughed. "Some say that the words contained within are the last prophecies of Hellespontian Sibyl, rumored to be the most accurate in the world, aside from the Soothsayers."

"Why would the Soothsayers deny us access to these scrolls?" Adalia asked.

Creticus scowled. "There is an old legend about them. It is said that the Cumaean offered six scrolls to King Tarquinius in the days of the old kingdom and the foolish king refused the price. The old priest burned three of the scrolls and then demanded a higher price. This time King Tarquinius paid the ransom, and it is said gained much wisdom from their study."

Cicero coughed uncomfortably. "These scrolls were considered sacred and accessible only by the Senate in the days of the Republic. Some read them and interpreted the prophecy to mean the traitor Brutus would murder the imperator to restore the Republic to glory. Foolish notions that killed many innocents."

"The Soothsayers requested the scrolls as the reward for saving my life," Caesar explained. "How could I deny them? If only you had not killed all of your tormentors. It would have been quite useful to drag their secrets into the light. From where did they come? Who are their masters? Were they involved with the beast that dared to touch my person?"

"I am told the answer is forthcoming this very evening," Marcus revealed.

"How are such things possible?" Creticus asked.

"My younger brother may have a means to discover their secrets."

"How?" Caesar asked.

"I feared to ask, imperator. He took their severed heads to the Soothsayer Academy."

The mere mention of the Soothsayers seemed to draw a shadow over them. Even the mighty senators of Rome trembled at the thought of beings so completely out of their control; they blanched at the mere mention of their names. Adalia took note of their reaction for the future, as even the most alleged stoics among the Romans had their own taboos and superstitions.

The Consul of Rome returned to his chair and considered the map. "I have heard word from the Soothsayers that indicates the answer to all of our mysteries lies within Egypt and the shortage in the grain shipments."

Senator Livius nodded, deep in thought. "The report to the Senate indicates that pirates were causing problems, but we have yet to locate them despite our efforts."

Caesar stood once again and walked across the Mediterranean on the floor. "Pirates kidnapped me on the Aegean Sea when I was merely a man. They tried to ransom me for a mere twenty talents of silver. Can you imagine that? Of course, I insisted they ask for fifty or I'd be humiliated. While their prisoner, I promised I'd return with a fleet of ships and see that each and every one of them were crucified."

"Did you?" Adalia asked, before she realized she interrupted the imperator.

Caesar laughed, but she felt a real menace under the mirth. "The governor wanted to let Rome handle it, but I raised a fleet with my own funds. It nearly set me to economic ruin, but the honor of Rome was at stake." He stepped over the Aegean Sea on the map. "They were pirates, and not trained to fight armed men. They relied more on terror than tactics. I routed them quickly and then yes, I kept my promise. It was the first time I ever saw a man crucified. Horrible way to die. It can take days for a strong man to suffocate, if mercy is not shown. And I was not feeling particularly merciful then. So believe me when I say that I understand the desperation of the pirate, and find it difficult to believe any would dare assault a ship under the banner of Rome. There is a pattern to their miscreant behavior, and this has not the stink of it."

"If pirates are not the cause, then what is it, imperator?" Creticus asked.

"It is an excuse to send a team of investigators, which is what the Soothsayer suggested," Caesar answered. "Centurion Marcus has family in Alexandria and has my complete confidence in this matter."

"It would be a terrible thing to ask of a man about to earn his year to abandon his military service," Senator Livus replied. "What do you say, Marcus?"

"I serve the people of Rome and the Senate," Marcus replied.

"My brother died because we did not fully heed the Soothsayer's words, imperator," Creticus stated coldly. The mention of Marcus Anthony brought a moment of tension between the Romans that Adalia didn't quite understand. "How can we refuse their wisdom this time?"

"The Soothsayers strongly suggested we send the three Valeria siblings to investigate this matter. It would seem each is considered vital to the resolution of this problem in favor of Rome," Caesar revealed. "I am inclined to follow their advice pending your words and support for what must be done."

Cicero nodded. "Proper excuses could be made to push the Senate into a motion of support for such a plan."

"Better to seize the moment now," Creticus agreed. "I'll choke the life out of any fool who tries to protest, right there on the Senate floor."

Livus raised his hand in objection. "Discretion is required. The real problem is the Senate will protest that a Vestal Virgin is leaving the Eternal City. It would be seen as a loss of face for the entire city, especially since the assassination attempt. The mob would be furious. This could be seen as an attempt to hide her from our enemies and a sign of weakness."

Marcus cleared his throat. "I would take this mission, provided I may petition the Senate for a release of service for Claudia."

"Under what pretext?" Cicero asked dismissively. "The mob would riot at such a thing. Rarely has a Vestal Virgin been allowed to leave office."

"I seek to create a branch family, which is why I have been attempting to earn my name in the field," Marcus revealed. He glanced over to Senator Livius. "My sister has arranged for a match, pending approval of my future wife's paterfamilias. Claudia would be needed at home, since my mother is quite ill. It is the duty of a woman to return to the hearth when she is needed. What Roman could protest such a thing?"

Livius smiled. It was the first sign of emotion Adalia had detected from him. "I have little doubt such a paterfamilias would be honored to have you as a son."

Caesar listened to each of his advisors speak in turn, at length, until their words merged together in a chorus of passionate tones devoid of meaning. Adalia ignored everyone else and concentrated on Caesar.

His face conveyed he carefully weighed the opinions of his advisers and he valued their opinions. They revealed themselves before him and thanked him for the opportunity. *This was how a jarl should rule.*

In time, the imperator raised his hand, silencing the room. "I will consider the matter carefully and send word when I have made a decision. Your support has been noted and Rome shall not forget such patriots."

The tribunus tapped the floor with his spear three times, signaling that the room was dismissed by the consul of Rome. Marcus and Adalia were escorted out of the curio by two of the Praetorian Guard, where Milius and the Third Cohort of the Seventh Legion awaited them.

Marcus turned to Adalia on the Senate Curio steps. "Any debt that once existed between our blood has been more than paid. You have done everything I asked and more, Adalia."

She read the doubt in his face. "And yet the future is still uncertain for all of us until the face of our enemy is known."

The centurion reluctantly nodded. "I am bound to seek out our collective destiny in Egypt, and I would feel better if you decided to come with us. No ties of honor or obligation move you towards this end. And yet, I would ask that you come with us."

"This tide shall not leave myself nor my brother untouched. I would see to the safety of the Teutonics and deal with this threat myself, rather than hope others dispatch it for us." Adalia laughed, "And if nothing else, I wish to see your wedding to this hoofed woman I have heard you lament about."

"I shudder to think of the children. It is a crime against the gods that the beauty of the Valeria shall not properly be passed unto the next generation."

Adalia laughed. "Perhaps the youngest Valeria brother shall have children, and thus shoulder the burden for you."

Marcus paused, horrified. "Am I the homeliest brother of the Valeria? Surely not."

"Do not fret, centurion." Adalia patted him on the arm, much in the same fashion she once did with her own brother. "You have a strong arm and are in many ways clever. Let us meet up with your handsome brother and steal what secrets we might from the enemy."

Chapter Five: To Keep the Flame

The cook tucked the swan's neck under its wing until it quit moving, and then snapped it with a practiced, fluid motion of her wrist. Hermana served as the overseer of Domūs de Valeria for nearly two decades. Years ago, this stern woman, whose face never seemed to express joy or sorrow, taught Claudia the rudimentary skills required to be considered a proper and noble lady of Rome and keep the hearth burning. Her mother rarely made an appearance in the kitchen save to order the servants about, and so Claudia had never understood the strange alchemy of baking bread or preparing a proper stew.

Hermana stretched the swan's neck out over wooden blocks and then severed its head with a single, clean chop with a sharp knife. The swan's blood pooled in a crimson halo around the severed head. She stepped away from the table and glanced aside at Claudia for guidance, hesitant as to what was expected in this unusual circumstance.

Claudia gingerly stepped forward to peer down into the pool of blood, desperate to glimpse some sort of sign of the future. Marcus would have laughed at this crude display of superstition. He believed in the teachings of Zeno of Citium and a natural world with laws that could be understood with proper study. She would have shared his beliefs before she joined the Vestal College.

She became a Vestal Virgin to escape this very house rather than embrace a religious faith. The mysteries and auguries were but a means to control the masses, or so she thought, until it was time for her to speak the words before a devoted believer. Her first attempt at haruspexy involved dipping her hands into the warm flesh of a dead chicken. She had never felt a dead thing before, and yet it felt familiar and ancient.

The augury came naturally to her, bringing insights Claudia had never realized possible. Marcus might have argued this knowledge was innate to her nature and that she could only force herself to rely on those resources when caught in the moment. Yet, Claudia knew there was magic in the world. She had seen proof of the alchemy produced by the Soothsayers; it kept the patrician families healthy beyond their years.

"Domina?"

Claudia waved her approval to the unasked question. The overseer used her hand to sweep the blood into the cooper bowl and poured the remains into the simmering brazier.

"The time of my brothers' arrival is uncertain, but I imagine that at least Marcus shall be hungry."

"Do you wish the house to prepare another meal for the cohort?" Hermana asked.

The cohort had placed a strain on the resources of the family, especially with the cost of grain dramatically rising, but it was an important investment for the future. "Yes. Use your best judgment on the portions, but we shall not be seen as shirking our duty."

"You may use my father's discretionary funds, Hermana." Claudia flinched at the sound of the voice of her childhood tormentor. She had focused so intently hoping to see the future in the blood of the swan that she had become blind to the present. Decimus turned to the overseer. "I would speak alone with my cousin."

Hermana glanced from Claudia to Decimus, conflicted, but in the end, she deferred to the son of the paterfamilias: his proxy. Disobeying any order from Decimus could bring severe punishment if his mood was foul. "Yes, domitor."

Claudia nodded to the overseer as she ushered the servants out of the kitchen. She scanned the table to ensure the knives were well within her reach and turned to Decimus.

He had grown a great deal in the last few years. His thick jowls of baby fat had thinned as exercise from the legions shaped his form. Decimus was no longer the rotund boy who chased her and pulled her hair. She could no longer slap him with impunity when he pushed her to the ground. He was dangerous.

Claudia smiled, as though she were happy to greet him. "It is a pleasure to see you, brother. The years have been kind to you."

"I appreciate the honor, dearest Claudia, but alas we are merely cousins, despite the marriage of your mother to my father," Decimus stated. "You were never adopted."

Was he trying to remind her that Orca refused to claim her siblings as his own? "I recall quite well."

"It was his hope our branches would be joined through marriage," Decimus continued. There was a flush about his cheeks and he scratched his head absentmindedly. "Rumor has reached me that Marcus petitions the Senate for a motion of release."

"He will need my guidance for his new branch of the family," Claudia countered. "If it is the will of the gods, I shall sacrifice for him.

He did as much for me during our childhood."

"I did not wish to make your life miserable, Claudia."

"What did you wish, then?" Claudia asked. "What world did you imagine you created for me?"

Decimus slammed his fist upon the table. "I wanted you to look upon me without repulsion."

Claudia flinched. "Do you imagine this as a means to accomplish that?"

"I offered amends for what I tried to do, but you refused to even speak with me," Decimus said, quietly.

She plucked a brown, ceramic plate from the table and held it up for inspection. "This dish has been in our family for years, taken from Egypt." Claudia threw it upon the floor, the concrete shattering it into pieces. "Apologies shall not put that plate back together."

Decimus stepped back. His face flushed crimson, and his hands shook. "I was young and stupid. It is difficult to be told you can master the world and to witness another take what is yours."

"Destiny belongs to those who win it." Claudia folded her arms. "None are entitled to Nike's blessing, save those who earn it."

Decimus nodded in agreement, much to her surprise. "A hard learned lesson in the Thirteenth Legion during my tour in Africa. I enlisted only to demonstrate that my bravery matched your brother's. The Thirteenth cared not that I was the pampered son of the paterfamilias."

"I am pleased you have grown, Decimus."

"I do not expect you will ever find joy in my face, given childhood torments, but there is no need for us to be enemies," Decimus said. "My father will not oppose your branch, as long as you do not attempt to take what is ours."

"We have no need of your coin, but the thought is appreciated." Claudia turned towards the door. "If that is all…"

"You were hostile to me long before I vented my frustration. Why? I would have looked upon you as family. Why did you make me into your enemy?" Decimus asked.

Claudia stepped onto the plate shards, grinding them into dust. She refused to look towards Decimus. "Did you believe we would befriend the son of the man who murdered our father?"

"You believe such a thing?" Decimus asked, horrified. "That my father would slay his brother?"

Claudia pointed an accusing finger towards her cousin. "You believe the mighty Titus Valerius Perseus would fall to a sickness of the body without cause?"

"Do you love Marcus and Nicomedes?"

"They are of my flesh."

"Then why is it so easy to believe that my father would kill his brother?" Decimus leaned upon the table, as though he needed help merely standing. "Twice in this life I have witnessed my father's tears — the day he discovered my mother dead in bed, and the night that the mighty Titus died walking through the great door of Domūs de Valeria. Their faces were pale and their lips were blue. What story does that tell you?" Decimus asked.

Claudia folded her arms defensively. Decimus and his father turned their home into Tartarus, ruining their childhoods. *How dare he imply that Orca was innocent of kinslaying?* "That your father used the same weapon twice."

"You think my father bothered to poison my mother?" Decimus tilted his head. "Do you even remember her? You and your dead sister were named after her."

Thinking of Decimus's mother brought forth a warm flood of memories for Claudia. Licia Terza had been a beautiful woman with an elegant neckline and thick lips, as was common amongst the women of the Aemilii. Claudia blinked a moment, feeling like a dull knife without purpose. She had thought Nephele, the materfamilias of the Aemilii, had been scrutinizing her looking for weakness, but may perhaps have merely been gazing upon the namesake of her youngest sister.

"I remember her fondly. She gave me a beautiful doll on a night when I was quite scared." Claudia smiled at the reminder of the kindness. "I had heard the story of my twin sister dead at birth and often imagined she haunted me."

Decimus reached across the table. Claudia flinched and stepped away, having palmed the knife Hermana left behind. He snatched one of the ripe pomegranates from the wooden bowl, cracked it on the side of the table, and bit into the juicy seeds. The juice stained the sides of his lips. "She loved you dearly. Mother wanted more children, but father feared for her health. She was precious to him, and so she looked upon all of you quite fondly, especially since you were distant cousins. I remembered her fear when Nicomedes was born, afraid that there would be yet another dead twin."

Septima Valerius Orca had once been Septima Axia Pulchra before her first marriage. She earned the agnomen Pulchra for her dazzling beauty, which sadly only her brothers inherited. Her mother never spoke of a blood relation to the Aemilii, but then again she did love her secrets.

Claudia pondered his words, realizing that there was a hidden piece of information that could not possibly be true. "You speak as though it was somehow expected that Nicomedes would also have a dead twin."

He offered her the remaining half of the pomegranate. "Considering both you and Marcus were both born with a dead twin, it was not an unreasonable fear."

"Why would you say such nonsense? If Marcus had also been born with a dead twin, why would I not know of this? There were several years when the mere sight of Janus frightened me."

Decimus shook his head. "The very subject became taboo after your birth. I still recall the screams from Hermana when your mother had her whipped after telling you. It is not uncommon in the history. Darius would know better than I, but the Valeria have a long history of twins, dating back to Romulus and Remus, if the stories are true. Why else do you think we revere Janus above others?"

"And Nicomedes was born without a twin?" Claudia asked.

"It is whispered he was born with a caul the doula had difficulty removing," Decimus answered. "Considering his current ability, that is hardly surprising."

"Sentiment is not a quality known in your father. These trivialities mean nothing," Claudia spat. She stepped towards the door, careful to keep the heavy table between them. "He wanted to be paterfamilias of the Valeria, and he did not let conscience or honor stand in his way."

"My mother was from the main branch of the Aemilii. She drew an inherence worth well more than the entirety of the Domūs de Valeria," Decimus revealed. "If that was his plan, it was poorly made. He could have had the wealth and the title."

Claudia scoffed. "He mourned just enough to claim the title and did little to provide for his brother's children."

"Do you think it is my father that makes these decisions?" Decimus asked. "Why do you think I hated you so? You and your brothers? Spawn of the Iron Queen herself. Look upon the face of your mother and ask her who killed your father. You may be surprised by what you see."

She paused, fearing to make any move that might encourage her cousin's predatory instincts. Despite her fear, escape now seemed secondary to wringing secrets out of Decimus. "Do you know why they called your father Orca? All animals kill because they must, save the orcas. Sailors have spied them from afar. Do you know how they train their young to hunt? An orca pod hunts down a herd of seals and isolates the largest one for a select purpose. Their leader will pummel that poor seal until its back is broken. Then young orcas learn to hunt while the poor seal desperately tries to remain afloat. Do you know what the orcas do while this happens?"

Decimus grimaced. "They laugh."

"Just as you did when you held your father's knife at my throat." Claudia lifted the kitchen blade, just enough to show Decimus that she would never again be caught unaware by him. "You thought you were special, but you were merely the first little boy to fail at taking my life."

He shoved the table to the side. Claudia blinked, surprised Decimus had the strength to even budge it. "It is true I failed," he said. "I thought she would care."

"Who?"

His eyes watered as Decimus clenched his hands into fists. "Septima! Do you think I could deny her Lorelai call any more than my father, even then? She stared into my eyes and laughed."

A hard woman's voice called from the hall. It was Adalia. "Claudia!" Adalia strode into the kitchen, spry and energetic. Her brother's magic was indeed potent to have healed such grievous wounds so completely. Adalia could almost pass for a lady of Rome in the blue stola, if one ignored her pale skin and braided blonde hair. "Marcus bid me to pass along a message."

Decimus growled. "It is poor form for a slave to speak such to a domina."

"Adalia is no base slave, but a guest of this house and my savior, on the word of my brother." Claudia reached out and embraced Adalia. "Let us retreat to my chambers, so this message may be properly considered and measured."

Claudia entwined her arms around Adalia and led her out of the kitchen to the atrium, where a portion of the Third Cohort kept watch. Decimus would not dare to harm her while her brother's soldiers were present. However, it was certainly better to avoid a confrontation, lest Marcus choke the life out of their childhood tormentor just when they were about to claim the right to their own branch family.

Adalia grinned slyly. She smelled of lilacs. "It may be my destiny to forever separate you from those who might wish to do you harm, or at the least to keep Marcus from dirtying his hands with swine."

"Does this mean you have agreed to venture with us to Egypt?" Claudia asked, taking the stairs to her personal chambers.

She nodded enthusiastically. "I have been convinced the answer to both of our families' misfortunes lie there. And I would see these pyramids that the legionnaires whisper about at night."

"Where is my brother?"

"Marcus and Milius have ventured to the Aventine to resupply the cohort," Adalia explained.

Claudia stopped before the balcony and offered Adalia her chair, a gesture of thanks one would give to a friend rather than a body-slave. "I have treated you poorly."

It was always difficult to read her face. "You treated me as a slave," Adalia stated. "As any Roman lady would for a new untested member of her household. My father had many thralls, though our way is different from yours."

She offered Adalia a bowl of dates. "You show me a kindness not reflected in my treatment of you."

Adalia carefully selected one, sniffed it, and then took a small bite. She smiled at the taste of it. "Who amongst us ever truly receives what we deserve? Let it pass from your mind. Never chase prey with a hunter you resent. My father said that, and I believe him."

Claudia bit her lip. *How honest could she be with Adalia?* "I would speak with you on another matter, which may birth that very resentment."

"Marcus must marry Drusilla for the good of the Valeria," Adalia stated. "And even if that were not true, it would be impossible for him to marry a savage from the north."

Claudia had ignored Adalia's great cunning and wisdom before. This time the lack of insight had been benign, but Claudia resolved to be more aware in the future. The plebeians and savages could be far cleverer than she had estimated. "Truthfully I expected you would fume at the news," Claudia admitted.

"Shall I rail at the injustices of the world?" Adalia asked. She took another bite of the date and swallowed. "Marcus is certainly brilliant as a lover, especially once I broke his innate Roman training and taught him the ways of the north. I shall find other lovers and build my own family."

The thought of a woman teaching Marcus the art of coitus was somehow amusing. He enjoyed bragging and implied he had been sprung from the womb with all of the knowledge required to be a man. "You taught Marcus?"

Adalia grinned wistfully. "Such was not a hardship, I assure you. I taught him the things a woman needs, and he proved to be a devoted student."

Claudia laughed. "This subject might return often in conversation with Marcus."

"I presume you were born with all the knowledge you shall require when you marry?" Adalia asked.

She felt her face flush. "I presume I will marry an experienced husband who shall teach me how to please him."

Adalia snatched yet another date. "I can teach you that which you must know."

Claudia gasped, dropping the date she had been munching upon. It was not unknown for Vestal Virgins to indulge in the secret delight of the flesh with each other. Such did not violate the vows of chastity required to maintain the sacred flame of Rome. She looked upon Adalia and tried imaging kissing those lips. "Thank you for the offer, but I should decline, as it should complicate the matter."

"As you like, domina." Adalia tilted her head slyly and grinned. "Does not your great Caesar claim that the application of knowledge is a lever towards power?"

"Power comes with a cost I am not certain I wish to pay at this time," she answered the unasked question. "And you are to call me Claudia. The ruse is over, and we shall be friends if you will allow it."

Hermana knocked lightly upon the door to the chambers. "Domina, a visitor at the great door requests the hospitality of the Valeria and the honor of your company."

The Valeria had received few visitors since the attempt upon her life, though many sent gifts and coin. For days, the mob camped outside of their walls, angry that a bride of Rome had been assaulted. "Who would dare come at this time?" Claudia asked.

Hermana quietly answered. "Livia Drusilla Claudius Appius."

Adalia tilted her head and wrinkled her nose. "I would meet the future bride of the legendary Centurion Marcus Valerius Perseus."

"What word shall I pass to the doctore?" She looked from Claudia and at Adalia and the bowl of dates, confused. "Shall I escort her here?"

Darius had ordered the Domūs de Valeria locked down. No one outside of the line of Valeria or their direct guests was allowed entry. Drusilla risked much socially and politically to venture forth. The mob was angry, and the target of their ire could shift quickly to a daughter of a senator who failed to protect the Vestal Virgins. And yet, if the Valeria refused entry to a future daughter, what did that say of their honor?

"No. Her foot has been healed by physicians at the Soothsayer Academy, but she still has difficulty walking. We shall meet her in the atrium, surrounded by her beloved's men," Claudia declared. "And remember, she is to be my sister if the gods are pleased. Ensure that the freeman know she is my personal guest and her security is the same as my own."

The overseer bowed and quickly departed. Her harried steps echoed down the stairs. The Claudians were not known for their abundance of patience. Claudia turned to Adalia. "Drusilla is wiser than many credit. Her father trusts her to run his household."

"Livus did not strike me as a foolish man," Adalia admitted. "I expect any daughter of his to be formidable, and I would know her intentions."

They met Drusilla in the atrium, where she waited on a wooden bench that rested in the shade of a vast olive tree. She wore a long purple tunic that reached to her ankles, with a grey stola that wrapped over her shoulders and her waist. Her lips and cheeks were painted, and her chestnut hair curled in the latest fashion. It must have taken a dozen slaves skilled in cultus more than an hour to prepare Drusilla for this visit, Claudia mused. If only the Valeria had the wealth to spend on such luxuries.

Drusilla stood greeting her host. "Dia!"

Claudia kissed her upon the cheek, greeting her like family. "Dru! Surely it is too dangerous on the streets to risk venturing here."

She blinked, flashing her large almond eyes. "Father assures me that the danger has passed," Drusilla replied. "And he insisted upon an armed escort."

"Have you met Adalia of the Rhine?" Claudia asked.

Drusilla turned towards Adalia and embraced her as she would a Roman woman of family and honor. She kissed her upon the cheek as Claudia had welcomed her. If there was cause for tension between them, she failed to show it. "Father speaks very highly of you and your aid to the cause of Rome."

"Claudia has told me of your wisdom," Adalia replied in kind.

"I trust that we shall be brilliant friends," Drusilla said. "It would seem that we have more than merely Marcus in common."

Adalia laughed. "It is a pleasure to converse with a woman that speaks plainly, as my people do along the Rhine."

"Would that we had the time for proper conversations about the hearth and dreams of tomorrow," Drusilla lamented. "Fate has other plans for us this day. Nephele of the Aemilii intends to visit the Vestal Virgins this day, while Claudia remains protected here."

This was unexpected. Services were suspended by order of the Senate. "Why?"

Drusilla smiled slightly. "Mannius Aemilius Vetus opposes my father in the Senate. An alliance with the Valeria branch would grant us strength."

Her words were a polite fiction to mask her embarrassment. The Claudians were considered a dying breed — a cursed line destined to fade away. The injection of Valeria blood might stabilize their descent. Though the Valeria were a poor family amongst the patricians, few doubted their courage and vitality. "Surely, the needs of Rome come before old feuds?"

Adalia tilted her head and wrinkled her nose. She always made that expression when pondering an issue and coming to an uncomfortable solution. "Is Minerva about to split your skull? Or do you have insight into this matter?" Claudia asked.

"Marcus claimed that Vetus was the richest man in Rome. Is that accurate?" Adalia asked.

Claudia nodded. "If he is not the richest man in Rome, than Pluto himself has taken residence."

"The Aemilii have many copper and silver mines in the territories and possess the slaves to make them produce," Drusilla added.

"And what of grain?" Adalia prompted.

Drusilla shook her head. "Farming is not lucrative enough for the Aemilii, but they do possess many transport ships."

Adalia grimaced and then sighed. "Vetus accused the heir of Caesar of tampering with the supply of grain, causing the shortage. It would be a tidy coincidence if the Aemilii controlled the grain. The first to accuse is typically guilty of the crime in question."

"The Cornelii control much of the farmland in Italia," Claudia observed. "They opposed the imperator's war in Gaul, because it broke their monopoly on feeding Rome. Caesar won them back to his side by granting Messalina Cornelius Scipio rights over Egypt and distributing their grain. If the manners of their materfamilias are any indication, the two families have been at odds for the last couple of years."

Drusilla shook her head gently. "My father claims that such is a ruse and the Cornelii are now secretly allied with the Aemilii in the Senate."

Was it possible that there was a conspiracy within the Senate to weaken Rome? "Nephele of the Aemilia has been organizing the noble women of Rome to ignore Messalina for the last year," Claudia said, thoughtfully. "If this has been a stratagem of such effort on the part of two major families of Rome, then to what purpose? Might Vetus have been attempting to divert suspicions for his ally? My own paterfamilias tried to force a marriage between myself and the third son of Vetus," Claudia said, thoughtfully. "I could not refuse the match until I arranged to join the Vestal Virgins."

"What can Nephele achieve at the temple that Vetus cannot achieve in the Senate?" Adalia asked.

"The Vestal Virgins are by law limited to authority over the hearth, marriage, and the family," Claudia explained. "We once gave prophecies, but that duty has been taken over by the Soothsayers."

Drusilla nodded. "The Pontifex Maximus approves the selection of new Vestal Virgins and the retirement of those ready to return to the world."

She suddenly remembered whom the Senate recently vetted to assume the role of the Pontifex Maximus. "They would not dare!"

"Enlighten us."

"The Pontifex Maximus is Mamercus Aemilius Paullus," Drusilla revealed. "Brother to Vetus and potentially spoiler of my marriage to Marcus. They seek to cast doubt on our marriage before the vote from the Senate."

"If they oppose your alliance, then can they not simply vote against the notion?" Adalia asked.

"To directly oppose my father is to draw his wrath, and his influence is great within the Senate," Drusilla explained. "And yet, he is a religious man, and he will not go against the word of the Vestal Virgins."

"Then we shall go to insure that matters are not unjustly swayed against us," Claudia declared.

"We should find Marcus," Adalia suggested.

Claudia shook her head slyly. The elements of a proper strategy began to form. "It is not my elder brother who is required for this purpose. Nicomedes, on the other hand, is an apprentice of the Soothsayers, and it is against the will of the imperator to act against their prophecies."

Drusilla sighed. "The Soothsayer Academy is on the other side of the forum, and unless he has the speed of Mercury, then it shall be too late to assist the cause."

"My voice means little at the Atrium Vestae, but perhaps at the academy I might sway Nicomedes to lend his weight to the matter," Adalia suggested.

"Are you not injured?" Drusilla asked, concerned. "Will you be able to reach him in time?"

"Nicomedes healed my body, but my soul had not yet processed the miracle this morning. Necessity forces strength upon us all," Adalia declared. "I shall make haste at this very moment. Take the guards and delay whatever plans these Aemilii might conceive."

"I came to this villa to attempt to discern if you would oppose my marriage to Marcus," Drusilla admitted. "And now I have only come to admire you and your strength, and learn best from you how to win his heart."

Adalia laughed. "It took courage to come here to take my measure, knowing that I am a barbarian from the north. Such strength is what will attract him."

"Thank you."

Adalia leaned forward and whispered into Drusilla's ear, such that Claudia had to strain to hear it. "Should that fail, there are things I can teach you to bend his will to yours."

* * * *

The Atrium Vestae remained closed and under the protection of the Praetorian Guard. Vendors and merchants returned to outlying areas on the forum to hawk their wares. Claudia and Drusilla rode in the lectica, surrounded by a cadre of soldiers made up from the Claudian freedmen and the Third Cohort.

The tribunus stepped forward, hands upon his gladius. "The Atrium Vestae is closed by order of the Senate."

"Have your eyes failed you?" Drusilla asked. "This is Claudia Valeria Terza. The very Vestal Virgin that foreigners tried to murder in that sacred place. Would you dare to anger Hestia?"

The tribunus noted the soldiers and then the size of his own compliment of troops. It was forbidden to prevent a Vestal Virgin from her tasks, lest the sacred flame of Rome fade. Yet, he was clearly given specific orders he did not wish to disobey. "Gentle protectors, it is only myself and Drusilla who seek entry," Claudia said. "Surely you could find room in your watch for my protectors to aid you?"

This seemed to satisfy the orders of the tribunus and the honor of both groups of soldiers. The tribunus helped Claudia and Drusilla rise from the lectica and personally escorted them to the gates of the Atrium Vestal. They stood under the shadow of the great marble statue of Numa Pompilius.

"The gods never blessed me with a sister despite my prayers." Drusilla entwined their arms together, protective. "If all goes well, I shall have one, along with a husband."

Claudia almost apologized for how her family treated Drusilla over the years, but then bit her tongue. Why spoil the moment with her guilt? She thought of the poisoned words that came from the lips of Decimus, and her own sister allegedly born stillborn.

They entered the temple via the door reserved for the Vestals and immediately heard her sister Vestals singing the Sacred Hymns of Hestia. The ceremony had already started. Claudia rushed past the inner sanctum, ignoring the protocol of sanctifying herself before entering the great atrium.

Her stola swayed in the gentle breeze, as Claudia stopped at the sacred flame burning at the center of the Atrium Vestae. She knelt in reverence. The singing stopped as Claudia stood, revealing her presence to the congregation. She noted a number of the important patrician women of Rome present, especially those who were connected to the Aemilii and the Cornelii, along with a smattering of the Mucia, the Horatia, and even the Fabia. The wisdom accepted from such a gathering of the noble women of Rome would be very difficult for even the Senate to overrule without just cause.

The Virgo Vestalis Maxima stood before the entrance of Ariadne's Maze alongside the Pontifex Maximum. Nephele knelt before them, her hands upon the earth and the dirt, symbolizing her feminine connection to Gaia and the world. She stopped, blinked but for a moment, and then smiled. "Claudia! Truly it is a blessing that you have come to us at this time."

"I would not wish to interrupt the ceremony, Maxima." Claudia glanced about the great atrium. Rarely, the Vestal Virgins performed smaller ceremonies for the major families of Rome. Though it was costly for coin, it paid great dividends in prestige. "I am surprised there is a blessing ceremony when the Senate ordered the temple be closed for the protection of all."

The Pontifex Maximus grimaced. "Closed for public ceremonies," he corrected Claudia. "The Aemilii have come for spiritual guidance from the Vestal Virgins."

"It is always a blessing from the gods when a daughter of Rome returns to the hearth," Virgo Vestalis Maxima said kindly. "I am pleased that you have arrived at the precipice of the revelation."

Nephele craned her neck to glance upon Claudia. She blinked her eyes innocently like a peacock about to pounce. "And you brought the beloved Drusilla. Surely this is a sign from Hestia that my dreams held meaning."

"It is true dreams can on occasion be a gift from the gods," Claudia replied. "And yet it is also true a dream can be a wish or desire forever unspoken lest one suffers the consequences."

"Then it is just and proper that Nephele of the Aemilii asked the Vestal College to verify her dream," the Pontifex Maximum replied. "Who else should she turn to about matters of family and the hearth?

"What dream is this?" Claudia asked sweetly. "I would guide any daughter of Rome who seeks to protect the family hearth. The Soothsayers have told my brother the foreigners attacked me on these very sacred grounds to prevent the proper interpretation of a prophecy. Perhaps it is this very one our enemies would prevent."

"Do you believe yourself the Virgo Vestalis Maxima?" the Pontifex Maximus asked.

She had spoken around the truth, without directly contradicting it, and who here would risk gainsaying her absent proof? "No, Maximus. I am but a chosen vessel of Hestia. Attacked and violated within these walls under your protection. If I can strike back at those who tainted this sacred place, I beg of you to allow it."

The Pontifex coughed, clearly flustered. "Absent the objection of the materfamilias of the Aemilii, I fail to see why we cannot indulge you."

Nephele smiled. Her painted lips reminded Claudia of a viper. "Mannius Aemilius Perini, my eldest son has lost his wife in childbirth. Twin grand-daughters are now in my care, and require a mother as much as my grieving son needs a wife."

"I knew Perini, when I was as a girl before I joined the temple," Claudia replied. "My wishes and prayers are with him and your family. I have faith that the horde of young women clamoring to be his new wife shall number several score."

Nephele tilted her head sympathetically, as though to suggest she felt pity. Claudia could not grasp the meaning of her words. "The selection of a wife is but a triviality compared to what is truly at stake, Claudia. The future of a great family rests upon this decision. Perini's wife shall be marked to become the materfamilias when I have journeyed to the Elysian Fields."

"And your dream revealed the identity of the future materfamilias?" Claudia asked.

"Never have I been so surprised than to see the face of Livia Drusilla Claudius Appius in my dreams, tending to my grandchildren and the next generation," Nephele revealed.

"Me?" Drusilla muttered with shock.

It was a genius feint, Claudia observed. Nephele would sever the

Valeria's alliance with the Claudians in a single stroke and capture a valuable hostage. And who could dare be offended Nephele selected Drusilla to replace her? "A worthy offer, of which I am certain Drusilla is honored."

The shock of the revelation left Drusilla stunned. Claudia squeezed her arm to catch her attention. Drusilla recovered quickly. "Yes. I am quite honored the Aemilii would consider me worthy. My family is under other obligations."

"And such obligations would pale and fade if the gods had other wishes, yes?" the Pontifex Maximus stated.

Drusilla answered honestly, yet completely avoiding an answer. "I obey the will of my paterfamilias."

"Do you have an answer to my dream, Claudia?" Nephele asked.

To say that the dream was false was to accuse Nephele and the Aemilii as false. This would start a public feud and end any advantage that Livius hoped to gain from the marriage. To support the dream effectively killed the marriage arrangement with Marcus, and ended any such proposal of a branch family in the Senate.

The only way out was to propose a third option. "A matter such as this should be brought to the Soothsayers. The fate of one of the pillars of Rome should not be left to the winds of fortune."

"And yet it is the Vestal Virgins to which Nephele of the Aemilii have come seeking guidance." The Pontifex Maximus gestured towards the Vestal Virgins surrounding them. "Should this college be disbanded in favor of the Soothsayers? Should we surrender our divine purpose of protecting the hearth and the family of Rome?"

Claudia opened her mouth to speak, hoping against desperation the answer would become clear to her. It was then that one of her Vestal sisters pointed up into the sky. She glanced upward to see a mighty eagle, the very symbol of Rome, circling overhead. It swooped down towards the Atrium Vestae, screeching loudly.

"An eagle! I have not seen one grace the skies of Rome in a decade," the Pontifex Maximus proclaimed.

The eagle landed on top of the arc that led to Ariadne's Maze and gazed with great intensity at the Virgo Vestalis Maxima. Claudia whispered into Drusilla's ear. "Adalia must have reached Nicomedes."

The plump woman, garbed in the traditional Vestal Virgin robes, foamed at the mouth, spitting out black vile. Her eyes turned up white as she dropped to her knees. Her head flung back and forth, knocking her hair from the traditional sini crenes on her head, dropping strands of her brown hair across her face.

She spoke in a broken voice that seemed to come from Tartarus itself. "Hither shall come a new house forged from the branches of the old. Praise be to the Valeria Claudians. Let any that oppose such a union be outcast as an enemy of the Sacred Flame."

The trembling stopped and the Virgo Vestalis Maxima's eyes returned to normal. "Hestia spoke through me. Thank you, Claudia! Thank you!"

Nephele rose from the muck and two body-slaves brushed away the dirt. She nodded gracefully, accepting her defeat. "The gods have spoken."

"She will not forget this day lightly," Drusilla warned.

"Neither shall we, sister."

Chapter Six: The Senate and People of Rome

The optio of the Third Cohort, Seventh Legion pushed through the noon-time crowd upon the Aventine, and the centurion followed. Blackbirds and ravens dominated the skyline, flying from the docks along the Tiber River, up to the two peaks of the Aventine, and then down to the gully. Marcus kept one hand steady on the hilt of his gladius, ignoring the law that stated any soldier was a civilian once he crossed the Rubicon.

A flock of the black birds managed to defecate upon Milius midflight. "Tartarus take you birds!" He wiped the white muck from his shoulder and washed his hands in dirt. "I hate this place. Couldn't wait to leave here as a child."

"The Aventine has a long and honored history in Rome," Marcus protested. "Every patrician male with a worthy family name is taught the story of Romulus and Remus, and the destiny of Rome. Remus selected the Aventine to live on and proclaimed it was the best location to build the seat of the new city. Romulus chose the Palatine and claimed it would be the better option. The brothers decided to hold a contest of augury to claim the right to name this new city. Romulus selected his home upon the Palatine Hill, whereas Remus placed his augural tent on the Aventine. Remus only saw the blackbirds and failed in the eyes of the gods. Romulus naturally discovered thirteen birds that signified divine approval. The very name Aventine represents that host of inauspicious birds."

"It was vultures, not blackbirds, or so my mother told me at her teat." Milius scoffed. "It matters not, centurion. It is merely a story to justify the patricians living in the higher hills and the plebeians slaving away in the muck."

"Did you not say just moments ago that this hill is where your tribe settled?" Marcus asked.

Milius grimaced. "And I quickly left this hill, which the gods themselves forsake, to see the world. We're venturing into the less-noble sections of the hill. Keep your hands upon your purse and your eyes upon the crowd."

They passed under the old gate in the Servian Wall, which led to the Trigemina Way. The narrow streets turned and twisted like the interior of a hornet's nest, with every step an opportunity to be stung. How could people live so closely together? He had not seen such squalor in all of Gaul.

The Temple of Ceres towered over the ramshackle settlements and hovels where beggars, merchants, and dutiful slaves mingled. Sigils of foreign gods hung from shuttered windows.

Milius casually stepped over rotting refuse and shallow puddles. "The Clivus Publicius runs through the center of the Aventine, from the docks all the way back to the Circus Maximus. Anything a mortal man can conceive can be purchased here, if he has the will and the coin to pay for it."

The swarm of plebeians around them stank worse that the field of Mars after a bloodletting. "And this is where you would outfit the entire legion?"

"Where do you think all of the great families of Rome seek out that which is forbidden or hard to acquire?" Milius gestured to the ships upon the Tiber River slowly sailing into the ports and warehouses that lined the shore. "By hook or crook, the Collegium has their grimy paws on every port along the Aventine. Every ship that comes to Rome gives them a taste, to stay in their good graces. We'll find everything here: weapons, armor, supplies. And if we desire the answer to this grain mystery, then here is the logical place to begin to seek it."

They passed through the Temple of the Moon, built at a steep angle on a cliff leading to a plateau over the docks, where men crouched down near the steps throwing dice. They wore red cotton tunics and wool cloaks dyed green, fastened with bronze clasps in the shape of owls. Milius grinned widely and tapped the bridge of his nose.

They glanced at him and returned to their dice. These grim plebeians were of Roman stock, judging from their curly hair and the shape of their aquiline noses. *Strange that these men would not acknowledge a patrician in their presence,* Marcus thought. *Perhaps it is the custom in the Aventine to ignore others clearly on clandestine errands?*

The optio stopped just short of passing them and reached for the hilt of his gladius. "We are not the victims you imagined this day," Milius stated. "Move along and you may still live to engage in banditry elsewhere."

The gamblers quit any pretense of throwing dice and threw aside their cloaks, revealing swords and javelins. Their leader was a lean man with a hungry look in his eyes. "You've made a good deal of noise in

Rome, centurion. That's bound to attract the wrong sort of predator."

Marcus drew his own gladius and took a step down the stairs to support his optio's tactical position. This was no mere robbery, but a planned assassination from an enemy who knew they would be coming to the docks. If Milius had not caught the deception, they would have been surrounded.

The high ground typically was the best position to mount a defense, but that was on a hill or on top of a battlement designed to repel your enemies. Their position was precarious, as the stairs were parallel to the base of the cliff. This allowed these ruffians the opportunity to potentially attack from two sides. If they wanted to escape, Marcus would need to push towards the docks, where the crowd swelled and potential allies might be found.

The gods did not favor them in the odds on this day, Marcus thought. *Three to one against us.* And they were legion-trained from the manner in which they welded their weapons and took formation — former soldiers ready to murder to them. "Who are these bastards who are about to die horribly?"

Milius shrugged his shoulders. "I know only that they wear the clasp marking them as members of the Aventine Collegium, and yet failed to provide the counter-sign."

He looked behind them. The way up was clear, but there were men at the top of the cliff. If they climbed the stairs, they could be trapped without any place to retreat. "The top of the stairs are guarded," Marcus said quietly. "We shall have to make our stand here."

Their would-be assassins maneuvered into a three-man attack

position to the front and the side: standard legionnaire tactics, especially for those fighting along the coast of Africa. *Was this a Scipio tactic? Had the Cornelii set these men upon them?*

The front line attacked with their javelins. They were too close to throw effectively, but in a close-quarters fight, they extended the reach of the attack, especially when the targets were in such an awkward defensive position – the very tactics the Caledonians used to lay siege against Gaul.

Milius knocked aside the first thrust, deflecting it against the wall. Marcus grabbed the shaft of the javelin and yanked it free. They slowly allowed their assassins to push them backwards up the stairs, until gravity and distance forced their enemies to follow.

Marcus and Milius stood shoulder to shoulder, forcing their opponents to fight one or two at a time. Marcus harried them with the javelin over the shoulder of Milius, defending the ground with a ferocity and patience that surprised their attackers.

An errant jab from a man on the front line gave them the opening they were waiting for. Milius deflected the javelin once again, leaving the body vulnerable to an attack. A Roman line would have had shields preventing this sort of attack, but absent such protection, Marcus found vulnerability. He caught his target just shy of the neck, hitting above the collar bone. Blood splattered wildly, causing a panic in the enemy's line.

Wild-eyed and crazed, Milius laughed. Their enemies had landed several glancing blows, bloodying their arms and shoulders, but they drew the first real injury.

Marcus took advantage of the momentary lapse and stepped back up the stairs until he had a distinct height advantage. He pointed to their leader with the javelin. "Once we've killed all of you, I'll send your severed head to the Cornelii, after I've fed your eyes to the blackbirds."

The leader of the bandits opened his mouth to retort, but Marcus flung the javelin before he could reply. The tip of the spear caught him in the throat, slicing his jugular and sending him reeling down the stairs. He flopped upon the plateau like a gutted fish desperate for one last breath.

The battle had lasted too long to remain secret. A woman screamed from the market at the edge of the plateau. The crowd murmured, uncertain of what to do. The bandits claimed membership in the Collegium via the colors they wore, but such indiscretions were bad for business, and unlikely to earn the Collegium's protection.

"You lot are more fucked than Proserpina on the first day of winter. Didn't your man tell you who you were fighting? This is the centurion who killed a bear in Gaul with only his two hands." Milius cackled again. "And you think you'll be paid for botching this and causing a spectacle?"

Marcus pointed at them with the blade of his gladius, as though trying to decide whom to murder next. Killing the leader of a cohort sometimes toppled their fighting spirit. Roman legionnaires were trained to maintain rank, but if the bandits lacked another leader, Marcus might be able to bend their wills to his. "Do not bother, optio. I smell piss and blood. Keep one alive for the Soothsayers."

Their eyes widened at the mere mention of the Soothsayers. Marcus glanced over his shoulders; the men above them had already fled. He allowed the bandits to cautiously step backwards until they reached the plateau, leaving behind their dead leader and wounded comrade.

"Mercy!" he pleaded through bloody lips.

Milius relieved the assassin of his weapons and tied his hands with a leather strap from his belt. Marcus ignored the plea and stepped past them until he reached the dead body of the leader. He grabbed hold of the head by the scalp and held it rigid, as a cook might prepare a goose. Then, he raised his gladius and chopped several times at the neck. *It might be easy for Hercules to chop the head off a hydra,* Marcus thought, *but in practice, it required much more effort.*

He raised the severed head of his enemy before the crowd. "This is what happens to the enemies of Rome!"

Milius shrugged his shoulders and whispered to the captive. "He does seem to be in a forgiving mood."

Marcus climbed the stairs, careful to avoid slipping on the blood, carrying the severed head. He stopped short of the prisoner and then paused to consider his prize, as though he had clearly forgotten something. He took a single forefinger and jabbed it into the eye-sockets until he dug out the glazed eyeballs. He looked at them in the palm of his hands and then flung them to the blackbirds.

"What is your name, legionnaire?"

The wounded man stuttered. Blood caked his lips and teeth. "Gallus Licinius Nonus."

"A celebrated plebian family," Milius noted.

"Allied with the Cornelii." Marcus lowered the severed head to eye level with Gallus, leaving him to stare into the bloody holes. "What is his name?"

"Centurion?"

"What is this soldier's name?" Marcus demanded.

"I'd answer him while he retains his patience," Milius said with a grin.

Gallus swallowed. "Centurion Nepos Murena Macer of the Eighth Legion."

Milius flinched at the news, and Marcus immediately understood why. Every legion had a quartermaster who kept the history of the legion — where they fought, who lived, and who died bravely. These tales were shared by the campfires at night. The Eighth Legion had been the Seventh Legion's brother-in-arms since the end of the Punic Wars, when they salted the very ground where Carthage once blighted the earth so that nothing would ever grow there again.

He turned towards their prisoner. "Why would loyal soldiers of the Eighth attack me?"

"I know not, centurion." Gallus raised his hands as though to repel a beating. "Do you explain your orders to your legionnaires?"

Milius opened his mouth to comment, but then glanced aside towards Marcus and quickly shut it. He patted down the prisoner and relieved him of a pouch of coins. "The best thing you could do in this situation is to give the centurion a reason to allow you to live."

The prisoner coughed, blood caking his lips. "Upon my honor as a citizen of Rome, I swear if you spare my life, I shall do all that is possible to make amends."

The optio looked towards Marcus and nodded. Milius always leaned towards mercy, especially when it came to handsome young soldiers pleading for clemency. Marcus lifted the severed head of Nepos Murena Macer. "Swear upon the lives and health of your family to obey every order given until your fate has been measured and weighed, and I shall allow you to live."

"I swear!" Gallus cried. "I swear!"

"Know that should you fail to keep your oath, Optio Milius Hortensius Lex here is ordered to seek out every member of your family to collect their heads." Marcus lifted the head of Macer to his eye level and kissed it upon the cheek. "They will suffer the same fate. Do you know of my brother?"

Gallus stuttered an answer. "The Soothsayer apprentice?"

"My brother collects the heads of those that disappoint the Valeria. Their shades will be his to consume. They will be denied the afterlife," Marcus stated. He avoided looking at Milius. "Do you understand?

The prisoner nodded. "Yes, centurion. I swear it."

The crowd thickened at the edge of the plateau. A score of green cloaks swept through them and advanced. Marcus nodded towards Milius.

The optio left Gallus and ran forward to greet the advancing men with his arm stretched wide and his hands empty. "Hail unto the Aventine Collegium. Hear my words before rash deeds take place. My name is Milius Hortensius Lex. You know that name. The Hortensi have worked the docks for generations."

One of the cloaked men removed his hood. Marcus noted the leader of the Aventine Collegium had the same bearing as Milius, especially the nose and the chin. "Heard tell that he died three years ago, back in Gaul."

Milius laughed. "Tartarus is too afraid to accept me. Quint, is that you?" They embraced like brothers, or at least how Marcus imagined brothers should embrace. Nicomedes rarely liked to be touched. "This is my nephew, Quintus Hortensius Florus, a rising star amongst the Aventine Collegium."

"You've been gone too long, Uncle." Florus pointed to the golden caduceus pinned to his tunic. He was a handsome, younger version of Milius, without the weight of years or the battle scars. "I'm the new dominus, and while a family reunion is something I've long wanted, might you explain why your friend is holding the head of one of my men?"

"That is not your man, Florus." Milius gestured towards Marcus. "That is Centurion Marcus Valerius Perseus of the Seventh Legion, here on imperial order. The head said centurion is carrying is from a soldier who betrayed the Empire and likely wronged you and the Aventine Collegium."

"Should that prove to be true, the Collegium would be in your debt for punishing them," Florus said carefully. The mood of the crowd was difficult to read, but the cloaked men were on edge, uncertain if there would be a fight. "I would hear words on this subject, but removed from public view, lest business continue to be disrupted."

"That should prove wise on a number accounts," Milius replied. "The centurion and I traveled here to see you and yours for business of a nature both private and profitable."

Marcus sheathed his gladius. He often allowed Milius to negotiate on his behalf while he loomed in the background and studied their opponents. The Collegium soldiers could not help but stare at the severed head in his hand.

Florus gestured towards him. "Would the centurion object to covering up his trophy? I fear that business is slowing, and we cannot have women fainting in the streets."

He nodded towards Milius, and his optio answered. "I think such could be agreed. However, he is leery of leaving said head behind. Perhaps you could arrange for a sack of some sort?"

Mediation went quickly once one of the Collegium soldiers emptied a burlap sack of baked bread, passing it out to the remaining men. Once empty, he shook it free of crumbs and then offered it meekly to Marcus. Pleased, Marcus dropped the severed head into the sack and tied it to his belt.

Florus and his men escorted them down to the warehouse district on the outer edge of the docks, where sailors and workers moved cargo from ships. Marcus had occupied many villages and cities over the years, and there was a palpable sense of power that followed the man in charge. Women smiled more in the presence of Florus, and children stopped to wave at him. Clearly, the patricians and the Senate looked away from the Aventine for far too long.

They stopped at an old brick building marked with the sigil of brass caduceus and the sign of the god Mercurius. Florus signaled the guards, and they opened the gates, much in the fashion a centurion might use to identify himself before the battlements with a cohort.

Florus brought them to a set of comfortable couches near the hearth, where a serving boy brought them flagons of honeyed wine. "Cestus." A large Collegium soldier with a broken nose and crooked smile stepped forward. He was clearly named for the gladiators so savage they fought and murdered in the arena without weapons. "Take this prisoner to the cell and ensure that he is not comfortable."

"Know I shall want him whole when I call for him later," Marcus stated. Cestus looked to Florus to confirm the order, which he did dismissively. "If he returns bruised and bloody, I shall not ask the why of it."

Cestus cackled and pushed Gallus away from them. Several of the Collegium soldiers followed. Florus waved for Marcus and Milius to sit. "I would hear the story of why two imperial officers would deign to come to the Aventine without the benefit of uniform or escort."

"I promised the centurion the coin from the treasury to resupply the Seventh Legion would be better spent with the Aventine Collegium," Milius interjected. "Eliminate the bottom feeders and ensure a good deal for all is made."

"Then why were your fellow soldiers seeking to murder you?" Florus asked. "Surely, the competition for my wares has not yet reached that level of frenzy from my customers."

Marcus finished his wine and studied Florus. It might be possible for a nephew to betray an uncle. Such happened with common regularity. He judged himself a good reader of the complexities of the human face. "We have come to seek answers to a recent mystery presented to us by the imperator."

The mention of possible imperial involvement in his affairs quickly soured the friendly face Florus projected. "And this mystery concerns the Aventine Collegium?"

"The grain silos of Rome are dangerously low. Who better to shed light on this than the Aventine Collegium?" Marcus asked.

"This is important, nephew, upon the life of my mother and the family," Milius added. "There is a stink about Rome over this. Empires will fall. You want to be on the right side of this when it is over and earn the imperator's favor, I promise you."

"How is this a mystery?" Florus asked, confused. "The shipments have not been at full capacity for nearly a decade. The city grows with each passing day, and yet the shipments have not increased."

"We have been told that pirates seized recent shipments," Milius explained.

Florus scoffed. "There are no pirates in the Mediterranean. Caesar crushed them under his boot heels years ago. What pirates would dare to seize a cargo ship flying the flag of imperial Rome? I've received two hundred shipments this year alone, and not a one of them have been harassed at sea."

Marcus recalled the story Caesar told and nodded. "Yet there are some noble voices that say otherwise."

"A good number of them I imagine claim such to avoid taxes. Who could naysay such august company?" Florus asked.

"If the Senate believes that pirates are harassing the supply line, then shipments can disappear." Milius asked slyly. "And you keep records of all of this, yes?"

Florus laughed. "The Collegium keeps detailed records. I have three Greek slaves who keep the tallies. We have records spanning years in storage. Otherwise the patricians would rob us blind. Worse than street thieves, some of them are."

"How would that be possible, and yet the Senate of Rome not be made aware of it?" Marcus asked. "Can you prove this?"

"Why would the Senate of Rome be informed about the private affairs of common businessmen? Those who run a business keep the details quiet, lest competitors take advantage," Florus explained. "Were you not family, we'd not be having this conversation. The patricians and businessmen pay their taxes and business runs through their senator or the tribuni plebis."

"Would you be willing to open these records to us?" Milius asked.

"To open the records of the Collegium is to reveal the sacred business of all who trade with us. Should such become revealed to the public, our reputation would be forever ruined," Florus revealed.

"I can assure you of the imperator's favor in this matter should the information prove useful," Marcus promised.

"Power is fleeting, especially here in Rome. Even mighty Caesar may fall in time," Florus replied. "Milius might want a place outside of the muck, but this is my home."

Milius shook his head. "You want something, nephew. I know that look. Out with it!"

Florus grimaced. "My daughter Florentina came down with the fever over winter. It nearly killed her. She survived at the cost of her sight. They say the Soothsayers have strong healing magic to cure such afflictions, but they refused to see us. Swear your brother will leverage this magic on our behalf, and I shall have my accountants retrieve the tablets from storage immediately."

"I know not the limit of the magic wielded by my brother, Nicomedes. Should it be within his power to cure your daughter, I swear if you aid our cause, I will move Olympus itself to make this happen," Marcus promised.

"That is an oath to secure a foundation," Milius added.

Florus extended his hand. Marcus took it, pulled him close to his chest, and they exchanged kisses upon the cheek. "Let it be written before the gods."

Marcus remembered what his brother had told him – how important this mission was to the Soothsayers. "Nicomedes will undoubtedly need to see these shipments of grain himself. Can you make this happen?"

"If he can manage to remain discreet, then all things are possible," Florus answered.

He imagined studying dusty wax tablets with numbers and shipment information, and hoped that instead there would be another assassination attempt. "Milius will examine your records alone to ensure that your secrets not related to this mystery will be secure. And during that time, he can negotiate a fair price for the delivery of the supplies needed by the Seventh Legion. Some inflation will be allowed, so long as the supplies are of good quality."

"That might take the whole of the remainder of the day and night, sir," Milius reported.

Florus poured another cup of wine. "The Aventine Collegium would be honored to host you, centurion." He noted the blood caked on his face and the evidence of the day's battle stained on his tunic. "We have a bath house that is quite pleasant, if not quite up to the standards of the Forum."

"I have other business that must be completed this day, though I'd appreciate the use of one of your cloaks as a disguise and the loan of some of your soldiers. Cestus would do quite nicely," Marcus revealed.

"This can be done, but for what purpose?" Florus asked.

"I must propose marriage this night."

* * * *

Marcus crossed the Cyprian Street and turned towards the Orbian Hill, in the direction of the Esquiline Hill, where stood the Domūs de Claudia. He passed near the statue of murdered King Servius Tullius, where his mutilated body had been ground into the street from the chariot driven by his own mad daughter.

He stopped at the great door of the Claudian villa, studying Neptune's Trident carved into the wood. It was an impressive sight, but it could not hold long against a siege like the great door of the Domūs de Valeria. The privilege of the Valeria still meant something in this day of the Empire, and only they were trusted with the ability to fight off soldiers of Rome.

The centurion knocked three times upon the door. One of the Claudian house guards answered the knock. "No beggars this day."

Marcus withdrew the cloak revealing his face, including the blood streaking his face. "I am no beggar. Before you stands Marcus Valerius Perseus, and I would speak to the dominus of this house."

"I will see if Senator Livius is available," the guard answered politely. "Would you care to wait in the Atrium?"

"It would please me to have wine to sate my thirst," Marcus stated.

The Domūs de Claudia was thrice the size of his own ancestral home. The Claudians came from the Clodia, a Sabine tribe the men of Rome conquered. He supposed it was possible Valeria blood, thinned as it might be, ran through their veins.

He was escorted through the great door to a grand atrium with a concrete fountain in the center, half a dozen peach trees, and statues honoring heroes of the Republic. The sheer audacity of the wealth overwhelmed the senses.

Marcus Livius Drusus Claudianus awaited him, resting in a chair under a peach tree. "Centurion, you honor our home with your visit." He smiled softly, noting the blood. "Though, I would expect that you would have washed yourself first."

"I come to you anointed in the blood of our enemies." Marcus lifted the wet, dripping burlap sack containing the severed head of Nepos Murena Macer. "Along with a gift."

Livius signaled for wine. "A tale I'd be quite interested in hearing."

He told the senator everything they learned in the Aventine and opened the burlap sack to offer proof. Livius waved away the evidence. "I trust in your word, centurion."

"The lack of surprise upon your face is concerning," Marcus admitted.

"That the Aemilii and the Cornelii are allies and conspiring to achieve power?" Livius asked. "This I've known for years. They are not as subtle as they believe. I admit I am impressed you learned so much in a short amount of time. I would not have considered meeting directly with the Collegium."

"An accident of fate, senator."

"Nonsense. You found a way to gain an advantage," Livus argued. "Nothing wrong with that. Fortune grants opportunity so rarely that it must be seized when offered."

"That is why I have come, senator." Marcus downed his cup of wine and continued. "I have come to seek your approval to marry Drusilla."

Livius regarded him a moment. "Why would you come now?"

"The political and social interests of our two families are aligned in the present and likely will be in the future," Marcus said.

"It is true such a marriage would present certain opportunities," Livius admitted. "However, I am disinclined to put Drusilla in danger again for such a purpose. Her elder sister's husband engaged in politics quite poorly, and I lost the both of them."

Such was a dry understatement. Senator Tiberius Claudius Nero had barely married Drusilla the Elder before joining Brutus and the Senator Liberators in their failed assassination attempt upon Caesar. It had taken years for the Claudians to regain their political power. "I am told that she was quite beautiful."

"Sweet Drusilla is quite taken with you," Livus admitted. "She is typically quite stoic on such matters, but you have enflamed her blood."

Marcus blinked, uncertain how to respond. "I am honored she would find me appealing."

"She was a sickly child. Brilliant. The Soothsayers wanted her," Livius revealed. "They would have made an exception to their edict in order to claim her. They sent one of their magisters to cure her foot and affliction, but I could not bear to part with her."

Marcus only remembered the girl who followed him around as boy. He tolerated it at the time out of respect for his father's friend and the protection of his patronage. He did remember quiet conversations between Nicomedes and Drusilla, and now he began to wonder what topics they spoke of. "I did not know this."

Livus sighed. "She is a treasure I would not lightly part with. Yet I know she has a powerful will and shall make this happen with or without my blessing. Divorce is all too common in the Empire. I would not see her discarded once the political necessity is over."

"She will be the materfamilias of my branch and of my heart. Family and honor is all to the Valeria," Marcus stated. He had to admit even he was surprised by the sentiment swelling in his chest. "Should the vote favor my intention in the Senate?"

"Have you not heard, centurion?" Livus asked. "The Virgo Vestalis Maxima issued a prophecy about the merging of two families."

Marcus resisted smiling. He imagined Claudia and Nicomedes had something to do with this latest revelation. "I am pleased to hear this."

"The villa has been filled with whispers of the final words. 'The Valeria Claudians shall rise.'"

He had not considered changing his agnomen. Marcus had long identified with the Greek hero Perseus, but it would be expected that he would honor his new father and family. "I would be honored to carry your name."

"I was adopted also," Livus admitted. "But it has served the family well."

"Then you will give your blessing to the marriage?" Marcus asked, hopefully.

"Drusilla shall not give me a choice in the matter. She is quite willful, as you will discover." Livus toasted Marcus and then continued. "I believe this union shall strengthen both families against the enemies of the Empire. With the Virgo Vestalis Maxima and the Soothsayers supporting the branching of your house, overruling the paterfamilias, I believe the Senate shall have no choice to but to quietly approve."

Marcus returned the toast. "If only we survive the expedition to Egypt, then all shall be well."

"What can be done to secure this?" Livus asked. "Speak plainly."

"Clearly, there are forces arrayed against our cause. I would have my cohort with me to protect my back. Can you arrange that?" Marcus asked.

"Such would leave the Seventh Legion undermanned in the war against the Caledonians," Livus observed.

"I have considered this. There is an answer, though it twists my stomach," Marcus admitted.

"Ambition must be your only master if you wish to survive," Livus stated.

"My cousin Decimus has trained with the Thirteenth Legion," Marcus replied. "He could lead a cohort back with the supplies and hold the line until after the mission."

"And your rival could gain the glory you earned," Livus added.

Marcus nodded dejectedly. "The needs of the legion should come before personal advancement. If the Caledonians secure that beachhead, then we could lose Gaul and the Rhinelands."

"I will see if it can be done."

"Thank you, senator." Marcus swallowed more wine. "I know I am not at my best appearance, but I would speak to Drusilla."

"You are at the wrong house for that, centurion," Livus revealed. "Drusilla left to console Claudia for the evening."

Chapter Seven: The Materfamilias

A gentle breeze rustled the leaves of the oak trees in the sacred grove of the Atrium Vestae. Livia Drusilla Claudius Appius politely accepted the congratulations of the patrician women of Rome who would have barely given her a second glance mere days before. Such was her fate in the days when she was simply known as Livia Drusilla Minor.

Drusilla Major could command the attention of a crowd. With but a glance and a word, her sister could twist its desires to match her own. She had not been kind to those who could not match her wit. The death of her elder sister brought about Drusilla's apotheosis into patrician society as her own person, and unfortunately she drew the consequences for the actions taken by her namesake.

Marcus had a gift to lead men into blood and battle, but she was more like her father. She felt lost in the mob. Drusilla shined in private, where she could grow to the level of a titan.

Drusilla turned her head to gaze upon the marble statue of Numa Pompilius, just before the opened vaulted hall of the Vestal Virgins.

Nephele greeted her with the traditional kiss upon the cheek. "It would seem the very gods themselves thwart my intentions to have you as a daughter, dearest Dru. I trust in Hestia's hand to guide you to make the proper choices for your new branch family."

Messalina of the Cornelii followed, blinking like a lost peacock, surprised by the adulation that she had long considered her due. Drusilla supposed the need for secrecy about the alliance between the

Cornelii and the Aemilia was past, and they were once again permitted to act the best of friends. "Perhaps this is really an opportunity given to us by the gods to pull our families together for the benefit of Rome, with all of the lesser families under our guidance."

She glanced aside at Claudia, wishing she stood next to her in the face of their enemies. The sister of her soon-to-be husband whispered fervently into the recovering ear of the Virgo Vestalis Maxima and then flashed a serpent's smile, sweet as a sugar cake. Drusilla hoped that whatever Nicomedes did to the matron of the Vestal, she would only suffer the uncomfortable effects temporarily. Somehow, it felt gauche to punish her with such pain over petty politics.

Nephele gently placed her arm on Drusilla's shoulder and said in a sickly sweet voice. "Perhaps you will do us both the honor of visiting us once your family is situated. We would love to host a party for you."

Messalina nodded intently. "I have always wanted to be your dearest friend, Drusilla."

"And perhaps the gods have not completely thwarted my intentions," Nephele added quietly. "You might not have married my son, but you could still be as my daughter. It is sad both your mother and your sweet sister have ventured to the Elysium Fields. Perhaps you could look to us as your kindly aunts who love and adore you."

Her father once told her something she understood in her bones: never confirm your disdain of an enemy. "You both honor me above reason."

Nephele laughed loudly, stronger than any woman she had ever heard. "I shall take that as an acceptance. Once you have settled into your new life, of course. I can only imagine it will be lonely for you while Marcus Valerius is away in Egypt."

"Egypt?" Drusilla asked.

"You knew that, of course," Nephele stated. "We are the materfamilias, and our higher duty is to ensure the hearth fires remain and the family grows stronger."

"Family is our life," Claudia spoke. Somehow she left the Virgo Vestalis Maxima and inserted herself into the conversation without any of them taking notice. Drusilla envied how Claudia seemed born to this world. "Drusilla, we should really return home to greet Marcus, so that we might share the joy."

Messalina kissed Claudia upon the cheek. "Take with you our love."

"And pray, do not forget to share our congratulations with your mother," Nephele added.

Claudia's eyes shifted slightly, but her demeanor remained the same. Drusilla knew that somehow Nephele had landed a blow, and her soon-to-be sister seethed. *Why would the mention of Septima cause such anger?* She resolved to discover the root of this divide within her new family.

Word had spread beyond the Atrium Vestae of the new prophecy, the first from the Vestal Virgins in two decades. The Praetorian Guard formed a skirmish line to block the plebeians from entering the temple. The cadre of soldiers, made up from the Claudian freedmen and the Third Cohort of the Seventh Legion, surrounded the Valeria lectica.

The mob murmured the moment Claudia gracefully appeared

under the columned porch of the Atrium Vestae. Drusilla followed, amazed at the intensity of their gaze, wishing that she could hide in the great marble statue of Numa Pompilius.

She followed Claudia to the lectica and joined her upon it. The cadre of bodyguards lifted them into the air and left the Forum, heading down the winding streets of Rome towards the Palatine.

Claudia stared listlessly into the faces of the crowd. "We revealed too much of our intentions to our enemies, and now they wish to invite us into their homes."

Drusilla turned onto her side and shielded her eyes from the setting sun. "There was little choice in the matter, and perhaps we might turn this to our advantage by learning their intentions in return."

"Are you certain that you wish to join your future to ours?" Claudia asked. "The Valeria have stumbled in the dark for so long, I do not know that we would recognize the light."

* * * *

Drusilla studied the sigil of Janus upon the great door of the Domūs de Valeria. The Claudians were always associated with the sea and the bounties that came from it. The Valeria were an ancient family, even by the standards of Rome. Their blood walked with gods and kings. They were one of the last pure-blooded Roman families, and after the marriage, she would be its materfamilias.

The great door opened outward to the street, and the remainder of the Seventh Legion ran out to guard their flanks. Adalia stood among them, towering over them like an amazon goddess, her golden hair braided in the fashion of northern women. At that moment, Drusilla understood why Marcus was so taken with her.

Claudia slipped off the lectica and greeted the freedmen of her house and Adalia. She exchanged a glance with Adalia and turned towards those who had ferried them across Rome. "The Valeria thank you for keeping us safe on our journey home."

Drusilla remembered Claudia as a young girl, slightly younger than her, but adroit in maneuvering the social waters of patrician society. The woman before her, dressed in the ceremonial stola of the Vestal Virgins, commanded the attention of the men. The weight of her words inspired them, and once she was finished speaking, their chests were out and their steps just a little quicker.

Adalia greeted Claudia warmly. "Word has spread onto the streets of Rome that the Vestals have blessed this union for the good of the Eternal City."

Claudia motioned for Drusilla to join them. "It would seem you made very good time on your journey to see Nicomedes."

Drusilla slid out of the lectica, adjusted her stola, and stood inside the walls of the Valeria villa. "The display was truly terrifying. Few shall cast aspersions upon this prophecy."

She remembered Nicomedes as a quiet boy frequently ignored by his peers. Often they read together while the other boys engaged in the type play amongst the patrician children. His mind was keen, sharp as a knife that could cut through any nonsense, but the idea that he wielded such power was truly frightening. If an apprentice could achieve this, then what was the limit of the Soothsayers?

"Apologies for the interruption." The optio of the Claudian freedman approached her. "Do you wish us to stand guard, domina?"

She glanced over to Claudia, who seemed to consider the matter for a moment and then nodded. "It would seem our aid would be welcomed in this time of turmoil."

"You must stay with us this night," Claudia insisted as she embraced Drusilla. "We shall share stories like sisters."

The Claudian freedmen took positions alongside the Valeria, protecting the Domūs as the great door closed. Once the walls were secured, Adalia beckoned the other women to move closer and whispered, "Nicomedes bid me to tell you the skulls of our enemies have been properly prepared, and this very evening we shall have the answers we seek. Darius has opened his cottage for this purpose, where Nicomedes is meditating."

"Where is Marcus?" Claudia asked, clearly worried. "He should have returned by now."

"Be calm and listen to the entirety of my words before reacting," Adalia admonished. "Marcus and Milius just survived an assassination attempt in the Aventine. They are both safe and well. Marcus is now with Senator Livius."

Drusilla felt her heart palpitate. "Was my father attacked as well? Were either injured?"

Adalia shook her head. "Details are somewhat sparse. Nicomedes only thought to scry upon Marcus after he completed his incantation for the Atrium Vestae prophecy. Marcus and his optio survived some sort of assassination attempt. Then after securing aid from the Aventine Collegium, they ventured to the Domūs de Claudia where his sight could not follow."

She forced herself to breathe, trying to take control of her nerves. If Marcus reached Esquiline Hill from the Aventine by foot, then surely he must not have suffered too grave a wound. "If he found sanctuary with the Claudians, then he is safe."

Adalia nodded. "The thought is he shall try to return this night to allow darkness to cover his movements."

Drusilla sniffed, wiping away tears that she hadn't even realized that she had shed. "Apologies. This has been a day of much unexpected excitement."

"You bore the gaze of two gorgons of Rome this day," Claudia said, with mirth and admiration. "Never feel shame for what you feel, only how you control it."

Drusilla embraced Claudia once again. It felt proper to have a sister with whom she could share such a burden.

"I hesitate to interrupt such bonding, but there is a further problem that must be addressed, lest we have division in the house," Adalia revealed. She gestured to the soldiers defending the walls, consisting of the normal Valeria freedman regiment, the Third Cohort, and the cadre of Claudian freedmen. "I spoke with Hermana to make provisions for the evening and to ensure the men were properly clothed and fed, but Decimus countered said order before he was summoned to the quaestor."

This visibly concerned Claudia greatly and Drucilla understood why. Decimus served his tenure in the Thirteenth legion, the traditional short term of office for a young man seeking to earn his name within his year. Marcus sought higher honors, and thus had to serve twice the length to gain the same consideration. "Do you know why they summoned him?"

Adalia shook her head. "The guard told me the messenger carried with him the seal of the Senate."

Was this part of a plan to derail the mission to Egypt? "There is little to do about it now," Claudia admitted. "However, I am the domina of the house and will make proper arrangements for our guests. Would you care to rest in the atrium? I can have Hermana bring out refreshments."

Drusilla realized that she had not eaten this day, and her stomach rebelled against her will with a growl. "Food would be received with great gratitude."

"It shall be done," Claudia said as she left for the house.

Adalia gestured to the very wooden bench situated under the olive tree where they had first met just a few hours ago. She wondered if this was a symbolic gesture, or if it was simply the most convenient place to discuss the future away from the prying ears of the soldiers. "If it pleases you, I would keep you company in comfort."

Drusilla blinked. "I admit to being surprised by the offer."

"Did you not wish that we would be brilliant friends?" Adalia asked. "Your offer of friendship touched my heart. Not since Marcus saved the life of my brother have I seen a Roman reveal herself as a friend in such a manner. It is an offer I would see returned in kind."

Drusilla could not help but glance up into Adalia's pale eyes and feel shame. Was she not the victor in her machinations to marry Marcus? Should she not remain magnanimous? Drusilla followed Adalia to the wooden bench, which rested in the shade of a vast olive tree, and awkwardly sat next to her. "Apologies. I have been surrounded by conspiracies and assassinations such that I forgot what friendship felt like."

Adalia laughed. It felt unnatural for a woman to laugh so fully and loudly, and Drusilla pondered why. "I was once an imagined rival, and thus it is natural to feel such. Our hopes and futures are bound together, and I would assist you if you will allow it."

Curiosity got the better of her discretion. "How?"

"I did not idly boast when I said that I could teach you to bend Marcus to your will." Hermana brought them a platter of dates and pomegranates. Adalia snatched one of the dates and took a healthy bite out of it. "You came to age without sisters or mother. The closest friend you can claim is a priestess who knows nothing of men or natural relations."

"I had a sister," Drusilla protested. She wanted to say something kind, but found herself lacking the words. Drusilla Major had been as cruel and capricious as the sea. Her mother had been much the same way, although as her father tried to deny it in later years. "But she died while I still played as a child."

"You are wise to the world, and yet never comfortable in your skin," Adalia said without judgment. "My brother Armin was much the same way after our father died. He became a man in a house of women and learned much from our extended family. Such reliance on kin is considered a weakness in Rome, I've come to understand."

Drusilla found it difficult to argue with the statement. "Please understand I had a great affliction as a child that marked me as a follower of Vulcan." The amazon's face furrowed, as though she was attempting to understand the context. Drusilla lifted the hem of her stola, revealing the slight discoloration of her right ankle. "A fever struck me a baby, and when it came time to learn to walk, I had difficulty because my foot swelled unnaturally. It was gross in size and color."

Adalia reached down to touch the ankle, but paused. "May I touch it?" Drusilla blinked at the kindness of the question and nodded. The amazon probed gently at the tender muscles, feeling the newfound strength in the limb. "Such has happened to the very young in our village – a malady that cannot be cured. How is that you walk as well as anyone else?"

"My father called upon the services of the Soothsayers," Drusilla explained. "They claimed such a thing could not be cured until I had matured into adulthood."

"It must have been difficult."

Drusilla swallowed, trying to choke back tears. "Venus is revered in Rome. Her beauty is a symbol of her grace. Patricians forced their children to remain in my presence to please my father. Some called me Vulcana when they believed I could not hear. I had but one friend."

"And this is why you adore Marcus? He was your friend. A tale as sweet as honey." Adalia said with a smile.

"Only indirectly," Drusilla admitted, smiling at the memory. "Marcus treated me with kindness and ignored my affliction, but he had fire in his blood. He could not contain such energy. The boy ran everywhere, fighting imaginary monsters with such passion."

"Claudia then?"

"You would think that we would naturally bond, but she adored Marcus nearly as much as I. She followed him everywhere, seeking to join in his adventure," Drusilla explained. "Marcus ensured that every patrician girl in Rome wanted her at their parties and games."

"Then who showed such kindness?"

"It was Nicomedes who served as my first friend." Adalia tilted her head, as though Drusilla had told her that the world had inverted. "Many would be surprised by such a statement. Nicomedes was a quiet boy, content with the protection of his brother's shadow. He learned to read without being taught, and by the age of nine, there was little his tutors could teach him. He read Horace to me under this very tree."

Adalia glanced about the atrium, as though to verify that none of the soldiers listened to their words. "And he was your friend?"

Her words seemed entirely too weighted with interest beyond mere camaraderie. "You seem curious regarding my friendship with Nicomedes. Why?" Drusilla asked.

"Nicomedes seems like a man who needs few others," Adalia admitted. "His very voice once set my teeth to edge. However, I am forced to admit I find his countenance appealing. Marcus told me that he has no desires of the flesh. If you are his friend, then perhaps you know more of him than his elder brother."

Was it possible that Adalia preferred Nicomedes to Marcus? "He visited me often as a child. I always imagined the unfettered access to father's library first attracted him, but later our discussion of great philosophers and the words we read bonded us as friends."

"Marcus believes his ambition for knowledge is his only desire now. He implied Nicomedes has taken a patron as a lover to further said cause," Adalia revealed. "He would not share the identity of this person."

"Such would be a revelation to my world, if it was indeed true," Drusilla admitted. "Who can say? We have not spoken intimately in years, not since he joined the Soothsayer Academy."

"I suspected as much," Adalia said, with an air of disappointment. "Your battle for Marcus shall be much easier. You have won already before the engagement."

"How can that be true?" Drusilla asked. "Marcus has tasted the world and all that it has to offer. Why would he be satisfied with me when he has known you?"

Adalia raised a finger as though she were a Greek tutors and smiled. "Once he is yours, place one hand upon his neck and then the other upon his cock. Then you simply have to speak a command to win his heart. He is a leader amongst men and requires permission to worship that which he desires."

"Surely, it is not that simple?"

"Romans are taught all things of the flesh are possible, so long as they can control their urges," Adalia explained. "Men may do as they wish to others, as long as they are not the passive partners. That which is denied becomes much more desirable in private."

Drusilla shook her head. "I shall ever only be Vulcana to him."

Adalia slid off the bench and knelt before her. The amazon lifted her stola until her knees were revealed. She placed her hands on Drusilla's calves and smiled. "Look at yourself. Yes, there are imperfections. Every man or woman, save perhaps Nicomedes, has them. Desire is commanded by intent and will."

"Such is beyond the content of my nature," Drusilla protested. "I love him for who and what he is."

"Then you shall have to seduce him as an old man would a young girl by surrendering your power." Adalia ran the tips of her fingers along Drusilla's leg, grazing the thighs and landing at the knees. "You desire him. You crave his touch. You wish for him to conquer you. Such is a foreign concept for his nature to believe. Show him that you worship his flesh and spirit, and he will be touched."

"And will I not simply be another whore to be possessed?" Drusilla asked, bitterly.

"Marcus has possessed whores from around the world. He has known more women and men than can easily be counted," Adalia conceded. "And such leaves the soul bored for that which can excite the mind. He has been taught to worship the sacred hearth. If you prove yourself devoted to him and willing to worship all that he is, then he shall be moved."

"And you did this?" Drusilla asked.

Adalia laughed. "No. I put my hand upon his neck and commanded his worship, but you are a sly woman with advantages that

I did not have."

"What possible advantages do I possess?"

"You can be wife and mother, and if you will it, lover and fellow adventurer," Adalia explained. "He expects a wife shall be passive. Take what you desire and you will forever own it."

The great door of the Domūs de Valeria opened. The soldiers quickly took their positions and greeted the entrance of Marcus Valerius Perseus with an excited salute. His tunic was marked with torn spots and blood spatters, but the centurion seemed in fine spirits. He ripped off a green cloak and handed it to one of the guards.

Adalia smoothed out the stola and stood. Drusilla blushed and followed her example. Marcus noted the two of them together and tilted his head, as though presented with an intriguing puzzle. "I was unaware the two of you were acquainted."

"We are brilliant friends," Adalia declared. Drusilla realized Adalia had slipped her arm around her shoulders, as though they were sisters. "The real question is, did you horribly murder those who attacked you?"

"You are injured?" Drusilla added.

Marcus grinned and then tapped the burlap sack tied at his belt. "I have vented my wrath, and the insult added to the injury is not yet complete, if Nicomedes can do as he has boasted." Drusilla noted that the bottom of the burlap was stained with a red pulp. "And to answer your question, Dru, I was not harmed, save for the stain upon my clothing."

"We must see to cleansing you immediately," Drusilla insisted.

"I would speak with Nicomedes. Perhaps there is something from this he can leverage against our enemies," Marcus explained. "He explained a concept called 'sympathetic magic,' where like is attracted to like. I would follow those who escaped and end their lives."

Adalia gestured towards the back of the villa, where the cottage of Darius waited them. "Nicomedes arrived a few hours ago with all that he requires for the ritual."

"You were being literal about the skulls, then?" Drusilla asked.

"If such gore is beneath you, Dru, I would understand if you wish to retire to Claudia's rooms," Marcus offered, not unkindly.

"A woman of Rome does not shy away from blood when it is necessary," Drusilla stated, much cooler than she felt. "It simply strains credulity that such magic is possible in this world."

Marcus nodded sympathetically. "I was once a follower of Zeno of Citium. I believed in a universe that could be understood rationally, with effort."

"What happened to such a noble philosophy?" Drusilla asked, curious.

"I heard the voice of my younger brother come from the lips of an eagle," Marcus said, somewhat dejected. "And since that night, I have been forced to keep my philosophy more open to possibilities, lest I am attacked unawares."

"I would see such magic for myself," Drusilla said.

Adalia nodded empathetically. "Drusilla is in the same soup as the rest of us. If it gets any hotter, we'll all burn."

*   *   *   *

The cottage was quite spartan, but spacious enough to seat all of them. A large oak table was moved to the center of the central chamber. Five clay pots, inscribed with Egyptian hieroglyphics, were arranged within a circle of drawn purified salt — such a resource was comparable to a week's salary for a freedman. Beeswax candles flickered with a sickly green tint. A cracked stone mortar contained a mashed mess of grime and some sort of ground powder.

This was some sort of death ritual. Such clay pots — known as death urns — were decorated with foreign sigils and quite popular amongst the wealthy patrician families. Some patricians held public orgies, donning the masks of Egyptian gods and using these sacred artifacts as pitchers for honeyed wine. Drusilla found such behavior crass.

Nicomedes ignored their entrance to the cottage and continued to grind the material within the mortar until it was fine as sand. Her childhood friend had grown taller than expected. His chubby cheeks had thinned to handsome proportions, but he retained his boyish lips and wide eyes. She had heard stories of long savage-like hair, but now it was fashionably short.

A boy with red hair fumbled around the table as Nicomedes barked orders. He shyly looked up at Drusilla and smiled until Nicomedes rebuked him.

Not wishing to cause the apprentice more trouble, Drusilla turned her attention towards the host. Darius Valerius Egnatius was a bastard born of a Gaul woman, but raised Roman. Vitus Valerius Aetius, the paterfamilias, had two older sons and insisted that Darius, so named for the founder of the Valeria, be treated as one with full Roman blood.

Drusilla noted that Marcus stared at the household gods of the Valeria prominently displayed on the wall. These gods would soon be her gods, when she bore children for Marcus and the family. He spoke to her with kind politeness, but not as one who would be her husband. She resolved to do her best with the advice Adalia freely offered.

Adalia and Claudia joined them quickly. Darius offered refreshments and ensured all of the patricians had a seat, if they so wanted, before sitting himself. Nicomedes pointed at the clay pot at the edge of the circle. "Rubio! Bring me the skull."

The boy gingerly opened the lip of the clay pot and reluctantly reached into it, lifting out a skull that gleamed from a translucent fatty substance rubbed over it. He offered it to Nicomedes.

Nicomedes placed the skull in the palm of his left hand and held it over the circle of salt. Drusilla learned as close as she dared to examine the bone. The pure whiteness of it suggested it was cleansed rather recently. If this skull belonged to one of the assassins who attacked Claudia, then how did the Soothsayers remove the flesh so quickly while preserving the quality of skull?

Nicodemus pinched a small amount of the powder in the mortar and dropped it into the flame of the candle, sparking a burst of energy and power that crackled throughout the cottage. Drusilla flinched, and to her surprise, found Marcus and Adalia had each grabbed hold of one of her hands. The contact made her sweat, but neither seemed to object.

"The Egyptians are amongst the world's greatest necromancers. They believe the logos, the soul of a man, can be divided into five separate and distinct parts," Nicomedes explained. His voice was filled with wonder and awe, even while controlling the very elements of the universe. "I had dermestid beetles consume their flesh. Their eyes, their tongue, their brains. That essence is still within thier ground bodies. It will call back part of their souls into a gestalt being I shall compel to answer my questions."

"You are creating a spirit whole from the parts of their soul you can steal?" Drusilla asked.

"Indeed, the sum of their knowledge and experience is contained within these crushed beetle remains," Nicomedes explained.

"Will it place us in danger?" Claudia asked.

It was a fair question, but one Drusilla did not wish to ask in front of Marcus. Nicomedes laughed. "There is always danger when magic is involved. But know this, this spirit shall be mine. Three questions may be asked before I must send it back to the underworld."

He sprinkled more of the ground beetle into the flame and began to chant. "My mouth has been given to me that I may speak with it in the presence of the Great God. My mouth is opened, my mouth is split open by Shu with that iron harpoon of his, with which he split open the mouths of the gods."

The flames crackled and danced, turning into vaguely humanoid shapes, begging and pleading. The skull vibrated within his hand and opened its horrific mouth to shriek. A spectral image of five different faces flashed — all caught in a death scream

Nicomedes stared into its empty eye sockets and continued. "Get back you crocodile of the West, who lives on the Unwearying Stars!" He swallowed a pinch of the ground beetle. "Detestation of you is in my belly, for I have absorbed the power of Osiris, and I am Seth. Get back, you crocodile of the West! The nau-snake is in my belly, and I have not given myself to you, your flame will not be on me."

The skull screamed once again. This time Drusilla noted that Marcus flinched. He smelled of blood and sweat, yet she found being so close to his presence strangely compelling. She squeezed his hand this time.

Nicomedes raised the skull, as though he were about to cast it upon the floor, shattering it into dust. "Speak and be heard, lest I weigh down your hearts with the sin of murder against my flesh. Speak now, and you may yet discover mercy within my heart. Know this! To lie to me now is to blacken your heart before your gods, and you shall be cast out. Answer as completely as you are able to, and I shall not cast you out into the darkness. Please me."

The voice from the skull sounded akin to the wind on a blustery night. The language was strange and foreign to their ears, but Nicomedes waved his hand over the skull. Suddenly they heard words they intuitively understood. "We hear and obey, sorcerer. Ask that which you want would know, and we shall answer."

"What language was that, Nico?" Claudia asked.

"One I have not yet heard," Nicomedes admitted curtly. "What questions shall we ask then?"

"The first question seems simple enough. Who sent them to kill Claudia?" Marcus answered.

"You do not wish to know their names?" Drusilla asked.

"Soldiers have no true names, save for their loyalty to their dominus," Marcus said. "It is why the legionnaires always chant 'the Senate and the People of Rome' before a battle. If we truly wish revenge, then the names of their dominus is what we need."

Nicomedes nodded and then presented the question to the skull. The wails of the dead echoed around them. "The King of Kings. He That Placed His Boot Upon the Eagle. Orodes, second of his name."

"The Parthian Empire!" Marcus stood in the excitement, dropping Drusilla's hand. "Then the beast you killed is connected to the assault upon our family. Cicero was correct!"

"Why would they want me dead?" Claudia asked.

"This king is the only force in the world that has resisted Rome in many generations. Perhaps their Soothsayers found a danger presented by your life or that of your daughter that they could not countenance," Nicomedes answered.

"Imagine the world if they managed to slay a Vestal Virgin. Rome would have exploded with unrest and anger at those who failed to protect what was theirs," Drusilla observed. "Perhaps this is not a personal assault at all, and Claudia was simply collateral damage."

"Two questions remain. We might ask the motive behind the assault," Darius suggested. "Knowing that which might move our enemies allows us to predict their movements."

"We know this enemy is connected to what happened to Claudia and your imperator," Adalia stated. "What if they are connected to that which besets the Rhine? Would it not be worthy of asking?"

"We have a means to verify the theory without wasting a question from this spirit," Nicomedes revealed.

"How? Why was this not done?" Adalia demanded.

Nicomedes tilted his head towards Adalia. "Duties have prevented me from asking for your foreign coin for the appropriate research. I hoped to acquire it this very night. The Parthian Empire once used Greek letters for their coins, but if that has changed, there is much that can be learned from it."

"Ask them what route they took to reach the Atrium Vestae," Claudia suggested. "This would explain how they managed to reach the heart of Rome and identify the weak points in our perimeter."

Nicomedes nodded and asked the skull Claudia's question. It vibrated in his hand and the spirits wept. "We gathered in Alexandria from the sands of the south and the lands from far across the Atlantic. We hid in a shipment of grain through the Mediterranean and the Tiber River."

"What lands are across the Atlantic?" Adalia asked.

"There are lands that Rome trades with to the far east where we import silk. The Seres and the Indians lay upon the other side of the Parthian Empire," Nicomedes explained. "Perhaps the Parthians have managed find a direct route over the ocean."

"We could ask why they attacked in this manner now," Darius suggested. "Rome has been at odds with the Parthian Empire for centuries. They were last the victor on the Fields of Mars. Why such a desperate maneuver? What motivation would the Parthians have to start a war they might never win?"

None had a better question to propose, and so Nicomedes asked the skull. "The Magi — That Wait Beneath the Sands — sent their beasts to turn away the assassin's blade that would have killed the King of Kings. Mithridates would have killed his own brother while he slept. The King of Kings asked the Magi That Wait for advice on how to keep his empire forever strong, and they commanded that Claudia Valeria Terza must die before the birth of her first child."

Claudia gasped at the words of the spirit. She turned towards her brothers, tears streaking down her face. Marcus wrapped his arms around her, holding her close to his chest. "I shall have this man's heart and those of these Magi."

"Soothsayers, brother. 'Magi' is simply the word the Parthians known them as," Nicomedes explained. "This is the counter-strike that the Soothsayers have been waiting for since they became active in Rome."

"Why would such creatures bother with us?" Adalia asked.

"The Soothsayers of Rome struck the first blow when they changed the world. They play a game of infinite regress with the whole of creation. I believe I have learned enough to understand the factions of this secret war. Allow me to ponder it, to digest the changes, and I may be able to prepare proper defenses." Nicomedes lifted the skull into the air and gazed into the empty sockets. "You told the truth, beyond what was required. Know that you pleased me. But you attacked one of the Valeria. Tell all you pay the price for this sin." He threw the skull upon the ground, shattering it. The gestalt of the souls of her attackers screeched in agony unknown to the living. He turned towards Rubio. "Sweep up those bone fragments. They can be quite useful, now that I have gone through the trouble of casting their aspects into the outer darkness to be consumed."

"What can be done?" Darius asked. "What defense might we have against the magic of a Soothsayer?"

"We are safe within the walls of the Domūs de Valeria. The blood of our ancestors keep us safe. The bones of our people live within these walls. Such power can block even the prying eyes of the Soothsayers," Nicomedes explained.

"We are about to venture to Egypt, brother," Marcus observed. "A good distance from the walls of our ancestors."

"There is a Zoroastrianist ritual that might be cast to cleanse ourselves of any sympathetic bonds that exist within the world," Nicomedes explained. "It severs the mystical connection with anything that contains your essence until you touch it again. Others seeking to gain power over you often search for that connection through a favorite brush, a strand of hair, or an old garment. Normally, you would have to carry such items with you forever to defend yourself, but this ritual would prevent scrying and tracking, which assuredly these Magi That Wait have been doing onto Claudia."

"Such is easy for a soldier," Marcus said. "I would volunteer to go first."

Nicomedes smiled. "Your confidence is gratifying, but patience is required. We must prepare for the trip and discard those things that we have outgrown, lest an enemy steal them in our absence. Besides, you have been anointed in blood." He reached over and touched one of the blood splatters on his brother's face and brought it to his lips. "Roman blood, yes?"

Marcus nodded. He untied the sack from his belt and offered it to Nicomedes. "This is the head of the centurion who dared to raise a gladius against me."

"Thank you for the gift. We will have his secrets."

Marcus nodded. "I thought he might have answers for us at the least. And if nothing else, torment. We captured one of his men, a legionnaire by the name of Gallus Licinius Nonus. Milius is delivering this prisoner to a safe location for Senator Livius to question. His testimony will be what protects us, should we fail in Egypt."

Nicomedes handed the sack to Rubio. The boy's face turned sickly. "Arrange a pot for this head in my chambers at the academy. You know where to acquire the dermestid beetles. Have it assigned to my accounts."

Drusilla wondered if the boy was able to stand at all from the pallor of his face. "Yes, magister."

"Very well. If you will watch over Claudia, I shall retire to my chambers to wash," Marcus declared.

Nicomedes nodded. "I would have privacy with our sister to perform tests to see if I might discover what threads of prophecy these foreign Soothsayers see."

Claudia nodded, fervently. "Anything to aid the cause."

"A pity that the Sibylline Scrolls are unavailable," Adalia said.

Nicomedes blinked, curiously. "How do you know of this?"

Adalia smiled, pleased to have caused a reaction. "Senator Cicero mentioned the scrolls and their prophecy at the Senate Curio building."

Nicomedes nodded at them, dismissing them, contemplating the words of a dead man. Marcus turned to leave the cottage, the conversation over, but Adalia stopped him. "Drusilla and I would have words with you in private, centurion."

He tilted his head, confused. "Apologies to the both of you. With the events of the day, I have taken leave of my senses and the future. Shall we dine together this night?"

Drusilla was uncertain exactly what Adalia intended, but she was certainly intrigued. If allowed, Marcus would put off any personal conversation until the battle was won. Perhaps Adalia was simply priming the pump to help her as promised. "Such would be pleasing, but perhaps we could walk you to your chambers."

If the other members of the Valeria noted the conversation, they said nothing of it. Nicomedes whispered to both Claudia and Darius, while Rubio gawked open-mouthed. They wrapped their arms on either side of him and led him to the main villa.

They passed Hermana barking orders to several servants, as they started up the stairs. Adalia turned towards the overseer as they passed. "The dominus must be cleaned."

Hermana nodded, pleased that Marcus was finally seeking to bathe rather than strut about the villa dripping of his enemy's blood. More than one of the servants had fainted since his bloody arrival.

"Excellent. I will send up servants with warm water and scented oils."

"Have the servants leave it outside," Adalia instructed.

The overseer merely nodded and quickly departed. Marcus eyed Adalia and then Drusilla. "What mischief do you plan this evening?"

Adalia glanced aside towards Drusilla with a curious expression and a smile, as though waiting for her to respond. *Was this the amazon's way of helping?* The very thought of bathing Marcus brought a tingle to her body and a wetness that she had never experienced before. She looked at Adalia's lips and wondered what it might feel like to kiss them.

Drusilla laughed as demurely as she could possibly manage. "You visited my father this very day. Our union is certain, centurion." She pulled Marcus into his spartan chambers, which held only a comfortable bed and trophies from his march across Europe. Adalia followed with a knowing smile. "I would not have this be a mere political union. I would take your cock and your heart as well as your name."

"I am not certain that Senator Livius would approve," Marcus said, uncertain.

"Father has only wished me happiness," Drusilla countered as she closed the door behind him. "And, he need not know everything that happens in Rome."

He turned toward Adalia and then back to Drusilla. What happened with a slave was not spoken aloud in society, as it was considered to be the equivalent of masturbating. This act of daring could shame the both of them and their house, yet the desire was plain upon his face. It was a face he had never shown her before. "And you know that Adalia is not a slave, yes?"

Drusilla gingerly reached up to touch his cheek. It was softer than she imagined. "She is my brilliant friend. She knows much of the world. I asked her to come here."

Marcus tilted his head towards Adalia. "She asked you here?"

"This dutiful woman of Rome has loved and revered you all of her life." Adalia reached across Marcus to touch Drusilla. Her skin tingled. "You have always told me the women of Rome keep the hearths for the family. She has dreamed only of you above all men. Above all else, she yearns to learn how please you properly."

She knew not why Adalia agreed to this mutual seduction to secure her place as wife, especially if she truly desired Nicomedes. This was a dangerous gambit. Should Marcus refuse and play the insulted groom insulted by this improper offer, then she would be beaten and driven from her home for dishonoring her father. "I asked her here, and she kindly agreed to educate me in the world that I have never experienced."

Marcus looked at her strangely. It was though it was the first time that he thought of her as a woman. Adalia pulled her between them. They towered head and shoulders above her. "Look at this Roman beauty, Marcus! She would be worshiped in the Rhine." Adalia ran her fingers along Drusilla's arms and then cradled her hips. "Such beautiful curves and the size of these breasts would make Ostara swell with jealousy."

Adalia was tall and graceful like a gazelle. It had never occurred to

Drusilla that such a beauty would desire her or that feeling desired and having such words spoken about her would feel so intoxicating. The Vestal College denied her entrance because of her deformity, long-since cured by the Soothsayers. She had soft curves and wide hips that seemed to appeal to both Marcus and Adalia. Drusilla tugged at her stola as though to tease the both of them, drinking in the pleasure reflected in their eyes.

A knock at the door interrupted her tease. Adalia opened the door to discover that the servants had left behind a wooden tub of steaming water, a wicker basket filled with washing supplies, and a platter containing a pitcher of honeyed wine, bread, olive oil, and cheese. She tucked the basket under her arm and dragged the rest into the room. Adalia turned towards Marcus and smiled. "Centurion, I fear you shall not pass inspection with your uniform in such a state."

Drusilla unclasped the belt of his tunic. "We might have to have Hermana take these rags outside of the walls and burn them."

"No!" Marcus pointed to his other trophies adorning the walls and then pulled off his tunic. "This shall be amongst my most prized possessions, reminding me of the day I bested another Roman worthy of my name!"

She imagined Marcus naked a hundred times as a girl and more when she first became a woman. Drusilla had somehow pictured him to be smooth like a statue, but there were battle-scars and hair upon his chest. She soaked in the pleasure of his gaze, from his handsome face down to his torso, and the line of hair upon his perfect stomach to his already-erect cock.

Adalia dipped the rags into the warm water and washed them over every part of his body, until it was clean of the blood and grime of the Aventine. Then, they rubbed his muscles with sweet scented oils and scraped him clean with a strigil.

Drusilla dried him with a towel. Some believed the sweat of an athletic body was a cure for sickness. She only knew the scent of it excited her, and there was a twitch between her legs she had only previously experienced in private in the dead of night, where none could see.

"You have been quite patient with us, centurion," Adalia purred. She stepped towards Drusilla, holding onto her hand. She was naked as a baby. Drusilla could not help but admire the strength of her body. It was though she was Diana the Huntress, carved from ivory. Adalia grabbed hold of both of her wrists and pulled them behind her back. Drusilla yelped like bunny being caught by the scruff of her neck. "And now for your reward."

Hungry hands gently pulled the stola over her head. Marcus and Adalia took turns kissing her and biting upon her neck. They laid her upon the bed and parted her legs. Each kissed one of her thighs, and the anticipation of the moment brought shivers down to the core of her being. Tongues caressed her skin, tasting her, and fingers probed places upon her body that none had ever touched.

She gasped the moment that her labia was parted and probed. Fingers penetrated her so slowly that she pushed forward with her hips — greedy for more. Her body bent and flexed in ways she never imagined possible. She felt a swelling inside of her that slowly built until she climaxed.

Drusilla felt shame only for a moment, until Adalia raised her head from her thighs. The amazon wiped her luscious mouth and then moved up towards her face. They kissed, and the sensation of it was so powerful, she had realized the amazon had taken the leather belt Marcus had recently worn and wrapped it around her hands. She leaned forward allowing Drusilla to suckle at her breasts. It felt peaceful and natural.

The amazon cradled her neck under her arms and then returned the favor — feasting upon her breasts. Marcus finally lifted his mouth from her cunt, dripping with her wetness, and laughed. Adalia kissed her ear and whispered, "And now he will worship you forever, for you have made him a god."

He rubbed the tip of his cock along the outside of her cunt, becoming all the slipperier for her juices. He stared into her eyes for what seemed like hours. Perhaps it was as Adalia promised, and the act of worship bound him to her. He pushed forward, slowly, penetrating her. She opened the entirety of her being to him and cried.

Adalia shushed her like a mother rocking a babe. Drusilla fluttered her eyes open, determined to see their faces. She kissed Adalia, remembering all of the wisdom that had been shared between them.

Marcus smiled, almost shyly. It felt very strange to see such wanton desire on his face, and it seemed to be equally directed at her. Her body opened to his in time, and the pain of the new experience gave way to a hunger for more.

She slipped her hands out of the belt and reached around to the back of his neck, grasping her fingers in the scruff of his hair, pulling it back.

Drusilla imagined that she appeared to be no more fierce than a kitten growling at a lion, but if she wanted him, for him to truly be his, she needed to trust the words of Adalia. She whispered into his ear, "I am not something that you must take care not to break. I am of Rome and require your full measure."

He blinked, slowly absorbing the meaning of her words. Marcus said nothing in return. The only sound that escaped his lips was a growl, as though his body was ready and willing to react to her challenge. His eyes were ablaze with lust, conveying a new sensation: to be wanted and worshiped.

Adalia pushed him back and squirmed her way to her lips. Marcus grunted his disapproval. To be the focus of their desire felt like being a goddess in flesh. She lost the capacity of thought as her body adjusted to the paradoxical pain that tasted of pleasure. The warmth of his seed brought forth a new pleasure, complex with a sense of having been part of the cycle of the world. "The two of you should do nothing but this until the end of time."

"My body belongs to the people of Rome during the day," Marcus whispered. "The night shall belong to you."

Adalia poured a cup of wine and passed it to Drusilla. She took a sip of it and passed it to Marcus. "I am pleased we had this night before you left for Egypt, husband. I wish I could attend with you."

"I would take you to see the pyramids of that ancient land, but such was not the arrangement I made with your father," Marcus explained.

"To hedge his bets against you not returning from this mission," Drusilla admitted with a sly grin. "I am precious to him."

"Not only to him."

"I would fight my way out of Tartarus to return to you, my wife."

The word wife was more precious to her than gold or jewels. "It seems cruel that I shall not experience this again until you return."

Adalia snatched the cup, finished it, and then tossed it aside. "This lesson is not yet over, my student."

Chapter Eight: The Precipice of Knowledge

Nicomedes gazed upward into the black of night, studying the stars that reigned over the calm waters of the Mediterranean. He nested against the curved prow of the round-hulled ship, seeking protection against the brisk night air. It was his first time leaving the Eternal City, and it was adventure enough for Nicomedes. He measured the location of the stars on the horizon, and compared them to the position of the lighthouses that lined the coast of Africa.

There was a solar observatory on top of the Soothsayer Academy, where he learned to circumnavigate by observing the stars, but he never had the chance to put this knowledge to practice. He used the imperial lighthouse, first built by Pompey Magnus in celebration of his victory over the pirates in the Mediterranean during the days of the Republic.

Sailors worked quietly on the deck. It was third watch, and the majority of the passengers and crew upon the corbitas class merchant vessel were sleeping. A number of the Third Cohort lined the rails of the ship, eager for the night air to alleviate their sour stomachs and green faces. They occasionally vomited the last of the sour wine the men had smuggled aboard.

Tradition of the Seventh Legion demanded legionnaires toast their historical victory over Carthage that ended the Third Punic War. Drinking had started early in the afternoon, once the ship caught sight of the African coast. They sailed between the islands of Sardina and Sicily, and passed by the tip of Numidia, where once stood the enemy city.

"To Hasdrubal the Boetharch, may he never run out of salt."

"We rose up from her bone and ended the strife, may we never be as fucked as Queen Elissa."

Milius laughed the loudest. "Hail Publius Cornelius Scipio Aemilianus Africanus Numantinus!"

The insults and not-so-sly sexual bragging only became baser as day faded into night. Marcus ignored this breach in protocol because it was tradition, and he was taking the men away from their brothers-in-arms, away from glory at Gaul, and into the unknown.

Nicomedes had a store of caraway seed in his baggage, but hesitated wasting them on drunkards suffering from their own vices. He doubted that the soldiers would voluntarily take anything from him without strict orders from the centurion.

The historian Tacitus wrote the salting of the earth of Carthage was a mere tale the soldiers told. Nicomedes kept his gaze upon the stars. That land once contained a great power not unlike the Lupercal Cave. Were there once Soothsayers in Carthage? Was that why Rome and Carthage warred?

Adalia slowly climbed onto the deck from the passenger rooms deep in the hold. She stretched and scratched her head. "Have you forever forsaken sleep, Nicomedes?"

"Magic refreshes my flesh and nourishes my soul." Nicomedes was surprised that he deigned to answer this woman, but Marcus asked that every courtesy be extended to her. It certainly proved useful when they needed to counter the plans of the Aemilii. She had a keen perception that both of his siblings lacked towards the whole world. "I only need a few scant hours each day. I typically slumber in the early afternoon, to keep alert during the night when the walls between worlds are thinnest."

"Do you miss it?"

Nicomedes pondered that astute question a moment. Few would have dared to ask him such a personal question at the Soothsayer Academy. "There is peace in slumber – a time when you can release the obligations of the world. Seeking out the divine always comes at a price. I knew that before my first lesson. I have not been disappointed with what I have purchased at such a cost."

"What do you see when you look out at night?" Adalia asked, craning her neck to attempt follow his gaze.

Nicomedes gestured towards the stars, wishing that he could express the visual cacophony of colors he percieved. "I see the pulse of creation. All that was or will ever be is out there."

"I heard tell from Milius you still carry one of the skulls from the men I killed. Why?" Adalia asked.

Nicomedes opened his satchel, fished out the remaining skull, and presented it to Adalia. "It whispers secrets to me and begs for forgiveness. It knows nothing of consequence, but I am learning Arsacid Pahlavi."

"I envy your gift." Adalia gestured towards the soldiers vomiting over the sides of the ship. "My uncle believes that 'he who controls steel and gold can move the world.' I have seen the thoughts of Caesar, and it is secret whispers that make the world turn."

He looked down from the heavens to study Adalia. She was not unattractive. Nicomedes could see why Marcus had taken her for a lover. His brother overlooked her natural intelligence, almost a match for himself or Drusilla. "Many believe the sun rises and descends upon their mastery of the secret world. There is a chaos that exists at the center of all things, and sometimes the best that can be done is to weather the storm."

Adalia continued to stare at the stars. "I envy your rotund apprentice and the wisdom he must learn from you."

"Rubio?" Nicomedes asked. The thought of that boy mastering wisdom almost brought a smile to his face. He would have laughed if he remembered how. "He serves a proper purpose."

"He lives in fear of disappointing you," Adalia stated.

"I brought him only because he is related to the Aemilii, and I feared they would take him from the academy to seek out answers regarding my research." Nicomedes caught the sly grin on her face and snorted. "I am not a pederast as has been rumored. Such needs of the flesh are rare for me, and I have lovers should that be required."

"Do you?" Adalia asked. She turned towards him with a grin. "Marcus told me once that he thought that flesh delighted you not."

Nicomedes shrugged. "I do not let such passions rule my spirit as does Marcus. There are magics that require certain sacrifices, and I pay the price when required."

Adalia seemed satisfied with the answer as she returned her gaze onto the stars. "And what do you think we will discover in Egypt?"

Nicomedes decided that perhaps this woman from the Rhine deserved a brutally honest answer. "We shall be drenched in opportunity and blood in equal measure. The Soothsayers would not have sent us otherwise."

"Why did you agree to come?"

He sat shivering in the darkness upon the deck and was silent for many minutes, careful to select his words with great care. "Because I am willing to pay the price."

* * * *

Nicomedes opened his eyes with a violent start.

He sniffed the air, surprised by the great and potent magic he had not felt since leaving Rome and the Lupercal Cave. He turned to his side, discovering Rubio snoozing loudly on the floor. Nicomedes slid out of the hammock and washed his face in the basin to come quickly to his senses. He crept out of his cabin and climbed to the upper deck.

The sun beamed brightly through the clouds, as the vast coast of Africa appeared upon the horizon. The glorious port of Alexandria opened before them like a flower unfolding, as ships — blackened by the shadow of the setting sun — buzzed around it like bees.

Alexandria was the geometric opposite of Rome. The layout of the Eternal City was round — forced by the geographic curve of the seven hills. Alexander the Great took advantage of the African coast to design an elegant rectangular layout that was simultaneously beautiful and imminently practical.

The soldiers cheered while the sailors went about their duties, eager to reach port. Nicomedes glanced about the deck, peering through the crowd, until he located Marcus and Claudia speaking with the ship's captain near the back of the vessel.

Captain Abasi was a native Alexandrian well versed in the etiquette of the port and the city. According to Drusilla, her father had made this man quite rich over the years, and it was in his best interest to make the future son of the Claudian financial empire happy. "I mean no disrespect, centurion, but it is customary that ships ferrying emissaries sail past the Pharaoh's Lighthouse, so the city might prepare a proper welcome."

Marcus scoffed. Nicomedes noted the pained expression upon the captain's face. "We wish to arrive into the city without such honors."

"Brother! Sister!" Their conversation halted as he stepped closer. "Might I speak with you, Marcus?"

Claudia tilted her head and smiled sweetly towards the captain. "Captain Abasi, I have questions about this lighthouse you spoke of. Could we take some air to look at it closely?"

She took the captain by the arm and led him towards the front of the vessel, while Marcus turned angrily towards his little brother. The centurion turned away from the captain, clutched his arm, and pulled Nicomedes to a quiet place near the back of the ship. "Why would you dishonor my word by interrupting one of my commands?"

"This man shall be whipped if he breaks tradition. This is his home, and he must live here after we have gone," Nicomedes explained. "He will betray us, for he must. This is not the Seventh Legion, brother. In this, we should follow the advice of our sister and ply all with sweet words."

"How shall we discover the problem with the grain, if our movements are immediately known?" Marcus asked.

"It is too late for the fly to worry about the spider when he already caught in the web, brother." He swallowed his pride and spat out the truth. "My presence was felt. I had not imagined that it could happen so fast without foreknowledge of my arrival."

"How do you know this?" Marcus asked.

"I felt the power of their magic upon my flesh," Nicomedes admitted. "If I had not been sleeping, I might have absorbed it, and they would be none the wiser."

Marcus smiled and puffed out his chest. "If your enemy knows that you are coming, then always walk as though you are Atlas about to lift the world upon your shoulders."

"Agreed. The appearance of power is often better than actually having it."

"Then I shall assemble my men, and we'll present quite the spectacle," Marcus declared.

Nicomedes nodded, quite pleased that his elder brother could be brought to reason. "I shall see if I can aid your presentation."

The centurion spun on his heels and nodded to his optio, Milius Hortensius Lex, who pulled out a whistle and blasted three shrill calls to the men. The Third Cohort of the Seventh Legion of Rome assembled into parade formation, and when the corbitas class merchant vessel passed by the white tower of the Pharaoh's lighthouse, they saluted with their spears — an honor only given to the most august leaders of Rome.

Bells rang in the distance on the shore. The other ships in the eastern harbor parted, much like that Hebrew story of the Red Sea. Marcus pointed out the warships docked in the harbor and near the lighthouse. "I fight on the ground where the gods intended. Look at that fleet of warships – almost fifty – as though Octavius expects a fight."

A small rowboat met them and directed the ship towards the Royal Harbor. Once the ship docked, the cohort seized control of the dock via the traditional flanking carry position every legion practiced to seize a trigger point and make an impression. Shields were maneuvered into position via a series of cascading motions that made it seem to an observer like a wave of red and gold metal was about to wash over him.

The royal guards of Alexandria met them at the edge of the dock. They came with bare chests and wore brightly colored loincloths, protected with straps of hardened leather. Nicomedes noted they painted their faces with a faint gold tint and lined charcoal under their eyes. Their leader wore an elegant headdress with a large feather of brilliant plumage. He sneered, displeased at the arrogance of the display.

Nicomedes readied himself for a battle, until a whistle blast sounded three times somewhere behind the Egyptians. The thunderous sound of marching boots, thick Roman leather, boomed against the cobblestone streets. The Egyptian guards parted to allow for the Roman legion to meet its brethren.

Marcus seemed to recognize them immediately and shouted. "Hail unto the Eighth Legion of Rome."

A tall Roman with leathery skin and frayed features grimly nodded. He wore the helmet of a centurion. "Hail, centurion. What is your name?"

"Marcus Valerius Perseus. I am glad that Governor Thurinus has sent an envoy of his father," Marcus stated calmly. He used the governor's agnomen as a sign of respect for his rule over Egypt. "Might I have your name, centurion?"

"Lucius Domitius Ahenobarbus. This is the First Cohort of the Eighth Legion." Nicomedes noted that the centurion seemed careful to choose his words correctly. How much did this centurion know of their purpose here? "Allow me to greet you in the name of Gaius Octavius Thurinus, Governor of Egypt, and his wife Arsinoë, Queen of a United Egypt. I am certain they shall wish to greet you personally when they return from their tour of the Nile tomorrow. We were ill prepared for your visit, but if you have not made arrangements for your stay, quarters at the Royal Palace shall be placed at your disposal."

"That would be most generous. Thank you. Know I have not come alone." Marcus gestured to Nicomedes and their sister Claudia, who wore a proper stola and a shawl. "My brother Nicomedes Valerius Corvus, student of the Soothsayers. My sister Claudia Valeria Terza, she who recently left the Vestal Virgins."

Nicomedes studied the legion, trying to read their faces. Marcus told them that the Eighth Legion had been assigned to Egypt for five years or more. The shade of Nepos Murena Macer had whispered many secrets of the Eighth Legion, and few of them were pleasant.

He searched for a young face amongst the legion with a light complexation, dark hair, and the ears of a certain Roman patrician. Nicomedes smiled upon locating the boy holding the legion's standard, a fine position for the son of Octavian and the Queen of Egypt boldly named — Gaius Julius Octavius Ptolemy — after two mighty conquerors, one Roman and one Egyptian.

"Egypt is surely honored to have such august guests. I will send a runner to inform Senator Orca and his wife that their children have arrived." Centurion Ahenobarbus flashed the customary legionnaire's salute to a fellow centurion. "Might we escort you to the Royal Palace?"

* * * *

A snarling stone lion perched upon a royal standard greeted them at the gates. They were led down a path lined with colossal red granite columns, with a decorated crown on top to create magnificent entrance — fit for a living goddess.

Roman politicians had the courtesy to deify each other only after death. Egyptian royalty were the living avatars of their gods, carrying the virtues and vices of the spirits that theoretically lived within them. Nicomedes imagined such divinity made political discourse somewhat difficult.

The palace of Alexandria rested at the edge of the city overlooking the eastern bay. The sheer opulence of the grounds was astounding. Their apartments were on the outer ring, near the cliffs that overlooked the sea. They were flanked by two sphinxes — statues with the body of a lion and the face of a man — fiercely protecting the royal guests.

Their chambers were vast, especially compared to their home in Rome, where space was at a premium. Their apartments collectively were almost the size of the Domūs de Valeria. Nicomedes paced along the borders of the atrium, squinting up into the bright desert eye, carefully stepping around the palm trees. He noted each of his siblings acted in accordance to their natures.

Marcus immediately ordered his soldiers to protect the key entry points and then assigned them barracks. His optio Milius began to cajole a callow legionnaire — named Cossus if Nicomedes remembered correctly — to play a game of dice.

Claudia turned her attention to the servants — smiling like a serpent — trying to discover the gossip of the day and feel out the rhythms of the palace. Adalia watched quietly, her hands firmly gripping the hilts of the daggers on her belt. "Ancient and terrible gods ruled here once," she said. "You can smell it in the air."

"Once? Where did they go?" Marcus asked.

"They were murdered, of course." Nicomedes stopped his pacing suddenly, inspired by the thought. He opened his mouth to verbalize the strange sensation he felt since they landed at Alexandria. He felt a bump against his back, forcing him to stumble forward. Nicomedes spun on his heels to discover Rubio gaping up at him, his lip trembling. "Do you now feel it, boy? You've studied at the academy for years. I must have taught you something."

Claudia turned towards them. "Feel what, Nico?"

He ignored his sister's question and glared down at his student. "The precipice of knowledge. The tension in the air, crackling from the oncoming storm."

Rubio nodded. "I feel emptiness. Cold. Like I am falling off a cliff and there is no bottom. What is it, magister?"

Nicomedes sniffed the air. "Death."

Marcus scoffed. "I've faced dying before. This is no different."

"Not dying. There is no trick to that," Nicomedes snarled. "All that is flesh dies, no matter how slow, not matter how strong. This is the essence of death. The hunger at the end of all things."

"By the words of Jove, speak plainly, brother, please." Marcus extended his arms and waved about the palace.

Nicomedes paused for a moment. His brother lived in a world bound and trapped by the frail human senses. How could he possibly explain that which could never been seen, but only felt? He turned to Rubio. "Answer his question."

The chubby boy blinked, wide-eyed and terrified. "The cold hand of Dis Pater is about us all!"

"Calm yourself, Rubio." He placed his slender fingers upon the boy's cheeks. "Describe what you feel."

"It feels as though we're at the edge of the world," Rubio tried to explain. "As though we are gazing into a hole in everything.

Somewhere nearby is a portal to the otherworld, where the Soothsayers gained their immortality."

Nicomedes nodded, satisfied his student had at least grasped the fundamentals. He thought of his last conversation with Spurinna and the promise of his own ascension. Was this why they sent his family to this place at this time while the royal family was away from the palace? "There is power here, the likes of which I have only felt in the presence of the Soothsayers themselves, upon the very steps of the Lupercal Cave."

Marcus pondered this a moment. "Do you believe the Egyptians know of this?"

"Select sensitivity and training is required to feel these energies. Rubio has adjusted his susceptibility to such magic. I suspect that Adalia comes by it naturally," Nicomedes explained. "Octavius believes in a natural order as you do. However, this is an ancient and wise land. It would strain the limits of credulity to believe there are none here aware of the power. And that alone suggests it is guarded and protected somehow."

Claudia tilted her head, as though trying to hear a muffled melody. "Such power might well inspire devotion, such as Rome feels for the Luperical Cave."

"Such is also academic, as it is not our mission to seek a place of power in this land," Marcus stated. "We are here about the grain."

"You are here about the grain, brother," Nicomedes corrected him. "I am here at the will of the Soothsayers, and this may be the root of why they sent the three of us here."

Claudia stepped between her brothers, holding her hands up in an attempt to broker peace. "Did not the Soothsayers promise the resolution of all of these mysteries would aid Rome?"

Marcus softened his features when he glanced aside towards Claudia. "I am not opposed to taking advantage of opportunities as they arise, sister. I merely wish to remind us all of why we risk this venture."

"Our goals are united, brother," Nicomedes soothed. "The Soothsayers plucked the threads of fate to bind our causes to theirs. The laurels of victory shall be yours when we return to Rome, brother, and we shall all rest in the shade under the protection of our new branch house."

His elder brother sighed. "I merely advise caution towards such things we do not understand."

Nicomedes took petty pleasure from the flicker of fear in his brother's eyes. "Fear not that we venture unarmed. The Soothsayers have trained me well for this. It might very well be this is the source who summoned the ghoul that attacked Caesar."

He noted the swell of patriotic fever in his brother's chest. "Then clearly, we should investigate this immediately."

Nicomedes opened his mouth to agree with his brother, when he felt a palpable sense of dread at the base of his skull. He spat onto the ground to rid himself of the copper taste that overwhelmed his tongue.

Marcus drew his gladius. "What is it? Poison?"

Claudia snapped her fingers and one of the palace servants ran to pour a goblet of wine. "Something caught in your throat?"

Nicomedes waved away the servant until he finally spat out the answer. "Mother!" Marcus and Claudia questioned his senses at once. Their voices merged into a wave of nonsense. The shrill cry of the falcon overhead silenced them. The legionnaires drew their spears and raised their shields. "No! It is merely a message."

It cried once more, flew through the atrium, and landed upon the stone lion. Falcons adorned the sigils of the royal family of Egypt, every bit as precious as the eagle was to Rome. It studied them a moment, looking from Nicomedes to Claudia and then finally ending at Marcus.

The falcon opened its beak and instead of a shrill squawk, they were rewarded with a familiar feminine voice – one he would know in his deepest dream or the furthest depths of Tartarus. Claudia blinked, seemingly recognizing the words of their mother immediately. Marcus furrowed his brow, clearly not believing what his senses revealed to him.

Their mother, Septima Valerius Orca spoke through the falcon. "Children! Heed well my warning. There is a power in the palace you will be attracted to. Your father and I shall be arriving in morning to reveal that which was previously hidden to you. Stay safe or all is lost."

The falcon blinked twice and took flight into the sky.

Claudia turned towards Marcus. "If this is how Nico communicated with you in Gaul, I well understand why the legion was spooked."

Marcus ignored the comment. His face flushed red. "Did she dare to refer to Orca as our father?"

Nicomedes ignored his brother's ranting and pondered the situation. Their mother had managed to learn the Art without instruction from the Soothsayers by will alone. She had lived in Alexandria for the better part of five years. Surely, she had managed to discover much about this strange energy.

His sister's next comment snapped him out his thoughts. "If Mother does possess powers akin to Nicomedes, then perhaps what Decimus warned me about is true after all."

"What did that cretin warn you about?" Nicomedes asked.

"I did not think it was worth sharing, truthfully," Claudia admitted. "He has said so many lies."

"What did he say, sister?" Marcus asked.

Claudia's lip trembled. "He said that each of us had been born with a twin, save for Nicomedes."

"It would explain your two-faced household gods," Adalia interjected. "A family of twins is considered lucky in the Rhine."

"It is true you were born with a twin, but she did not survive the night. I recall, for I was there outside of the room," Marcus said, not unkindly.

"If Decimus speaks rightly, then so were you brother. And your twin did not live past the hour of your birth," Claudia revealed. "Only Nicomedes was born alone, and it is said his birth was marked with a strange caul."

Nicomedes grinned at the very possibility of this story. If it were true, there would be a number of implications about the potential limits of his own power. "I have learned much of the body: birth onto death. Sometimes a stronger twin will kill the weaker in the womb. It is the way of nature."

"What of it, if I had a womb-brother who died shortly after we first took breath?" Marcus asked.

"Nothing, if they died of natural causes," Nicomedes explained. "If she drank of their blood and ground their bones into dust, then she may have drawn strength from the flesh born of her flesh. Such practices are known amongst the Caledonians."

Marcus turned his back to them. "Unthinkable!"

Claudia walked around the pillar until she faced her elder brother. "We've always assumed it was Orca who forced her to turn away from father."

"Our mother is a creature of ambition and will, comparable to my own. She learned the secrets of the Art forbidden by the Soothsayers," Nicomedes revealed. "There is little she would not dare, should she feel it would lead to knowledge or power."

"Monster! She listened to me cry about being forced to join the Vestal Virgins! She rebelled against propriety by breaking the law. Why would she not protect me?" Claudia demanded. "Why would she not share such knowledge with her own daughter?"

"My earliest memories were at her knee, feeling the essence of her power while sucking from her breasts," Nicomedes explained. "It was our secret. She started my education before Darius arranged for my entrance into the academy."

"What parent would do this to their child?" Marcus asked. "She watched Orca and his son abuse their privileges and lord their position over us."

"Did not Saturn consume Jupiter's siblings to gain their power?" Claudia asked.

Nicomedes nodded towards his sister, recognizing the legitimacy in the argument. She might have joined the College of the Vestals to avoid marriage to Decimus, but Claudia learned well the theology of the various temples. There was power in these stories and traditions. "Quite right, sister." Nicomedes turned to his brother. "How else could mother be immune to the passage of time? There are natural ways to heal. Those skilled in the Art can slow the aging process, but it always comes at a price. Only life can bring life. The more related by blood, the stronger the magical connection."

"Should this be spoken of out in the open?" Adalia asked, her eyes focused upon Rubio.

"Rubio, would you care to explain why we can speak openly in front of you?" Nicomedes asked.

"Yes, magister." Rubio stood straight, as though he were a probatus in the legion. "I have a geis upon my soul. If I betray the Valeria in word or deed, I shall suffer a terrible calamity."

Claudia's face twisted with concern. "What will happen to you?"

Rubio's face turned white. "My innards shall transmute into scorpions, and I shall shit them out."

"Is this true?" Adalia asked.

"No," Nicomedes answered sharply. He paused a moment, realizing the others had misunderstood his answer. "The scorpions would sting him to death long before he could defecate them."

Rubio's knees buckled. Claudia took the goblet intended for her mouth and brought it to the boy's lips. He drank slowly, nearly choking in fear of his body's ultimate betrayal. "Nico, torturing the boy doesn't help the matter."

Nicomedes scoffed. "The boy is immaterial. There is a great and terrible mystical power anchored someplace within the palace. I assure you this is a rarity unknown within my lifetime. We have the opportunity to seize upon it."

"You speak of mystical power, but what does that mean in a practical sense?" Claudia asked. "I've been led to believe magic is a function of will and discipline. Is that not true?"

Nicomedes explained. "Yes, magic is a function of will and discipline towards directing energy. All life has some energy, a life-force. This does not dissipate upon death. Someone or something very powerful once ended their mortal existence here, and that energy was hidden away. If I can locate it, I can absorb it, and my own power would increase exponentially."

"Surely it will be guarded," Marcus argued.

"I doubt Octavius would believe in its power," Nicomedes countered. "You would not have, before your return to Rome."

"What of the Egyptians?" Claudia asked. "Surely, they would know of this? There are multiple orders of priesthoods in Alexandria."

The double doors to the palace opened with little fanfare. A cadre of palace guards parted, allowing entry by a gaunt man who towered in height, over even Adalia. He wore a tanned leather loincloth and priestly vestments.

Marcus stepped forward, keeping his hand upon the hilt of his gladius. His soldiers did likewise, keeping pace with their centurion. Claudia rushed forward, lifting her stola in her hands, ensuring that she was the first to greet their Egyptian guest. "I am Claudia Valeria Terza."

"I am called Megabyzus." The priest had perhaps a decade of experience on Nicomedes, but he had an inviting, seductive smile. There was brilliance behind his dark almond eyes, almost hidden with splashes of green mascara. He spoke Latin with a strange southern Greek accent. "Please allow me to personally welcome you to the royal palace of Alexandria."

Nicomedes noted the symbolic representations of the crocodile upon his gold jewelry. Claudia spoke while he pondered the implications. "It is a truly a pleasure to meet a priest of Sobek the guardian." He turned to Marcus. "An aspect of Apollo here in Egypt."

"And I am honored to be in the presence of one of the fabled Vestal Virgins of Rome," Megabyzus replied. He turned towards Marcus and then finally Nicomedes. "And there are few places in the world that have not heard of the honor of the Valeria, even if your names were not commonly bragged by your mother at court. Centurion Marcus Valerius Perseus of the Seventh Legion, your deeds are known to us. Magister Nicomedes Valerius Corvus, it is a privilege to meet a teacher of the Soothsayer Academy."

Marcus did not move his hand from his gladius. The palace guards watched them carefully. "You seem to have us at a disadvantage."

"A mere temporary flux of events I fear I must leverage while the advantage is mine." Megabyzus gestured towards the palace guards, dismissing them. They stepped back into the main section of the palace and closed the gate. The priest smiled confidently and stepped forward. "The majority of the court is away with our queen to take care of an important matter of state. This will be the only time that we can truly speak privately."

"What is this matter of state?" Marcus asked.

"You spoke of our mother," Claudia added. "Do you know her?"

Megabyzus raised his hands, as though to protest their questioning of him. "All in due time. We must establish our relationship first to a mutually satisfying rhythm."

"He wishes to bargain with us," Adalia stated. Nicomedes had forgotten she was present. Somehow, she moved to the edge of the conversation, yet placed herself between himself and the priest. "We have something he is desperate to acquire."

"Your northern barbarian servant is not wrong." Megabyzus knelt before Nicomedes, offering his hands outward with palms reaching towards the sky. "I felt your presence from a great distance, magister – power that outstrips any of the priests of my order in wisdom and understanding. I would learn from a magister of the Soothsayer Academy."

"What?" Marcus asked.

Nicomedes raised a finger to silence his siblings. "Why would you not seek a teacher amongst your homeland?"

"My mother came from an important Nubian family. My father was a trader of Parthia blood," Megabyzus explained. "Such things are very important in this land. I have learned from the scraps offered onto me from the orders, but none of the real masters will accept me."

"Megabyzus is Arsacid in origin, is it not? Why give yourself such a name?" Nicomedes asked.

"Such a Roman question, magister." Megabyzus stood, wiping the dust from his knees. "They say the men of Rome do not possess a True Name, for it changes with their deeds and families. In Egypt, the True Name of a man has power. They would not let me forget my blood, so I wanted to remind them that I was a conqueror."

"I only take personal students that show great promise," Nicomedes stated. He glanced aside at Rubio. "To do otherwise is a waste of time."

"And how would he know that you would be loyal?" Adalia asked.

"I would submit to the geis," Megabyzus answered solemnly. "I would not wish scorpions in my stomach for the world."

Nicomedes blinked. The echoes of the source of power clearly blinded him to lesser spells. "You scried upon us without attracting our notice."

"This place is my home. I know these columns and this sand quite intimately." Megabyzus gestured towards the palace. "My senses have adjusted to the uncontrolled broadcasting of the Three Gates of Agony."

Nicomedes nodded. "This is the great power locked in the palace, some sort of portal to the underworld I presume?"

"Our Soothsayers are called the Eternal Dreamers. We built the pyramids for their slumber. They left knowledge in the hands of the priesthood, but we've lost much of their techniques, especially with the Library of Alexandria burned. It is said they left their power here in the palace for the worthy to claim them, if they can brave the Three Gates of Agony."

A brilliant flash of insight blinded him for a moment. It was though he had been trapped in a dark cave for the entirety of his life, and only now understood the power of fire. The concept of infinite regress rebounded in his consciousness. Spurinna had been trying to guide him into mastering the concept, and now he understood their subtle hand in events.

Decades ago, Caesar chased Pompy Magnus to Alexandria at the end of the Civil War. The priests who puppeted the boy Pharaoh Ptolemy XIV ordered Pompy's execution to please Caesar. This lead to Rome interceding on behalf of Cleopatra. During the Siege of Alexandria, Caesar murdered hundreds of priests who supported his enemy. A wing of the Great Library burned to the ground when the forces of Ptolemy attempted to seize Caesar's ships, forcing the wily general to set fire to his own ships to harry the enemy. Rich citizens moved certain scrolls to private hands, and the reputation of the institution had fallen since then. Had the Soothsayers planned for this very day decades ago, before the Valleria were born, to remove rivals in Egypt? Nicomedes pondered this while his siblings continued to question Megabyzus.

Marcus shook his head and his face lined with doubt. "You claim that Egypt has its own Soothsayers and they slumber while your country suffers Roman rule?"

Megabyzus merely smiled through the challenge of veracity. "The world of flesh does not consume the thoughts of the Eternal Dreamers. They surrendered their ties to this world to explore the next and prepare the way for us all. They left behind their power should Egypt need it again."

Nicomedes nodded, if only to placate the zealot. He knew by Spurinna's own admission the Soothsayers had broken some sort of accord with others of their kind when they saved Caesar from the assassination. This was a war fought with the perspective of infinite regress. Why would the Soothsayers not simply include him in their plans? It was akin to trying to discern the will of a hurricane.

"I admit his words make a certain amount of sense, considering the tales I have learned of the Egyptian gods," Claudia stated. "But why then do you press our brother to teach you now?

Megabyzus merely smiled. "You arrived at a time none here expected — during a crisis of the state where there are tremendous opportunities for us all. There is but a limited window of time where my advanced knowledge is useful to the magister, and I would claim a reward before offering the prize."

"You outmatch me in years, Megabyzus," Nicomedes stated.

"And yet, your knowledge and power vastly outstrips my own," Megabyzus countered. "The reach of Rome is far. It is said the Soothsayer Academy was founded upon the scavenged bones of the Library of Alexandria. You have access to secrets and methods that were once the sole dominion of Egypt. I would learn them and bring them back to my people."

"It would be irresponsible to simply agree to accept you as my apprentice," Nicomedes replied thoughtfully. "However, I give you my word that should you be forthcoming with us and aid us in our causes, I will ensure you are properly weighed and measured. Should you prove to be worthy, I will take you back to the Soothsayer Academy and arrange for your studies. I cannot promise what the Soothsayers might elect to do or not do in this matter or any other. Their will is paramount."

"Agreed, but we must hurry if you are to take this gift offered by the gods," Megabyzus said.

"Why is that? What hurry is there?" Adalia asked.

"You have not heard?" Megabyzus asked. "Parthian ships have been sighted in the Red Sea. Alexandria faces attack from the south. War is upon us."

Chapter Nine: Deep Calleth Unto Deep

Claudia gawked at the wonders of the Royal Palace of Alexandria, as Megabyzus led them through a series of iron gates until they reached a large square open-sky atrium where courtesans and priests murmured and turned their heads to gain a peek at the guarded visitors from Rome.

Patricians traditionally wore respectable colors in public, such as blue or grey, benefiting the glory of their families. Egyptians held no such taboos, displaying every color of the rainbow as a sign of their love of nature and the gods. The influence of the Aemilii was such that when Nephele demonstrated a clamor for Egyptian-style auguries, many of the Vestal Virgins mastered it to attract the wealthiest patrons. Rome always had an appetite for the new. The scope of the divine was unlimited, and why should their forms be locked? The gods allowed men to know and understand their different aspects. Great Jupiter was known to the Greeks as mighty Zeus.

The Egyptians held a vast number of daily rituals designed to uphold maat, the divine order of the universe. The fashionable patricians of Rome took to mimicking the more colorful of these rituals, holding exclusive parties reenacting these mythological divine interactions.

Claudia folded her hands together over her stomach, nodded respectfully, and bid the others to do likewise, demonstrating their piety. Adalia immediately followed Claudia's direction and whispered to Nicomedes, who scowled at the intrusion into his private thoughts.

The entourage of the court craned their necks at a distance to peek at the visitors from Rome. Courtesans whispered to one another in the shadow of the line of sacred pylons — thick, flat towers, engraved with hieroglyphs, that flanked the main gateway.

She tried to read their expressions, but whatever glorious intrigues captured their attention were alien to her. Would it benefit their cause to immerse themselves in them? Or if by remaining above the fray, would they increase the desirability of their company?

Claudia paused for a moment by a stone statue of a powerful man with the head of a noble falcon. Ra ranked amongst her favorites; the god of the sky and the earth clearly was some sort of analog for beautiful Apollo. Some stories claimed that man was born in the lonely tears of Ra. *Why would the gods choose to reveal themselves with such animus forms*, she wondered?

A collective hush of the crowd's roar attracted her attention towards her younger brother. Nicomedes knelt in the center of the hall, where a falcon had descended from the skies. Adalia and Rubio flanked him. He beckoned the falcon to scurry closer and then whispered cautiously to the bird. It took flight out of the palace and into the horizon. "What was that, brother? Claudia asked. "Were we not attempting to be circumspect?"

Nicomedes gestured to Marcus, who closely followed their host, flanked by two of his legionnaires. "Necessity overrode caution, sister. Marcus asked that a message be delivered for our safety, before we venture into the sacred space."

Claudia ignored her tinge of anger over whatever secret her brothers withheld from her and offered her hand to Nicomedes. She marveled with just a tint of jealousy at how slender his hands were. "Are we getting closer?"

"Close enough that I could lead us there now from the mere pull of the power emanating from it," Nicomedes replied confidently.

Adalia watched over them silently, keeping her eyes upon the crowd. Claudia noted the amazon was rarely more than three steps from her youngest brother's side. Was this mere affection, or had Nicomedes made a separate deal with her? Claudia had feared Adalia would protest the marriage bonding the Valeria and the Claudians, but instead a strange bond had somehow formed between her and Drusilla that Claudia envied. Why was she always distant from those so close to her?

Claudia suspected Adalia would soon discover yet another romantic disappointment once she attempted to seduce Nicomedes. Her little brother lived so much inside his own skull that he rarely took delight in others, and then he only chose those who could match his genius. How would Adalia react to his rejection? She made mental note to address it in the future.

Megabyzus called from the other side of the sky hall, where Marcus and his legionnaires awaited. "Time is not our ally in this matter, friends."

They adjusted their pace to match the others' and quickly passed through an egress protected with elaborate stone columns painted in a variety of colors. Megabyzus circumnavigated the palace through a winding series of hallways that ended at a colossal door made of ashen wood.

Twin guards with painted flesh and spears in their hands protested in Egyptian. Megabyzus shook his head and whispered to them. They eyed each other suspiciously and opened the door, revealing a long narrow chamber with gold-painted stone walls leading to a single four-columned kiosk.

"This is the sacred place I felt on the tide," Nicomedes whispered with an unfamiliar tone of awe and naked lust. "A great and terrible power is contained within these walls, and it will be ours."

Megabyzus smiled enigmatically. "Many have attempted to access the sacred energy here and failed because they were judged unworthy. The Eternal Dreamers created three tests to kill those who would seize that which belongs to Egypt and the world."

Nicomedes snorted, waving away the Egyptian's concerns and stepping into the chamber. "Nonsense. This is merely a vault to contain that which was most valuable to them. Those tests you have mythologized into a sacred duty are more security measures designed to keep anyone else out."

Megabyzus shook his head. "You believe you know the mind of the Eternal Dreamers better than those who have been the instruments of their will for millennia?"

"I have walked with Soothsayers. I have listened to their words and have seen their deeds. These creatures amassed power and influence through the countless ages of time." Nicomedes pointed to the golden kiosk and continued. "Their schemes advance in ways we simply cannot conceive with a limited mortal perspective. Spurinna once implied she was fabled Cassandra who foresaw the Trojan Horse crushing Troy and brave Aeneas fleeing the burning city to help found Rome. You believe they would leave their so-called inheritance for the future to chance? To those who can pass their test? If they wished their power to be absorbed by another, they would have groomed them from birth through the strands of fate."

"Do you believe you're immune to the strands of fate dictated by the Eternal Dreamers?" Megabyzus asked.

Nicomedes ignored the priest's taunt and entered the sacred chamber. He knelt down before the kiosk and placed his head upon the dusty floor. Egyptian doctrine contended the kiosk held blessed material from the gods, but her little brother seemed content to study the ground under it. Nicomedes closed his eyes and listened, as though the very earth would whisper secrets to him. Satisfied, he rose, sniffed the air, and beckoned for them to follow. "It is safe until the translocation circle is triggered."

Marcus stepped inside of the shrine. His usual bravado was strangely absent. "You've solved the mystery already, brother?"

"No. Not yet," Nicomedes admitted, as he caressed the stone walls, allowing his fingers to probe the engravings there. "But I have felt this energy before in the Luperical Cave. The Soothsayers step into a section of the cave and immediately transport themselves to the academy."

Hieroglyphics devoted to the gods and monsters of Egypt had

been carved into the stone over the centuries, much later than the structure had been built. Claudia pondered them for several minutes until she realized that they related a grand story celebrating the birth of a new god and the proper mortal offering and submissions to the new power in the universe. *Was this a sign of what was to come*, she wondered?

Marcus glanced about the room with a wide-eyed sneer. "This place will lead us to the Three Gates of Agony? Do we yet know what danger this shall pose?"

Megabyzus answered first. "In truth, we don't know what happens when the translocation circle is triggered. None have done so and survived."

Her elder brother crossed his arms and turned towards Nicomedes. "Did you know of this before we arrived, brother?"

"I highly suspected the Soothsayers would wish me to recover that which was lost in Egypt," Nicomedes explained without looking up from his work. "Mother has been preparing for this moment for a very long time."

The very mention of their mother brought a tick to her elder brother's face. "Mother! What does she have to do with this?" Marcus demanded.

Nicomedes gestured towards the kiosk. "That represents everything mother has sought since the Soothsayers rejected her entrance to the academy. I admit that clarity has eluded me until this very moment at the precipice of knowledge. The Three Gates of Agony present a test to determine if a mortal is worthy to gain the mystical power of the Eternal Dreamers."

"This is not a revelation, Magister Nicomedes," Megabyzus replied, with an undisguised air of superiority. "Anyone who has spent time at court has heard whispers of this."

Claudia blinked, realizing what her youngest brother was hinting at. "And does that include our mother?"

Megabyzus nodded, with his chest out and his chin firm with confidence. "Of course. I am the guardian, an aspect of Sobek. I often escort guests to the shrine."

"And you felt her power, yes?" Nicomedes asked.

"Indeed, it pained my eyes to lay them upon her," Megabyzus admitted. "Beautiful. Elegant. A giantess who walks the world of mortal men. I escorted her to the shrine several times and to the library. It seemed strange that she would be wed and chained to such a doddering old man, barely able to talk."

Claudia turned towards Marcus, hoping he had caught the nugget of valuable information. He raised his eyebrows and nodded. She placed her clammy hands upon her chest, as though to contain the beating of her heart. Was that joy for the suffering of the monster who tormented them, or anger that she had been absent the cause?

"You speak of Orca?" Marcus asked Megabyzus.

"Clearly the old gods and the new have great love for your mother." Megabyzus touched his head and bowed before the kiosk. "I am her junior in years, but I would have sworn upon my very soul that she was younger than Magister Nicomedes. Imagine her as a mother of four."

"You said mother of four?" Claudia asked.

Megabyzus blinked, as though sensing that there was danger about his words. "I have already met your youngest sibling, Caecilia. Barely able to walk, yet graceful beyond her years."

Claudia exchanged knowing glances with her brothers. If there was another sister, they needed to protect her, even if she was born of the tainted seed of Orca. If it was true that her mother ate her children as had been suggested, who knew what terror awaited their youngest sister.

She ignored the subject for now, promising herself she would revisit it when they were alone. "It seems strange that our mother would reveal her secret powers only to warn us against attempting to seize this power without her. Why?"

Marcus sneered. "She either has special insight about this room with which she wishes to bargain, or she is afraid we should seize her prize."

Megabyzus nodded in agreement. "She spoke quite confidently of her children and their potential. I knew as soon as Nicomedes entered the palace he could guide my own progress."

Adalia scowled. "What did Septima say when you asked her for patronage?"

Megabyzus coughed. "She laughed at me. Septima claimed she had to fight for every scrap of knowledge, and said if I wanted to achieve real glory in this world I would have to do the same."

Claudia placed her hands upon her hips. "We have no choice but to press forward. We know not if Octavius or Queen Arsinoë shall allow us in this shrine without complications. Mother has given us no reason to trust her, if she has prepared for this challenge. Absent our knowledge, she may be able to sway the outcome if she is present."

Marcus nodded reluctantly. "The Parthians have a number of reasons to seize Alexandria first on the way to Rome, but if they have magicians such as Nicomedes, then they surely would see this shrine as an asset. Egypt no longer has the knowledge or Megabyzus would have already seized upon it."

"I have held certain suspicions about mother that seemed unfounded until she was desperate enough to speak through us via the animus spell. The Soothsayers claimed I had the potential to grasp great power in time, if united with my family," Nicomedes explained. "Why they did not choose to come here and claim it for themselves is a mystery. Having examined the translocation circle, I believe I understand the reason they insisted all three of us must attend this mission."

Marcus groaned. "If you have the answer, brother, then enlighten us. Dealing in these secrets and mysteries hammers my brain."

Nicomedes gestured to the hieroglyphs and sigils carved into the rock. "Mother knew of this place, and if she is as wise as I believe, then she solved the puzzle of said tests long ago."

The language of land was a mystery to Claudia, but she learned enough about Egyptian culture to satisfy the curiosity of her clients through the writing of the Ptolemies, a line of Greek conquerors who formed a dynasty of mixed blood. Their influence dictated all official court documents were recorded in both Egyptian hieroglyphics and Greek. She had been quite interested in the Egyptian expression of the gods, and she memorized the symbols of the old gods along with their sigils. There was an overabundance of the presence of certain death gods in this story. Anubis and Ammit she expected, as they were masters of the realm, but Shezmu the Executioner gave her pause.

She had a queer feeling in the back of her neck, the same one she had when giving auguries and seeking the right words. "There are tales untold carved into the walls, brother. We should learn them to be better prepared for what we might face."

Nicomedes scoffed. "Such stories are merely a way to describe the divine to the uninitiated who cannot manipulate such power. It is immaterial. Do you think that the Soothsayers actually believe that mighty Hercules carved the landscape of Rome, or that the Hearth of Rome requires virgins to tend it?"

Claudia opened her mouth to argue, but then decided it would be a waste of time. Nothing could turn Nicomedes or Marcus from a decision once they believed they were right. She turned towards the hieroglyphs, trying to discern their meaning.

"Then you know how to access the power?" Marcus asked.

"Activating the translocation circle is simplicity itself. The key is the nature of the trap," Nicomedes explained. "I can only bring those bound to me by blood."

Claudia thought of the accusations against mother made from a safe distance by Decimus. "Hence she had to ensure there were three of us strong enough to face the Three Gates of Agony."

Marcus snapped his fingers and pointed to the spear and shield of the closet legionnaire. The soldiers immediately surrendered them to his centurion. “Run back to camp and acquire a legionnaire’s pack from Milius. Ensure it has enough supplies for a few days. I refuse to become an unwilling bride like Proserpina over a few pomegranate seeds.” The soldiers saluted and immediately disappeared down to the hall, running double time. Marcus turned towards Adalia. “It is vital this door remains open while we are gone, lest the Egyptians attempt to trap us there. Murder anyone who attempts to close it.”

Adalia folded her arms and raised her chin definitely. “You need me with you,” she protested.

“You are needed here as an anchor should we become lost,” Nicomedes explained. “The sexual energies between you and Marcus might help me pry open a doorway when it has been shut.”

Adalia blinked. Claudia resisted the urge to smile. Her youngest brother’s customary bluntness finally caught the amazon by surprise. “I would protect your family with my life.”

“And so you will, if you obey my commands,” Nicomedes said curtly. “Distract me not, lest we suffer the indignities of death due to inattentiveness.”

Marcus glanced from Adalia to Nicomedes, clearly confused at the strange tone of the conversation. He opened his mouth to complain, but Claudia placed her hand on his shoulders and shook her head.

Nicomedes beckoned Rubio to his side. “When the falcons return, you shall have to answer any questions that might arise. You know what to say?”

Rubio trembled. “Yes, magister.”

“Excellent. Perform well and you shall be rewarded, Rubio,”

Nicomedes promised. "If nothing else, it will ensure you outrank Megabyzus, should I survive to accept him as my apprentice."

Once the tired and breathless legionnaire returned with the pack, Adalia ushered the others out of the shrine. Marcus slipped it on and prepared his shield. He clashed the blade of his gladius against his shield three times and nodded, satisfied. "A good shield and a strong arm is all we shall need in this world or any other." He offered the spear to Claudia. "This is for your protection, dear sister."

She gingerly accepted it and tilted her head as though to study it. "I have no training in this weapon."

Nicomedes snorted. "Point the sharp end at the person you wish to end, sister."

"It can give you some leverage against an enemy long enough for me to protect you." Marcus extended his arm so as to demonstrate the advantage of distance in a melee. "It might delay any enemy for a few moments, which will hopefully be all that is needed to protect you with my blade. If only I could bring along some of the men, I'd feel better about leading you into danger."

"I endured great danger every night after you left me behind, brother," Claudia countered. "I suffered it bravely, knowing you faced danger out in the badlands. I did it knowing Nicomedes might be murdered at any moment in the academy. I joined the Vestal Virgins to buy us all time. I do not fear this Underworld. It is but one of many I've visited."

Marcus sheathed his gladius and then wrapped his free arm around her. "Never have I realized how strong you have become. Adalia said as much, but I did not believe her until this moment."

Claudia cast a curious glance towards Adalia, who merely shrugged. "This has indeed been a day of pleasant surprises, brother."

"Let us hope fortune continues to smile upon us into the next world," Nicomedes retorted.

Marcus nodded and raised his shield to cover Claudia, while Nicomedes knelt before the kiosk and placed his hand upon the ground. Pressure formed in the very air, pressing against their ears, making Claudia dizzy. Bolts of eldritch power crackled through the air like lightning, forming some sort of mystical web over their flesh, burning and shocking them into the darkness.

*   *   *   *

Claudia retched bile onto the sand. Her chest burned as she coughed, desperate to take a single breath to fill her lungs with soothing air. It felt as though every bit of breathable air had been transmuted into an oily mucus. A panic bubbled in her very blood as she struggled to breathe. She continued to vomit until her throat ached, worn raw from the acid in her stomach. Her eyes burned in the smothering darkness, yearning for the light. She felt around her, breathing finally once she ran her fingers through the sand. "Marcus? Nico? Can you see?"

Nicomedes called out in the darkness. "Fear not, sister. Light I can manage, if nothing else."

Emerald flashes of crackling energy burst into ephemeral globes of light, revealing the faint outline of delicate hands shaped to form strange symbols. They floated upwards to cast her younger brother's face in a pale light, making him appear almost skeletal. She gasped at the sight of it all.

Once the energy spheres reached a sizeable orbit above them, they exploded into dozens of lesser sparks and floated like leaves in an autumn wind. The emerald light reflected on the canopy formation above them, revealing giant stone fingers closed as though they were clutching the world.

Marcus coughed. Now that her eyes were adjusting to the light, she could see that he was standing next to Nicomedes. "Perhaps I have taken leave of my senses, but are we inside a giant stone hand?"

"It is said that Anubis judges all mortals who venture into the Underworld," Nicomedes said. "This realm is not a mere physical place, but a dimension where the symbology is more important than the laws of nature. The Eternal Dreamers created constructs designed to terrorize the weak of will and soul. We might as well be within the hands of a god, as far as we are concerned."

She often counseled petitioners about the afterlife and the wishes of her patrons' ancestors. Seeing the reality of it made her ashamed of the paltry words she'd spoken about it. Claudia wished to return to her life as quickly as possible. "Do you see the way to return?"

"I see only what you see, sister," Nicomedes said.

Claudia pushed herself up from the ground, dusted off her stola, and picked up the spear. *Perhaps it could be useful as a walking staff if nothing else*, she thought.

She thrust the point of the spear into the ground. To her surprise, it crunched as it struck something hard. Now that her eyes had adjusted to the light, it was much easier to explore. She poked the sand with her foot until she cleared a mess of sand, revealing the bleach-white bone of a skull.

Claudia reeled back, dropping the spear. Her hands shook and her lips trembled, until finally she could scream. "Marcus!"

Marcus pulled her backwards and stepped forward to shield her from danger, then laughed once he saw the skull. "It lacks the gumption to bite you, sister."

Nicomedes scooped a handful of the sand and then threw it at the horizon. It scattered into a fine, glittering mist. "It is not alone." The sand swirled into a wave of shimmering illumination that swarmed over the ground like a host of angry bees, seeking and locating dozens of rotten corpses in tattered, faded cloth. "Those who have failed the test of the Eternal Dreamers, I imagine."

Marcus unloaded the legionnaire's pack and unrolled it to reveal a cornucopia of medicine, rope, and other valuables. He found what he was looking for — a weathered leather flask — and held it high, as though it were victory laurels. "Milius, I shall see you promoted if it is the death of you." He sucked from the flask, wiped red wine from his lips, and passed it to Claudia. "Drink! It will flush that venom from your mouth."

Claudia did not need to be invited twice. She drank the wine, and never before had it tasted so sweet. "It felt like I swallowed death."

"Blood of the old gods long ago burned away, according to

legend," Nicomedes replied. "Or fluid from the sea that exists between worlds – a phenomenon I hope to study one night, should we survive." She offered the leather flask to Nicomedes, but he waved it away. He was too busy examining the remains. "They died decades ago, and not peacefully. Note the age of their weapons and armor."

"How long have they been here?" Claudia asked.

"Difficult to say exactly. Dermestid beetles are native to this part of the world, and the Egyptians use them in a number of their sacred places." Nicomedes dug his hands through the sand to closely examine one of the skulls. "I fear expending too much energy while here."

Marcus rolled up the pack and examined the weapons and armor. "Judging from the armor and weapons, I perceive ancient Romans, Egyptians, and even fabled Spartans."

Claudia asked the obvious question. "What killed them?"

Marcus grunted, as though to say that the answer should be obvious. "Nothing special by the look of it. I have seen all manner of deaths in this world — murderous and otherwise. By the nicks on the bones, nothing seems unusual. Typical wounds you would find from a blade or spear."

"I suspect we will find the answer there." Nicomedes pointed to the opposite end of the chamber, where there were dozens of ebony obelisks, covered with hieroglyphs. They were organized in a perfect formation, heading towards a large arch that had two crocodiles holding the roof. "That might be the first gate."

Claudia studied the closest obelisk with great interest. The hieroglyphics mirrored those she had found in the shrine from the royal palace. If she could decipher the hidden meaning locked in these stories, then perhaps they would learn clues about the so-called Three Gates of Agony.

Marcus glanced over her shoulder and sneered. "Typical dreck from a temple. The gods subjugate mortals into worshiping them. Never works. The world is ruled by the blade and flesh."

"If such were so, brother, then we would not be here, would we?" Claudia retorted.

"The powers wielded by Nicomedes are merely another weapon I fail to understand," Marcus said. "The means is unknowable, but the hand behind it is mortal and finite."

Nicomedes stepped close to the arch. "I feel the power this way."

The space under the arch shimmered, and the dead walked once more through it. The gibbering, hungry horde of the dead of the underworld shambled towards them, reaching for the warmth in their blood and their bones. Claudia felt a dread in her stomach as they approached. Their faces were withered, as though dried in the presence of a thousand suns, and yet she somehow sensed that they hungered for her very flesh. White and clouded eyes glowered ravenously at them.

Marcus raised his shield and waved for his sibling to move behind him. "Get back!"

The Gate of Agony was large enough that five men abreast could march without touching. Nicomedes extended his arms and commanded the elements in a powerful, terrifying voice. At his command, shards of sand and rock flayed their putrid flesh from their bones. Shimmering ribbons of yellow light shot from his fingers and exploded when they touched one of the dead.

Despite this awesome display of power, Nicomedes could not drive them away alone. The few that made it past the barrage were quickly put down into the dirt by Marcus. He bashed them backwards with his shield and then sliced and diced his way through their heads as opportunity presented.

Claudia held back, defending Nicomedes with her spear. Wielding the Art brought bouts of weakness to Nicomedes. The very act was a violation of nature, and it reasoned that there would be a cost to the flesh. She stood over him, defending him with her body and spear when the pain grew too much and Nicomedes staggered to the ground.

Marcus leaned against one of the obelisks, breathing heavily. "Is that all of them?"

Another wave of the dead came at them from the portal inside of the gate. Nicomedes blasted down their numbers with destructive mystical energies, and Marcus moved in to end their miserable existences quickly before they recovered and became serious threats.

This bloody cycle continued and repeated for more than an hour. The dead continued to charge fanatically at them in waves of twenty, thirty, or more. "Must we kill every soul in Tartarus?" Marcus asked.

She noted sheer exhaustion in his voice. He glistened with sweat, and his breathing was labored. Heavy fighting required rest between battles, or he would die from sheer exhaustion. Claudia once delighted in her brother's tales of battle, but now that she personally witnessed the trembling in his hands, the bleeding from minor cuts, and a savage wound on his thigh, the poetry of battle faded in light of the grim reality. If those were not dressed properly, and soon, he would quickly lose strength.

Nicomedes grimaced, his eyes focused upon the gate, lost in the power of his magic. He wielded the power of the gods in his mortal hands and seemed content in the moment. "This is a cauldron intended to purify our souls!"

This was not a situation that they could simply power their way through, and neither of her brothers would admit to this. Their egos would get all of them killed if she didn't find an alternative solution. Claudia glanced down at the warriors that had died here before. Why had they failed? What were they missing? The answer must be in the obelisk. *Why else have them?*

The prominence of Shezmu concerned her. He was the sacred executioner of the gods, striking down the unworthy. Yet, he was also a god of balance, serving neither the darkness or the light. If this was a test from the Soothsayers, then what did Shezmu represent to them?

She looked upon the images of Shezmu lording over the mortals as Marcus described. Her brother lacked finesse when it came to understanding theology. Could it really be so simple?

The first thing she learned as a Vestal Virgin was the gods were jealous and cruel. They wanted people to love and submit to them above all else. If the Eternal Dreamers wanted to ensure only the worthy took their power, would they not want someone who could submit to a higher power?

The very concept of submission was alien to Marcus and

Nicomedes. They understand power only as a means to conquer, not a subtle tool. Sometimes, you lost power the more you used it. What was the proper way to show humility to the gods here?

Claudia dashed back towards the pack and found the flask of wine. She turned towards her brothers just as the next wave of the horde entered through the gate. "Brothers! I have the answer."

"There is no time!" Marcus cried as he prepared for the fight. "We have more souls to send back to Tartarus!"

If they did not break the cycle, they would be overwhelmed. If not this time, then surely soon after. She knocked Nicomedes down to the ground to prevent him from spellcasting. The unexpected blow staggered him. He cursed, rolling in the dirt. Marcus raised his shield and gladius, holding on to a tactical position from which to protect the both of them. "Stay back!"

Claudia ignored his command. She dropped her spear and ran forward into oncoming onslaught. The hungry dead advanced reaching for her. She knelt and poured the flask of wine onto the sand. Then she bowed her head in humility and prayed.

"Claudia!" her brothers cried.

Marcus screamed, hoping to draw her attention before the dead set upon her. She ignored their warnings and extended her arms. Claudia tilted her head back to offer her neck as an honorable sacrifice. The dead ceased their relentless march. They turned towards each other and murmured together in a tongueless language. A deafening horn blasted from the portal, and the dead knelt in homage to their lord.

A terrifying monstrosity strode through the so-called sea between worlds. It had the pallor of death stained wine-red and wore a loin-cloth of sewn entrails. Claudia knew this beast from the obelisk and her hands trembled at the knowledge.

The dead stood at attention one by one as their master passed them on the way to reach Claudia. Shezmu towered over her menacingly. He sniffed the air and cackled, revealing horrific fangs. She could smell putrid flesh on his breath and imagined what he would do to her. She fought back tears; even in hell, she would not cry before her enemies.

Marcus ran forward to shield his sister. "Claudia!

She snapped her fingers and held up her hand, as though to command her brother to wait. If she spoke before being given permission, the sacrifice would mean nothing. *Please let Marcus understand*, she prayed.

Nicomedes waved his hand, catching Marcus with invisible threads. "Stop! Claudia engaged him. Interrupt and she may be flayed for eternity."

Her elder brother looked upon her, lost and helpless. Claudia nodded, as though to tell him that all would be right in this world and the next.

Shezmu cupped her face with its rough claws and turned her towards him to gaze into her eyes. He kissed her upon her forehead. It burned like acid, but she kept still and bit down upon her lips. The god laughed — it sounded like broken bones and cries of the damned. *"A worthy offer with a delectably sweet taste. To be kissed by Shezmu is to forever be loved by that which shall break you."*

And then Shezmu and the dead were gone. Marcus and Nicomedes lifted her to her feet. "Are you well?"

The whispers of the dead still reached her ears, but now she understood their speech and cried for a simple taste of the pleasure of life. "It will be some time before any of us can make such a claim."

"How did you do this?" Nicomedes asked, oblivious to her distress.

She blinked, trying to regain her sense of self. Claudia smelled death upon her brothers. She knew each of the lives they had claimed or would claim, and the cost frightened her.

Claudia answered their question, if only to focus her mind on anything else besides the screams. "You claimed that this was a test. If the Eternal Dreamers wanted someone to gain their power, they would only want someone they considered devout. This realm — a symbolic mystical construct of the Dreamers or the Underworld — works on the story logic of the myths, not numbers or formulas that you can quantify. That was Shezmu the god of blood and wine. I offered him submission in the only way he could understand."

Marcus flushed red. "We should have listened to you."

"I had not thought of this challenge in terms of myth and story." Nicomedes furrowed his brow and paced. "I had thought the concepts of the metaphysical tests were something the priests told themselves to believe they were worthy of the power."

"Who could believe someone would surrender this sort of power in the world?" Marcus added.

Claudia ignored their observations and found battle-field bandages within the legionnaire's pack. She cleansed and stitched her brothers' most grevious wounds and covered the rest as best that she could. The act of nurturing her family in this sacred place of death soothed her soul. It was a final defiance against Shezmu and the knowledge that she would always feel touched by that monster.

Nicomedes stood at the precipice of the Gate of Agony, waving his hand just short of it. "I believe we can face the next gate when you are ready."

Marcus nodded to Claudia and stood. His legs were shaky, Claudia noted, but she said nothing, as her hands quivered from terror and exhaustion. She rolled the pack into traveling order and tried to sling it over her back, but crumbled under the weight. *Adalia would have been able to take this weight*, she thought.

Her elder brother laughed and took it from her. The pain of shouldering the load forced him to grit his teeth. "I would sleep in a grand bed this night and fuck every whore in Egypt."

Claudia rolled her eyes. If she argued for carrying the pack, it would only wound his ego, and they all needed to believe they were invincible in this horrible realm — perhaps if they believed that they were immortal, then reality would bend to their will. "I would settle for returning to the land of the living."

Nicomedes gestured towards the gate. "And I would see that we reach the end of these insufferable challenges before we kill each other."

*   *   *   *

The distant roar of wind and tide could be heard. If she craned her head at just the proper angle, she could discern screams crying out for oblivion. The transference weighed lightly upon her lungs, and this time she felt no need to vomit out the sea between worlds.

Twin pillars of shimmering light illuminated their path through ebony obelisks, arrayed in a similar formation to the previous realm. She glanced upward, expecting to see the configuration of stone fingers, but instead discovered twin oval portals akin to mammoth eyes looking down upon an endless sea of sand. It was as though she was inside of the head of a giant gazing upon her dominion.

Her breathing intensified as panic struck, giving way to vertigo. She poked the spear downward to keep her sudden dizziness from causing her to crash down onto the ground.

Nicomedes' sharp voice snapped her back to reality. "Keep your eyes focused upon the horizon! The perspective can be deceptive, and in this realm that is as dangerous as the dead."

Marcus stumbled forward, dropping the pack. "I feel as though I am standing upon the shoulders of the Titans themselves," he grumbled.

Nicomedes pointed towards an array of obelisks. "I believe that the second test has been revealed. Observe!"

A behemoth-sized stone cauldron bubbled with a brew of steaming orange vapor, the likes of which Claudia imagined only could be found in Vulcan's foundry. The searing heat from the overflowing, burning liquid was sweltering.

Claudia felt drawn to the cauldron. Something inside of it beckoned to her. "What is that?" she asked.

"The essence of power," Nicomedes whispered with awe.

Marcus fumbled to his feet and drew his gladius once more. "Where is the gate?" Marcus asked.

Nicomedes held up his hand. "Patience, Brother. It should appear once this test has been successfully defeated."

Marcus set himself to guard them while they examined the area. Nicomedes stood before the cauldron, peering deep into the liquid, lost in thought. Claudia turned again to the obelisks.

This time the symbols referred mostly to Ammit the Soul-Eater. She was a goddess of truth trapped in a body that was part lion and crocodile — man-eaters. Her purpose in the Duat was the measurement of the soul, represented as an ostrich feather. "This test is about truth," she said with certainty.

Nicomedes grunted, as though he resented having to speak at all. "The power is contained in that cauldron. If only I could reach in there, I could seize it."

"That would burn your hand to the bone!" Claudia protested.

Marcus pursed his lips. "It would at that. Perhaps that is the test of these Eternal Dreamers. There is truth in pain. Darius taught me we see the world as it is when we suffer. A warrior has to acknowledge the pain his flesh must suffer, but also know the truth."

"What truth is that, brother?" Nicomedes asked.

Marcus laughed. "That pain is just an illusion."

Neither brother would ever admit to fearing pain. They would burn their bodies to ash before admitting weakness in front of the others. "All creatures feel pain," she protested. "How can that be false?"

"All animals feel pain. We are made of the logos," Marcus explained. "The divine spark of the universe gives us the ability to reason. Our reason is stronger than our pain, if our will is strong enough."

"The second gate shall not appear until summoned," Nicomedes said. He stepped closer to the cauldron, as though to test himself against the waves of heat that wafted from it. "I can feel the power there, and if I can touch it, just for a moment, it will be mine."

She flinched, imaging the suffering her little brother would have to endure to take that power. Claudia recalled well the moment of his birth, and when she was first allowed to hold him. It was the first life she had ever held in her hands. "Could you heal yourself aftwards? Or would you be immortal such as Achilles without the fatal flaw?" she asked.

"The process is bound to be intense," Nicomedes admitted. "I may not have the presence of mind to direct the power initially.

"Surely, this is part of the test. Could there be another method?" Claudia asked. "Perhaps you could simply will the power to come to you?"

Marcus shrugged. His shoulders slumped, resigned and dejected. "If there is an enemy to battle or outwit, I would feel happier, but this task is for Nicomedes to face. I have been to lands where warriors must prove themselves, enduring pain. Perhaps the Eternal Dreamers would know the mettle of the one who would claim their power."

"There is little choice now."

Claudia prepared the remains of the dressing from the pack to dress Nicomedes should he survive. Her hands tingled with sympathetic pain. She could not bear to look at her youngest brother and what this trial might do. Marcus stood grim-faced at the ready with a blanket to smother any fires that might happen.

Nicomedes stripped down out of his robes to a cotton loincloth. His arms were thin, surprisingly feminine, but strong. He closed his eyes for a moment, murmuring words of arcane power Claudia did not understand, and when he opened them once more they were black as coal — smoldering and ready to burn.

He delved his hand into the molten liquid and screamed as did Prometheus when the vulture consumed his liver. His flesh sizzled and blackened. And yet, she felt an explosion of the divine — power the likes of which seized upon her heart.

His scream turned into something inhumane and profane. The ecstasy etched upon his face was akin to the oracles of Delphi prophesying the future. "I have touched the logos!"

Marcus knocked Nicomedes back with the blanket, flapping it against the flame that consumed his flesh. To their surprise, Nicomedes did not flinch or scream, but tilted his head back with his lips quivering.

Claudia covered her nose, least she retch from the smell of cooked flesh. She couldn't look directly at him, lest she weep. The knowledge that she allowed him to make this attempt sickened her. "Does he live?" she asked.

Marcus stepped back as a burnt, skeletal hand waved him away. The flesh of the arm appeared as though it belonged to one of the burnt dead creatures that had attacked them in the other realm, yet to seemed to possess the full mobility of a healthy, living arm. Her eyes swelled with tears to see the suffering of her brother. The arm was hideous, as though it belonged to a beast that crawled out of Tartarus.

Nicomedes spoke calmly, but his voice was deeper than normal. "The pain is gone."

Their youngest brother arose from the ground. His hideous arm motioned and maneuvered without difficulty. Claudia bit down upon her lips to prevent herself from retching. "My power sustains this dead thing," Nicomedes stated.

He reached out with his dead hand towards the end of the room and pantomimed pulling something down to the ground. The second Gate of Agony appeared before them. "I have the power. Let us see what new fresh hell this place can bestow upon us."

* * * *

Tides of energy and waves of power swirled around them — Claudia felt them upon her skin like a warm wind during the final days of autumn. The ceiling was an oddly shaped dome that seemed to constrict and expand like a fist. She noted that the borders of the realm were curved like an oddly-shaped inverted pear.

She winced that it had not been obvious to her from the start; she had felt enough hearts from her haruspexy. Claudia felt the edge of the chamber and jerked her hand back. It was flesh and muscle, as though from the inside of a human heart.

There were no windows to the outside, only the sound of energy and souls pumping through an unknown system. Eldritch light shimmered from the center of the chamber, hidden behind gargantuan towers of muscle and flesh. *Those must be the arteries of this metaphoric heart*, she thought.

The light emanated from a dais of flesh, upon which was a throne made of weeping skulls. The figure that claimed the honor of this seat was a man with a physique powerful enough to shame Atlas. His head was that of a snarling jackal. Claudia recognized this ethereal being from his sigils: Anubis, Lord of the Dead.

Nicomedes sneered and dismissed the figure before them with a gesture with his dead hand. "Remember this is an artifact of this test, not a real god. I can see the energy that animates it as plain as sunlight."

The power of the of the theoretical artifact's voice shook them. Their words displeased it. "Respect!"

Claudia recalled what she learned of this aspect of Pluto, Lord of the Underworld in Rome. He judged the hearts of those who sought to pass on to heaven, and he consumed the unworthy. "Which of you will submit to judgment? Which of you has the bravest heart?" Anubis demanded.

Nicomedes laughed. He summoned azure flames that flickered over the fingers of his dead hand. "I have the power to crush him."

Anubis snarled and pointed to Nicomedes from the throne of bones. "Test me not, Dreamer, or I shall consume your heart and cast your soul into the darkness. I smell great power, but you have yet to master that which you have taken."

"Then test my soul," Nicomedes commanded.

Claudia and Marcus shouted. "No!"

"Do you think I am unworthy?" Nicomedes snapped.

Claudia thought of what Nicomedes had done as a child to their cat and decided to avoid answering the question. "I think you are driven. I am a Vestal Virgin. I am pure."

Marcus stepped forward and raised his palm to halt them both. "No, sister. This test is not about purity. It is about courage. And who better amongst us than I?"

The Lord of the Underworld sniffed the air and licked his snout as though hungry for the hunt. "Are you ready?"

Marcus unbuckled his armor and dropped it. He slipped out of his tunic and offered his bare chest. "The heart of the Valeria is pure."

"We shall see."

Anubis plunged his hand into Marcus' chest and ripped out his heart. Marcus fell to the ground, dead. Anubis sniffed the heart and then savagely consumed it. Claudia screamed and ran to the body of her elder brother. A pregnant silence stilled the chamber. Claudia looked to her brother's face, noting the pallor of his skin and his dead eyes. "Is he worthy?" she asked.

"The sacrificed heart of a hero is always worthy."

Claudia tilted her head, trying to understand the meaning of these words. Gods had different definitions of the term worthy, than that of mere mortals.

Nicomedes narrowed his eyes at Anubis. "Then we have passed this test. Raise him," he commanded.

"I am only a construct as you said, Dreamer," Anubis explained. "You now have the ability and power to leave this realm and take your place amongst the worthy."

"What of my brother?" Nicomedes asked.

"He shall venture to the Underworld as a hero."

Nicomedes remained defiant. "No. He is needed here."

"Others will take his place in service to you, Dreamer," Anubis explained. "You will rise in glory, and nations shall be yours to shape."

"Raise him," Nicomedes commanded once again.

"His heart is gone. It is impossible to cheat death in that way." If it were possible for a jackal to smile, Anubis managed it. "Unless you are a Dreamer."

Nicomedes scratched his chin thoughtfully, pondering this final test. "There may be a way to bring Marcus back to us."

"What is it, Nico?" Claudia asked

"If we wish our brother to live, I must give him my heart," he explained.

"How is that possible? Will you not die?" Claudia asked.

A tight-lipped smile crossed her younger brother's face. "The power within me shall keep me alive, much like this dead arm. Marcus will live, but there will be consequences."

Claudia felt her lip tremble. Tears welled in her eyes. She no longer cared if anyone saw her cry, as long as Marcus was safe and living. "Do it! It doesn't matter what the consequences are, so long as both of you survive."

Nicomedes raised his dead hand, slowing flexing each of the burnt fingers, as though verifying his control over them. It glowed with eldritch energies. He took a final breath and then plunged his hand into his own chest, emerging with a palpitating black heart.

The magic he stole from the Eternal Dreamers kept him alive. Nicomedes studied his heart for a moment, as though fascinated, and then knelt down beside Marcus. "This shall forever bind us. Only for you would I do this."

He plunged his heart into the empty cavity that in the chest of his dead elder brother. A spark of life enveloped the two of them, broadcasting a light so intense Claudia was forced to look away.

Marcus gasped for air and opened his eyes.

Claudia wept.

Chapter Ten: Argue Not Against the Sun

Marcus Valerius Perseus dared not open his eyes, not yet, but his other senses told him the ritual to return them to the land of the living worked. The air tasted fresh and real in a way that he never before noticed. The familiar musky scent triggered memories of the royal palace and the sea. The hard cadence of bootsteps in the halls outside of the shrine revealed that guards were posted at the entrance as he had ordered. This fact suggested that Milius and Adalia had managed to keep the area secure while he was away.

He opened his eyes and crowed upon seeing beams of sunlight from the hall. "Legionnaires, attend me!"

Two Roman soldiers leaned into the entrance, poking their heads into the room. One of them was Probatus Cossus of the Third Cohort of the Seventh Legion. "Centurion! We thought you were dead!"

Marcus laughed and dropped the legionnaire's pack and his chest armor. They clanged with a powerful force that made everything seem grounded. Claudia had bandaged the wound over his chest as best she could, but the injury was still visible. There would always be a scar from where his heart was ripped out of his chest. "You think I am a shade after a mere hour or two? Such lack of faith in me brings a tear to my eye."

Cossus saluted and remained at attention. "You and your family have been gone for three days, centurion."

Marcus glanced aside towards his family.

Claudia was not injured physically during the ordeal, but the horrific experiences were reflected in the pallidness of her skin. Nicomedes seemed to possess the bloom of health with the exception of his arm. He allowed Claudia to bandage it, not because it was wounded, but because he wished no one else to see it. Marcus had seen many wounds, from fire and otherwise, and he could not believe a limb so burned through skin and muscle to the bone could move about in such a manner.

He ran his fingers down the scar upon his chest. The imprint of his brother's hand was forever burned into his skin, although it had mostly healed. A desperate jubilation swelled in his throat. "Summon forth the palace physicians. My family is injured. And bring Milius. Once I am debriefed, I shall require access to the best whores in the city."

The other legionnaire saluted. Marcus failed to recognize him, so presumed he was a member of the palace guard under the command of Octavius. "Centurion, we have been ordered to take you directly to court. Our finest physicians and priests are there in consultation with the governor, and they will certainly see to your needs."

Claudia ran her fingers through her hair. "Surely Governor Octavius would not object to us cleaning ourselves before we present ourselves to him."

Cossus swallowed and stuttered an interjection. "Forgive me for speaking out of turn, centurion. The Parthians have crossed the Red Sea. We believe it might be only days before they come at Alexandria from the east. We were given explicit orders to bring you to the governor willingly or in chains immediately."

Nicomedes laughed — it was a hard, bitter, mocking sound that was totally inhuman. His younger brother was always harsh, but this was different. *Had the power of the Eternal Dreams already changed him*, he wondered. He pulled Marcus from the very edge of the abyss and gave him life with his will alone. "We should simply acquiesce to the command, brother. We do not wish to be put in chains."

Claudia cleared her throat. "If we have truly been gone for three days, there is no telling what has happened since then."

Could they have won the prize only to lose the war? Claudia was correct, of course, protocols and discipline were their best weapons here and now. "Very well." He pointed to the unknown legionnaire with the Sabine jawline and the sandy hair of the people of the Rhine, presumably from the Eighth Legion. "Is that how you address a centurion?"

The legionnaire snapped to attention. "First Spear Coriolanus of the First Cohort of the Eighth Legion, centurion."

Marcus gestured to his belongings on the ground. "You will assign one of your men to take these back to my quarters. Once there, they are to command Optio Milius to attend to my needs at court. He is to bring along Adalia."

"Optio Milius is already at court, centurion," Probatus Cossus interrupted. "He is helping organize the Third Cohort towards the city's defense."

Of course, Milius would be defending the city to ensure the gate back would be open if nothing else. "Then ensure Adalia is there." It was unlikely the Romans or Egyptians would have anything to do with her in public court if it could be avoided. "I would have news from her."

"And my student Rubio." Nicomedes interjected softly. The sheer power behind his soft voice forced both soldiers to flinch. He raised his dead hand to chest level, indicating the boy's height. When they noticed the shriveled hand, Nicomedes smiled enigmatically. "A short, fat boy not good for much but making deliveries. I have need of him immediately."

The soldiers simply stared, confused. Marcus snapped his fingers to catch their attention. "You have your orders. See to them."

Coriolanus flashed a salute in acknowledgement. "Yes, centurion."

"I presume that Centurion Ahenobarbus is present as well at court?" Marcus asked.

"Yes, centurion."

"Then let us proceed."

Marcus took the lead, refusing any offer of assistance from Claudia. He tried to keep from looking into her eyes, where he still saw fear and pity. *Tears are better spent upon the dead*, he thought.

He clapped the legionnaire upon the back and laughed as they entered the hall. His head felt light. Too much had happened and he felt strange breathing air as though he were a normal man, one who did not contain his brother's heart in his chest. A wellspring of laughter had been trapped in his throat since he first opened his eyes in his second life. It was as though his body needed to feel mirth to live.

His gladius clanged against his leg as he spun around towards his siblings. It was against protocol to meet a general or governor outside of the battlefield while armed. Neither legionnaire dared to ask for his gladius. Their eyes lingered upon his bare chest, where several cotton bandages had been stained with black blood; any soldier knew it came from the heart. Such wounds were always fatal on the battlefield.

Anubis had ripped his heart from his flesh and left him to the Underworld. He had felt the sweet wind of the Elysium Fields upon his face for a glorious eternity. A voice called to him. He believed it was his father for a brief moment, until the withered hand of Nicomedes thrust into the hole in his chest and seeded a new heart that quickly took root.

Marcus recalled the shocking sensation with a shiver. The weight of the heart chained his soul to his body. It felt wrong immediately, a foreign object in his body, keeping him alive. His brother's fingers felt like death, more bones than flesh. "We have always been of two minds, brother. Now we are of one heart."

Nicomedes defeated the Three Gates of Agony and absorbed the mystical energies of the Eternal Dreamers, practically ensuring his apotheosis. Yet he surrendered the core of his being, his heart, to keep Marcus alive. Had he crushed his brother's chance to be a Soothsayer? Nicomedes explained the power he absorbed would keep his flesh alive just as it maintained his dead arm. It boggled Marcus' soul that his youngest brother was now no more than a shade kept alive by the stolen power of the Eternal Dreams.

Their lives were now forever linked. Nicomedes was limited to the mortal lifespan of Marcus until he discovered a suitable replacement for his heart. What did that mean for the future? How far could they be apart? What if he died on the battlefield? What would that mean for Nicomedes?

But all these questions were secondary to another, deeper query – one that left dread in Marcus' still-beating heart. Why did Anubis declare him unworthy? Was he secretly a coward? He faced death many times at the hand of his enemies, always terrified until overcome with heat of battle. Would his taste for fleshly delights fade until he was a sexless statue like his younger brother?

The familiar sharp snap of the lash quickly followed by the scream of the guilty forced him from the prison of his thoughts. To hear such a sound in the royal palace felt wrong. Such punishment was common for deserters or traitors out in the field. "First Spear Coriolanus, is that the sound of a man being scourged?"

The legionnaire blanched. Witnessing a scourging was not easy even for those comfortable with bloodletting. "Governor Thurinus decreed that Megabyzus would receive lashes every day that you and your siblings were gone from this place or until he died."

The servants of the royal palace crowded around the arch that led into hall, seeking an illicit peek at the deeds of the court. The guards watched the crowd with lazy interest until First Spear Coriolanus tapped them angrily. They spun around with malicious intent until they gazed upon Marcus and his siblings. Then their jaws dropped with fear.

Marcus scoffed and commanded they part the crowd with a mere gesture. He stepped out into the hall as though he was commanding his cohort upon the battlefield – powerful with life and death in his hands.

Megabyzus screamed at the snap of the cat of nine-tails. The priest hugged the large stone column at the edge of the court, where he was chained in place. Milius grimaced as he continued his work upon the crimson pulp that once was the back of Megabyzus.

He felt as much pity for Milius as he did Megabyzus. The last time the Third Cohort of the Seventh Legion had to discipline a man in such a fashion, they spent the night away from the men drinking to strike the horrid memory of it. This was a public punishment to remind everyone that Octavius was in charge here and that to disobey him was disobeying the gods. He turned to his siblings, seeking advice.

Nicomedes shrugged his shoulders, as though to imply this was beneath his concern and Marcus should simply resolve it. "I need Megabyzus to contain and control the energy from the Eternal Dreamers. He has studied these arcane energies and may have some insight into how these foreign Soothsayers acquired it."

Claudia whispered into his ear. "He is a Caesar, but even he must bow to the will of the gods if it is presented properly."

Marcus kissed his sister upon her forehead and strode towards Megabyzus. Milius looked up between blows and stopped once he noticed him. The old man's shoulders were slumped together, and he was breathing exceptionally hard.

"Why have you stopped?" demanded Octavius.

The royal palace court reminded Marcus of the Senate Curio room with its curved walls and vaunted seated positions outlining the perimeter. The influence of Octavius in the design was obvious. He might have ruled Egypt for ten years, but in his heart, he was still a Roman, despite the Egyptian iconography.

The noted difference, which would never be tolerated in Rome, was a raised dais in the center with two golden thrones resting upon it. There sat Gaius Octavius Thurinus, Governor of Egypt and heir to the Roman Empire. He was a stern, thoughtful-looking man of four decades with thin brown hair and a prominent brow. He wore his armor, that of a general of Rome.

By his side sat Queen Arsinoë IV of Egypt. It was said her sister Cleopatra was the most beautiful woman in the world, able to charm both mighty Caesar and Marcus Anthony. She wore an elegant golden gown so beautiful that the ladies of Rome would weep at the knowledge that it was not made in the Eternal City. Arsinoë was a handsome if reserved woman, perfect for a man who valued propriety.

Milius coughed, uncomfortable with the attention. He looked to Marcus for permission to speak, and it was granted with a simple nod. "Governor Thurinus, I am merely following your orders. You commanded each day I personally scourge Megabyzus in court until the return of Centurion Marcus Valerius Perseus and his siblings." He saluted his commanding officer. "I present him to you here and now, along with Claudia Valeria Terza and Magister Nicomedes Valerius Corvus."

A collective gasp escaped from the court at once, sounding like the roar of the sea. Marcus studied their faces. A proper example of the whole Egyptian empire was represented in this room - from the Nubians and Temehu, to the descendants of the armies of Alexander the Great. He noted the nobles were seated opposite of the priests. Legionnaires and Egyptian soldiers lined the hall. He had withstood such a mob while serving in the legions — furious and ready to explode into violence.

Claudia tapped his shoulder and leaned close to point towards the collection of Egyptian nobles. His eyes followed her finger until he caught sight of their mother. The youth of her face would have made him believe that he was her elder by several years, if he did not know that she birthed him. The tired husk of the man who once terrified him as a boy slumped next to her. With his large belly and withered bones, Quintus Valerius Orca was a threat now only to his drink and meals. He found himself delighting in the sight of it.

Octavius nodded towards his guards. Their tribune tapped the butt of his spear three times onto the ground, silencing the crowd. "Heed the words of Gaius Octavius Thurinus, Heir to the Empire, Governor of Egypt."

Marcus knelt as he would before the imperator, despite his wounds. Claudia and eventually Nicomedes followed his lead.

Octavius waited a moment, allowing the crowd to digest the symbolic gesture of supplication. He had clearly learned oration from his adopted father's knee and knew well how to bend a crowd to his will. He spoke slowly and deliberately, as though explaining how he wanted a meal to a stupid slave. "Centurion Marcus Valerius Perseus, what do you have to say for yourself?"

He recalled his lessons from Sextus Clodius, the renowned Sicilian rhetorician who had once taught oratory to Antony himself. Sextus

Clodius recommended such open-ended questions to trap your opponents into a corner. It forced your enemy to pick a position and defend it, and then you had time to use their words against them. Whatever was said would be determined to be wrong in some fashion.

Marcus turned his back upon the governor, and the crowd murmured over the insult. He turned to Milius. "Optio, if this centurion has displeased the governor in how he acted to strengthen the Empire and save the city of Alexandria, then you will remove this wretch and scourge me until the proper apologies have been made. Megabyzus acted upon the orders of myself, given authority under the Imperial Seal. All that has been done under my name is my responsibility."

Octavius stood, casting his drink upon the ground, a symbolic gesture to demonstrate his anger and his authority here. His guards raised their weapons in response, ready to kill them all upon a single word from the governor. "Do you think to rob me of my right to punish those who have broken the law?"

Marcus cast his eyes towards the ground with false humility. "I merely wish to serve the Empire. If I have displeased you in the manner by which I have attempted to perform my duty, then I would rend the very flesh from my bones."

Octavius returned to his throne. The tension dissipated, and the guards relaxed their grip on their weapons. "Tell us how you have served the Roman Empire and Alexandria this day?"

Octavius blessed him with an opportunity to state his case without arguing against the governor's words. There was hope he could provide a proper justification that would work to both of their advantages. Marcus tried to imagine how Claudia would have said the next statement, and hoped he had the tongue for such sophistry. "Imperator Gaius Julius Caesar received word from the Soothsayers that Egypt would face a worthy challenge, and that his son would achieve a great victory if he were to receive wisdom from Rome in time."

"And Rome sent three siblings to halt six legions from Parthia?" Octavius asked. "My father must have great faith in me."

Claudia stepped forward and bowed before the thrones of Egypt. "Governor Thurinus, please forgive the rudeness of my interruption. Our present appearance does no credit to my family. I have been sent to carry a spark of Rome to great Alexandria as a Vestal Virgin. You have been chosen as the champion of Rome to defeat Parthia."

"You violated the law set forth by Queen Arsinoë," Octavius stated. "The shrine of the gods is sacrosanct without the presence of their divine avatar on Earth. You defied earthly law as well as divine, and Arsinoë as Isis must judge you."

The problem became clear. They had violated a taboo and disrespected the Queen. Octavius likely did not believe in the mystical power of such a place. If he wanted to rule this land without constant bloodshed, the governor had to appease those under him. They had to present an argument that would allow Octavius to forgive them, while protecting his dignitas and allowing them to turn to the matter of protecting Alexandria.

Nicomedes knelt to the thrones of Egypt with his dead hand firmly upon the ground and visible to all. "Governor Thurinus, may I speak?"

The flock of priests to the right of Octavius chortled. Their leader was a tall, gaunt man with a small nose and shifty eyes. He wore gold from his headdress to the buckles in his sandals. "What right does the imperator's catamite have to speak of the business of Egypt?"

"Any right that I grant him, Typhaon," Octavius stated. "And you would do well to remember this, lest you receive the same punishment as Megabyzus."

"Is that man under your protection, governor?" Nicomedes asked calmly.

Octavius studied Nicomedes for a moment. He looked at the withered hand, clearly curious as to how it still moved deftly. "You are a magister of the Soothsayer Academy, yes?"

"I have that honored distinction, governor," Nicomedes answered. "And I am a favored friend of your father."

"What would you do if I said the mighty Typhaon is the high priest of Alexandria, and thus under the protection of myself?"

"Governor Thurinus, I have heard of your exploits and your keen mind. Even if you were not in command of Egypt, if such a man were under your protection, I would not harm him," Nicomedes said.

"Harm me? That pathetic gimp can no more strike the sun out of the sky then dare to think that he can touch my person," Typhaon called out. The priests harrumphed at his words. "I beg of you, Governor Thurinus, let the boy try to harm me, and he shall learn of the power of Egypt."

Octavius was unmoved. "What would you do if I gave you

permission to act?"

"I would present you with a taste of the power I took from this land – the very power the Parthians would seize and leverage against you and Rome. The very power these charlatans could not leverage, due to their feeble minds. I would show you how their boastful promises almost burned this ancient city to the ground."

Typhaon crowed. "You dare to challenge me!" His fingers rose into a weird arcane formation. "I'll skin your other arm!"

Nicomedes did not speak. Instead, he calmly waited for Octavius to deign to reply, as though the words of anyone else, especially the priests, meant nothing. They laughed and taunted him from a distance, hoping to break his composure.

Marcus firmly gripped the hilt of his gladius. The guards noted this gesture and responded in kind. He hoped his younger brother would have leaned more upon the reputation of the Soothsayers rather than antagonize the local priests, who clearly carried a great deal of political weight in Alexandria.

Octavius sighed, as though the matter was completely out of his hands. "If Typhaon refuses my protection as the high priest of Alexandria, then it is his concern, so long as my laws are obeyed and he is not killed."

The priest began to murmur and shake some sort of golden idol towards them. Nicomedes raised his dead hand towards Typhaon and spun his wrist, as though flicking something towards him. Silver strands of mystical energy shot out from his withered fingers and snaked across the room, until they struck Typhaon. They wrapped around him like one of their infamous ceremonial mummies and dragged him to the ground, wiggling and crying like a worm.

Nicomedes turned his attention towards the thrones. "By your will, Governor Thurinus. It is important to my family to obey your will in all matters concerning Alexandria."

"Governor, we came to Alexandria under orders from your father," Marcus said, hoping to change the tone of the conversation. "I have the imperial seal in my diplomatic pouch, along with a personal letter to you. May we confer in private so that we might relay his wishes and other information which may help you better defend this city?"

Octavius seemed to consider the matter. He glanced over towards Typhaon, who was fighting the mystical restraints. The priests were weakened politically and hardly in a position to present a problem for the moment. Queen Arsinoë whispered into his ear. They quietly spoke for several moments and once they reached an accord, they turned towards the court.

The governor of Egypt stood. The remainder of the court did likewise. "Queen Arsinoë and I shall hear your words in private after court. Megabyzus is granted a stay of punishment by Queen Arsinoë pending private considerations."

"You have our eternal gratitude," Marcus said.

Queen Arsinoë joined her husband standing before the dais. "We formally grant you permission to return to your quarters for recuperation." She did not mention the word bathe, but it was certainly implied in the tone. "Guards, escort our guests back to their quarters and ensure that every honor and comfort is given unto them, until they are summoned."

Marcus showed her proper honor as a sovereign and knelt once more. Gratitude swelled in his throat. This encounter could have gone so much worse had the sovereigns wished it. "My gratitude, mighty Queen of Egypt."

"May we bring Megabyzus with us?" Nicomedes asked. His voice sounded strange, trying to be humble and contrite. "I would apply my own limited knowledge upon him."

Octavius nodded his approval to the legionnaires, and Milius unchained the poor bastard. Megabyzus stumbled to his knees. His back had been savaged. His muscles has been torn and ripped asunder.

Nicomedes placed his dead hand in the muck that was once skin and muscle. Megabyzus yelped from the pain, but when Marcus' younger brother removed his hand, the muscles had somehow knitted themselves together and the skin began to recover, growing anew. "Enjoy a taste of the life-force stolen from Typhaon. It will not last, but it should soothe your injuries until I can apply the proper salves."

Once they exited the court, they heard the tribune tap his spear three times once again to hear the very next business on the docket. The noise of the court quickly elevated once more, as the nobles and priests restarted an old argument.

They met Cossus coming from the opposite direction, with Adalia and Rubio in tow. Adalia was less than pleased. "You are late!"

"We did defeat the Egyptian Lord of the Underworld," Marcus protested weakly.

Adalia ignored his quip and offered her arm to Nicomedes. He waved her away and beckoned Rubio to come closer. "Yes, magister?" the boy spoke, hopefully.

"Did any of the falcons return, boy?" Nicomedes asked, irritated.

Rubio answered quickly. "Yes, and I heard them speak, magister."

"Both of them?" Nicomedes asked, cautiously.

"Yes, magister."

"What was their response, Rubio?" Nicomedes asked.

"For the Senate and the people of Rome."

That meant that the message was received, and that soon help would be coming to Alexandria. "Then the dice is cast," Marcus said.

"What does this mean?" Claudia asked, clearly annoyed that her brothers were keeping secrets from her. "To whom did you send the message?"

"Such news should be shared privately, sister," Marcus said with mirth. They now had a chance to defend Alexandria, and wanted nothing more than to celebrate. "Know this. We have great leverage now, and the tide of battle promises to be favorable on the morrow."

The Third Cohort of the Seventh Legion cheered upon the return of their centurion, as seemed appropriate to Marcus. They clapped him upon the back, which he tolerated through strained smiles. His chest and back ached — the thing that Nicomedes placed in there seemed foreign, but he could feel it palpitate, keeping him alive.

Claudia called for the palace servants. "Prepare the baths."

A lovely Egyptian girl gestured towards the apartments. "We prepared the balneums once we heard of your return, domina. Would you follow us?"

Claudia looked over her shoulders before she left. "Do not dally, brothers. We have a brief respite, but the hour of the queen and the governor's arrival is not yet known."

Marcus agreed and turned towards Adalia. He needed to speak of what happened to him, and of all of the people in the world, she was the only one he felt he could unburden himself upon. "I could use a friend to wash my back."

She glanced aside towards Nicomedes and shook her head almost reluctantly. "We have shared much in this world, but I believe that part of our life together has ended. It pleased me to help you find your true beginning with Drusilla, but now I must look to my future."

It had been the wisdom of her heart that he sought, but Adalia's rejection stung his chest. Marcus recalled well their first kiss at the encampment near the Gaul front and the passion that quickly followed in his tent. He fucked many slaves and timid patrician girls before enlisting in the legion. Adalia initiated him to the mysteries of intoxicating intimacy and the delights of the flesh.

She blinked, clearly uneasy with this topic. Had he finally managed to rile the ever stalwart Adalia? "I would not wish to place my body in a place different than my heart," she stated not unkindly. "Would that shatter the bond we share?"

He pursed his lips to hide his disappointment. He shook his head and then wrapped his fingers around the top of her head like a crown and pulled it down to his lip. He kissed Adalia upon her forehead, much like he would Claudia. What happened between her and

Nicomedes was a mystery to him, but he could not deny her a chance at happiness, even if he imagined it would end bitterly. Vulcan himself could not shatter that which binds us."

She embraced him with a strength that surprised and almost staggered him. Once he released her, Adalia quickly went to Nicomedes to examine his arm. The skin on the younger brother's arm had blackened into the bone, but she did not blanch. Nicomedes handed her a salve, which she began to apply to the surface without flinching. "Do not fear harming me. The flesh is already dead, but maintained through my magic. I feel no pain," he explained. "This salve shall preserve the remains of the flesh and keep it from rotting. The stench would be foul indeed, otherwise."

"Is there nothing we can do?" Adalia asked.

Nicomedes flexed his dead hand. "This is the price willingly paid for power. But, I will need your assistance in treating Megabyzus. The deed must be done quickly or he shall forever lose much of his mobility. His value to us would be forever diminished."

Marcus turned towards Milius. "It would appear I shall need a bathing companion. Perhaps two. Conquering death tends to awaken baser appetites."

Milius forced a smile. Marcus supposed the memory of the scourging was too fresh in his old friend's mind. "I'll arrange it immediately."

*   *   *   *

His skin felt alive once Marcus dipped into the warm water. It seemed divine, as though the sins of the world were cleansed from his very soul. He allowed the two slaves to wash his body, but almost stopped them when they touched his chest. He flinched by reflex, afraid to let any other touch him there.

A lithe bathing attendant with a shaved head had a beautiful smile with lips he wanted to kiss. She tilted her head coyly and drew her hands to her breasts. Her words were soft and musical, but he did not understand more than a few words of Egyptian.

His shoulders slumped from exhaustion. Despite his boasts, he did not wish to be touched. He stopped their amorous advances and shook his head. They looked at each other and whispered fearfully. "You have not displeased me. I am simply tired. Dim the lights. I wish to soak in meditation."

Marcus sank back into the water and waved them out. They snuffed out the candles and left. He closed his eyes for the first time since he returned to the world and tried to let everything go. The last time he cried was the day they put his father into the ground. He allowed his head to sink beneath the water and sobbed.

It felt safe, much like he imagined the womb felt to the unborn. Not his mother's, of course, but he imagined other women's were noble. He imagined Drusilla pregnant with his child. Would she still love him, now that his body was not perfect? He had once been as close to perfect as a mortal could be: beautiful as a boy and handsome as a man.

Drusilla had chased him for his beauty when they were children.

He snubbed her advances because of her foot. The very idea that her family had a taint from the gods signaled they were beneath his perfection. She came upon him crying the day they buried the great Titus Valerius Perseus.

Orca had already taken over as paterfamilias of the Valeria, and Decimus had the good grace to somewhat hide his gloating. Their mother changed her name to Septima Valerius Orca and refused to see anyone due to her grief. Marcus Livius Drusus Claudianus invited all the children of Titus to his villa outside Rome for a time of grieving.

They played and danced in his olive orchards for his last summer of childhood. Drusilla lost her mother the previous winter, and she was glad to have company. Rumors of her deformity caused many parents to forbid their children to acknowledge her, for surely such an affliction was a sign of devotion from Vulcan. The wealth of the Claudians leant weight to the rumor, but none wanted the taint of his favor.

Marcus hated the sight of her at the time without knowing why. The boy he once was had been a terrible monster no less than the infamous Minotaur. His father had been born to the agnomen Perseus. It spoke of his heroic ideals and the desire to conquer monsters. He was known by the agnomen Pulcher, meaning beauty, and it had been his pride.

It would have been natural for Marcus to have taken his new step-father's agnomen. Mother asked him to do it for the health of the family, to show that there was unity and love within the Valeria.

Livius came to him as a friend of his father. He had changed his own agnomen for his own adopted father and counseled Marcus to follow the tradition for his own protection. Such devotion would reveal a deep respect for Orca, but Marcus could not surrender that final indignity to him — not when he knew that his uncle had murdered his father.

It was after that conversation, when Marcus felt alone with the great weight of responsibility to take care of his younger siblings, that Drusilla brought him sweet honey cakes. She read to him one of the early scrolls of the Aeneid — the part where Aeneas lead the Trojans to Latium, where he met the beautiful Lavinia, daughter of King Latinus.

He read every new book from Virgil until the Aeneid saga had been completed. He consumed the final book while patrolling the shores of Gaul. The boy he was could not understand why Drusilla read this part, only that he was glad for the company. In truth, it had not been Drusilla's affliction that cast his affections against her, but when she saw him that day and wiped away those tears.

A thought occurred to him. If the Soothsayers could heal her foot, could they not heal the scar upon his chest? Perhaps they could even sever the link between himself and Nicomedes and give him a new heart.

The door to the balneum opened. "I prefer to be alone at this time," Marcus called out in the darkness. "Leave me!"

"It has been years since I have laid eyes upon you, Marcus," a light, feminine voice said – one that triggered the deepest of memories. "How often does a mother get the chance to visit with her eldest son?"

"Mother?"

Marcus wiped the sweat and water from his eyes to get a better look at her. He knew it was her even from the shadows. She snapped her fingers and the candles relit. "Did my first born forget me?"

The woman before him was beautiful. Her face had the roundness that a girl had before she really became a woman. Her eyes were painted like a peacock. She wore an elegant gown. It was his mother as his childhood memories would portray her — untouched by time or circumstance. Her hair was short and curly, in the fashion of the ladies of Alexandria, rather than a traditional Roman style. "You have become as strong and as handsome as I had hoped, Marcus."

"How is it possible that you stand before me younger than myself?" he asked. "The magic of the Soothsayers themselves slow the process of aging for the highest-ranked amongst us. Mighty Caesar appears to be a much younger man, frozen in amber at the age he started his treatments. I remember you older than how you now appear. I thought it was a trick of their knowledge, a previously undiscovered curative that retarded the aging process. How is such a thing possible?"

Septima blinked with false innocence. "Megabyzus revealed under his scourging that Decimus told stories. Do not blame him. Your optio is a force to be reckoned with that whip. What do you believe? That I consumed your twin like Chronos swallowed the Olympians?"

He dipped into the bathing pool down to his neck. Marcus had never known shyness about his own nakedness, especially when bathing. It felt wrong to feel so vulnerable in her presence. He resolved to banish such thoughts; after all, she was the first to see him naked in this world. "I thought all stories of magic were told to frighten the weak, those who did not wish to free themselves to properly know the universe. The imperator himself claims divinity from Venus. Yet you appear young as the dawn and beautiful as the goddess of love stepping from the conch."

Septima laughed with delight. He remembered those soft dulcimer tones, triggering memories as a boy. She stepped to the edge of the bathing pool, knelt down – showing a good deal of her bronzed leg and thigh – and dipped her finger into the water. "I have studied the secrets of the Art since before you were born. Had I been a man, I would have been accepted immediately into the academy. Father took me on a trip to Alexandria before the Civil War. We stayed with the Cornelii and had the run of the city, including the Great Library."

He had imagined his mother two decades older than himself, but on that timeline she would have to be at least fifty years old. "How is that possible, Mother?"

"Few took the curiosities of a girl seriously," Septima explained, and then sighed. "I could sense the power held in the royal palace, but I lacked the skill to access it. We had such coin in those days. Father bought me everything I asked for, that trip."

"You failed to answer my question, mother." Marcus stated coolly.

"Am I to be treated so harshly after all I have done for my children?" she asked.

Marcus stood from the water, revealing his nakedness to his mother. "You married the man who murdered my father. Or you killed him yourself, according to Decimus," he accused.

"Oh, I knew that Orca paid the former overseer to poison him," Septima revealed. "I fed your father the antidote as often as I was able, but he refused to believe that his precious younger brother could have such ambition. In time, I came to care less for his welfare and more for yours, especially after Nicomedes was born."

"How could you believe such nonsense?" Marcus asked. "Orca left us with virtually nothing and spent everything on his children. I had to watch over Nico and Dia every night lest Decimus lay hands upon them or worse."

"The future required that you bond to your siblings under the worst conditions, or you would fail at the Three Gates of Agony," Septima explained. "Or did you believe that all of your impressive success stemmed solely from your own deeds?"

His face flashed crimson. "You threw us to the wolves!"

Septima shook her head sadly. "I sought to make you strong enough to seize your destiny and birthright. Had Titus lived, you would have been a poet and historian – a good man who lived a quiet life of pleasure and leisure. You never would have joined the legion and fought for your name. I pushed Darius into accelerating your training as boy, but he refused, explaining you were simply too happy to devote yourself as needed to become what you are now."

"Darius knew of all of this," Marcus muttered.

Septima waved her hand over the water, skimming it with her fingers, creating waves. "Darius is very astute and he loved me. I knew you would need to be strong to survive the storm."

Had Darius been in league with her this entire time? Could he ever trust that man again? "He protected us from Orca and even Decimus."

Septima scoffed. "I protected you when it was required, and I still can."

"How can you protect us?" Marcus asked.

"The Parthians will attack Alexandria at first light. They will kill everyone within these walls loyal to Rome," Septima explained. "Stand with me. The storm will pass you by, and we shall restore that which once was. My children will take their destiny as those who returned Rome to the Republic."

Marcus resisted the urge to smile. He feared Septima knew of his battle plans and of his special advantage. He pushed such thoughts from his mind. "How can you abandon Rome? To allow the Parthians to claim Alexandra will weaken her and leave her open to invasion."

Septima blinked, clearly disappointed. "The portents revealed long ago this city would be the first nexus point in the resistance against Rome. Octavius betrayed Rome years ago. You already know this, if you are a clever as I believe."

"The grain shipments."

"Exactly. Octavius has the patience of a god. He knew the Soothsayers would notice any major action taken against Rome immediately, but the tiny ones, the ones that make quiet ripples, were the most difficult ones to detect. He made arrangements with the Cornelii and the Aemilii to move so slowly that Caesar failed to notice until there was potential for danger."

Marcus felt appalled. The taste in his mouth turned sour. "And you and Orca support this move against the imperator?"

Septima waved away the accusation. "We supported that which would give me Alexandria. This feint will fail. Nicomedes alerted Caesar before he could be politically weakened. However, it did weaken Octavius — distancing him from Rome — just enough to allow for the Parthians to attack. If you had waited for me, then our family would have power enough to make changes in this world."

Marcus reached his hands towards his mother, as though to seize her neck, but stopped at the last moment. "You have been working with the Parthians this whole time. You sent them after Claudia."

"I needed you together. I needed you to stop that senseless fighting in Gaul and return to Rome. I needed you to come to Alexandria in the whole of your power. And I needed you to understand the danger of it all."

"You betrayed us?"

"I betrayed nothing! The Soothsayers have locked our blood into a dangerous path for their glory and dominion, not ours. Rome started this war against Parthia long ago. The Soothsayers cannot allow anyone who could threaten their hold to exist in this world, lest their plans be disrupted. They killed those who slept under Carthage. They tricked the Eternal Dreamers to submit to their vision of the world. If they are not stopped, their influence will creep to the corners of the world."

Marcus folded his arms, lest he do something he regretted. He needed to allow his mother to continue to share these secrets. "And the Parthians are better? Noble in spirit?"

"The Soothsayers are not the only ones with this power. The

others — those who held to the promise to remain aloof from the world — have started to ally against them. They understand the danger of living by the Soothsayers' design. Our destiny is not our own."

Marcus sneered and turned his back upon his mother. He could no longer bear the look of her. "I think you care more about your destiny than ours. You wanted us ready, so you could seize that which Nicomedes won."

"Nicomedes was always destined to seize the power of the Eternal Dreamers," Septima revealed. "The Soothsayers would never allow anything else. However, the burden you hold would have been mine. Look at you, weeping alone, ignorant of the gift you have been given. If you had a mere shred of the talent that your brother claims, you'd feel the power flowing towards you. You could have been a god. Nicomedes and I could have stopped them."

"And for that you sacrificed my brothers and sisters?" Marcus asked.

"Dead lives that had no meaning, boy. There is strong power in blood, especially those related to you. I used that which came from my womb to my own purpose to save the family," his mother explained. "The Soothsayers heal by stealing life-force and putting it into others. All of those fat patricians living beyond their years — that comes from life. You live because Nico gave you his heart. You live by his life-force. I need that blood and that life to break the chains put upon us in this infinite war of regress."

"To what purpose?"

"To restore the Republic. To give the world a chance to evolve into something new."

"You have been part of this conspiracy from the start," Marcus stated, finally understanding.

Gentle hands caressed his shoulders. A mother's touch never felt so alien. "You speak as though you are separate from it. I gave you the chance to be free of these chains."

He flinched from her touch and forced himself to face her. Septima dragged her fingers along the length of his shoulders and stopped just short of his chest. "You would allow the Parthians to rule Rome?" Marcus asked.

Septima smiled, lifted up her gown, and dipped her long legs into the water. "They are an honorable people, wise in lore of medicine and the stars. They have learned to harness the elements and forge great steel."

"What of Brutus and Gaul? Are they part of your plan?" Marcus asked.

Septima unclasped the top of her gown and lifted it over her head. She laughed in the revelation of her own nakedness. "Yet another faction arising to fight Rome. The people on that island are real monsters. Cannibals. Savages who worship dark gods to freeze the soul. And Brutus has made alliances with their Soothsayers, called the Divine Devourers. They shall be dealt with in time."

"We have made oaths of service," Marcus protested.

She reached over and put her weight on Marcus, just enough to allow her to descend into the pool. "And what of your duty to she who gave you life?"

Marcus stepped backwards until his back was against the edge of the pool, escaping her grasp. "What would you have of us?"

"I would have you shed your moral inhibition and acknowledge you have the seeds of the gods within you." She gingerly touched his chest, tracing the scar, where Anubis ripped out his heart. His body tingled from the nearness of her flesh, despite his revolting stomach. There was a strength to her will that somehow diminished him. He had always imagined her in his brain as a giant, even though now he towered over her. "I would have you shatter the foundations of Olympia and take that which the Soothsayers stole from us, as did Prometheus deliver onto us fire."

Marcus wanted to push her back, but his body remained frozen in place, as though held by her will alone. "He paid a steep price to the gods, mother."

She kissed the wound on his chest. "All glory comes at a price, Marcus."

Septima turned suddenly towards the entrance, her neck craning towards oncoming footsteps.

"Marcus!" It was Adalia.

He wanted to call out to her, to warn her, but his lips would not move to his will. Septima sighed. She stepped out of the pool, and purposely maneuvered her shapely ass to within a foot of his face so that he could smell her sex. "We will have the remainder of this conversation another time."

Adalia burst into the balneums. She paused, blinked. "Apologies, I did not realize you had company."

Septima slipped her gown over her head and smiled as she clasped it around her neck. "No apologies are required. Marcus may need help finishing his bath. I am finished here for now. You are the barbarian wench from the Rhine, yes? I have heard much about you. Thank you very much for taking care of my sons. Or trying at the least. Very ambitious."

Adalia reached for her dagger. Marcus wanted to warn her, but could not speak. "And who are you?"

"Septima Valerius Orca." She glanced over her shoulder at Marcus. "I am his mother."

Adalia sideways towards Marcus, careful to keep Septima in her line of vision. "Are you well?" When he failed to respond, she raised her dagger and stepped towards to the pool. "What did you do to him?"

Septima raised her hands to show that she carried no weapons and smiled sweetly. "Merely made him susceptible to listening to what I had to say without interrupting me," she explained. "I was quite impressed with his stamina. Few can resist me alone. He will recover in a moment or two. Give him some wine, and he shall be cognitive by the time Octavius arrives."

Adalia looked from Marcus to Septima and then back again with narrowed eyes. She eventually reached for the cask of wine and poured a cup, forcing Marcus to drink it. Septima took this moment to make a graceful exist from the balneums. She paused at the door and glanced over her shoulder. "Whatever happens next, know this: Your mother is proud of each of you."

Chapter Eleven: The Avatar of Sobeck

Megabyzus awoke in a confused haze, as he was dragged through a row of colossal red granite columns. The light of the sun burned his eyes and his back. He had never expected to see it again by order of the queen, a fit punishment for his betrayal. The soft cries of the sea birds and the distant roar of ocean waves could be heard about the atrium. It took a moment to realize that he had been moved to the guest residence on the outer ring of the royal palace.

They laid him down upon a couch under the shade of a palm tree near an ebony sphinx. He glanced upward towards the sky. The effort of moving his neck brought devastating waves of pain.

The soft, yet intense, voice of Nicomedes called to him. "I have prepared a salve that will kill any potential infection. This will hurt as much as the scourging, but it is required."

Milius offered a small sanded stick to him. "Bite down on this, and you'll feel the pain less."

"You will need to hold him still if he is to heal in time for the battle," Nicomedes instructed.

"I'll do what's necessary, magister."

"I see why my brother places such trust in you, optio."

Megabyzus felt a strange energy near him through the haze of pain, as though the gates of the Underworld had been opened and the dead walked the earth. "Rubio, apply the salve."

Gentle, diminutive hands rubbed ointment into his raw flesh. The salve itself was soothing, but the touch triggered a fire of agony across his limbs. Milius and other foreign hands held him in place. His body rebelled against this imprisonment, but lacked the strength to move against them.

He felt the icy touch of Nicomedes and his dead hand upon his back, forcing a swell of healing magic that stitched muscles and skin together. Such growth was painful, living through the months it would have taken to heal in but moments.

"How is such magic possible?" he asked through the pain.

"I have taken the life-force of your Eternal Dreamers," Nicomedes said, matter-of-factly. "I give but a drop of that onto you for your oath. You kept to it and told them only what I wished."

The Royal Guard marched into the atrium and took positions at every entry point alongside the sentries of the cohort. Their uniforms were traditional legionnaire attire, but their colors were blue and grey, to honor the Greek historical tradition of Alexandria. Gaius Octavius Thurinus, Governor of Egypt and heir to the Roman Empire, strode into the atrium once it was secure. Queen Arsinoë IV of Egypt followed in an elegant golden gown. Her arms were wrapped around her son Gaius Julius Octavius Ptolemy.

Claudia greeted them first. She offered the traditional Vestal Virgin greeting and knelt. "Blessings onto you from the hosts of the Sacred Fire."

The cohort saluted Governor Octavius and then reluctantly knelt before the queen. Megabyzus tried to get to his feet, but Nicomedes pushed him down with his unexplainably strong dead hand; it seemed to swirl with a black aura. Nicomedes remained standing, in his robes, waiting to be addressed.

Adalia returned with Marcus, bathed and dressed in a silk tunic appropriate for the occasion. "Thank you for granting us a private audience, governor. I know that your time is valuable in the best of circumstances, but more so during a time of war."

Octavius waved away the pretense. "You implied that you had ways and means for us to win this war. I would hear of that first, centurion."

Nicomedes raised a single finger, signaling the group to wait. He knelt down, scraped some sand with his skeletal hand, and cupped it a moment as he chanted over it. Megabyzus felt the arcane energies shift the properties of the sand into a pattern hitherto unknown to him.

The magister tossed the sand into the air. It spiraled into a large dome, encapsulating their section of the atrium. Megabyzus no longer heard the cries of the birds or the crash of the waves from the sea. "None may scry upon us via mystical or mundane means within my circle of protection," Nicomedes explained. "Please signal that all is well to your guards, so we are not horribly murdered when this is noticed."

Octavius almost smiled. Instead, he turned towards his guards, their hands steady upon their weapons, raised a single eyebrow, and nodded. Centurion Marcus Valerius Perseus did likewise, and his soldiers lowered their weapons. The potential standoff ended with the safety of silence and promise of a real discussion.

Claudia offered wine and seating within the globe of protection. Marcus waved away the offer and addressed Octavius directly.

"Governor, time is short for all of us. Just a few moments ago, an envoy of the Parthians sought to buy my loyalty away from the defense of this city."

"And the identity of this envoy?" Octavius asked dispassionately.

"Not important for the moment. You have five legions ready to defend this city and a hundred warships protecting the harbor, yes? The Parthians have how many legions coming to Alexandria from Cairo?" the centurion asked.

"Twice that number, along with equipment and water for a long siege," Octavius conceded.

Nicomedes sneered. "Along with monsters this part of the world has not seen since the fall of Troy."

"It matters not. Unless you have a means of conquering more legions, we shall have to retreat, until we can contact Rome for reinforcements," Octavius admitted. "They claimed Cairo a little more than a week ago. They could be upon Alexandria as soon as tomorrow, or the next day if they decided to be leisurely."

Marcus now took a goblet of wine and toasted Octavius. "Three legions in fact are closer than you or the Parthians suspect. That redistributes the odds considerably when you factor the might of my younger brother and our ability to manipulate the field of battle."

"You would have had to send a messenger weeks ago to ensure that any reinforcements could arrive from Rome in time for the battle," Octavius said, his words heavy with doubt.

"It is true that it would take weeks for word from Rome to reach the legions." Marcus gestured towards Nicomedes and the bowed.

"Thankfully, I sent word directly, or rather Nicomedes, magister of the Soothsayer Academy, conjured the method to relay said message."

"You would have had to know where these legions were deployed," Octavian argued, shaking his head, refusing to believe that circumstance could favor them. "A mere centurion would not have such information."

Adalia turned towards Marcus with great respect in her eyes. "You learned these new positions from the map in the Senate Curio building when I gave testimony to Caesar – to keep the Parthian Empire from sending supplies to Gaul."

Nicomedes snorted, as though such was a trivial matter. "And I sent a falcon to each position, relaying orders from the centurion in Caesar's and the Soothsayers' names."

"I have a diplomatic pack in my quarters that would have notified you of these changes, Governor Thurinus," Marcus explained. "Alas, I was ordered to attend court before I could retrieve it. Once we have finished this conversation, I would be most happy to deliver it as ordered."

Octavian pondered a moment, staring directly at Megabyzus. He swallowed fearfully. "Megabyzus shared the information about the impending siege against my orders, because he knew you could ensure that the reinforcements would arrive."

Megabyzus opened his mouth to speak, but Nicomedes countered him. "He accepted a geis from myself with a penalty of death to protect the plan."

Octavius turned to Nicomedes. "If you possess a talent to see through falcons, then you can spy upon our enemies and note their locations and fortifications." Nicomedes merely nodded in agreement. "And what do you want for all of this? No gifts fall from the sky without a price."

"We wish for the grain shipments to resume without trickery or delay and to know the reason you would turn against your own father," Marcus answered.

If the governor was surprised by this accusation, he showed nothing of it. Megabyzus had family who worked those docks. The queen ordered an increase in production in wheat, grain, and all manner of supplies towards Rome sold at a significant discount. How could Egypt be lowering the supply to Rome?

"How did you discover the deceit?" asked Octavius.

"The deliveries have continued unabated, and yet the general stores of public grain have been slowly decreasing," Nicomedes explained. "The Aemilii and the Cornelii lack your patience. You slowly sold more and more of the greater share to them, and they paid less and less into the general coffers. It was an impressive gambit, moving so slowly and subtly that the Soothsayers themselves might not have noticed, save for the greed of your partners."

"Why would you betray your own adopted father?" Marcus asked.

"It is natural for a son to wish to succeed his father, but this becomes ever-more difficult in a time of immortal Soothsayers. I do not wish him harm," Octavian explained. "I merely wish to weaken his position by advancing the position of the Optimates, so that the mighty imperator will continue to need me and need the power of

Alexandria."

"Why then did you attempt to ally with the Parthian Empire?" Nicomedes asked.

"Egypt has long traded with the Parthians," Octavius replied stiffly. "Alliance would be too generous of a word to describe this situation. They are a civilized people known for great craftsmanship and knowledge. Besides, there has been peace between Rome and Parthia for almost seventy years."

Megabyzus nodded his agreement. Parthia traded with India along the route Alexander the Great first trod. And in turn, India provided the secret route to the mysterious Serres and their lucrative silk trade. There was little mundane reason for Parthia to attack now. They had won the last war and claimed considerable territory they had yet to properly settle.

"You allowed them to trade steel to the Caledonians for their war against Rome in Gaul. Why?" Marcus asked.

Octavius shrugged. "It seemed harmless enough. A distraction for the Senate. I find it difficult to believe Rome has not squashed them already."

Marcus placed his hands on his hips. "They are backed with coin and steel from Parthia and led by Brutus and other Romans. They have their own Soothsayers, called the Eternal Devourers. This is larger than we can understand."

Octavius pursed his lips. "You speak of magic and gods, as though they touch the world on a daily basis."

Nicomedes locked his arms behind his back and began to pace the length of the atrium. "I have claimed the power the Parthian Soothsayers — Those Who Wait Beneath the Sands — craved, but absent their prize, they will still attack. Parthia must move against Rome or surrender to its will, and we mortals must be burned or harvest the fire."

Octavius scratched his chin, pondering the words of the magister. "It would appear then it is in the interest of Rome to once again remember the importance of Alexandria and myself."

"What more could you possibly wish from Rome?" Marcus asked. "You are the second-most powerful man in the empire! What has been denied to you?"

Octavius beckoned to his son, calling him over from guard duty. Megabyzus had not noticed his presence, despite having tutored him as boy. "Caesar has accepted barbarians from Gaul into the Senate, and yet Roman law does not recognize my wife nor my son."

The particulars of Roman law were foreign to Megabyzus, but he well understood the pain of a heritage denied. He decided speaking would only remind them of his presence and there was much to learn by watching silently.

"It would take an act of the Senate to approve such," Marcus argued. "Caesar might be imperator, but his will is not absolute."

"He would not recognize his own foreign-born son, Caesarian, before Brutus murdered him and my sister," said Queen Arsinoë. "It is fashionable for the men of Rome to have mistresses far from home, but never wives."

Adalia glanced aside towards Marcus and Nicomedes. Megabyzus did not know what sin she mentally accused them of, but he would not wish for that one to be angry with him. Claudia stepped forward, gazing into the eyes of the queen. "Family and marriage are sacred in Rome. It is shameful some are allowed to ignore any spark that adds to the Eternal Flame."

Queen Arsinoë nodded with some gratitude. "As it is likewise in Egypt. It saddens me the Roman people do not consider my marriage real, and yet demand the bounty of Egypt."

"If we were in Rome, you could reaffirm your marriage at the Atrium Vestae before the Sacred Flame," Claudia offered. "I could talk to the sisterhood."

Octavius held up his hand. "The offer is kind, Claudia, but you are no longer a Vestal Virgin. Even if married before the Sacred Flame in front of all of the gods of Rome, it would not matter. I am born of plebian blood. So is Caesar. We are a plebian house raised to greatness. Such is the law of Rome."

"What of the Sabine women in the days of legend? The patricians took brides from neighboring tribes, and their children became true Romans." Claudia turned to her brothers. "I know why the Soothsayers insisted all three of us be present in Egypt at this time. It is obvious, is it not?"

Queen Arsinoë nodded. "You would agree to marry my son?" she asked.

"That would only add a daughter to my house," Octavian objected. "It would not make my son a true Roman in the eyes of the law."

"Not if the paterfamilias of my branch house adopted your son for his own," Claudia explained. "The law is clear; adoptions carry the weight of blood. The most powerful senator in all of Rome is Marcus Livius Drusus Claudianus. Appius Claudius Pulcher came from a plebian house, but when he married the daughter of Marcus Livius Drusus, he changed his name to reflect his new station. A paterfamilias of a patrician family has the right to marry anyone and name them patrician, if their blood is pure and their deeds are many."

"Surely Senator Orca would refuse to accept that burden, even if I were willing to have another claim the title of father over my own son," Octavian argued.

"My paterfamilias stands before you, and I suspect he is much more open to your cause than Orca." Claudia gestured towards her brother. "The price for Marcus leaving his post and forever surrendering the chance to earn his name within the year was a formal declaration from the Senate granting the approval of the branching. The Valeria Claudians stand before you. I am half a decade senior to your son, but a worthy bride prophesied to give birth to an important daughter of Rome. To reject your son's status as a patrician and son of Rome would be to reject the word of the Soothsayers."

"Claudia, is this your will to marry this boy?" Marcus asked.

"You married Drusilla for the family. Can I do less for the family and Rome? Claudia asked. She reached out to Ptolemy and took his hand. "I am older than you, but I would swear to be a dutiful wife and to make you happy."

Gaius Julius Octavius Ptolemy glanced from his mother to his father. Such strange customs did not hold political weight in Egypt, but

Megabyzus knew it would hurt the queen greatly to accept such a fate. Octavius seemed to consider the matter. "This would merely be political sophistry at best."

Marcus placed his hand upon Ptolemy's shoulder, as a father would a son and grinned at the governor. "Yes, but to publicly deny the marriage would be the ultimate casus belli allowing for war. The best argument is one that cannot be repudiated without cost, even if it is meaningless."

"It is certainly an option to consider," Octavius stated.

Marcus offered his hand to the governor in the fashion that Megabyzus had seen Roman legionaires do as a sign of respect. "If you agree to properly resupply Rome once this battle is over, I will agree on my honor that my house will aid your cause via this proposed method or another."

Octavius accepted the offer. "That you would offer your own beloved sister to this cause shows me your intention. I agree to this proposal for this coming year. Should I have reason to alter my plans afterwards, I will inform you before taking action."

"Agreed."

"And now let us plan for the defense of Alexandria."

*   *   *   *

The stormy sky was as black as coal, yet it could not be later than midday by his calculation. Megabyzus poked his head out of the makeshift tent on the hill that overlooked Tanta valley. The Nile forked in several places along the Egypt Delta, but this was the best route for an army to march upon Alexandria. The ground between the hills and the Nile had the perfect texture — soft enough for an easy walk and hard enough to ensure that none of their equipment would be bogged down in the muck.

There were other routes to Alexandria over land between the various rivers, but they took more time to traverse, and Nicomedes ensured those lands and valleys were flooded, as happened often during this season. The town of Tanta was the economic heart of Egypt where the hub of the Nile Delta delivered goods to the whole of the region.

The storm made it difficult to directly observe the positions of the legions, but dozens of small campfires signalled the outline of their presence. Milius joined him from the tent. "The rain makes it impossible to note whether it is one legion there or ten."

Megabyzus sensed the incredible power expended to conjure this storm. "Such was the intent of the magister. It may indeed save Egypt this day."

Milius snorted and clapped Megabyzus on the shoulder. "Parthians defeat a combined army of Egypt and Rome? They're more fucked than Proserpina on the first day of winter."

Megabyzus pointed south, where the Nile twisted and turned. "You underestimate the Parthians. They have defeated both Egypt and Rome in the past. Hundreds of miles south past Cairo is the valley of Pelusium. There Cambyses II defeated Egypt, leaving a field of skulls and a river of blood."

Cossus Crassus had been listening to the story from the tent. He brought them water and asked, "What happened?"

"Cambyses became Pharaoh over Egypt, and for the next two hundred years, Parthian blood held the throne," Megabyzus continued. "That was a long time ago, but their children never forgot that victory. Egypt never forgot the humiliation of that battle, even as it passed into forgotten memory. If this battle goes poorly, Orodes II of Parthia may rule both Egypt and Rome in time. Do not scoff at this king. His father claimed the throne by putting to death thirty of his brothers in a single night."

Milius rejected the water and poured himself more wine. "I heard tell that Cambyses ordered his men to nail cats to their shields on the eve of battle. The Egyptians hold cats sacred, and so they didn't want to get in trouble with their gods. Their archers refused to fire upon them for fear of wounding the animals."

"It is true that such stories are told by Parthians," Megabyzus acknowledged. "But the Egyptians tell a different story of betrayal, poison, and a horrible ambush."

Milius snorted. "The Egyptians have long been conquered. Rome has stayed strong against the Parthians for hundreds of years," Milius said.

Megabyzus shrugged. "Rome lost Armenia to the Parthian dynasty because mighty Caesar agreed to a treaty. Some say Rome fears the Parthians and their impressive culture."

Cossus looked out into the darkness and visibly shivered. "What of the coming battle? Coriolanus said that the odds were vastly against us."

Milius finished his wine. "Coriolanus has never had the pleasure or the honor fighting along side the Bear Centurion."

"I have not heard of this title," Megabyzus admitted. "What does it mean?"

The optio answered the question with great mirth. "My father once told me this joke. 'Where does a bear shit in the woods?' I once thought the answer was simple. 'Anywhere he wants.'"

"And now?"

Cossus and Milius delivered the punchline together. "Anywhere that Marcus Valerius Perseus is not."

Milius laughed so hard it ended with coughing. "Near a year ago, the centurion was visiting the privy, when he came upon a large black bear in Gaul."

"What happened?"

"The centurion wears that bear's skin into battle," Milius explained. "You'll see it. The men will see it, and so will the enemy."

"I wish we were down there," Cossus muttered. "To fight alongside him."

"There will be battles aplenty in the coming days." Milius clapped the probatus's shoulder. "He placed me here, because he needed to know our task would be done."

"Why did he place me here?" Cossus asked.

"Because he wanted me to have something pretty to look at," Milius quipped.

The blast of horns cut off their conversation. The sound echoed off the hills, making it difficult to determine the source, but it was clear that it came from the south. The wind from the storm muffled the brunt of the horns, yet carried their call throughout the valley.

Milius pointed towards the southern mouth of Tanta, where the movement of shapes could be discerned. Foot-soldiers and horsemen spread out their front line. "And that will be their famous cavalry — the Acheamenid Horsemen. I fought those bastards once: quick and hard to kill. They can jump breach defenses and attack weakened flanks on the open plain."

The Parthian legions halted and broke rank into formations. They clanged their swords together in the dark, daring the Romans to attack them. "They have taken position over the mouth of the valley," Cossus reported. "Should we light the signal fire?"

Milius shook his head. "The plan relies on them going further into the valley. And, if nothing else, we were ordered to wait until the centurion offered them a chance to surrender."

"How will we know if that happens?" Cossus asked.

The optio gestured towards Megabyzus. "Remember, this one is now the familiar of Nicomedes. The magister can see everything that he sees; he hears all that Megabyzus hears. I have no doubt an order shall be passed, should it not be obvious to us."

"Our main function is to ensure they do not try to flank us on the hills and warn the centurion should there be problems," Megabyzus replied. "Nicomedes will use my eyes to coordinate efforts on the ground with the governor and to focus his magic."

The sky stormed above them, swirling dark sand clouds into

magnificent shapes. Slowly, those clouds condensed and then rounded into an oval shape. The edges smoothed and bent into the angry face of Marcus Valerius Perseus — floating above them as though he were a god.

"By all of the bastards in Tartarus!" Milius cried.

The avatar of the centurion spoke, and the strength and terror of his voice echoed around them. "I am Marcus Valerius Perseus. I come from the Valeria, descended all of the way from Aeneas. Some of you may know me as the Bear Centurion. You have sent your monsters to kill the imperator and failed. You have sent your assassins to kill my sister. This land is under the protection of Rome. I offer you a single chance to lay down arms and leave the way you came. It will not be offered again."

There was silence in the valley, as though it were a sacred grove, until a volley of arrows fired high into the sky. The winds of the storm slowed and deflected their progress, yet many of them still landed on target. The sounds of dying men fell into the muck.

"I can't believe they managed to hit those shots in this storm," Milius complained.

"Parthian archers are the best in the world," Megabyzus muttered. "They have been key to many victories. Some archers possess the talent to kill a man from horseback a league away."

Cossus took their torch and lit the signal fire. Megabyzus had previously treated the wood with special minerals and powders he had gathered during his time in Seleucia. It burned quickly and exploded into a cloud of blueish hue that could be seen for many leagues in any direction.

A cadre of heavy cavalry with giant armored horses charged across the battle lines. "Why do the Romans not attack?" Megabyzus demanded. "They will only have one chance to defend themselves, and if those Sassanian Cataphracts break the line, this battle is over."

"What you are about to witness is the classic battle between the lion and the killer whale," Milius explained. "The Parthians are strikers. They move fast and attack at a distance. The Romans prefer to fight in close quarters, where we can see the faces of our enemies."

A shrill whistle emanated from the Roman ranks. It blasted three times, and the legions broke into smaller units, then maneuvered into a phalanx position, where the front line created a shield wall. The men inside of the protection raised their shields to form a protective barrier. "That would be the turtle position. It protects the men and allows the spear carriers to attack in safety."

The initial clash brought forth cries of the wounded and screams of the dying as steel tore flesh and ended lives. Megabyzus understood now the metaphor Milius used for the battle. Each army was the ultimate predator in its realm. The Romans were slow to move, but deliberate in action. The Parthians were quick and bold, prepared to fight passionately.

Sassanian Cataphracts struck against the shield wall, and while it did not savage them, it landed many mighty blows. The Romans fared less well, but their long spears harried both horse and rider.

The Sparabara — the shield-bearers of the Parthian legions — fought with spear and shield. They wore dark, lightweight linen trousers and tunics under a Greek-style Linothorax and a veil across their faces. Their ranks charged under cover from the archers, but the so-called turtle formation blunted the majority of that attack. "Those are the Immortals, the elite warriors of the Parthian Empire. Kill one and another appears instantly."

"Look at those weak shields. They won't hold against Roman blades," Milius observed.

Megabyzus agreed. "They are perfect for deflecting spears and arrows, but nothing more. The Immortals count upon speed and skill to kill their enemies."

Sassanian Cataphracts attacked the Roman line once more, this time knocking down several shields. The battle lines of the two armies engaged in the muck, staining the mud with the blood of the dead and dying.

A blue flame flickered upon the horizon behind the Parthians. "The legions from the west have arrived," Milius replied. "Signal to Nicomedes that the trap has been triggered."

Megabyzus projected the situation in his mind, hoping that Nicomedes could hear it. The storm began to fade, and light from the sun shone down upon the battlefield. The Fifth, Sixth, and Twelfth Legions gathered from the corners of Africa and closed off the southern mouth of the valley.

The Parthians were fighting a battle on two fronts. Their reserve forces had to turn towards this new, advancing enemy. The hills were rough terrain that would be closed to their cavalry. They closed ranks around the archers, hoping to thicken their defenses. The Roman legions marched slowly, knowing every inch claimed would be paid for in blood.

The Parthians held fire until the enemy marched forward at a solid pace and were no longer able to hold the turtle position. The archers moved to the side, revealing traveling catapults. "What is that? What use are siege weapons on the battlefield?" Milius asked.

The first catapult launched a single barrel, and it exploded into a wave of fire upon the first cohort that maneuvered close to the range of the explosion. Hundreds of Romans died in burning glory, and the explosion threatened to blind any who dared gaze upon it.

"Greek Fire. It burns through water," Megabyzus explained.

He felt a tingle in his eyes at that very moment. Nicomedes was using his perspective from the hills to judge the field of battle. There were five catapults and several wagons of ammunition, no doubted created by the Parthian Magi and their students.

Roman soldiers broke rank and tried to extinguish the fires by jumping into the Nile, but it did not blunt the flame. A small cohort advanced. Milius pointed out the standard of the Seventh Legion – the Bear Centurion and his escorts. Why would the commander risk being so close to the front lines?

They formed a shield wall around two men. He could not be certain from this distance, but it seemed likely to be Marcus and Nicomedes themselves. The magister raised his arms, and Megabyzus felt an increased wave of power emanate from him.

The catapults fired more barrels, but this time they splashed against shields and broke without an explosion. Nicomedes had transmuted the Greek Fire into some inert substance.

Fire shards blasted from the ranks of the Parthians, targeting Nicomedes. They exploded high over his head, as though he were protected by the very gods of the heavens.

The Roman legions charged forward and the sound of men fighting and dying increased, as the foot soldiers engaged in a fierce battle of shield versus spear and gladius. From their location, the lines of skirmish appeared as little more than ants fighting over a hill of dirt.

A rumbling overtook the earth as horrific monsters — scorpions the size of horses — freed themselves from the muck and attacked the Roman lines. A single snap of their massive claws had the force to chop a man in armor asunder. Their stingers were potent enough to shatter shields and penetrate armor.

The beasts ripped through the line while the Parthian soldiers followed closely behind. Nicomedes blasted them away with a wave of his hand, commanding a mighty gale force of wind and lightning. A number of the scorpions were smashed against the rocks at the edge of hills.

Three of the scorpions scrambled upright and began to break rank. They skittered up the hill towards the encampment. "They're coming right for us!" Milius shouted.

Megabyzus realized that the Parthian Magi must have realized how Nicomedes was leveraging his position and decided to kill that advantage. Usinging his perspective allowed Nicomedes to attack anywhere on the field of battle. "They can sense me."

"There's a backup position to the south. Follow me," Milius

commanded.

They scrambled across the edge of the hills, running desperately. Cossus raised his spear and sword, cocking his head. "Do you hear it?"

Before he could answer, a giant stinger plunged out of his chest, splattering blood over them. Milius chopped quickly with his gladius, killing the scorpion, but two more skittered towards them. Milius raised his gladius and shielded Megabyzus. "My orders are to keep you alive at all costs."

Megabyzus took the shield and spear from Cossus. He had no need of them in the afterlife. "We can run."

"The Bear Centurion needs you. I'm just an old man too ornery to surrender his life just yet. Take position over the field of battle." Milius slammed his shield against incoming attacking stingers. He pushed Megabyzus farther behind him. "Alright, you sons of bitches. Prepare to be escorted to the gate of Tartarus."

Megabyzus had never seen such skill in battle or bravery. The old legionnaire stood his ground against the monsters, defending against their claws with his shield and dodging their stingers. He cut and sliced them only when he had a clean opportunity, giving them reason to fear him.

He fought them with a fierceness that only came from knowing death was certain. One of the stingers grazed his arm. His hands shook and from his misses; it was clear that poison had started to affect his vision. Still, he ended the abomination that was the scorpions' lives with a solid stroke of his gladius, severing the head of one of them and then puncturing the other in the back. Milius Hortensius Lex, optio of the Third Cohort of the Seventh Legion, dropped to his knees. He glanced about the field of battle, counting dead scorpions.

The sounds of battle from the valley below them had muted. Megabyzus surveyed the damage. "Many died on both sides, but it looks like Alexandria won."

Milius laughed. "The whores of many lands will weep bitter tears. This seems like a good time to leave. Do me a favor?"

He was not certain he would survive the night. His own vision began to blur. One of the scorpions must have stung him, and the poison blunted the pain. "Anything."

"The next time you make sweet love, shout my name unto the gods," Milius asked.

"Shout your name?"

Milius dropped his sword and lowered his shield. His eyes fluttered. "The world should be reminded that I was here."

Chapter Twelve: Dawn is a Friend to the Muses

Claudia went from tent to tent, tending to the wounded legionnaires. The woes of the living drowned out the whispers of the dead, and thus she felt alive. The blessing from Shemzu's kiss fendured even after she returned, and now voices of the dead would forever surround her. It felt worthy to see the brave soldiers who saved Alexandria, rather than wallow in her misery.

Under the watchful protection of Adalia, she asked each of them if there was anything that could be done to help them be comfortable. They spoke of wives and daughters left behind and their dreams of the future. She did her best to imbue these conversations with joy, especially amongst those who had lost a limb or felt close to death. Claudia might have left the college of the Vestal Virgins, but to the legionnaires, hers was a voice from home.

Once word spread as to her identity, the tenor of the conversations changed radically. The legionnaires fervently praised the courage of the Bear Centurion and his leadership against the Parthians. They whispered of the frightening power of Nicomedes and his command of the elements and the sky. Some quietly asked if it was proper for them to pray to the magister.

She countered their requests by reminding them of the foresight shown by Governor Octavius who led Alexandria and Rome to their first victory over the Parthians since the days of Alexander the Great.

Life could become very difficult indeed if the Valeria were seen to openly encourage such worship. Few wished to discuss the horrors they had endured in Tanta, but they spoke kindly of the wives and loves they had left behind.

The wounded trickled into Alexandria from the Nile on barges. Queen Arsinoë ordered the royal palace to erect a series of open tents in one of the outer rings to house the soldiers who bled for her country. Royal physicians triaged the wounds according to the methodology of the Greek Pikoulis. The palace service staff went about the fundamentals of aftercare, cleaning and dressing wounds to avoid infection.

A young girl — perhaps ten or eleven at the most — with braided black hair and beautiful almond eyes pushed through the physicians and orderlies. Claudia recognized her as one of the queen's handmaidens, even though she wore a simple slave's tunic far below her station. Adalia's hand swiftly moved to the hilt of her dagger with a concerned scowl. "Remember the weapons of choice in the royal palace are crocodile tears and poison."

Claudia thought of the night after the legions left for Tanta, when a young girl much like this one had presented her with a poisoned chalice in the royal hall. Were it not for the vibrations of the silver ring that Nicomedes gave her long ago, she would have put it to her lips, drank, and died.

Claudia raised a finger to delay Adalia from pushing the girl away. Her instincts told her to trust this girl. She knelt down to her eye level and beckoned for the young girl to approach. "I remember you, little one. You are Ipy, yes?"

The young girl smiled sweetly and tugged at her stola, which Claudia noted had been accidently stained crimson from the wounded she tended. "Domina, I have been asked to bring you a message from Queen Arsinoë, daughter of Isis. She would hear your wisdom in private."

Claudia remained behind in Alexandria, along with Adalia, to protect the queen and ensure the Valeria interests were maintained in Egypt. Yet Arsinoë had not yet deigned to speak to her privately or otherwise since that first night. The priests seem to wall Claudia away from the world, fearful of revenge.

They only learned of the victory in Tanta from the cheers in court, and even then it was not until the next morning, when a message had been delivered via falcon, that Claudia had been informed of the survival of both of her brothers. "I am honored that the queen would think my insight valuable."

"Domina, if you will follow me, I can take you to her by a path known only by the handmaidens." Ipy tugged at her stola once again, trying to direct them back to the palace. "Forces conspire to keep you separated, and she would speak in complete privacy."

Adalia wrinkled her nose at the very thought. Claudia knew her friend distrusted all of the secret passages and doors in the royal palace, and this would be the best opportunity to kill them without witnesses.

She considered the matter carefully. Since returning to Alexandria, Claudia felt oddly confident at weighing the deception of others when they tried to lie to her. The handmaiden believed this was an honest attempt at clandestine communication away from prying eyes. "We would be honored to visit with the queen."

"This invitation is only for you, Vestal Virgin," Ipy said meekly. She squealed like a mouse when the amazon stepped over, growling at the thought. "The queen did not give permission for any others to come."

"Then Claudia shall have to refuse the kind invitation," Adalia said. She leaned down until her eyes were but a foot away from the girl's. "I have taken an oath to not leave her side until her brothers' return."

"The queen should consider her one of my handmaidens," Claudia added, hoping her words soothed the frightened child. "Surely the queen would not ask me to visit her without my handmaiden and protector. Why, I would be dead without Adalia."

Ipy looked from Claudia to Adalia with dread, but eventually nodded her consent. "If you would follow me, domina."

The handmaiden led them into the royal palace through a series of winding pathways Claudia was certain were meant to confuse and disorient them. The smell of roasted meat permeated through the pathways, suggesting that they were near the kitchens. The loud clang of pots and pans echoed around them, confirming her suspicions.

Adalia grumbled. "We're skulking about in circles."

Ipy stopped at a tapestry that reflected the life of Cleopatra, and pulled it aside to reveal a hidden door. They followed her through dozens of twisting and winding secret passages between the halls and rooms of the palace. Only the handmaiden knew the way. During their walk, they listened to those considered of interest by the queen.

Adalia covered her mouth to indicate she wished silence and waved Claudia over to a strange, plugged hole within the stone. She gestured that Claudia should peer through it, only to discover it was an obfuscated spy-hole designed to discreetly observe some sort of assembly room where Typhaon and a mass of priests argued in an unknown dialect.

Ipy beckoned them to follow her deeper into the passages. Claudia and Adalia exchanged worried glances, but the opportunity to learn about the palace outweighed the risks.

Claudia's mind reeled from the dust and the continual turns. It reminded her of Ariadne's Maze under the Atrium Vestae, akin to creeping along a single thread in a complex spider web, seeking out flies caught within it. It was not unlike visiting the death realms with her siblings, only this time she understood the tongueless murmurs and comprehended their purpose.

In time, they came upon a large sounding chamber, where the distance echoes of all who traveled through these passages could be heard by a small cadre of armed guards protecting a large door with the seal of the phoenix upon it. Ipy signaled the guards, and they allowed them egress into the queen's private chambers.

The soft trickle of water filling the heated baths reverberated off the stone walls. This so-called private chamber of the queen had been built with unlimited wealth, vast fortunes of manpower, and limited modesty. Erotic murals and tapestries depicted acts of carnal love. Golden statues of forgotten pharaohs and ancient gods stood in formation along the walls and bath, as though they were a legion ready to spring to life upon given the proper order. The sheer audacity of the wealth contained in this room would have turned the Aemilii green with envy and paid for the whole of all of the legions of Rome.

Queen Arsinoë lay upon an exquisite reclining couch with plush pillows and drapery, drinking a golden goblet of wine. "This is the private chamber of the pharaohs. I am told by my handmaidens, it was here my sister once seduced mighty Caesar. Here our words are only for each other."

Claudia placed her hand upon her heart and bowed in the Egyptian fashion. She tried to ignore the whispers of those who had died in this chamber. "A high honor indeed to be invited here. Thank you for allowing Adalia to keep her vow and attend."

"The legend of the amazon from the Rhine has already spread throughout the palace," the queen said. "My handmaidens were afraid that she would eat them."

Adalia glanced down upon Ipy and turned up her nose. "Too scrawny. Not enough meat on the bones."

Ipy squeaked and hid behind her queen. Arsinoë waved, gesturing to the low table where the kitchens had supplied the best meals that Egypt had to offer — olives, roasted pheasants, and stuffed mushrooms. "Share in the bounty of the harvest. All are safe, upon my honor as queen."

Claudia noted her ring remained silent and so accepted a cup of tart wine from Africa and one of the strange-looking fruits that tasted similar to a pear. "I am pleased your undoubtedly busy schedule allowed for such a meeting."

"I feared to remain alone with you," Queen Arsinoë said. It must have been difficult for a sovereign to admit such, deep in the bowels of her own palace. "Trust is not easily earned. My eyes have been upon you these last three nights."

"Eyes upon me?" Claudia asked.

"Please forgive me for the transgression," Queen Arsinoë said with conviction. "I needed to take your measure. There are many passages in the palace as you have seen, and privacy such as we have now is a rare commodity."

Claudia made a show of sipping the wine and then offering some to Adalia. There was no malice in the queen's voice, and the offer was genuine. The amazon refused politely. "Trust is earned, as you said. Though why you feared to speak with me is a mystery."

The queen threw her head back and laughed. "You truly do not know? How delightful! The powers of the Vestal Virgins are known even in the dark recesses of Egypt. Our priests feared you far more than either of your brothers. I was uncertain if you had your mother's gifts. Octavius was blind to your threat, not believing a woman could take such power in the world."

She scowled at the mere mention of her mother. "I note she kept the knowledge of such gifts from her own children," Claudia said.

Arsinoë placed her goblet upon the low table and made herself comfortable on the couch, encouraging her visitors to the same. "It would seem she kept this knowledge from you and Marcus, but not Nicomedes. One of my handmaidens witnessed the conversation between Septima and Marcus in the balneums and learned much about your family."

Claudia sighed visibly, unable to hide the disappointment in the news. "A story that has not yet been shared in full with his siblings," she admitted.

"The Bear Centurion should be made aware that amongst my handmaidens, the duty of watching over him is considered a prized affair, which had caused many fights amongst them," Queen Arsinoë said dryly.

Adalia snorted. "That alone will take the sting from the knowledge he was spied upon."

"And now?" Claudia asked.

Arsinoë laid her head upon a silk pillow and stretched out along the couch in the Greek fashion, her arm laid upon her forehead. Claudia was uncertain if this behavior was a sign of strength or trust. "Your brothers have kept their word to my husband. Egypt is secure, with less than a thousand fatalities."

"And triple that in causalities," Claudia observed.

"Such is the cost of war, and we both know that without the help of the Valeria, the cause would have been entirely lost." Queen Arsinoë reached over, took her goblet once again, and sipped her wine. "Marcus and Nicomedes are becoming legends already, and yet all of you defer any such deification in favor my husband."

Claudia merely smiled tightly, hoping to avoid that topic as much as possible. "Such a victory will surely require the Senate to approve a triumph through Rome, an honor your husband well deserves as general."

"A sign of loyalty, honoring your pledge to my husband," Queen Arsinoë acknowledged. "And I am told we shall have almost five thousand new slaves once the ransom to Parthia is complete, enough to man the fields for a new generation."

"And yet there is hesitation in your voice," Claudia noted.

Arsinoë smiled through strained lips, acknowledging the truth of the statement. "I am the Queen of all of Egypt, the upper and lower Nile. I am the daughter of Isis. You give to my husband everything he wishes in the world, and all you ask is for that which is most precious to me."

"Does not the merging of two families add to the life of all?" Adalia asked.

Claudia nodded sympathetically, finally understanding why Arsinoë protested this marriage. "If this marriage and adoption were to happen, Ptolemy would have to move to Rome to help us establish our new branch family."

"I have reluctantly come to accept that sometime in the near future, I shall have to surrender him to the world." Arsinoë frowned. Her shoulders slumped from the knowledge of what must be done. "I hoped he would establish himself in Alexandria first. Ptolemy is of age certainly, but in many ways he is still a boy. Mothers never wish for their children to leave them."

Claudia thought of her own mother and what she sacrificed to achieve her nebulous goals. "I think I understand your pain. It seemed that I would never have children, due to politics. Now that the opportunity has been given to me, I feel blessed."

Arsinoë forced a smile for her guests and began to speak. Claudia knew well the language of the smiles often demanded of women. "I was the youngest daughter of the pharaoh of pharaohs — my son's namesake — Ptolemy XII. I was the younger sister of the most beautiful woman in the world, she who brought the Eternal City to its knees with her mere smile. I am the eternal last resort of royalty. I first became queen when dissidents hoped to leverage me against the Romans when they first came to our shores. They raised an army against mighty Caesar and rebelled."

"I have not heard of this rebellion," Adalia said with great interest. "What happened?"

Arsinoë had difficulty swallowing, so she poured herself another drink. "It is said that General Ganymede almost defeated the imperator, until they decided they would rather have my idiot brother as pharaoh. Caesar won the battle and took the entire court prisoner back to Rome for his triumph. In those days, it was customary to strangle prominent prisoners when the festivities ended, to sanctify the blessing of the gods. Octavius convinced his father to spare me. I found sanctuary at the temple of Artemis in Ephesus, where I lived and studied the stars."

"I have visited that temple. It is quite beautiful," Claudia said.

Arsinoë shook her head. "No prison — however gilded the cage — is considered beautiful by the prisoners who must remain there."

Claudia thought of the Atrium Vestae and reluctantly nodded in agreement. Arsinoë toasted the both of them. Adalia reached for her own goblet, and filled it to have something in her hand while the queen continued her story. "I might have lived out the rest of my life there, with my eyes raised towards the stars. Had the Senate Liberators not failed in their attempt to murder mighty Caesar, my own sister might have sought my life. When Brutus fled Rome, he wanted a final strike at Caesar. His men broke into the villa where Cleopatra slept with Caesarion and had them dragged into the streets to be murdered by the mob."

"How horrible!" Claudia whispered.

"It was then Caesar remembered that I existed. My future husband insisted I come with him to Alexandria to be installed as queen for the glory of Rome."

"I have seen the love in his eyes for you," Claudia said sweetly.

"I think it disappointed Caesar that his adopted son made the same mistake and openly loved a foreign queen," Arsinoë said sadly. "The people of Rome are very jealous of their heroes and suspicious of foreign women who would bring them down."

"You believe your son will have difficulty in Rome," Adalia observed.

"He has the blood of two conquerors in him," Arsinoë stated. "How could Rome look at him with anything but fear? And you would take him to the lion's den. Can you protect him? Can you love him, as I have loved Octavius? You are five years his elder, and women always mature faster. Will he be anything but a boy to be controlled by you?"

Was she comparing Claudia to Septima? "I admit I have little experience with men outside of those in my family. However, I have counseled the patrician women of Rome on marriage and the best matches for their family, and I have learned much on this topic."

"What have you learned as a Vestal Virgin?" Arsinoë asked.

She wondered if the queen was asking as a mother concerned for son or a soverign trying to asset her threat. Claudia bit into a fruit and chewed it while she pondered her words. "I have learned a marriage is more than a simple contract. It is more than a union of families for the benefit of power and financial gain. It is a blending, where neither family is ever the same. Each family absorbs the character from the new member and grows. This has been the same from the mighty patricians to lowly plebeians."

"What of love?" Arsinoë asked.

"I have witnessed love and affection grow in marriages I thought barren and cold. My brother is a devoted reader of your husband's words. Did you know this? He says that your husband is a dispassionate man of logic. How did you fall in love?" Claudia asked.

The memory of it brought a smile to the queen's lips. "He visited me once at the temple, and we talked of the stars I studied. I knew he wanted a Roman wife to improve his chances in the Senate. The promotion to Governor of Egypt was a mighty thing to this man, and yet it was also an exile. When he chose to marry me before his gods and mine, he thought it would forever sunder his chances at succeeding Caesar."

"A father and mother desire great things for their children," Adalia stated. "It is the natural way of the world."

Queen Arsinoë stared at Claudia, as though reading her soul right through her eyes. "This match between our families would go far towards forwarding my husband's ambitions. It would secure relations between Egypt and Rome. It would give my son an opportunity otherwise impossible. But it is not without risks for both of us."

Claudia had considered those same risks. "The Optimates will scream bloody murder in the Senate. Those who hoped to weaken the imperator will seek to undermine us."

"And then there is the matter of your mother and her own plans for her children," Queen Arsinoë said. "She has her own intentions towards Rome and Egypt, and her crusade against the Soothsayers."

"We have worked for years to separate ourselves from the sins of our mother. Marcus has strived to earn his name within his year solely to get permission to branch the family and escape Orca as the paterfamilias," Claudia explained.

"And yet, now you begin to suspect Orca was not the architect of your father's fate. Your mother is cunning and quite potent. My handmaidens have witnessed her power. With but a few words she was able to befuddle Marcus — a man known for his will and ability to command others. She is a woman who would hurt her son to break him to her will."

Claudia blinked. Clearly, the queen knew more about her mother's meeting with Marcus than she did. "I would not be surprised at any tactics that woman might use." Adalia swallowed, almost choking, and reached for more wine. What horrors could make this amazon pause? "Time has not been our ally since we have arrived in Alexandria."

"Marcus lost his optio in the battle — a friend and mentor of many years. It might be wise to wait before probing too much into sensitive matters," Adalia suggested.

Claudia glanced aside to Adalia. She envied her easy friendship with her big brother. "Agreed. Suffice to say that her children oppose her machinations against Rome and the Soothsayers. If you discovered the truth, then why have you not acted against her?"

"She is the wife of a senator from a powerful patrician house. We would require proof, and the word of a single slave would never be enough," the queen explained. "And how would we contain her? She has the power to entrance others, and the priests actively support her. She has spent many years as their patron, teaching them trivial tricks. No, it is better we watch her from afar."

"And so how did you come to finally trust me?"

"I admit I had doubts, but your actions the last few days have shown otherwise," the queen revealed.

"May I ask what you have learned?"

"You have shown virtue in difficult circumstances," the queen answered. "I was uncertain if you had your mother's gifts. If you have them, I knew not if you would abuse them. You showed a special gift for divination. You have selected the right door more often than not."

Claudia had not considered that she actually had the gift of divination. She had always thought it was reason that guided her intuition, and yet these words felt true. "Then why did you avoid me?"

"Politics and pride are often conjoined twins," the queen said with a sigh. "Nicomedes humiliated Typhaon before the court. The priests were quite angry. One tried to poison you. It took time to soothe their fury and keep them in line. Egypt much as Rome needs their priests, and compromises were required."

"What did you promise them?" Claudia asked.

"Much of the lore of this land was sent to Rome," Queen Arsinoë said. "I promised to return it to the priests, so they might learn what our ancestors knew."

"Megabyzus."

Queen Arsinoë smiled. "Yes. Once his apprenticeship is over, he will return to Egypt and teach others what he has learned."

This would appease the priests and make it easier for the governor to formally pardon Megabyzus. "That may not be for years."

Arsinoë toasted them once again. "Time moves slowly in Egypt. We plan a crop for our grandchildren."

"You speak of planning for our grandchildren. What of Ptolemy? Do you oppose this match?" Claudia asked.

"You seem as though you would try to be a proper wife to my son, and he does not find you unattractive," Queen Arsinoë said. "I fear that he would marry you, if only to get close to your eldest brother. He longs to transform himself into the soldier who wins an empire and destroys monsters."

"I have heard he acquitted himself well enough in Tanta," Adalia said.

Claudia nodded. Adalia would not have said it if it were not true. "If he wishes to be imperator, then an interest in battle is natural, is it not?"

"Perhaps, but he is also his father's son. He has a mind sharper than any sword. He has the talent to see what others fail to notice," Queen Arsinoë revealed. "This is not mother's pride, but observation. Ptolemy sensed the energy in the shrine before he heard the stories."

"It seems exploring both possibilities is good for any man – to take account of his strengths," Claudia said.

Queen Arsinoë nodded. "A wife is muse to her husband, encouraging dreams never spoken and awakening forgotten ambitions."

"You have your own ambitions for your son, not unlike my mother," Claudia stated. "What do you expect of him?"

"Ptolemy has the potential to be Alexander the Great reborn and to unite the world – a dream of lasting peace and prosperity to all men."

"What of the Soothsayers? Might they have their own plans?" Adalia asked.

"Why else did they send the Valeria as their catspaws at this time, if not to create a world not yet planted? Your mother spoke the truth. There is a secret war waged in the shadows amongst the great and powerful, and the Soothsayers shall need agents of their destiny to fight their battles. This battle changed the political map of this side of the world. Caesar, through his son, has finally won a victory over Parthia. This may give him the political power to claim that which has been denied to him."

"And that is?"

Claudia alreay knew the answer, but she wanted to hear the Queen say the words.

"A crown."

*   *   *   *

Claudia lay upon the feathered bed in her apartment, slowly eating salted olives, reclining her feet upon the pillows. It was the only time she was allowed any real privacy. Adalia insisted upon being in her presence outside of these walls.

She closed her eyes, trying to sleep, when she felt a presence. It felt like a shift in the wind, the breath of a familiar person. Claudia started up and reached for her dagger.

"A daughter should never fear the presence of her mother." Claudia lifted the dagger and rolled to her side. Septima stood before her, wearing a purple gown with a stola made from the feathers of a peacock. "It has been quite difficult finding a time to speak to you alone.

Claudia did not lower the dagger. "Do you fear being in the presence of Adalia?"

Septima raised her eyebrows and a tight-lipped smile appeared on her lips. "I think Adalia would have stabbed me when last we were together, if I had allowed it. It would seem that she is quite jealous of my boys," she said.

Claudia put the bed between them, careful to keep her dagger raised, as Adalia taught her. "They are no longer 'your boys,' mother. They have grown into men in their own right, and they owe nothing to you," Claudia snarled.

Septima waved away her anger as though it was nothing. "Jealousy sours your face, daughter. I warned you against scowling if you wish to keep your youth."

Claudia stood at the ready, facing her mother without blinking and feeling braver than she ever expected. "I could always learn your methods," Claudia said. "If I can shred my soul and learn to consume my children, I might look as young as you."

"You have a bitter bite, daughter," Septima said, with a surprising amount of respect. "Good. A woman needs such to make her way in the world."

"You do not deny the allegation, do you?" Claudia demanded.

Septima shook her head sadly. "You listen to the words of Decimus against your mother? What else can I say?"

It pained her to admit that there was truth in her mother's words, and yet she refused to deny the accusation. Patrician women in Rome were taught to suppress their anger. To allow another to anger you is to allow them to touch you.

Claudia seethed and could not contain it. "You can say it is untrue. You can explain how you regained your youth. You can tell me why you would refuse to teach your daughter and leave her to choose between the mercy of your stepson or joining the Vestal Virgins."

Septima maintained her composure. "You had talent as a girl, but no gift for the Art. I tested you, but you lacked the innate ability of Nicomedes."

"And Caecilia? Does she have this talent?" Claudia asked.

Septima shook her head, very disappointed. "No. She is blind to the energies as you were at her age, but she has other talents that will become apparent in time."

"It should be obvious we shall not betray Rome by now. You know of the victory your outcast children have managed in her name. What could you possibility want now?" Claudia asked.

Septima sneered. "You turned away a single tide. This is true. It is an impressive feat that shall be known through the annals of history. And what now? Will you allow Octavius to claim credit in Rome? Walk in a triumph? This resolves nothing."

"The Soothsayers protect Rome, and we are Rome. Why would we act against them?" Claudia asked. "Because you said they are dangerous? Because of some unknown threat you fail to explain?"

"There are always consequences to any action. Do you think the wielding of such power and influence will not have some consequence in the world?" Septima asked.

Claudia raised her dagger. Her hands shook. *Was she ready to stab her mother?* "There are always consequences. Fear only leaves you a slave to those with discipline to seize power. What do you want?"

"The three of you are brilliant — each in your own fashion. Seek out the truth in what I have shared with you. Do this, and when you discover the truth behind this war of infinite regress, seek me out so we might ally our causes. Promise me this, and I shall swear to leave you and yours out of my plans until you consent to them," Septima swore.

Thus far Septmima had been careful to speak only the literal truth in vagaries. Could Claudia trick her into revealing more? "You have only one thing to bargain with, mother. Are you willing to surrender it to ensure your good behavior?" Claudia asked.

"You wish to murder Orca for your petty revenge?" Septima asked, laughing. "I care not what happens to him now."

Claudia couldn't help but flinch at the brutal truth spoken. "You always underestimate us, mother," she sneered. "Perhaps it is because you lack the capacity for love or loyalty."

"You want Caecilia?"

"She is our sister," Claudia said. "You are not fit to be a mother. I would not trust you to raise a goat."

"She is not what you believe."

"Is she our sister?" Claudia asked.

"She is my daughter," Septima answered.

In this, her mother spoke true. "Then, that is all that matters," Claudia stated resolutely. "If you wish for us to consider your words and not seek your destruction, then you will give her unto us. If your words prove to be true, we will meet once again."

"Perhaps I was wrong about you. I imagined that you failed to live up to your destiny, but there is steel in your spine." Septima appeared to consider her words and finally nodded in agreement. "Done. I shall have her belongings packed and delivered to your apartments by morning. I hope in time we can be family once more. Blood always tells."

Claudia sheathed her dagger. She had managed to secure her sister's safety, yet it felt too easy. Was it possible for Septima to lie to her? Nicomedes had said no mortal would ever be able to shield the pure truth from her again. "One last thing, mother. I wish you to know this here and now. If you ever ensnare Marcus with your magic again, I shall kill you."

"I find it difficult to believe you have such malice in your soul, daughter."

"I might not. Adalia has more than enough malice for the two of us, and she would most pleased with the opportunity."

"I really am quite proud of you in this moment."

* * * *

Claudia enjoyed the sweet briny smell of the sea as she lay upon her couch and gazed at the stars. *They seem to shine brighter this side of the Mediterranean, away from the lights of Rome*, she thought.

She had come to enjoy spending her evening sipping tart wine in the atrium with Adalia. The amazon's tongue loosened considerably once properly plied with copious amounts of drink, and after several goblets, Claudia no longer heard the whispers of the dead. They toasted to the health of Marcus and Nicomedes far away in Tanta. Claudia shared stories of their childhood together, while Adalia told tales of the Rhine and its people. She hoped that fortune allowed her to visit those mysterious lands sometime in the future.

Adalia's words slurred together slightly, but it only made her stories much more entertaining. "You Romans keep such mysteries between your men and woman. It divides your lives and keeps you alone. It is different in the Rhinelands. We mark the grave of heroes who die for their people with the rune Uruz. It means courage. Uruz is also given to the honored women who have died in childbirth."

Claudia bit her lip to prevent speaking about the fear that rose nightly in her chest and haunted her dreams. It was said mothers loved their children all the more because of the pain and blood spent bringing them into this world. Childbirth was not a risk any woman who entered the College of the Vestal Virgins planned to face within this life. As a wife and materfamilias of a patrician family, it would be expected for her to have regular relations with her husband, and in time to give birth to children.

Adalia had yet another drink and then continued. "It is true. Our men are greeted into this world by a woman, and if they are brave and noble of spirit, a woman shall see them to the next realm."

Claudia tilted her head incredulously. "Dis Pater comes as a woman to the people of the Rhine?"

The amazon held her hand to her heart, as though to pledge it then and there. "If a man should die upon the field of battle, the Valkyrs, the beautiful war-maidens, come and carry him on their swift horses that ride the sky to Valhalla."

"Valhalla?"

"A hall in Asgard where the brave feast, fuck, and fight on, to the end of time."

Claudia laughed. "I am surprised Marcus has not forsaken all Roman gods to live amongst your people long ago."

"There was a night years ago when I held to that hope." Adalia blushed, realizing the thought had given way to words better not spoken aloud. "Drink has taken hold of my sensibilities and released that which is better not spoken of."

Adalia was a taciturn woman, rarely given to speaking of feelings. *Was this the time to probe further about Nicomedes?* "And perhaps your eye had turned towards another?"

"You speak of Nicomedes? That would be a fool's errand."

This truth burned from Adalia, and Claudia did not require the blessing of Shezmu to understand it. "Then why turn your attention towards him?" Claudia asked

"To learn from one whose mind burns like fire is a gift," Adalia said wistfully. "And perhaps despite all evidence to the contrary, I am a fool."

Claudia opened her mouth to speak, but the loud grinding of the gates to the guest wing of the palace drowned out her reply. Servants rushed over to greet the guest. Adalia drew her daggers and waited. One of the guards left behind by Marcus announced the name of their visitor. "Gaius Julius Octavius Ptolemy."

Claudia glanced aside to Adalia, who immediately sheathed her blades and helped Claudia prepare her appearance. Once she had learned the value in the methods, Adalia had grown quite skilled over the last few months, assisting her.

Ptolemy stepped into the atrium wearing a legionnaire's uniform with markings from the Seventh and Eighth Legions, no doubt a gift from Marcus. The armor was dirty and scuffed from battle, but his face was washed clean and shaven. He was young, but handsome and pleasing, with the features of his grandfather. Ptolemy wore his hair short in the Roman fashion, but it made his large ears stick out on the side. *A feature of his father that would surely argue against any idle speculation about his paternity*, Claudia noted.

"Please forgive the interruption at such a late hour," he said with a gentlemanly bow worthy of a patrician. Octavius had been certain to teach his son the manners of a Roman. "The centurion bid me to bring an invitation to each of you."

Claudia offered him a seat next to her. Ptolemy refused politely. "I have been asked by my father to immediately attend my mother afterwards."

A slight fib on the priorities of his orders, but she found it endearing. "You came to me before your own mother?" Claudia asked coyly.

Ptolemy blushed. She found it endearing. Her smile only deepened the crimson in his cheeks. "Inappropriate. Please do not tell her."

The pained expression on his face was so adorable that she had to bite her lip to avoid laughing. To hold such power over him was quite intoxicating. "I suspect she already knows. She knows everything that happens here in the palace."

"I shall gladly accept any punishment to lay eyes upon you."

His devotion was clear, and he feverently meant every word spoken to her. "What invitation did my brother offer?" Claudia asked.

"Centurion Marcus Valerius Perseus wishes to give the men a proper Roman funeral. It would be a kind thing to the soldiers if a Vestal Virgin blessed their ashes. I am to escort you back to Tanta via barge in the morning. My father wished me to assure you that it will be completely safe."

She thought of Caecilia and the promise that her mother had given. "I am to take custody of my sister. Her youth argues against taking her to a battlefield."

"The queen has a number of handmaidens who would be honored to entertain one of your blood," Ptolemy offered.

A daughter blinded with love would surely miss even a mother such Septima. If she was gone less than a day, then surely Caecilia would understand. "Perhaps if a proper spectacle could be arranged with girls of her age."

"I shall ask Ipy to make this, so as to please you."

Claudia laughed and placed her hand upon his arm. She could feel the goosebumps on his skin. "And should I agree to attend, shall you be there to protect me?"

Ptolemy raised his arm over his chest and swore to the gods in the Egyptian fashion. Her hand slipped to just above his heart where she could felt it palpitate from her mere presence. "With my honor and my life."

"Then I accept the invitation," Claudia said.

Ptolemy smiled and blushed once again. He turned to Adalia. "I was asked to carry a special message to the amazon. The centurion asked that I request you bring that which Optio Milius Hortensius Lex loved most."

Adalia tilted her head, confused. "Whores and wine?"

"I am certain that you will resolve this mystery to his satisfaction," Ptolemy quipped. "And now I must attend to the queen to answer any questions to her satisfaction."

"Will you return?" Claudia asked.

"Will you be ready to leave in the morning?" Ptolemy asked.

"Of course, I have a bag prepared this very moment, and my slaves can attend to anything else required." Claudia gestured to the stars gleaming in the night sky. "I love the sky in this land and I would have company this night. I have a jug of this especially tart wine."

Ptolemy glanced aside to the low table and took one of the goblets to his nose and sniffed. "It is called Desert Blossom from the Sahara Vineyard. It is owned by my family on the queen's side. It is very difficult to grow such grapes in this environment, though the flavor is quite worth the cost."

"I would share it with you this night, Ptolemy. Should our families come to an agreement, we will be wed this year or the next, once the formalities of the union between the Valeria and the Claudians are complete."

"Such would be a pleasure."

Ptolemy might be young, but he was quite handsome and growing into a striking figure of a man. She knew that she should remove her fingers from touching him, but she simply didn't have the will. She wanted to rule his heart and claim dominion over his flesh. "But that is all that we can share. The walls have eyes and ears, and it is important to both families that you marry me as an honored Vestal Virgin."

He forced a smile, but it was clear he was disappointed. Claudia understood as she shared it. "A taxing challenge, but one important to both families."

"Will you return to me once you have spoken with the queen?" Claudia asked.

He took her hand in his and raised it to his lips and kissed it. "If the queen can spare me, then nothing could please me more."

And in this, Ptolemy spoke only truth.

Chapter Thirteen: No Tears for Milius

Winning the battle had been the least exhausting part of the Tanta campaign. It had taken the better part of three days to sort though the prisoners and recommend a plan to Octavius about their ultimate fate. The common soldiers were bonded into slavery, to be sold in Egypt and Rome. The sweat from their backs would help seed a new generation of crops for the future of the empire.

The officers were questioned as to the state of the Parthian Empire, the logistics of their journey from the Arabian Sea, and the number and location of other legions. Those who survived interrogation would be taken back to Rome and displayed before the Senate in the Triumph of Octavius before they were ransomed back to their family or executed.

The last of the wounded had been sent to Alexandria this morning, and now Marcus Valerius Perseus had a personal debt to settle for an old friend. His back ached — spasms of pain crawled along his spine — from the digging. It had been many years since he had a real turn with a spade, and this trench needed to be exact for the funeral pyre.

Marcus tried to imagine life in the legions without Milius, and he shivered as he did when he thought of his brother's dead fingers probing his chest. This night would be difficult, but he resolved to honor his friend in the manner Milius often spoke of during long nights near the campfire.

When a Roman died at home, his family would place a coin in his mouth — Charon's obol — to seal the passing of the spirit from the body and pay the ferryman to convey the souls of the newly dead across the River Styx. The family held the body at the local atrium with its feet pointed towards the door. It would be washed and anointed by the family, or if they could afford it, priests of their household gods.

A legionnaire who died in battle could not expect such impractical niceties in the wilds of the world. The common practice was communal cremation, and a portion of the ashes were delivered back to Rome. The legionnaires who survived dug large crematorium pits for the dead.

The body of Milius Hortensius Lex lay covered in a cenotaph tent near his quarters. Marcus could not abide his friend being burned alongside everyone else, as though his life had not mattered. Milius would have a grand funeral, furnished with all that was within Marcus' power to acquire. It felt right to indulge his old friend one last time.

"Marcus!"

The work distracted him from the world. His name had to be called several times before it penetrated his fog of grief. This authoritative voice could not long be ignored, however. He turned towards Governor Gaius Octavius Thurinus. "Hail, general."

Octavius still wore his pristine blue and grey leather breastplate, cut in Greek fashion to honor the history of Alexandria. It was strangely clean of dirt or scratches after such a battle, but none would dare to call attention to it. Octavius had remained in deep in the flank of their legions, learning what happened on the field from Rubio, who spoke with Nicomedes' voice upon his lips.

The general climbed the hill where Milius had served and died for the empire. Nicomedes ordered some of the slaves to gather the monstrous scorpions and butcher them for their parts, leaving only blood and scuffle marks in the muck as the evidence of their existence. "You honor my name, centurion. We both know your leadership was the key to victory."

Marcus thrust the spade into the dirt once again. The lie came easily with practice. It was as though Octavius wanted to be certain he would be convincing enough in Rome during the triumph. "I merely served as directed, general. I am told soon you shall be changing your agnomen to Tantius for this great victory."

"I could say the same thing of you, centurion." Octavius turned his nose up at the work, glanced about the pit, and asked, "Do we lack the manpower for digging holes? Surely there are men who could be assigned to this task while we celebrate our victory."

"This one is special. My friend and optio Milius Hortensius Lex died securing our victory." Marcus found it difficult to glance over towards the cenotaph. "I would honor his memory in absence of other duties."

"I have never had a talent for manual labor. It seems to require so much stamina." Octavius sighed and wiped his brow. "I would speak to you of the future."

Marcus glanced aside at the cenotaph tent and nodded. "Milius was a legionnaire. He understood the business of Rome was paramount. Besides, the wine and mourners are not yet present."

It was known that Octavius approved of practicality even more than piety. "Excellent. My legions are disorganized. We lost a thousand men. More are wounded. My officers took a substantial hit. Many will cashier out of the service."

"I might be able to assist you there, general." Marcus had already worked with a number of the men, assessing their strengths and which should be allowed to leave the legions. "I know their spirits well and can make recommendations on who to promote."

Octavius scoffed at the thought. "My best legate is dead. The other two are worthless political appointments. I need a soldier in the role who the men respect and fear. I need a voice in the legions none will doubt. You know some of the men consider me to be effeminate, yes?"

The general was offering him the position of first legate with command over the legions of Alexandria. Such a position would bind him to a military career for years. He hoped to leave the service once his term was over and after he had earned his name within his year. "Your generosity is too kind, general."

"Kindness has nothing to do with it. I need you here," Octavius stated.

"I am to be married when we return to Rome."

"Alexandria is not Rome, Marcus, but it has pleasures of its own your bride might enjoy. There is no reason you cannot establish your branch family here as well as Rome. Mighty Caesar himself lived many years in Gaul. The difference is you would be based where your family may live in luxury and safety."

"I have an obligation to the Seventh Legion, general," Marcus replied. "A month's leave has expanded into three months. I promised

Legate Agrippa upon my honor I would return to defend the borders of Gaul."

"Agrippa is a childhood friend. If I can persuade him to release you from such a promise, then would you consider the position?" Octavius asked. "Greatness is rarely thrust upon a man twice in a lifetime."

"Certainly I would be a fool to not consider such a generous offer from such a worthy man as yourself," Marcus said.

"Excellent." Octavius looked back at the pit. "Does your man require anything?"

"Adalia is acquiring what I need at this very moment, but your presence at the ceremony would honor him greatly, and I would consider it an act of friendship."

"It will be done."

*   *   *   *

Adalia arrived from Alexandria with two dozen whores, ten casks of wine and assorted drinks, and a fat cow that wandered through the field aimlessly. The legionnaires of the Third Cohort of the Seventh Legion hailed her arrival as a conquering hero. Marcus eyed the quantity the wine delivered, concerned that come moonrise all of the casks would be empty, leaving angry soldiers. Adalia assured him the store of drink would be more than enough and that more was coming on the last shipment.

He had expended all of his remaining coin ensuring the prostitutes were properly motived to see to the pleasures of his men. A portion of every soldier's pay was set aside for his funeral by the legion's assigned quaestor, whose job it was to maintain an account for such expenses. The problem was that the Seventh Legion and its lictors were in Gaul, and thus Marcus had to pay for the celebration out of his own resources. He had felt tempted to ask for money from Octavius, but did not wish to indebt himself further.

Tradition held that heroes were always celebrated upon the battlefield. This was difficult in Tanta, because supplies were scarce. Fresh water could be found easily enough upon the banks of the Nile, but they could hardly gather enough food to feed all of the captured soldiers. Clearly, the Parthians intended to gather supplies after they raided the valley and gained control of the barges that sailed the river.

Vermin and flies littered the battlefield, scavenging meat and blood from the dead. The muck and the heat did little to stem the horrific stench. It took almost two days to clear the field, but the pests were quite persistent until Nicomedes called down a potent wind to clear the stench from Tanta.

It was gruesome work, and the appearance of the men reflected it. Once the new slaves were organized into labor parties and under control, Marcus ordered a rotating liberty for the soldiers bivouacked in Tanta, allowing them time to properly wash themselves in the Nile.

Adalia organized the festivities with her accustomed efficiency and through sheer intimidation over the palace servants, who had come along with her by order of Ptolemy. The soldiers gulped the wine, kissed the whores, and cheered the names of their fallen comrades to let the gods know that Roman legionnaires were coming to Elysia. They gathered around a dozen smaller campfires to keep warm and sang mournful dirges for lost friends, calling out to household gods and honored ancestors. A few of the more learned legionnaires recited favorite passages of Virgil, recalling the fall of Troy and how the tragedy led to the founding of Rome.

Marcus waved Adalia over to him once she had finished. They shared a potent embrace that seemed to release their pent-up anxiety, leaving only the sorrow. "I miss that old goat," she said.

"He died well, so I am told."

A collective yelp escaped from the servants and the whores once Nicomedes had been spotted in the valley, ascending up the hill. Marcus scanned the horizon until he spotted his younger brother, clad in Soothsayer robes with his hood down — giving the ghastly appearance of Charon coming for his due. The visible skin on his dead hand was still black and ashen. It was as though they were staring at the very embodiment of Dis Pater.

The men were silent, having seen his power in action, and wished to avoid offending him. The mystical might of Nicomedes saved them all. He waited solemnly near Marcus, studying the soldiers from under the hood.

Marcus turned towards his men. "Is this not a party?" he asked them, with a bit more ire than intended. Revelry continued, just a bit further away from the presence of Nicomedes. "How is your new student?"

Nicomedes replied in a low whisper. "Megabyzus transmuted a

good portion of the scorpion venom in his blood. He leeched just enough power from our connection to ensure his survival. I have prepared a healing poultice that should drain the remaining poison in his system. Rubio is watching him presently, under protection of certain wards I have put into place."

It felt wrong that Milius died while this priest lived. He surrendered his own heart, securing it, and if there was justice in this world or the next, it would have been enough to heal Milius. "Do you believe Typhaon's followers will strike at him to punish us for humiliating them?"

Marcus once caught Nicomedes examining the dead corpse of Claudia's former cat. When asked why he would do such a thing, his younger brother — barely a decade in age — merely grinned at the experience of seeing that which was hidden by skin and fur. The smile Nicomedes flashed reminded him of that very moment and beamed with malevolence. "The very attempt would inspire legends of sorrow and suffering to be compared to brave Prometheus."

He worried Nicomedes swelled with the high of power and might forget it should be used judicially, lest others rise up against them for fear of it. "Gaining the fear and respect of the local authorities here might not be a terrible loss for the family, but remember if we must harm, it should be so terrible others would dread the thought of the performance vested upon them."

Claudia stepped off the barge docked at the bank of the Nile in her Vestal Virgin vestments, her sacred veils, and the traditional sini crenes, never before seen outside of the walls of Rome. Palace servants cleared a path through the mud and the muck with straw brooms. They laid down wooden planks over the larger puddles. General Octavius and his son Ptolemy served as her honor guard until they reached Marcus. They exchanged proper familial affections, and Marcus snapped his fingers until one of the servants brought Claudia a chair on the dais.

Some of the more astute men stood at attention and saluted. Octavius waved away the need for formality. He was known for his speeches about Roman virtue, but on this night, he merely smiled and greeted the men as equals. Marcus nodded his approval, shared a drink with the general, and then toasted the men's victory over the Parthians. The men cheered heartily. Octavius was trying to win the hearts of the men, and his approval would help secure that.

To a common soldier, the mere presence of a Vestal Virgin was akin to hearing the very commands of Jupiter. It did not escape notice that the general escorted her to this procession, and now she tended one of the fires as though it were the sacred hearth of Rome.

The funeral procession slowly transformed into a party, as the sun began to set. Octavius turned towards Marcus expectantly. Roman tradition demanded the host give the laudatio. Great oratory skills were required for prominent men of Rome. If Marcus was going to serve as legate, he would need such skills, and this was clearly a test by Octavius. If he could not speak well of his friend, then what good could he be as legate?

Sextus Clodius, the renowned Sicilian rhetorician, once taught Marcus that a well-delivered funeral oration could be a way for a young politician to publicize himself. The imperator made his introduction via a speech in honor of his aunt Julia, the widow of Gaius Marius. It is said the speech helped launch his career as a politician.

The cohort brought forth the body from the cenotaph and crowned its head with the honor of the victory wreath. They carried it to the pit, which had been prepared with tinder and wood, and then lowered it from a dais. Claudia knelt down and kissed Milius upon his swollen face. Marcus had forced the body to close its eyes earlier. He remembered how cold the skin was. Now it was almost grey, akin to a statue.

She anointed his head with sacred oils and whispered a prayer. "Great Vesta, please take this son lost so far away back to the Eternal City. Let the sacred flame of your hearth warm his soul on the Elysian Fields."

Marcus led the cow before the funeral procession. She was fat and full of life, staring blankly at the people around her and chewing her cud. He raised his gladius to the heavens and then finally began to address the funeral procession about his friend. "There were nights when we starved in service to Rome. We were alone in the wilderness, where even the gods themselves had forsaken us. Milius made us all laugh when our bellies ached. I remember a time when the cohort had been separated from the legion by a swath of Caledonians. We were lost and chasing rabbits to survive. It was kill or be killed, and yet, my spirits were rarely higher. That was life with Milius. His spirit lifted us all. He embodied motto of the legions: *the Senate and People of Rome*. He loved Rome, and his love lifted us all. Now it is time for all of us to lift his spirit. His one request was that, at his funeral, we indulge in what he loved and shout his name to warn all of the gods and devils on the other side that a Roman was coming."

He pulled the blade of the gladius under the throat of the sow and killed it immediately. "We sacrifice this beast to Ceres to help our friend journey."

Slaves butchered and cut the animal into two portions. The portion given unto the gods was burned on an altar. The remains were roasted on a spit and given to those who grieved for the fallen Roman.

Octavius joined Marcus once he washed his hands, and the feast began in full. "Such a feast would be an honor to the greatest amongst us. I only knew your optio for a short time, but he was a good soldier of Rome."

"It would have pleased him greatly to hear you speak of him thusly," Marcus replied.

Octavius nodded. "I must attend to other matters back in Alexandria, but consider my offer. We can discuss it en route to Rome for my triumph."

"Will you honor me by taking my sister back to the city?" Marcus asked.

The general agreed heartily. "I imagine the debauchery might upset her delicate sensibilities. All men and beasts must act according to their natures. Soldiers have base needs that must be filled in times such as this, but there is nothing under the heavens that says it must happen in front of civilized men."

Once the general left to gather his honor guard, Marcus pulled

Claudia close to him and kissed her upon the forehead. He tried to think of words to express the gratitude that swelled on his chest. "Thank you for your attendance. This night is bound to get quite wild."

"And the governor is bound to disapprove of the attendance of a potential new daughter," Claudia replied bitterly, cutting him off before he arrived at the same point. "I understand and agree the political situation is complex. I would rather spend time getting to know Ptolemy."

"He fought bravely, if not always wisely." Marcus squeezed his arms around her body, lifting her high into the air before setting her back down. "I well remember my first battle, and I fared no better. He is young, but he will learn the wisdom of battle. I will teach him personally."

"You are his hero. He respects you greatly," Claudia said. "And I would ask that you send him back with us."

"He will not take kindly to the thought that I do not count him amongst us," Marcus argued. "And he should bond with the men in their victory."

Claudia smiled coyly. "Not if you ask him to guard that which is most precious to you: me."

"I will ask Adalia to follow you," Marcus offered.

She shook her head and gestured to their friend toasting the night with the rest of the cohort. "Adalia loved Milius nearly as much as you. She deserves this night. I will be safe. If not, you will horribly murder the governor and everyone he has ever loved in revenge. He knows this. I have yet to experience a night of romance and seduction. Ptolemy is young and inexperienced, to hear his mother speak of it, but I am quite satisfied to witness the attempt. We both might even learn something from it."

It was difficult to imagine his sister — the Vestal Virgin — as a seductress. There was a lust resurfacing in her eyes, one which she had long been forced to deny, and it caused a queer feeling in his gut. "Remember his mother sees everything in the palace, and there is power in discretion."

"Victory denied only makes a real warrior much more eager for true victory," Claudia said with a knowing smile.

Once Claudia positioned herself a discrete distance from Marcus, he called the boy over. Ptolemy proudly strode towards the centurion. "Hail! You honor me."

Marcus nodded solemnly. "I have a special mission that needs doing this evening, and it will mean you will miss the festivities, but it is vital to our interests."

Disappointment flashed over the boy's face. The celebration orgy of a Roman cohort was nothing less than the stuff of legend. He quickly regained his composure. "Anything for you, sir!"

Marcus put on his officer's scowl, designed to intimidate new recruits. He thought of Cossus, and the weight of his sorrow burned upon him. "I need you to escort my sister back to the palace. There has already been one attempt on her life. I place her life in your hands. I expect you to safeguard her with your own."

Ptolemy flashed a quick salute. "Yes, centurion."

"Let her not escape your sight for any reason!"

The boy saluted, having never been more pleased by an assignment. He turned to find Claudia in the crowd, only to discover her whispering to Nicomedes. Something happened in the other realm that restored their childhood bond, and Marcus found himself envious. There were moments that he could barely stand the sight of either of them.

General Octavius gathered his honor guard and promptly exited the wake with his special guests. Marcus knew that Octavius would ensure the protection of Claudia, lest his honor be violated and his son's reputation forever stained for failing to protect a Vestal Virgin. Once they had left the hill and crossed half-way through Tanta valley, the tension that hung upon the party dissipated.

The whores began to giggle freely and poured drinks into the soldiers' mouths. This naturally aroused the men and their laughter bellowed as night reached the sky. No soldier wanted to get drunk or be seen as a degenerate in front of the general, especially one known to disapprove of such things. Marcus gulped his wine as he surveyed the performers of the night.

Adalia brought forth a cornucopia of delightful pleasures, both subtle and gross. A trio of enchanting women clad in sheer scarlet veils danced, revealing every curve and ripple in their bodies, even by flickering campfire light. They posed and flexed their bodies with such fluid precision that every movement brought forth an undulation of flesh and dulcimer chimes from the tiny brass bells they wore on their belts. The soldiers cheered, reaching crescendo frenzy once the dancers selected lovers for private performances.

Next, living statues strode out into the open with great aplomb, surrounding Marcus. They knelt before him to pay homage, as though he was their pharaoh, to crazed applause from the soldiers. He glanced upon the tantalizing entertainers — men and women — and then raised a single eyebrow, indicating his approval. The living statues were avatars of the gods and heroes of old — wearing only tragedy masks of their ideal forms, painted gold or silver, that glimmered in the torchlight. Such beautiful spectacle typically only came to the lavish parties of the patricians and the grossly wealthy.

The soldiers began to chant "Bear Centurion! Bear Centurion!"

Marcus pointed to the men and then turned aside to the living statues. "Pleasure is your business. Seek it with the men, for tonight they are all gods!"

The living statues obeyed the command with the practiced discipline of a legionnaire. Soon their silhouettes fell against the backdrops of the campfires, embracing and seeking pleasure in all of the forms the human body could experience in this world.

Marcus stood in the fashion of the imperator at the games and threw the thumbs-up signal, formally announcing before the gods that the orgy was to begin in earnest. "This night is ours. Eat, drink, and fuck your way to oblivion. Remember this night is to honor Milius, and we will celebrate him in the manner he requested of us all."

Sweet words were expressed in whispers from the shadows until they became load moans and finally screamed in homage of Milius, crying his name in the darkness. Some might have considered this blasphemy, but what happened at an orgy was never spoken of during the light of day, lest the betrayer feel the eternal wrath of Dionysus. Milius had been a loyal friend for years beyond measure, and this had been the chosen manner of celebrating his death, so the gods themselves would be prepared for his entrance in the afterlife.

The palace servants crept quietly between the campfires, quietly ensuring every cup was eternally filled and bringing anything the men desired until dawn. Marcus sat upon his chair like it was a throne, near Milius, watching the grinding flesh before him and directing the flow of the orgy, ever the officer in the cohort. He searched through the crowd for Adalia, only to finally locate her at the outer edge of the orgy, whispering quietly to Nicomedes.

It felt strange to be jealous of his younger brother. Adalia helped him ease into loving Drusilla. Perhaps it was her way to say goodbye to that aspect of their relationship, but the mere thought of being overlooked for Nicomedes still burned. Would he even acknowledge her? Mighty Caesar was the only lover he had known Nicomedes to accept, and even then it was the imperator's brilliant mind that seduced him. Adalia was wise and wily, but would she even attract his attention?

The centurion pointed to a fresh-faced whore with gentle lips like Cossus, commanded him to sit upon his lap, and then proceeded to feed him slices of grilled steak. "What is your name?"

"Heru."

"Where are you from?" Marcus asked.

"I am a Nubian from the lower Nile," Heru answered.

"Can you sing?"

Heru smiled slyly. "My voice is one of my most sought-after qualities."

How was it possible his chest ached without feeling pain? This rotted thing in his chest belonged to Nicomedes. His eyes watered from the well-spring of conflicted emotions, but Marcus refused to sob in front of his men.

Nicomedes raised his hood from across the orgy, confused. Adalia mouthed something towards him, likely asking if he needed them. Marcus waved away their concern, freeing them from all obligations for the night.

Marcus slapped Heru on the ass and bid him to rise before the funeral procession. "Then sing. I would see my friend to the gates of Hell with a song in his ears."

Heru swallowed the last bit of steak and began to sing a beautiful song about Alexandria and the Nile. The lad had a sweet voice and though he sung in a strange language, Marcus had been moved enough to release gentle tears.

He drank his wine and stared out at the stars. This was what his friend had desired, but Marcus wanted to be alone to remember all that had happened. His melancholy tainted even Heru, who eventually snuck away while he was distracted and found another lover in the night.

By dawn, the orgy had mostly dissipated, and the soldiers retreated to their tents. Marcus walked between the darkened embers of the campfires and poked them with a stick to keep them stoked. The servants moved about listlessly, but Marcus did not berate them. They had managed to keep the flow of the orgy moving, despite limited resources. He made a note to praise them before their masters when he came across a familiar face.

Coriolanus, First Spear of the First Cohort of the Eighth Legion, lay upon his back in his breastplate like a turtle that had been tipped. A voluptuous woman with curly black hair buried her head in his crotch and wiggled her plush ass in the air as though taunting him.

"Centurion, please join us." He pointed to her bottom. "The honor of Rome is at stake, sir."

It would not be fitting to allow any one of these prostitutes to say the men of Rome would not take up any challenge. Marcus scanned the remains of the orgy until he spotted a seasoned member of the Third Cohort. "Longinus!"

The legionnaire startled at hearing his centurion command him, flinched, and drunkenly flipped over. Longinus was naked, save for his helmet and one of his boots. He stood at attention and saluted.

"Centurion!"

"How dare you leave a job undone, Longinus!"

The soldier blanched. Marcus stepped away, lest he be vomited upon. "What task is required of me, centurion?"

He pointed to the challenge before them, still wiggling. "Never let it be said that a legionnaire of Rome leaves a man or woman on the battlefield. Have at it!"

Longinus did as commanded with great fervor. Marcus left them and returned to Milius. The servants lowered Milius down into the hole on a bed of leaves. The wood was already smoking from the embers and coals he collected. He found the last lit torch and waited over the pit until Longinus cried out. "Milius!"

The centurion dropped the torch into the pit and sat back upon his chair to watch his friend burn.

*　　*　　*　　*

Tradition held that legionnaires became citizens of Rome once they crossed the Rubicon. Soldiers were forbidden to wear armor or wield weapons in the Eternal City, unless on duty or on the day of their triumph. Lowly legionnaires arrived at the Field of Mars well before first light to prepare their armor and ensure the legion was at parade best. Centurions arrived at dawn to ensure that their cohorts were presentable before the city, and that their standard had been properly polished and treated.

The general of a triumph always received the lion's share of the coin and the adulation, but every soldier who marched in the triumph had opportunity thrust upon them, even if it came in the form of free drinks and the adulation of the women.

Marcus knelt down upon the wild fields and dug his hands through the soil of his home. It felt strange to muster with the Eighth Legion and the survivors of his cohort. These were not his men, yet he had replaced their legate.

The Parthian prisoners were kept in chains or portable cages on wheels like animals in a zoo. Seven Roman legions had participated in the Battle of Tanta, but Egypt and other parts of the empire required protection, and so General Octavius assigned three to protect Egypt and returned the others to their new assignments to watch the borders of the empire.

Triumphs were lackadaisical affairs —unforeseen interruptions and accidents caused such delays that it might take the entire day to travel from the Fields of Mars to the Capitoline temple. Marcus prepared a leisurely itinerary that had several planned stops for drinking and sampling of local Roman cuisine. Some speculators would wipe down the soldiers to collect samples of their sweat to cure ailments and vitality. No soldier of the Eighth Legion would hunger or thirst or want for anything this day. Marcus found the prospect quite pleasing. *The men deserved this adoration*, he thought.

August members of the Senate of Rome arrived hours later, once the soldiers prepared the prisoners and settled into marching formation. They wore traditional white togas with a red trim to indicate their citizenship and authority.

The triumphator — General Octavius — had the right to invite any patrons he wished to share in the spotlight. Marcus noted Senator Marcus Tullius Cicero was the first to arrive with a small staff. He was the leader of the Optimates — the so-called Best Men — a collection of patrician senators that opposed many of Caesar's great reforms.

Lucius Antony Creticus — brother of Marcus Antony — came along with Manius Aemilius Vetus, sharing wine and laughing together. Creticus was the leader of Caesar's faction — known as the Populares, for they were of the people of Rome.

Other men with unknown faces in noble togas arrived and took their places in the triumph. Marcus had no idea Octavius had so many friends in the Senate, but then he supposed on this day, he was the most important man in Rome.

Senator Marcus Livius Drusus Claudianus arrived in a lectica. He had not realized his father's friend looked so frail by daylight. This was who Marcus had chosen to include with his one invitation, and Octavius had been quite pleased to approve it. He immediately went to his future father-in-law and offered his arm. "It is a pleasure to see you, senator."

Livius struggled to his feet. "I am to be your father on the morrow. It would seem foolish to stand upon pomp and circumstances now. Bread and circuses are for the plebians, not men of worth."

Riding the lectica in the triumph would imply the senator was frail. Yet, Marcus doubted the man could endure the grueling day of walking and standing around. He turned to one of the guards not involved in the triumph and snapped his fingers. "You! Fetch my steed. Senator Claudianus is going to do me the honor of riding her during the triumph as my father."

The foot-soldier swallowed. "What will you ride, sir?"

Marcus growled at having his order questioned and gestured wildly towards the horses drinking near the stream. "If deeds do not replace words quickly, I shall insert my boot in your ass and ride you through the streets of Rome for questioning me!"

The foot-soldier departed quickly to find his horse. Livius smiled gratefully. "You surrender a great honor for the sake of my vanity, son.

Perhaps I am simply too old for a triumph."

Marcus shook his head. "This victory is as much yours as mine. I would not be here without you. My family would not be here. You have given me a new life, and it will never be forgotten."

He helped Senator Livius mount the steed. It was a great honor, but none could gainsay the offer to his new father. "I confirmed with the prisoner everything General Octavius told you."

The prisoner Livius referenced was Gallus Licinius Nonus of the Eighth Legion. He was captured when he and Milius ventured to the Aventine. Octavius had sworn upon his son's life he had nothing to do with the attack. They had long presumed the cohort had been ambushed and killed in secret by the Parthians. "Did he know anything about who might have sent them to Rome?"

Livius scratched his chin thoughtfully. "I suspect Macer kept such knowledge strictly to himself. A pity your brother could not wrest the secrets from his skull, as he did from the assassins."

"I am told such information shall be provided tomorrow, as a present for the wedding." Marcus shrugged his shoulders upon seeing his future father's twisted facial expression and glanced up to the heavens. "Listen, I am quite grateful he promised to bathe properly and wear fresh clothing."

A murmur amongst the senators alerted Marcus to a new arrival amongst their ranks: Senator Quintus Valerius Orca. Marcus felt his hand move slowly towards his gladius. Separating that monster's head from his body would be an insidious crime inside of the walls of Rome, but here in the Field of Mars it might be forgiven.

Livius directed his steed between Marcus and his intended prey. "There is a time for every deed imaginable. Is this the time to surrender all you have gained, son? If nothing else, do you not wish to see him suffer the entire route? He might very well die from the effort and in more suffering than you could visit upon him."

Marcus laughed, despite the shaking of his hands and shallow attempts at breathing. Octavius must have felt it was politically unwise to insult the senator by not offering an invitation to him. Who would have predicted Orca would have come to the event?

Orca walked with a limp, and his large belly made any exertion difficult. He acknowledged Marcus with a nod. "It would appear you have found a good patron."

"Sometimes fate is kind." Marcus spun on his heels and looked towards the procession where soon General Octavius would arrive. "Enjoy the triumph, senator."

General Gaius Octavius Thurinus arrived with great aplomb in a four-horse chariot with along with Ipy, his wife's body-slave. They would ride through streets of Rome together, and she would whisper a simple phrase in his ear — *"you are not a god"* — to ensure that he never forgot that he was only an avatar of Jupiter and still mortal.

He wore a gold-embroidered triumphal toga stained purple and the traditional crown of laurel wreathes. His face was painted with blood from a sacrifice given unto Mars.

Octavius noted Marcus and then Livius upon his horse with stern disapproval. "Hail, centurion."

Marcus met the general and saluted to show his respect. "General."

"Why is Senator Livius on your horse?" Octavius asked.

"I felt my new father deserved respect, rather than be carried via a lectica," Marcus admitted.

"That will have political consequences, but that is not unexpected." Octavius turned and pointed to one of the guards on a white stallion who rode alongside him. "Surrender your horse to the centurion."

"General?"

"You will still receive your appointment, son," Octavius promised. "If there is violence, do you believe you can protect me as well as the Bear Centurion?"

The unknown officer slid off his horse and offered it immediately to Marcus. The face of this man seemed familiar, but Marcus had been too far away from Rome to recall it. "Thank you, centurion. I am in your debt. What is your name?"

"Sosius Avidius Cassius, sir."

The son of a very rich senator known for ignoring politics and outside of both factions – what was Octavius planning? To allow this inexperienced man at his side was akin to publically sharing the honors with him. "I shall remember that."

The triumph started through the streets of Rome in a serpentine fashion at the pace of a slow walk. The captured officers were at the point of the parade where the mob jeered them. Any spoils taken from the Parthian leaders were displayed on carts. Octavius had managed to collect paintings, tableaux, and beautiful carpets and silks, along with their weapons and armor.

Next came the senators of Rome and their magistrates through the route. Senator Livius led them upon his steed, catching the eye of the crowd. They cheered for the Claudians, a feat not heard for several generations. They were allowed by the lictors of the legions, who walked quietly in their red war-robes with their faces wreathed in laurel.

At the last came General Octavius with his chariot, drawing the largest applause. Fear of the Parthian Empire had long been hiding in the mind of Rome. This was the first victory against that enemy in living memory, and for that Octavius was a hero of the people. The Eighth Legion followed chanting "io triumphe!" and singing ribald songs at their general's expense.

The triumph left the Field of Mars to circumnavigate the Eternal City's sacred boundary on the west bank of the River Tiber. Then, the procession entered the city through the Gate of Antony and crossed the pomerium, where General Octavius formally surrendered his command to the Senate of Rome.

The journey was long, often stopping to address the swell of emotions from the crowd, or giving the senators a chance to drink at one of the designated rest stops. The procession continued through the Circus Flaminius, skirting the southern base of the Capitoline Hill and the Velabrium. Next, they entered the Via Sacra and stopped at the Forum to pray at the Temple of Jupiter, where the imperator awaited them.

Caesar embraced Octavius as a son. The mob exploded with applause. The imperator raised his hands, signaling to the crowd that he wanted to speak. "Never in the history of Rome has a father been more proud of his son!" Marcus noted well the expression of relief from Octavius and his smile upon earning his father's respect. "Octavius has brought us grain from Egypt and slaves from Parthia. Rome is enriched by his presence. Our laws — our justice — our divine spirit reaches out beyond the borders of our empire. Let us rejoice here!"

The triumphator waited for the applause to die before he addressed the crowd on the steps of Jupiter. "Gratitude to the Senate and People of Rome for their fighting spirit that led to this victory. Thank you to my father for guiding my life. Egypt is a willing partner in the Empire, and I hope the people of Rome will see its love and return it in kind as sisters."

The reaction from the crowd was decidedly mixed. Every citizen of Rome, from the patricians to the plebeians and slaves who lived in squalor, held true to the illusion that Rome was the greatest city in the world. To share such a title, even in thought, was anathema to them. "Just as the ancient Romans took brides from the Sabine and made them Romans, we have done the same with all of Italia and Alexandria. Just as mighty Caesar has taken Gaul and Hispania and made them as Romans, we must to the same to the rest of the empire. There are dangers in the dark places of the world, and we must unite to conquer them."

The mention of the word conquer was always good for a cheer from the mob in Rome. Octavius held up his hands, mimicking his father. "I have made a promise before my ancestors and the divine Venus herself. This day was made possible by a single centurion. A man who put Rome before his own glory. Tomorrow, Centurion Marcus Valerius Perseus marries Livia Drusilla Claudianus Appius. I ask that all of Rome blesses their marriage in the face of the gods."

Marcus swallowed at the eyes of the crowd turned upon him, and realized at that moment his marriage might not be as private as he hoped.

Chapter Fourteen: The Stars Incline Us, They Do Not Bind Us

Nicomedes opened the lid of the large clay pot inscribed with Egyptian hieroglyphics. He dug his dead hand into it, and then presented to his students the skull of Nepos Murena Macer — centurion of the First Cohort of the Eighth Legion. A tenacious dermestid beetle determined to not yet release its meal skittered across the brow of the skull. Nicomedes snatched it with his other hand, sniffed it carefully, and then tossed it back into the pot. The other beetles shimmied up the sides of the pot, attempting to escape, but the magister clamped down the lid with a loud thud.

Megabyzus blinked and gazed into the empty sockets of Macer's skull, where once there were living eyes. "I knew him, magister. Not well, but he was a man of importance in Alexandria. And you say that he dared to attack your brother?"

He placed the skull within a circle of purified salt drawn in the center of his workbench. The old black wood had been stained dark crimson from his experiments over the years. Nicomedes unconsciously tapped one of the spots of blood that had come from the assassins who failed to kill Claudia. "And lost his head in the Aventine in the process. Now that the dermestid beetles have finally completed their task, we shall draw forth this man's soul and compel it to answer our questions. If there is time enough in the day, we will also cast him to Tartarus."

Rubio rested his head upon the workbench, peering at the skull through folded arms. He gingerly raised a hand until Nicomedes acknowledged him. "Magister? Why go through the bother? Are there any mysteries left to resolve the prisoners could not answer?"

His student was learning to see below the surface of things. If he survived the next few years, Rubio could truly be useful. "We still do not properly understand the motives of our enemies and why they decided to attack the Valeria," Nicomedes explained. "The attack upon my brother was neither commissioned by the Parthian military nor Octavius. Never let an enemy harm you without taking revenge, lest you invite further attacks."

"I would find it unlikely the priests of Alexandria even knew of his existence before you arrived and seized the power of the Eternal Dreamers." Megabyzus grimaced and studied the skull once again. "It is a pity the Parthian Magi were able to escape, or we could question them directly."

Nicomedes released a tight-lipped smile. He had felt the power of their translocation circles during the last stages of the confrontation in Tanta, but he did not wish to end their lives at that time, not when there was so much he could learn from them. He had shown his power and wanted them to tell the tale of what happened to those foolish enough to challenge him. "It was pity that allowed them to escape."

"Why did you not take the skull with you?" Megabyzus asked.

"These dermestid beetles are a rarity in this world," Nicomedes explained. "They are owned by the Soothsayer Academy, and thus it is forbidden to remove them from Rome. It can take the beetles more than a week to complete their task. The haste of our mission from the Soothsayers forced us to depart before we were able to perform the ritual."

Megabyzus glanced about the damp chambers Nicomedes kept at the Soothsayer Academy and wrinkled his nose. "Magister, might I ask a personal question? Why do you keep such chambers? Surely you have proven your worth to the Soothsayers?"

Nicomedes studied the walls of the chambers that had been his home and laboratory for many years. They were carved from the limestone that served as the bedrock of Rome. A faint layer of moss glistened in the candlelight; in complete darkness, it shimmered like stars. If he listened closely, he could feel the very flow of the Tiber River above. "A person leaves their essence in spaces they inhabit. They imbue it with their soul. The Magister Palatii Counsel offered memberships just this morning. I could have luxury rooms in the tower, but I have found solace in this place. In truth, I loathe the idea of letting it go."

A line of beeswax candles arranged on the workbench lit of their own volition, producing sickly green-tinted flames. Nicomedes offered a cracked stone mortar to Rubio. "It is time to put what you have learned into practice. You know the components of the ritual, yes?"

Necromancy required precision and discipline. Asking the student to perform this task was a great honor. Rubio's eyes grew wide like saucers and his lips trembled. "Yes, magister. First, we must grind iodine powder and toadstools with a high concentration of psilocybin into paste."

Nicomedes rarely offered praise to his students, preferring to dollop it at the right moment. Otherwise, the effort grew too taxing. "You have proven you can be useful on rare occasion, Rubio. Prepare the components. You know where I keep them."

Rubio rifled through the shelves at the far side of the chamber and began to grind the materials gathered with the mortar and pestle until it became a green mash. He opened the clay pot, snatched two of the dermestid beetles, and smashed them into the paste. Megabyzus turned his attention towards Rubio and the efforts to grind the components of the ritual. "Are you hampered by the restrictions of Egyptian death magic? Surely you have the power to sunder the veil and take that which you need as long as you have the skull."

Macer's skull gleamed in the candlelight, slick from a translucent fatty substance Nicomedes had treated it with that very morning to lubricate the passing between worlds. Nicomedes noted it was quite similar to the strange substance he dubbed the sea between the worlds. "I have the power to do as you suggest, but I am leery of channeling it until I have additional control. This is a delicate ritual that requires finesse."

Rubio pinched a small amount of the powder in the mortar and dropped it into the flame of the candle, sparking a burst of energy and power that crackled throughout the chamber. He bowed towards Nicomedes. "I think it is ready, magister."

Nicomedes sprinkled more of the ground dermestid beetle into the flame, and then began to chant the sacred words. The intonations were a mere crutch, a way to bridge will with reality. "My mouth has been given to me, that I may speak with it in the presence of the Great God. My mouth is opened, my mouth is split open by Shu with that iron harpoon of his, with which he split open the mouths of the gods."

The flames crackled as Nicomedes continued to chant the remainder of the ritual. They danced, mutating to a vaguely humanoid shape, pleading and prostrating itself before him. A spectral image of Nepos Murena Macer flashed on top of the skull and screamed. "Mercy!"

Nicomedes sneered and raised the skull, as though he were about to cast it upon the floor, shattering it into dust. Such would forever bind the shade to wander the material world and suffer until it finally faded into the abyss. "Speak and be heard, lest I weigh down your heart with the sin of murder against my flesh. Speak now and you may yet discover mercy within my heart. Know this! To lie to me now is to blacken your heart before your gods and you shall be cast out. Answer as completely as you are able to please me, and I shall not cast you out into the darkness."

The voice from the skull sounded akin to the wind on a blustery night. "Ask that which you would know, and we shall answer."

"Why did you attempt to murder Marcus Valerius Perseus?" he asked. "Speak the truth and mercy shall be yours."

Macer's soul flickered as he spoke. "We were given special orders with the seal of the Senate."

"By whom?"

"Publius Quinctilius Varus," the shade answered dutifully.

Why did that name seem familiar? It was so difficult remembering the name of all of the so-called important politicians in the Eternal City. This is why he needed his siblings to take care of such nonsense. "Why would a member of the Senate seek to murder Marcus? They would hardly know where he would be at that moment without divine help."

The shade answered immediately. "General Varus approved of the centurion's leave to return to Rome to resupply the Third, Fourth, and Seventh legions."

Nicomedes remembered Varus now. He was the general feeding the Senate strange reports on the war in Gaul against the Caledonians. "Did he say why this foul deed was to be done?"

"Only that this single death would restore the Republic."

* * * *

The great door of Domūs de Valeria opened upon his arrival. He traced his fingers over the sigil of Janus carved into the wood, surprised he had not seen the metaphoric connection between the probability of twins in their lineage and the two-faced household god believed to be the protector of the gates of Rome. *The universe appreciates irony*, he thought.

He found Claudia on their favorite bench under the olive tree. She cradled her arms around a child with curly black hair and the traditional Valeria nose that came with the blood. Caecilia turned her attention towards Nicomedes immediately before Claudia knew of his presence. "Is that my brother, Nicomedes?" she asked.

Claudia adjusted her position on the bench and welcomed him with a beckoning wave. Nicomedes lowered his hood and approached the girl with caution, as she was clearly precocious beyond what could be reasonably expected for a child her age.

His younger-half sister gazed up at him with her large almond eyes and then slowly focused upon his dead hand. She regarded it with a strange curiosity. "May I touch it, uncle?"

Nicomedes blinked and tilted his head. She meant his dead hand, of course. Adalia had been the only person who dared to touch his dead hand. He had always been the youngest sibling in the family. Save for Rubio, he had never dealt with a child, certainly not one this age. He looked to Claudia for guidance and she merely shrugged. "Why would a child wish to touch such a vile thing?"

Caecilia furrowed her brow, as though struggling to find the proper words. "Can you not hear it?"

"Hear what, Caecilia?" Claudia asked.

The child tilted her head. "Poppa once brought me to the sea and placed a conch shell to my ear. It was though the whole of the ocean was right there next to my head. It sounds like that."

Nicomedes studied her with careful regard. The girl was describing the synesthesia that came from sensing magic. Mystical energies existed beyond that which the human brain could properly understand, and often they were misinterpreted as one of the senses. He had felt magic as a boy as a variant of colors not existing in nature. "And you heard this even before I arrived here?"

Caecilia nodded. Curious, Nicomedes offered his dead hand to her.

She gingerly touched the bridge of the back of his hand with a single finger and ran it along his knuckles. The muscle had been burned away in the ritual, but there was a thin layer of burnt skin that had melded with the bone and remained fresh and fluid through the power of his magic. "It is cold."

He could not help but smile at the simple observation. "Yes. The magic that keeps the hand functional comes from the other side. Not many are brave enough to touch it."

"Is it true you lack a heart?" she asked.

"It is true. I surrendered mine to keep my brother, Marcus, alive." Nicomedes reached out to Caecilia and touched her curls with his living hand. There was a queer sensation in his chest that brought a shiver to his entire body. "The Valeria always protect their family."

The girl smiled. "Will you be living with us at Domūs de Claudia?" Caecilia asked.

Nicomedes shook his head. "I expect to visit there often, but the Art requires solitude. I have rooms at the Soothsayer Academy. Would you perhaps visit me there?"

The very mention of the Soothsayer Academy brought a pout to Caecilia's face. When Rubio made a similar expression, Nicomedes wanted to burn it from his face. Somehow this child could touch his spirit. "Mother said girls were not allowed at the academy."

He noted Caecilia used the familiar "poppa" when speaking of Orca, but the formal "mother" when referring to their mother. "A policy a member of the Magister Palatii Counsel has the power to change, or at the least make an exception for a remarkable student."

Claudia wrapped her arms around Caecilia. "Is that wise?"

Nicomedes understood the real question Claudia asked. *Did this maneuver give some sort of advantage to Septima?* "She has the gift. Her natural affinity might be stronger than my own. Better for her to learn to master this under my hand than any other."

His elder sister nodded reluctantly. Her expression reminded him of soured milk. "It is something to be discussed later for certain."

Some topics were bettered argued in private. Nicomedes nodded his agreement. "Where is Marcus? I have learned much from that final skull that should be discussed."

Claudia recognized the code for Macer and her eyes grew wide with caution. "Sadly, Marcus has already left for Domūs de Claudia. This is the day of his wedding. Can this information wait until tomorrow, when we have had time to settle into our new home? I would not wish to further inconvenience Orca more than we already have."

Hermana entered the atrium from the main house with a tray of orange juice and wine. "Dominus Orca thought you might enjoy refreshments."

Orca followed from the main house with a slow deliberate limp. He carried a cane, but clearly had yet to master it. Orca was a bear of man who spent too many winters hibernating and would clearly only survive one last spring. Caecilia hopped up from the bench and ran to her father. "Poppa!"

The old bear laughed and hugged her. Claudia blanched, perhaps remembering a less kind side of their stepfather. Orca acknowledged their presence with a smile and nod, as though the decade of terror had been forgotten.

What secrets are buried under that smile, Nicomedes wondered?

The opportunity offered by fate now seemed evident. Orca walked in the open without the mystical protection of Septima. He could not sense his mother, but if she were cloaking her presence, then she could not protect her husband.

Nicomedes reached out with thought-tendrils, burrowing deep into Orca's brain. A flood of memories — distorted and opaque — became available and flashed through his mind. It would take time and meditation to shift through all he had stolen, but he now understood why Varus was so important and why Marcus had been attacked on the Aventine.

The old man tried to fight against the psychic assault, but he was a feeble elder worn down by Septima over the years. Orca staggered, almost falling, but Caecilia swept under him, desperately trying to prop him to his feet. His eyes twitched as vessels in his nose burst, spraying blood down his face. The old man's words slurred as he tried to speak.

Caecilia twisted until she could see Nicomedes. Her eyes watered with tears for her father. "Mercy!"

Nicomedes withdrew his magic from Orca. The old man coughed blood, but he lived. "Know this: I have spared your life on this day solely because of the blood we share in Caecilia."

Orca had not the fortitude to speak. Hermana helped the old man to the bench and offered him wine. The old bear gulped it down quickly, trying to regain the little composure available to him.

Caecilia glanced from her father to half-brother. “Thank you.”

Her composure and intelligence were disconcerting. If there was not evidence to the contrary, he would have thought he was dealing with Septima. “I spared him because you asked, sister. That said, I cannot promise as to what Marcus might do in the future.” Nicomedes turned to Orca. “I know the truth of what you have done, and should the imperator learn of it, you would face unending torments in this world and the next.”

He swept out of the Domūs de Valeria with Claudia and Caecilia in tandem like ducklings, hoping against despair he found Marcus in time.

* * * *

Nicomedes gazed upon the great door of the Domūs de Claudia and ran his hands over Neptune’s Trident carved into the wood. He had lived here for a time as child and remembered it fondly. Those pleasant childhood memories bubbled to the surface as he skimmed his fingers along the walls of the villa. He imbued these walls with his own energies to provide protection against scrying from their mother or the Soothsayers.

Once such a feat would have taken days to prepare, and it would have drained him of much of his vitality. The effort was now mere child’s play and an interesting diversion from the noise of the crowd.

Upon their arrival, Claudia immediately shepherded Caecilia to her new rooms inside of the villa. His little sister had steadfastly refused to speak during their trek across the hill to their new home, and it bothered Nicomedes more than he would care to admit.

Marcus stepped out of the villa and called to him from across the atrium. “Nico! You are here!”

Nicomedes lifted his hood to better see his brother. They met in the middle near the plum trees. “Brother, I have been attuning myself to this place, creating barriers against scrying and later a translocation ward between here and the Soothsayer Academy. We have much to discuss about the future and why you were attacked on the Aventine.”

“Is this a tale that can told upon the ‘morrow, brother? Between the triumph and preparations for the wedding, I have not slept a full night’s sleep in three days.” Marcus gestured towards the mass of well-wishers collected outside of the walls. The roar of the crowd seemed to crash upon the walls like the sea upon the shore. “We might well have the whole of Rome outside expecting us to feed them.”

Claudia had argued the crimes of Orca would be better revealed after the wedding, lest their hot-tempered brother ruin the ceremony and damage the political gain they managed against Orca and their enemies. It would seem she had been correct in her assertion. “Be aware the Soothsayers intend to make their presence known at this wedding.” Nicomedes felt their presence, even from a distance. They either could not cloak themselves from his senses or wanted him to know they were near. “I would not wish to offend them by being unprepared.”

His eyes turned wide. “The Soothsayers will be here? At my wedding?”

“The imperator and General Octavius will be here. Does it surprise you that the Soothsayers would take an interest in one who contains some of their power?" Nicomedes asked.

Rarely had he witnessed Marcus so humbled. "I am honored."

Nicomedes frowned. "If the Soothsayers wished to honor you, they would have announced their presence openly. They only appear upon their terms."

Marcus grunted an acknowledgement. "Understood. There is no use borrowing trouble, when there is plenty ahead of us. If there is cause to be concerned about this night, I would hear of it before it strikes."

He lacked the foresight of the Soothsayers. The future was not yet his to divine and master. Yet, he found it difficult to imagine an enemy bold enough to strike a wedding under the protection of the combined effort of the Praetorian Guard, the Eighth Legion, and the freedmen of the Valeria and the Claudians. "It would seem to strain credulity to think our enemies would strike openly this night, but I shall be on guard for it."

"What of Megabyzus? Will he be well enough to attend?" Marcus asked.

His brother had not named Megabyzus since the funeral of his optio. He had feared Marcus held resentment over his student for surviving when his old friend did not. "The poison from the scorpions has almost dissipated from his system. Despite his lack of education, Megabyzus almost managed to transmute it merely based on observation of my own efforts." Nicomedes studied his brother's face, searching for any signs of malice. On occasion, Marcus could be rather ornery when angered. "Rubio asked for permission to attend with his family. I did not see the harm to extend a hand to them."

Marcus nodded his approval. "Will you speak with Darius about the arrangements? Ensure he understands the Praetorian Guard will be protecting the imperator, and he is restricted to keeping the crowds outside of the designated perimeters. If this task is too complicated, I shall do it myself."

This request was no surprise. Marcus had not deigned to speak with Darius since their return. "You shall have to speak with him personally, eventually, brother."

Marcus folded his arms across his chest. "He allied himself with our mother when she betrayed father. I am uncertain I can speak to him without choking him."

"If there is a lack of trust, then we should simply replace him," Nicomedes argued.

Marcus shook his head. "How would that look on the day of my wedding? Darius has ever been loyal to Rome, if not our father. What further damage can be done now? There will be a reckoning later, away from prying eyes."

"As you wish, brother. I will see that it is done."

Nicomedes tried to consider it a compliment that his brother trusted him implicitly rather than an insult to his education at the Soothsayer Academy. He sighed and left the safety of Domūs de Claudia and returned to the mob. Nicomedes discovered the fervor of the mob had reached mythological proportions, as traffic froze from the sheer mass of people seeking to bless the wedding of the Bear

Centurion and Livia Drusilla Claudianus Appius. Actors pantomimed tales of their love based on rumors and idle speculation that bore little semblance to reality. Plebian vendors freely offered a hearty selection of cold meats, flavored rice balls, and shellfish. Wine flowed freely as water, and it considerably brightened the mood of the crowd.

He eventually found the doctore of the Valeria directing the freedmen and legionnaires to strategic points along the route to control the crowds and ensure there was ample room for the actual guests to reach the wedding.

Darius seemed to have aged greatly in the last few months, as though the gods themselves drank his vitality, or perhaps as a result of this very celebration. His beard had turned completely gray, and his shoulders slumped as though suffering through a heavy burden.

Nicomedes called out to the doctore through the crowd. "Hail, Darius! I would speak to you about the security arrangements for the wedding."

Darius searched the crowd until he located Nicomedes. The old man laughed and wormed his way through the mob until he reached him. "It is good to see you, Nicomedes. None of my former students have greeted me this day," he complained.

Nicomedes could not help but sneer at the naiveté of his former teacher. "Some children prefer not to work with those who allowed our father to be murdered."

Darius blinked and his face dropped from the accusation, as though it had been struck by a mighty blow. It took several moments for Darius to recover. "What did Septima accuse me of?" he asked horrified.

The magister snorted. The doctore had not realized he had just verified the very accusation against him. "All such accusations shall be spoken of in detail at a later time, doctore. Your duty this day is to maintain the perimeter and ensure that only honored guests may reach the threshold of the Domūs de Claudia. The Praetorian Guard will arrive shortly to see to the protection of Caesar and his entourage. That is an imperial matter."

Darius slumped his shoulders with defeat. Hope faded from his eyes. "Is there any other way that I can be of service to the Valeria this day?"

Nicomedes flashed a thin-lipped smile. "I would suggest avoiding Marcus until his blood is calm. I am told he once choked a bear."

The doctore nodded, turned towards the freedmen at the edge of the mob, and began barking orders. "Push those bastards back to the edge of the street or we'll all be overrun by the wedding! Allow only guests past the perimeter or I'll know the reason!"

Nicomedes retreated from the suffocating enclosure of flesh and the erratic cacophony of voices to the open space of the atrium inside of the Domūs de Claudia. He returned to his previous route along the walls of the villa, imbuing them with a tiny fraction of his essence. It helped to drown out the stench of the mob and their heated emotions. He allowed himself to slip into the rhythm of the magic.

Adalia woke him from the magical meditation by tugging upon his robes. "Nicomedes, I found them. They are waiting two blocks away, at the corner, but not venturing any farther."

"Have they been noticed?"

Adalia shook her head. "The mob seemed content to ignore them, thinking that they are beggars. I felt their eyes upon me and it burned."

"Then let us visit our Soothsayer overlords and see what they have to say to us mere mortals."

Adalia led Nicomedes out the great door of the Domūs de Claudia. Darius had managed to achieve the herculean task of taming the crowd and thinning traffic to the perimeter. They followed the length of Cyprian Street Way into the crowd towards a corner just out of sight from the villa under a large marble statue.

"This is sacred ground to all Romans."

"Why?" she asked.

Nicomedes gestured to the mighty statue that towered above them. "Behold murdered King Servius Tullius in the very spot where his mutilated body had been ground into the street from the chariot driven by his own mad daughter. The last king of Rome. Curious that the Soothsayers would select this location to summon us to their presence."

The three Soothsayers came at them from behind the statue surrounding them. They stood in the shadows, just out of sight from the mob. "Your insight into the world has improved greatly, Magister Nicomedes."

Adalia flinched at the very sound of their broken voices, but she raised her chin defiantly and refused to look away. Rare was the mortal who could gaze directly upon a Soothsayer without bending to its will. He recalled the distant memory of boyhood where he had such a reaction and reached out with his living hand to comfort her. She gazed down into his eyes and smiled.

Nicomedes turned his attention towards the Soothsayers. "I trust that we played our parts to your satisfaction."

Again, they spoke as one. Their words were made of broken dreams and shattered hopes gleaned from staring into the fire of eternity. "Nothing is ever certain in a war of infinite regress, and there are moments when even a Soothsayer might be pleasantly surprised by the outcome."

Nicomedes had so many questions, but knew asking them was likely pointless. He asked the one most likely to be answered. "Why are you here? I could have met you anywhere."

"We must be seen here and now at the appointed time."

The Soothsayers rarely made public appearances and then only to mark important occasions. "What changed?" Nicomedes asked. "You never would have acted thusly in the past. It has been ten years since you have been seen in public. What is so important that you must attend a wedding of one of your catspaws?"

The Soothsayers seemed to converse through some sort of telepathic link. They turned inwards, as though debating their next words very carefully. Once they were finished, they turned back towards Nicomedes. "Would you know the terror of infinity? Would you know the secret hell at the end of existence?"

The nature of the question intrigued him. "You said I could join you in some futures. If you would have that happen, I must know the consequences of such a choice."

"And your friend?"

"Adalia is strong. She is trusted and will do as I require," Nicomedes said with confidence.

The Soothsayers nodded silently to each other. This time it was Spurinna alone who spoke. "The world as we know it was broken before the dawn of history by fire from above. The continents were of one body and the world was whole. Great and terrible beings ruled over the world, and the gods were weak and trembled in their power."

"What happened?" Nicomedes asked.

Spurinna continued her tale. "The world broke, and over the ages, the continents drifted and these Old Ones fell into a slumber. At the center of the world was a floating city of shimmering glass and magic: Atlantis. There, the first people learned the secrets of the Art and the terrible power of the Old Ones. We grew in power until we were betrayed by an agent who worshiped those who came before us. Then our own city crumbled. We came into the world and promised to live quietly to allow humanity free will."

"You speak of the other Soothsayers," Adalia said.

"Indeed, we agreed to an accord," Spurinna explained. "And we in Rome broke it when we learned the horrible secret."

"What is this secret?"

Spurinna answered this final question in a whisper. There was a stillness that echoed in the response and the murmur of the crowd slowly seemed to drown out everything else until Adalia screamed for the terror of knowing.

*   *   *   *

Nicomedes cast a glamour over the walls of Domūs de Claudia to mute the noise of the crowd. The hushed silence allowed him to collect his thoughts. Spurinna's final secret weighed heavily on his mind and what it meant for his family and indeed the world.

He stood guard over Adalia as she turned in her sleep. He laid her upon one of the couches in the atrium under the shade, and ordered the servants to fetch a pitcher of water and an apple to help her recover.

Adalia slowly opened her eyes and rubbed her temples as though she suffered a massive migraine. "What happened?"

Nicomedes helped her sit upright and then passed her the water. "Drink slowly." She brought the water to her lips and sipped. It had been a simple spell to wipe her memory, but it hurt to betray her trust. She could not endure this secret, not yet, when there was little hope for the future. "You drank too much, and I insisted that you lay down here in the atrium."

She tilted her head, as though trying to remember. "Such has not happened in recent memory. Last I remember I was on the street paying the vendors, watching out for the Soothsayers like you asked. How did I get here?"

"I carried you."

Adalia raised an eyebrow and scanned the magister's body. "You carried me here."

"Do not underestimate my will when a task must be done."

Nicomedes flashed a genuine smile. He hated the thought of lying to her, no matter how just the cause. "You have done as much if not more for me, and I have shamefully neglected to express gratitude for your deeds."

"You may repay me by speaking the truth without fear it will anger me." Adalia took another sip of the water, gargled it, and then spat it onto the ground. "You have never indulged in heavy drink. Certainly not enough to pass out, else you would know the sensation is quite unique. My head hurts as though I were struck from behind, and yet there is no wound. It leads me to the conclusion that perhaps you did this to me. I would know the reason behind it.

"Do you trust me?" Nicomedes asked.

Adalia cricked her neck, trying to release the pressure from her aching head. Nicomedes wanted to alleviate the pain, but such magics would restore her memory. "I hated the sound of your voice from the very moment it reached my ears. You were arrogant, sardonic, and cruel when you had little cause. Yet it was clear you loved your siblings and would fight the entire world if it prevented you from keeping them safe."

His entire body drooped from the very memory of that night. "The world has always been broken for us. Our love blossomed from our instinctive need to survive and find shelter in each other," he said.

"I knew from the moment I met Marcus, he had suffered a great loss he would never speak of. While I pretended to be Claudia's slave, I watched her from afar and noted the same grief echoed in her eyes. Then when I came to you in the Soothsayer Academy to ask for your help with the Vestal Virgins, I saw a flash of that brokenness in your concern for Claudia. Something horrific happened to the three of you, and none of you will speak of it."

"Yes," Nicomedes admitted.

"Will you share that tale?" she asked.

"There may come a dark night when you ask this question once again, and I will answer. We swore an oath, and the story is not mine alone to share."

"If you do not trust me, then how could I possibly trust you?" Adalia asked.

Nicomedes knelt down to gaze into her eyes. "I may not be able to return the affections I suspect you hold for me."

"It is true you are beautiful like the sun, and it hurts to look upon you directly," Adalia admitted shyly.

"You have earned my respect by deed and thought. I would have you know I only wish the best for you and your brother in this world and the next." A shimmering eldritch glow enveloped his dead hand, preparing for the geis spell to bind his will to hers in this matter. All he needed to do was touch her and speak the words. "If you wish, I shall swear a geis to always protect you and yours until the end of my life."

Adalia shook her head. "I can't allow such an oath. I'm a warrior born to bloodletting, and such a life is rarely safe. You would have to kill my spirit to keep me safe."

He reabsorbed the energy and negated the spell. "Then trust that I have dissembled to good purpose and your best interests."

She pursed her lips. "As you wish, but there will come a reckoning for all the secrets between us. And now, I believe we should return to the crowd. There's a growing dread in my stomach that says something is very wrong out there."

Nicomedes bit his lip. He could not argue with her logic. After all, the world had been broken long ago. The only logical action to take was to hold onto the pieces, try to make a life, and hope against hope that the universe failed to notice your happiness.

Flashes of black feathers and capes caught his attention. He followed Adalia back to the street just in time to witness the arrival of the Praetorian Guard. The imperator's personal guards quickly secured the area, fortifying every egress to the wedding, and then escorted the imperator — Gaius Julius Caesar.

All weddings were at once political and social affairs. Claudia once explained the Claudians were once the patrons who helped the ascension of the plebian family Julii to politics. The combined forces at this wedding could have turned the tide at the Battle of Tanta.

Nicomedes scanned the crowd, seeking a pattern and familiar faces. He noted representatives from all of the major patrician families of Rome. Rubio stood at the outer edge of the guests with a collection of the Aemilii and the Cornelii, including a red-haired woman who must be his mother by appearance. In the center of their clutch stood the two most powerful women in Rome: Messalina Cornelius Scipio and Nephele Aemilia Octavia.

He found the Claudians and branch families of the Valeria mixed in with the Avidia, Flavia, and Quinctia. Political factions whispered together such as the Optimates, including the vaunted Senators Cicero,

Aphthoniu, and Cassius. The Soothsayers remained at a distance. None dared to seek their company.

Every name worth knowing in all of Italia was present celebrating the ascension of the Valeria Claudians. This included the most important man in all of Rome.

The imperator and his entourage, which included General Octavius and his son Ptolemy, drank wine and laughed amongst the people while their soldiers watched carefully for any sign of trouble.

Caesar noticed him in the crowd. "Nicomedes! Come to me!"

Nicomedes obeyed, keeping his dead hand hidden under his Soothsayer's robes. "Welcome, imperator."

"I have heard of the travesty that marked you," Caesar stated. "May I see it?"

Strange that showing this man his hand should make him nervous, Nicomedes thought.

He offered the dead hand to the imperator. Caesar touched it cautiously and squeezed it tight. "You are still quite the handsome man."

"Thank you, imperator," Nicomedes said.

Caesar offered him wine. He did not dare take a gift from the imperator. "I am told you have mastered the Art. Octavius tells me your skill in the battle turned the tide. I would have private lessons."

Nicomedes replied cautiously. "That is ambitious for a man of your age, imperator."

"So was conquering your bottom in the bath house, and I did that well enough," the imperator retorted.

"I live to serve the empire, imperator." He noticed Claudia on the edge of the conversation. "Have you had the pleasure of my sister's company, Caesar? Allow me to introduce Claudia Valeria Terza, formerly of the Vestal Virgins."

Claudia flashed a wide smile and bowed before the imperator. "I am honored to me the giant who protects Rome."

Ptolemy immediately maneuvered to her side. Nicomedes regarded the boy a moment. He was young, but more perceptive than his handsome face would indicate. It might come to pass that both mighty Caesar and Octavius would have cause to worry about the new generation.

"It would seem the gods of Rome and Egypt have blessed me to have such a bride in my future," Ptolemy said.

Caesar studied them both a moment with great gravitas and then laughed. "And why not? My grandson should have nothing but the best."

Nicomedes noted the slight smile that appeared at the edges of the governor's mouth as the priests of Venus rang a brass bell to catch the crowd's attention. Claudia took her position inside of the villa and then escorted the bride from the inner sanctum through the atrium onto the street. Drusilla wore her hair styled in the traditional bridal manner — divided into six crines, six locks, and fastened with ribbons and fillets. It was said that such a fashion would discourage Dis Pater from taking any children born of this marriage.

Drusilla stepped to the great door of the Claudians, and there she offered old dolls and her maiden togas to the young girls in the crowd, symbolically forsaking the joy of childhood.

Nicomedes noted Caecilia was amongst them and claimed the largest doll. She turned toward him and scowled before returning to the gaggle of young girls.

Drusilla slipped a flame-colored veil over her face and accepted her father's hand. Livius led her to a wooden dais, where the priests of Venus awaited her. She knelt before them. "Wherever you are Marcus, goes the heart of Drusilla."

Marcus stepped forward to proclaim his love, but the murmured hush of the crowd turned his head as it parted to make way for the Soothsayers. They bowed before the icons of Venus and offered three pomegranate seeds — a symbol of fertility and fidelity — and then left silently.

The centurion stepped forward. "Your heart is the flame of Rome."

Drusilla giggled as she clutched onto her father, turning her back upon Marcus. This was the traditional reenactment of the seizure of the Sabine. "Take me not from my father, mighty Roman. You would cast me out as soon as you were done with me, and then I would be without family or honor."

Marcus placed his hands upon his hips. "Come with me and be my wife. Tend the flames of my hearth, and I shall conquer the whole of the world for you. Come with me and be my wife. All that I have will be yours. You will be Rome."

Then they signed the marriage contract provided by the auspex from the Vestal Virgins. The crowd cheered. Caesar was the first to shout the traditional bawdy jokes at the bride's expense. "Gone with the hymen!"

It was also traditional for the bride and the groom to take separate routes to the groom's family home, but since they were no longer living at the Domūs de Valeria, they merely parted around the stage and then entered the villa together holding hands.

The crescendo of the wedding brought a swell of emotion from the audience, and they rushed the dais like ants. The crowd beyond the perimeter burst through the barriers, hoping to catch a glimpse of the Bear Centurion before he departed into the villa. The celebration evolved into a crazed riot. The Praetorian Guard began to slam the blades of their weapons against their shields. A shrill whistle bleated twice, piercing through the screams of the mob.

Bodies slammed against Nicomedes from all directions. Adalia quickly came to his side, pushing other ways to give them space. It was just enough to allow him leverage to lift his dead hand into the air. He plucked the kinetic filaments of mystical energy that connected the world and sent a pulse of power through it that knocked the crowd to their knees. Now that the life-force of the crowd has been pushed to the ground, he sensed an ancient magic at the far end of the street just before the alleys that led between the patrician villas.

The Soothsayers acknolwedged him with a simple nod before they returned to the shadows and disappeared. It might have been his imagination, but he could have sworn that Spurinna smiled under her hood.

Adalia was the first to see it. "Caesar!" she cried.

The crowd immediately thinned, not wishing to be blamed. Caesar slumped to the ground, black heart's blood on his lips and a wound in his side. Nicomedes ran to his lover and sniffed the wound to verify what he already suspected. It bore the very same poison that once nearly killed Adalia when the assassins attempted to murder Claudia. Where Adalia was young and strong, Caesar was neither.

The imperator was dead.

Chapter Fifteen: An Honorable Man

The storm raged with great thunder and purpose until the dead of the night, almost capsizing the entire fleet to the ocean's dark waters. The sun had risen, much as it had every morning since the world was new, and the only evidence of its existence was the damage to the shores of Gaul.

A flock of albatrosses cried above them. One of the sailors pointed. "An auspicious sign for a landing, senator."

It has been nearly two decades since he had stepped onto European soil, and he felt the anticipation heavy in his chest. Once they landed, the senator and his guards secured the beachhead.

The Seventh Legion awaited them in parade formation at the edge of the beach, where the ground was hard enough for a quick march. A single officer broke rank and met them at the edge of the sand. He was a young man, stained with the bloat of boyhood still upon his cheeks. "Hail, Senator Brutus! Legate Decimus Valerius Orca commanding the Seventh Legion."

Brutus returned the salute. Military protocol tired him, but it was important for morale. "Where is General Varus?"

Decimus swallowed. "He had difficulty with my predecessor and had to kill him. I am told that he shall be joining us this afternoon with the Third and Fourth Legions."

"Excellent." Brutus gestured to the guard to his left. He was a handsome man barely of age, but taller than any other within his army. "This is Centurion Armin. He is my voice, and you shall react accordingly to his commands."

Decimus scowled. "Armin? Your second is one of the Germani?"

"Do you question my honor?" Brutus asked. "I have fought for the republic for two nearly decades and countless loyal Romans have bled for this single purpose, for which Armin is key."

The legate saluted the centurion in lieu of a formal apology. "Anticipation of the restoration of the republic has flustered my nerves."

Brutus laughed. "Nothing this day could tarnish my mood. I am home, and this is the day that historians will note that the restoration of the Republic began."

About the Writer

Jason Andrew lives in Seattle, Washington with his wife Lisa. By day, he works as a mild-mannered technical writer. By night, he writes stories of the fantastic and occasionally fights crime. As a child, Jason spent his Saturdays watching the Creature Feature classics and furiously scribbling down stories. His first short story, written at age six, titled "The Wolfman Eats Perry Mason" was severely rejected. It also caused his Grandmother to watch him very closely for a few years.

His short fiction has appeared in markets such as *A Mytho Grimmly: A Lovecraftian Fairy Tale Anthology* (Wanderer's Haven Publications)), *Frontier Cthulhu: Ancient Horrors in the New World* (Chaosium), and *Atomic Cthulhu: Tales of Mythos Horror in the 1950s Coins of Chaos* (Chaosium). In 2011, his story "Moonlight in Scarlet" received an honorable mention in Ellen Datlow's List for Best Horror of the Year.

In addition, Jason has written for a number of role-playing games. His most recent projects include *Mind's Eye Theatre: Vampire the Masquerade* (By Night Studios), *Shadowrun: Data Trails* (Catalyst Game Labs), and *Rites of the Blood* (Onyx Path Publishing). He currently holds the position of Developer for the Mind's Eye Theatre line published through **By Night Studios.** Check out his website at http://www.jasonbandrew.com

About Simian Publishing

Simian Publishing is a small press company devoted to primal dark fantasy and horror fiction. We're interested in seeing how the old gods, monsters, and Jungian archetypes work in the modern world. We want fiction that touches our souls.

With Print on Demand technology, Simian Publishing is able to take chances on a story or novel that might never see the light of day through a mainstream publisher. Currently, we looking for more direct distributors, but for now you can find our products on a variety of online stores.

www.simianpublishing.org